The brilli... ...t research DO
you have t...

Beautiful J... ...s to face up to that very
question. She i... ...ed to break out of her life as
a magazine featu... writer and become a novelist. But
having had rejection after rejection, she realizes that
the only way to get published is to write erotica.
However, her sheltered lifestyle just hasn't offered
up the right material to base them on and her un-
trained imagination can't fill the gaps.

So she must set out to explore the limits of human
sexual experience, to glean from the experts what
really floats their boat, and try it for herself. But,
as always, the question must be: once she has started
can she stop?

Also in paperback from New English Library

**Schoolgirl Lust
Depravicus
Sinful Deceit
Sexual Service**

Lust Quest

Ray Gordon

NEW ENGLISH LIBRARY
Hodder & Stoughton

First published in Great Britain in 2001
by Hodder and Stoughton
A division of Hodder Headline
First published in paperback in 2001
by Hodder and Stoughton

A NEL Paperback

10 9 8 7 6 5

A CIP catalogue record for this title
is available from the British Library

ISBN 0 340 76927 0

Typeset by Hewer Text Ltd, Edinburgh
Printed and bound in Great Britain by
Mackays of Chatham plc, Chatham, Kent

Hodder and Stoughton
A division of Hodder Headline
338 Euston Road
London NW1 3BH

LUST QUEST

Chapter One

He slid his male hardness deep into the hugging sheath of her sex-wet vagina as she squirmed and writhed in the adulterous union. The delicious squelching sounds of her lubricious love juices mingling with her gasps of pleasure, she sank her fingernails into his bronzed back as he repeatedly withdrew his granite-hard penis and thrust back into her tightening pussy.

'God, you're so big,' she gasped. 'Fuck me like you've never fucked before.' His heavy balls slapping the firm roundness of her tensed buttocks as the birth of her orgasm stirred within her young womb, he drove into her with a frenzied passion. Parting her thighs wider, the pinken nodule of her sensitive clitoris swelling and pulsating, she cried out as her climax erupted and gripped her very soul. 'Yes,' she breathed, his sperm gushing from his throbbing glans, bathing the soft hardness of her ripe cervix . . .

'I can't write stuff like this,' I sighed despondently, tossing the book onto the desk.

'Why not?' David asked, his dark eyes grinning as he stood beside me and gazed at my naked thighs. 'This particular book has done very well.'

'It's OK for a man to write that sort of thing, but . . .'

'A man?' he interrupted me. Shaking his head, he raised his eyes to the ceiling. 'It was written by a young woman, Jade. Didn't you notice the author's name?'

1

'Yes, but I thought it was a man using a female name.'

'No, no. Sex isn't a male-only thing.'

'I realize that,' I snapped. I felt that he was mocking me as he looked at my thighs again. 'I'm not a virgin,' I blurted out, immediately wishing I hadn't.

'Take Anaïs Nin, for example,' he continued, ignoring my remark. 'She wrote some wonderful erotic fiction.'

'I've never heard of her,' I murmured, wishing I'd not shown my ignorance.

'*The Story of O* was written by a woman. Why don't you give it a try?'

'Because . . .' I hesitated, my embarrassment rising as he focused on the rise of my nipples pressing through my blouse.

Travelling up to London to meet the literary agent had sent my hopes sky-high. I'd been like an excited child, bubbling over with enthusiasm. When he'd phoned, I'd thought he'd liked my romantic novel and was inviting me to his office to discuss the book. For him to suggest that I turn my hand to erotic fiction was the last thing I'd expected. And the way he'd stared at my thighs and nipples had left me cold. My dream of becoming an author of romantic fiction had been completely shattered.

Feeling self-conscious – and discouraged – I pulled my skirt down and crossed my legs. Folding my arms to conceal my breasts, I wished I'd worn a thicker bra. There again, I'd not thought my body would be ogled by the literary agent. And I'd certainly not thought that we'd be discussing dirty books. Stories of the casting couch came to mind as I looked around the plush office. What would it take to get published? Did he want me to write about sex or . . .

'This sort of thing sells,' he persisted, perching on the edge of the huge leather-topped desk. 'After all, we *are* in this to make money.' He paused, rubbing his chin as he stared hard at me. 'Or is it that you just want to see your name in print?' he asked accusingly.

'No, no, of course not,' I returned indignantly. 'I'd wanted to write a book I'd be proud of. A book I could show my parents and friends.'

'Your book's good, Jade.' He brushed his dark hair back and smiled. 'It's just that it lacks . . .'

'Sex?' I interrupted him, raising my eyes to the ceiling.

'Yes.'

'Why does sex have to come into everything?' I sighed. 'From selling cars to—'

'Like it or not, that's the way of the world. Have a go at writing an erotic novel. There's no harm in trying, is there?'

'I don't know anything about sex,' I confessed, shaking my head dejectedly as he laughed at me. 'What I mean is . . . Yes, of course I could write scenes like that. But not the bondage and spanking stuff.'

'What you mean is that you have no imagination.'

'Yes. No, I . . .'

'You're an attractive young girl, Jade. Don't try and tell me that you know nothing about sex.'

'Of course I know about sex. And I'm not a young girl. I can't write about something I have no knowledge of.' I felt confused as he gazed at me. I was coming across as stupid, naive. 'I'm talking about anal sex and . . . What I mean is . . .'

'What *do* you mean, exactly?' he frowned.

'OK, I can use my imagination to an extent. But whipping, spanking, anal sex, three men in bed with one girl . . . And as for lesbian sex.'

I grabbed my bag and stood up. That was that, I knew as he stared at my long legs. The end of my writing career had arrived before it had even begun. Raising his eyes to my cleavage, the agent gazed longingly at the half-moons of my breasts. All men were the same, I concluded. David seemed more interested in my body than my work. *That's why sex sells*, I ruminated. Men wanted sex and they were more than willing to pay for it. *Perhaps I* should *write about it?* I pondered.

'You've been more than helpful, David,' I said, walking to the door. 'I appreciate you giving me your time, and reading my manuscript. But if you don't like my novel, then . . .'

'Then you'll never be published.'

'That's encouraging.'

'Your book's all right, Jade. It's well written, the storyline is good and the characters are strong. But the boy-meets-girl scenario has been flogged to death. Times have changed. Closing the bedroom door on the horny couple just as they're about to—'

'Horny couple?' I broke in. 'They're a young couple who are desperately in love. They've fought tooth and nail to be together and—'

'People in love have sex, don't they?' he asked sardonically.

'Yes, but . . .'

'Then why not write about it? Give it some thought, Jade. Write a couple of chapters and let me have a look. Here, take the book with you. It might give you some ideas.'

'I suppose so,' I sighed, slipping the book into my bag.

'You can write, you've proved that. It's just that you're writing about—'

'About a young couple in love.'

'And leaving out the juicy bits.'

4

'Juicy bits? Perhaps I'm an old-fashioned prude,' I smiled. 'I'd thought that Romeo and Juliet . . .'

'To put it bluntly, Romeo and Juliet would have fucked rotten,' he chuckled, rising from the desk. 'As I said, give it some thought.'

'Perhaps I should buy myself a whip and a pair of handcuffs,' I quipped as he opened the door for me.

'Now there's an idea,' he grinned, eyeing my legs again.

'I think not. I'll see what I can come up with.'

'You do that. And good luck.'

Good luck? What chance did I have of writing about anal sex and spanking? I'd neither experienced anal sex nor had any desire to do so. And the only time I'd been spanked was by my mother, which couldn't have been further removed from a sexual act. Trying to look on the bright side, I supposed that I'd been lucky to have got as far as seeing a literary agent. It wasn't that I was ungrateful, it was just that I'd thought the meeting would be interesting, enlightening and fruitful. On reflection, it had indeed been most enlightening.

David had been helpful, but I'd put my heart and soul into my romantic novel. Having spent three years writing the book only to have it turned down had shattered my self-confidence, and I doubted that I'd ever write another word. But David knew the business, I ruminated. If he said that it was no good, then who was I to argue?

Walking to my car, I wished I'd stuck to freelance journalism. At least I'd earned a pretty good living. But now? I'd thrown it all away by wasting three years writing a book that was fit only for the dustbin. My savings all but dried up, I was going to have to do something to bring some money in. Did Romeo and Juliet fuck rotten? I'd always imagined them making passionate love, not fucking rotten.

Reaching my flat, I let myself in and mooched into my den. The computer screen reflected my blank stare as I flopped into my swivel chair and took the book from my bag. Flicking though the pages, I read about a young girl's naked body tied to a metal frame. Her buttocks crudely parted by two men, she gasped as one drove three fingers into her pussy and the other forced his finger deep into her bottom. 'Do my arse,' she begged the men crudely. 'Spunk my arsehole and then come in my cunt and fuck my mouth.' Did girls like that really exist?

My thoughts turning to Alan, my one and only boyfriend, I wondered whether we would have still been together if I'd behaved like the tart in the book. He'd left me for a so-called friend of mine, cruelly telling me that she was brilliant in bed. Apparently, she was heavily into oral sex. Alan had delighted in informing me that she enjoyed cocksucking and pussy-tonguing. 'Into anything and everything,' he'd said smugly. 'Unlike you.' I'd not only despised him, I'd hated his vulgar words, too. And now I was to use such words in a book?

I'd often said that I'd try taking Alan's penis into my mouth when I felt that I was ready, but I just couldn't bring myself to do it. Towards the end of our relationship I'd feigned headaches and goodness knows what else to get out of having sex with him. Every time he came near me, I knew that he'd expect me to suck his penis and I began to put up barriers. I'd enjoyed our lovemaking, the closeness, the burning passion. It was just the thought of him coming in my mouth that had revolted me. Perhaps I was too young? Were the barriers still there?

Dropping the book onto my desk, I realized the extent of my naivety, how inexperienced I was. Twenty-one years old, and I'd only had one boyfriend. If I was going to write erotic fiction, then I'd need to get out and about. I'd need to experience life, have a few relationships. Relationships wouldn't help, I sighed inwardly. I'd need to experience crude and illicit sex to write books like that.

Even if I'd had the experience, did I want to write that sort of stuff? More to the point, *could* I write it? I had to admit I felt somewhat aroused when I looked through the book David had given me. The notion of a naked girl having her young body pleasured by several men intrigued me, and I found myself wondering what it would be like. But the thought of writing filth went against the grain.

Not knowing what to do, I picked the book up and began reading from the beginning. It had a pretty good storyline, which surprised me. I'd imagined page after page of crude bonking, but no. The heroine, if she could be called that, came across as real. In fact, the book was very well written. The content was sexually explicit to the point of being disgusting, and I wondered why such books weren't banned. But it *was* extremely well written. Perhaps I was envious. Not only of the author, but of the heroine.

Just as I was becoming engrossed in the story, and pondering on anilingus, the phone rang. It was Jackie, my best friend. She'd been eagerly awaiting news of my visit to the literary agent and could barely control her excitement as she asked how I'd got on.

'Turned down,' I sighed. 'They want crude sex, not love.'

'Sounds great!' she trilled enthusiastically. 'There's nothing like—'

'Jackie, I spent three years writing that bloody book.'

'Bung some sex in it.'

'Bung some sex in it?' I echoed despairingly. 'I can't just "bung some sex in it". It's about love, not bondage and spanking. I can't punctuate every other page with filth.'

'I don't see why not,' she returned. 'Anyway, it's not filth.'

'Have *you* been tied to a bed and had your naked buttocks spanked?'

'No, but I wouldn't mind trying it!' she giggled. 'I'll come round and we'll talk about it, OK?'

'I don't want to talk about being tied to a bed and spanked,' I quipped.

'No, silly. I mean, talk about writing dirty books.'

'OK. I'll go and put the kettle on.'

Jackie and I had been friends since we'd been at school together. She was good company, vivacious and very attractive. Although radiating a childlike innocence, she was also a . . . No, 'tart' would be too strong a word to describe her: she was promiscuous. God only knew how many boyfriends she'd had since I'd known her. Dozens, I would imagine. How many penises had she had inside her? I wondered as I went to the kitchen and filled the kettle. Recalling the dirty book, I also wondered whether she'd ever had her arse done, as the author had crudely described anal intercourse. What an awful way to put it, I reflected. There again, what an awful act to write about, let alone commit.

Pouring the coffee, I pondered on lesbian sex. I could take a shrewd guess as to the things lesbians got up to in bed, but to bring authenticity to the scenes would take far more than a good imagination. Besides which, the last thing I wanted to imagine was licking another woman's vagina. Shuddering, I tried to push the vile thought out of my mind. My trouble was that I'd had a sheltered upbringing and had been a swot at school. While Jackie had been busy exploring the appendages of the opposite sex, I'd spent my time reading Shakespeare and . . . *Did* they fuck rotten?

8

Answering the doorbell, I caught sight of my reflection in the hall mirror. Attractive, with long golden locks flowing over my shoulders, I knew that I'd have no trouble getting a boyfriend. I'd been asked out often enough since Alan had dumped me for the tart. But I didn't want a relationship. My only relationship had ended in disaster and I'd decided to throw myself into my writing rather than waste time by going out with men.

Did I need to experience anal sex to write about it? I wondered. If I read enough erotic fiction, I'd be able to write my own, I concluded. There was no need to experience spanking to write about it. Bondage, whipping, group sex, anal sex, oral sex . . . Reading a few dirty books would furnish me with more than enough carnal knowledge. I'd have to earn money somehow, I reflected. The ageing washing machine was on its last legs and the television only seemed to work when there was nothing worth watching.

'Hi,' Jackie beamed excitedly as I opened the door. 'How's the dirty book coming on?'

'It's not,' I returned firmly as we walked into the kitchen. 'I do *not* write dirty books, Jackie.'

'Well, you should,' she smiled, brushing her long black hair away from her pretty face. 'God, I'd love to earn money by writing about sex.'

'That doesn't surprise me. You'd earn yourself a fortune,' I quipped.

'I don't know why you're reacting like this,' she frowned. 'If you can get a book published, which is something you've wanted to do since we were at school, then go for it.'

'What do you know about lesbian sex?' I asked pensively as she plonked herself at the kitchen table. God, what sort of question was that?

'More than you might think,' she replied mysteriously.

'*What?*' I gasped surprisedly, almost dropping the cups as I placed them on the table.

'Remember Jenny Hardbrooke?'

I feared the worse as she grinned at me. 'That skinny little thing who used to wear skirts up to her bum?' I asked.

'That's the one. It was during the summer holiday. We were playing around in a haystack down on Turner's Farm and . . . Well, you know.'

'No, I don't know,' I said, my eyes wide as I waited for her to enlighten me with sordid details of her lesbian encounter. In a haystack?

Gazing at Jackie's angelic face as she locked her dark gaze to mine, I dreaded to think what she was about to say. She was a beautiful girl with full red lips and huge eyes, and I knew that she'd never had a shortage of men after her. But a lesbian relationship? Had she licked Jenny Hardbrooke's pussy? I wondered. Had they taken their clothes off and licked each other's . . . There *was* material here for a dirty book, I reflected. Grimacing, I again realized how naive I was as I sat opposite Jackie and awaited her story with bated breath. I almost grabbed pen and paper to make notes, but decided against it.

'Jenny Hardbrooke,' she sighed wistfully, her pink tongue peeping at me as she provocatively licked her succulent lips.

'What happened?' I asked eagerly, wondering where her tongue had been.

'We brought each other off,' she replied unashamedly.

'Brought each other— My God,' I gasped. 'You actually masturbated each other?'

'Yes.'

'But . . .'

'But what?'

'Were you both naked? My God. Did you take each other's clothes off or—'

'Yes, we were naked.'

'My God.'

'I wish you'd stop saying "*my God*". There's nothing wrong with two young girls discovering their bodies.'

'*Their own* bodies, maybe. But not each other's.'

'You are a prude,' she laughed, flicking her long black hair over her shoulder. 'There were loads of girls at school who played about like that.'

'Well, *I* wasn't one of them.' Pausing, I tried to picture Jackie with her finger inserted in Jenny Hardbrooke's pussy. 'Tell me more,' I finally said, somewhat too eagerly. 'I mean, purely for research purposes.'

'So you *are* going to write smut,' she said eagerly.

'No, I . . . I don't know, yet. I haven't come to a decision. So, what happened?'

'We were rolling about in the haystack and she pulled her knickers down and showed me her crack. You know, "You show me yours" and all that.'

'No, I don't know.'

'Well, you do now.' Jackie's dark eyes gazed at me and frowned. 'Weren't you in the pube contest?' she asked.

'The what?'

'You weren't, were you?'

'No, whatever it is you're talking about.'

'We used to count our pubes every week to see who was winning. Christine Smith had a thick black bush while most of us were still as bald and soft as a baby's bum.'

'Jackie, your despicable behaviour surprises me,' I said admonishingly. 'Hang on a minute. Where was I while all this was going on?'

'I don't know. Masturbating, I would imagine.'

'Jackie!'

'Didn't you masturbate?'

'No, I did *not*.'

'All I can say is that *you* surprise *me*. I thought that everyone masturbated. Friday afternoons behind the kitchens was where the action was. Hands down knickers, fingers rubbing . . . There were girls frigging and coming like there was no tomorrow.'

Jackie had not only surprised me, but shocked me. And she'd finally driven home to me just how inexperienced I was. I began to wonder whether I was abnormal as I recalled spending Friday afternoons in the library reading Shakespeare. Perhaps I should have explored other girls' sex cracks. But no. To engage in lesbian sex wasn't normal. Of course teenagers experimented, but not with their own sex. Or did they? According to Jackie, teenage girls did far more than experiment with each other. Frigging and coming like there was no tomorrow?

'So, this dirty book,' she grinned salaciously. 'Want me to give you some ideas?'

'No, thank you,' I returned firmly. 'Jackie, we were best friends at school. We spent weekends together and had sleep-overs. How come I knew nothing about your . . . your lesbianism?'

'It wasn't lesbianism,' she giggled. 'For goodness' sake, Jade. Most boys wank each other off when they're in their early teens and—'

'Wank each other off?' I gasped in astonishment. '*You* should write filthy books, not me.'

'Now there's a thought. Seriously, Jade, most schoolgirls touch and frig each other. It's perfectly normal.'

'*Normal*? Do you . . . As we're on the taboo subject, do you still masturbate?'

12

'Since I dumped Ian, I've had no choice.'

'Well, I don't know what to say. I thought . . . I don't know what I thought.'

I thought that I'd led the life of a nun in comparison to Jackie. I realized that she was prone to exaggerating, but she wasn't a liar. Jenny Hardbrooke? My God. The last I'd heard of Jenny, she was working in the local library. And she was married with a child. The next time I saw her, I'd picture her naked in a haystack, her legs wide open and Jackie's finger in her pussy. What would her husband think if he knew of her sordid past?

I wanted to ask Jackie about her many sexual exploits, but decided against it. We'd never talked about sex before. Our times together had been spent enjoying shopping or having a drink in a pub. She'd always gone on about men, asking me what I'd thought of this one or that one, but we'd never discussed sex. I'd thought I'd known her so well, but now? I supposed she'd thought me too prudish to talk about sex. It had obviously been my talking about erotic fiction that had sparked her off. Gazing at her slender fingers, I imagined her masturbating, rubbing the solid nodule of her clitoris to orgasm. Did she finger her pussy?

Wondering about writing erotic fiction, I came to a decision, as we sipped our coffee. I'd write a couple of chapters, as David had suggested, and see how I got on. Lesbian sex would be easy enough to imagine. There again, I'd never masturbated myself, let alone another woman. Feeling that I'd missed out as I eyed Jackie's nipples pressing through the thin material of her tight T-shirt, I wondered what it would be like to explore her naked body. *Stop it*, I urged myself mentally. What the hell was I thinking?

'What's on your mind?' Jackie asked knowingly, following my gaze and looking down at her elongated nipples.

'Er . . . Nothing.' I smiled, my face flushing. 'Fancy going to the pub tonight?'

'Yes, why not? We'll celebrate the beginning of your new career as a pornographer.' She stared into my eyes and giggled. 'Or is it pornographess?'

'We'll celebrate nothing of the sort,' I stated firmly. 'Pornographess, indeed.'

'Have it your way,' she laughed. 'Right, I'll see you there at seven.' Leaving the kitchen, she turned in the doorway and flashed me a salacious grin. 'We'll get wrecked on vodka,' she giggled.

'I'm not getting wrecked on anything,' I snapped, following her to the front door. 'And don't be late. The last time you said you'd meet me at seven, I was left on my own for over an hour.'

'Don't worry, I'll be there on time.'

'You'd better be.'

When Jackie had gone, I went into my den and picked the book up. Reading the smut, as Jackie had called it, really did turn me on. The heroine had been stripped naked and was being attended by three men. One was doing her bum, another her pussy and the third her mouth. Sperm pumping into her anal canal, flooding her tight pussy and filling her gobbling mouth . . . Leaving nothing to the imagination, the author must have personally experienced the crude act, I mused. Three penises pumping sperm in a girl's orifices? I couldn't begin to imagine what it would be like to commit such a vulgar act, and found myself thinking that the girl was nothing more than a common tart.

'God,' I breathed, realizing that I was beginning to believe in the characters. The book certainly made good reading and, I have to confess, also made me very wet. My only sexual experiences having been with Alan, I'd never imagined sex with another man – let alone with three men at once. Reading about one man's tongue slipping into the girl's sex-juiced pussy as another man licked the rosebud of her tight bottom-hole, I realized that my arousal was rocketing. But this was what the book was designed to do, I reflected. A real turn-on, heightening the reader's libido to the point where . . . Masturbation?

Tugging my skirt up, I reclined in the chair and slipped my hand down the front of my panties. My vaginal lips swollen, my sex crack drenched with my lubricious juices, I couldn't believe how hard my clitoris was. Running my finger down the wet ravine of my opening pussy, I explored the moist entrance to my hot vagina. I'd never touched myself like this before, never explored the intricate inner folds of my vaginal crack. My finger instinctively slipping into my hot pussy, my heart racing, I gasped as my muscles tightened. Massaging my sensitive inner flesh, the beautiful sensations rippling through my quivering body, I felt an overwhelming need to come.

Slipping my wet finger out of the tight sheath of my pussy, I tentatively massaged the solid protrusion of my expectant clitoris. Breathing deeply as the electrifying sensations permeated my contracting womb, I moved forward in the chair and parted my thighs further. I'd never dreamed of masturbating, and became riddled with guilt as I rubbed my clitoris faster. Consoling myself with the thought that most women masturbated, I closed my eyes and pictured the girl in the book. Tongues were entering her creamy vaginal sheath, seeking the sensitive brown ring of her bottom-hole, licking her wet sex flesh, lapping up her juices of lust, taking her to orgasm. Fingers penetrated the secret entrance to her bottom, massaging deep inside her quivering body as she gasped and writhed in her illicit pleasure.

I'd had a few orgasms with Alan, but the pleasure I'd derived from our lovemaking had come from the intimate bonding of the union. He'd always come, of course. But his sperm gushing into my pussy had usually signalled the premature end of our passion. More often than not, I'd been left in a quivering state of arousal. Perhaps I should have masturbated, taken myself to orgasm when he'd gone home. He should have made sure that my needs were fulfilled rather than concentrating on satisfying his selfish male desires.

Should I have taken him into my mouth? I pondered as I thought of his hard penis entering the tight sheath of my pussy. Should I have sucked his purple knob to orgasm and swallowed his sperm? He'd once used the term *mouth-fuck*. It had revolted me. On reflection, perhaps it was Alan himself who had revolted me, not the crude words themselves. Mouth-fuck. Fuck-mouth. Mouth-sperming. I'd have to get used to such words if I was going to write erotica. Erotica? Or pornography?

'Ooh!' I cried as my orgasm suddenly erupted within my pulsating clitoris. Thinking about Alan's penis shafting my tight pussy, and picturing the naked girl with three men screwing and sperming her orifices, I experienced the most intense orgasm ever. My love juices gushing into my panties, waves of pure sexual bliss transmitting from my pulsating clitoris and spreading throughout my trembling body, I thought I'd never come down from my orgasmic heaven.

Slipping my free hand down the front of my wet panties, I drove my finger into my hot pussy as I sustained my shuddering orgasm. Massaging my inner vaginal flesh against the hardness of my pubic bone, gasping and whimpering in my new-found sexual euphoria, I fervently massaged my swollen clitoris and fingered the wet duct of my pussy. My juices of arousal flooding my hand, gushing into my panties, I writhed and whimpered in the grip of pure sexual elation. On and on waves of sexual bliss rolled through my quivering body. My heart racing, my breathing fast and shallow, I thought I was going to pass out as the almost agonizing pleasure peaked.

Finally slowing my massaging rhythm as the beautiful sensations began to subside, I lay dazed in the chair, panting as my body shook uncontrollably in the aftermath of my illicit self-loving. I now knew why Jackie masturbated, I reflected as I clambered to my feet and swayed in my orgasmic drunkenness on my trembling legs. Had I known of the immense pleasure masturbation brought, I'd have joined the girls behind the kitchens at school. There again, massaging my clitoris to orgasm in the privacy of my flat was one thing. To masturbate while other girls watched was something I'd never contemplate. And to masturbate each other . . .

To my horror, I found myself wondering what it would be like to watch Jackie rub her clitoris to orgasm. I'd never seen a blue movie, despite Alan's many attempts to show me one, let alone watched a girl masturbate. I'd always thought sex an act to be shared with the one you love, not alone or with an audience. Or with three men simultaneously. Did I really want to watch Jackie bring herself off? Thinking about rubbing her clitoris to orgasm as she lay naked on my bed, I sighed. Perhaps I'd wanted to satisfy a fantasy? But why was I having such fantasies?

Deciding to take a shower after my pioneering act of self-abuse, I walked into my bedroom and slipped out of my

17

blouse and skirt. Standing before the full-length mirror as I released my bra and tugged my pussy-soaked panties down, I admired the violin curves of my naked body. Whether it had been reading the book or talking to Jackie about sex that had driven me to masturbation, I didn't know. But I did know that my libido was again soaring out of control. I felt sexually aroused as never before. Focusing on the reflection of my creamy-pink vaginal crack peeping at me through my juice-matted blonde pubic hairs, I felt a quiver run up my spine.

Parting my feet and bending my knees, I peeled open the swollen lips of my vagina. The intricate folds of flesh unfurling, my clitoris emerging from beneath its fleshy veil, I gazed at the milky fluid trickling from my open sex hole. Parting my pussy lips further, I focused on the remnants of my hymen surrounding the portal to my sex sheath. Alan's penis had torn down my curtain of innocence, fucked my pussy and spermed my cervix. His balls had battered my firm buttocks as he'd fucked and spunked my virginal body.

'No,' I breathed, running my fingertip up and down the dripping valley of my yearning pussy. I couldn't masturbate again. I had to control myself, I knew as I went into the bathroom and stepped into the shower. I had to stop thinking about a penis fucking me, a purple knob jetting sperm deep into my pussy. The hot water splashing over my naked body, I couldn't drag my mind away from the amazing orgasm I'd had. How many times a week did women masturbate? Or men, for that matter? My fingers between the swell of my pussy lips again, I was like a child with a new toy. Was it bad for my health? I wondered stupidly, rubbing my ballooning clitoris as the water caressed my naked skin like a thousand tiny fingertips. How many times could I come in one day?

After leaving the shower and drying my naked body, I dressed and sat at my desk to write. If I could make a start on the first chapter, I'd get the feel of the book, I reflected, turning the computer on. Set the scene, introduce the characters and . . . I hadn't even thought of the characters, let alone a storyline. But I decided to see what I came up with and started bashing away at the keyboard. At least I could now write about masturbating, I reflected guiltily.

Chapter Two

Glancing up at the clock, I realized that I'd been writing for over two hours. Switching the computer off, I grabbed my bag and left the flat. I'd told Jackie to get there on time and now it was I who was going to turn up late. Walking down the street, I thought that it would serve her right to have to sit there waiting for me. Many times I'd had to sit in the pub waiting for her. Feeling self-conscious, not knowing where to look, I'd felt awkward and uncomfortable. Perhaps I was naturally shy, I reflected. Serve her right or not, I didn't like being late. But I'd been working hard on my new novel, I consoled myself. And, the terrible thought struck me, masturbating my clitoris to orgasm. God, what had I done?

'I thought you weren't coming,' Jackie complained as I walked over to a corner table and joined her.

'I've come now,' I replied, wishing I'd chosen my words more carefully. 'I mean, I'm here now.'

'There's your vodka,' she said, pushing a glass across the table. 'The ice has melted, but that's your fault.'

'I'm sorry,' I sighed, sipping my drink. 'I got engrossed in the book and lost all track of time.'

'The smutty book?' she asked, rather too loudly for my liking.

'No, of course not,' I lied. 'I'm working on the book they turned down, trying to improve it.'

'By adding lots of sex scenes to it?' she beamed excitely.

'"He forced his huge cock right up her tight pussy and fucked her hot cunt and—"'

'No, Jackie. That is *not* what I've been writing. As I said earlier, *you* should write filth, not me.'

'I might just do that. A book in the form of diaries,' she murmured pensively. 'I could call it *My Days in the Haystack*.'

'Don't be ridiculous,' I returned. '*My Days in the Haystack*, for goodness' sake.'

'How about *Preteen Pleasures*?'

'*Preteen*? How old were you when . . .'

'Quite young,' she sniggered.

Gazing at Jackie's loose-fitting blouse, the half-moons of her young breasts, I wondered why her libido ran wild most of the time. It probably had something to do with her discovering sex before she'd reached her teens. She seemed to think of nothing other than sex, unlike me. We were both the same age, so why was I so very different? Why was anyone different? I mused. Some girls wore skirts so short that their panties were on display, while I wore knee-length skirts. Give me a child for the first seven years . . . Was it my parents' doing?

'Anyway, I was quite pleased when you didn't turn up at seven,' Jackie giggled.

'Oh, why's that?' I asked, dragging my gaze away from the deep ravine of her cleavage.

'I was chatted up by that bloke at the bar. The one standing by the fruit machine with long hair and a leather jacket.'

'He looks like a nomad,' I whispered, eyeing his scuffed boots and torn jeans.

'He is. Well, he's living in a caravan until he gets his own flat. I told him that I was meeting a friend so he went back to the bar and joined his mate. I should have come here on my own.'

'Oh, thank you very much,' I returned. 'If I'm cramping your style, then—'

'I was only joking.' Her eyes lighting up, she leaned across the table. 'Jade, he's looking this way,' she whispered loudly, grabbing my arm. 'His friend looks a bit of all right. What do you think?'

'Jackie, we're not here to—'

'Shush, they're coming over.'

Raising my eyes as the two young men joined us, I knew that I really didn't feel like being sociable to strangers. Having been up to London and had my dreams shattered, I wished I'd stayed at home and gone to bed early. Jackie was soon in conversation with the nomad, leaving me to contend with his weird friend who seemed to think it necessary to enlighten me as to his name, age, state of unemployment and lack of money. *Great*, I thought. *Another waste of space called Alan.* This one was eighteen years old, on the dole and stone broke. At least my Alan had had some money.

'I'm a musician,' he enlightened me, holding his glass on its side to indicate that it was empty and in need of refilling.

'Really?' I sighed, forcing a smile.

'The guitar. I play lead with The Gremlins From Hell. We do pubs and clubs.'

'Where did you find the name?' I asked with more than a hint of sarcasm. 'A children's programme on the Cartoon Channel?'

'No, we . . .'

'I don't know how you can afford it, seeing as you're on the dole.'

'Afford it?' he echoed, hooking his long black hair behind his ears. 'Afford what?'

'Playing in pubs and clubs. Lugging your gear about and paying for petrol, and—'

'We don't play for nothing,' he laughed. 'We get paid for the gigs.'

'So people actually give you money to listen to you playing your guitar?' I asked mockingly. 'You obviously inform Social Security when you earn money from your musical exploits.'

'Of course not.' He frowned, looking at me as if I were stupid. 'We get a hundred each for a really good gig. Trouble is, they're far and few between. I don't suppose—' He broke off, grinning as he passed me his empty glass. 'I don't suppose you could . . .?'

'Your supposition is correct,' I smiled, wondering at his effrontery.

'It's just that I'm right out of cash. I'm trying to get into journalism but it's not easy. I've had a few short stories published but—'

'Short stories?' I echoed, sitting upright and taking an interest.

'The national women's mags. You know, romance, twist in the tale, that sort of stuff. The money's not bad, but . . .'

'How long have you been writing?' I interrupted him.

'A few years. Poetry, mainly. And songs, of course. You know, for the band.'

'Here,' I said, taking a five-pound note from my bag. 'Get yourself a drink. I'll have a vodka and lime, with ice.'

'Oh, right,' he grinned in surprise as he took the money. 'Thanks very much.'

Jackie was too enthralled by the Neanderthal lookalike to notice that I'd bought Alan a drink. Chatting about some nightclub or other, her eyes sparkling lustfully, she reached beneath the table and squeezed or touched some part of the man's body. I didn't dare think *which* part as he leaned forward and kissed her. I also didn't dare think what was lurking in the undergrowth of his full beard as he pressed his beer-wet lips to hers.

Alan returned and placed the drinks on the table – and pocketed my change. He was OK, I observed. He was scruffy and unshaven, but clean. His jeans had been washed and, although his Jimi Hendrix T-shirt was torn, it wasn't dirty. *I notice these things*, I mused, gazing into his dark eyes as he smiled at me and leaned forward. Thinking that he was about to follow the nomad's approach and kiss me, I sat back in my chair.

'Guess what?' he whispered, again hooking his hair behind his ears.

'What?' I frowned, tentatively moving forward as I realized that he didn't intend to wet my lips with lager by snogging me.

'The manager has just booked us.'

'Booked us?'

'The band. I was talking to him earlier about it. He wants us to play here on Saturday night.'

'Is *he* in your band?' I asked, nodding towards the nomad who seemed to have his tongue down Jackie's throat.

'Big Dave? No, no. There are three of us. Steve the drummer, John the bass guitarist and me. Why don't you come along?'

'I might just do that. What sort of things do you play?'

'Rock, heavy rock. Mostly our own stuff.'

'Do you write the music *and* the lyrics?'

'Oh, yes. I don't suppose it's your scene.'

'It might be.' I smiled.

'Come along and see what you think. Want another vodka?'

'You mean, you want some more money so you can buy me another vodka.'

'I got fifty quid up front,' he announced proudly. 'The manager has seen us play down at The Frog Pond, so he knows we're good. When he booked us for Saturday, I told him that we had to have some cash up front. Oh, I didn't give you your change, did I?'

'It doesn't matter.'

'I'll get you another drink.'

Despite his name, which brought sad memories flooding back, Alan seemed pleasant enough. But I didn't want a relationship. A friend, but not a lover. At least, I tried to kid myself that I didn't want a relationship. Glancing at Jackie, who by now was being indecently molested by the hairy nomad, I shook my head. She didn't want a relationship. Cold sex, or *raw sex*, as she'd often put it – but not a relationship.

After a couple more drinks, Jackie made her excuses and left with the nomad. No doubt she intended to pull her knickers down and have sex with the animal once they were ensconced in a shop doorway. I was quite pleased to be rid of the deviant pair and it didn't bother Alan when his friend announced that he was leaving. If anything, he seemed relieved.

'Are you two good friends?' I asked, downing yet another vodka.

'Mates,' he smiled. 'There's a difference.'

'Is there?'

'He's more of an acquaintance than a friend. To be honest, he's more of a pain in the arse than an acquaintance. He follows the band around. A sort of hanger-on.'

'He must like the music,' I proffered.

'He likes the free drinks he gets when he tells the bar staff that he's our roadie. Would you like another vodka?'

'I've had too much to drink as it is,' I giggled girlishly, and then changed my mind. 'Oh, go on, then,' I said, deciding to drown my sorrows. 'One more won't hurt.'

Feeling dizzy as Alan went to the bar, the room beginning to spin round, I knew that I shouldn't drink any more. But, after the disappointing news from the literary agent, I decided to have a good time. I needed to get out and about and meet people, I reflected again. Especially if I was going to write erotic fiction. But a good time didn't mean pulling my knickers down and having my arse done. God, what an awful expression.

'So, what do you do for a living?' Alan asked as he brought the drinks to the table and sat opposite me.

'I'm a writer,' I replied, knowing from experience what he'd ask me next.

'What do you write?'

'Books,' I smiled, wondering what to say in response to the next inevitable question.

'What sort of books?'

'I . . . I write romantic fiction but haven't been published yet. My agent . . .'

'You've got an agent?' he interrupted me eagerly.

'Sort of. He's seen my novel and has turned it down so, technically, he's not my agent. He wants me to write . . . He wants me to spice up my work.'

'Sex?'

'Yes.'

'And that's not what you want?'

'No, it's not.'

'Don't do it, Jade,' he advised me, hooking his hair behind his ears for the umpteenth time. 'Write what you want to write, not what—'

'The thing is, I need the money,' I confessed, wondering why he didn't have his hair cut. 'It's all very well writing what I want, but if it's not commercial and doesn't earn money, there's no point.'

'There's *every* point.'

'Alan, what's the use in spending all day, every day writing and not earning a penny? I'd starve, wouldn't I?'

'Yes, but . . . I suppose you're right. It just seems a shame to have to churn out that sort of stuff.' He paused, his dark eyes staring at me. 'Romantic fiction and sex . . . Can't you bring an element of sex into the romance? After all, the two go together.'

'They want more than an *element* of sex. They want unadulterated filth.'

'Oh, I see. What are you going to do?'

'Finish my drink, go home and have some coffee, and then think about it.'

'I wish you luck. Whatever you do, don't give up writing. Oh, about Saturday . . .'

'I'll be here.' I hesitated, pondering on the thought roaming my head. I was about to make a big mistake, I was sure. But I went ahead anyway. 'Do you want to come back for coffee?' I finally asked. 'Just coffee.' *Coffee, not sex.*

'OK. Thanks,' he beamed, finishing his drink.

Walking home, I wondered what I was letting myself in for as Alan laughed and joked about writing dirty books. I wanted him as a friend, but nothing more. He'd turned out to be good company and was genuinely interested in my work. I'd enjoyed the evening with him and was looking forward to watching him play in his band on Saturday. But . . . but what? My head spinning as the alcohol numbed my brain, I didn't know what to think. I *couldn't* think.

'This is it,' I said, trying not to slur my words as I led him through the hall and showed him into the lounge.

'It's a nice place.' He smiled. 'Really nice.'

'I like it,' I mumbled, leaning against the door frame to steady my swaying body.

'Ah, Lowry,' he grinned, gazing at the picture above the mantelpiece. '*A River Bank*. That's one of my favourites. Excellent stuff. Do you have anything else by Lowry?'

'No, that's the only print I have.'

'Shame. I think Lowry was misunderstood. He—'

'All artists seem to be misunderstood,' I broke in. 'Misunderstanding seems to be a trait among artists.'

'Now, Jimi Hendrix . . .'

'Where do you live?' I asked as he studied the painting.

'With my parents at the moment. I can't afford a flat. It's OK living at home, but . . .'

Managing to stagger across the room and flop onto the sofa as Alan rambled on about the trials and tribulations of living with his parents, I tried to focus on the mantelpiece clock as the room spun round. Finally joining me on the sofa, he talked about his music and how he hoped I'd enjoy the band on Saturday. I tried to make some sort of coherent conversation but the alcohol wouldn't allow my thoughts to turn into speech.

I don't know what possessed me to place my hand on his thigh as he moved a little closer. The alcohol, the dirty book, talking to Jackie about sex, masturbating . . . I'd not seen a man's penis for over a year, let alone clutched one in my hand. Were they all the same? I wondered in my alcoholic haze. I knew that they varied in size and began to wonder how big the musician's was. Fighting my uncharacteristic desires as I slid my hand further up his inner thigh, I wished I'd not invited him round. I should have gone straight to bed. I felt I had no control over my actions as I slid his zip down. What he was thinking, I didn't want to know. I didn't know what *I* was thinking as I thrust my hand into the opening of his jeans and groped for his penis. He probably thought I was pissed, which I was – and an easy lay. Lay? Whatever happened, he wasn't going to lay me. What a terrible expression.

Watching my hand as if it was disembodied, I hauled his erect penis out. What the hell was I doing? I wondered, kneading the warm shaft of his huge organ. He said nothing as I gazed at his fleshy rod as if I'd never seen one before. Pulling his foreskin back and exposing the silky globe of his purple knob, my vaginal muscles tightening, I knew that I'd crossed the threshold. There was no turning back now.

Focusing on the small slit in Alan's glans, my head spinning, I wondered what his knob tasted like. This would be a first, I ruminated. A battle was raging in my mind: I knew that I shouldn't have pulled his penis out and yet I couldn't help myself. Why was I so indecisive? I wondered, kneading the hardness of his warm shaft. The girl in the book had been mouth-fucked, I reflected, my vaginal juices flooding my panties. Did *I* want to be mouth-fucked? Did I want my mouth spermed? Why couldn't I make a decision? Who was whispering in my head, telling me right from wrong? My mother?

Remaining silent as I toyed with the loose flesh of his foreskin, Alan closed his eyes. I felt that, if I didn't grab the chance while I could, I'd regret it later. I either sucked a man's knob now, or for ever lived without the experience. Many times in the past I'd decided against doing this or that when I'd had the opportunity. I'd usually wished that I'd gone ahead when it was too late, when the chance had sailed by like a passing ship. Was Alan a passing ship? *Take what you can when you can*, Jackie had always said. Did that include sucking the ballooning knob of a virtual stranger's penis?

Moving closer to his erect organ, I studied the veined shaft, the shape of the rim running around the base of his bulbous knob. I'd never examined a penis in this way before. With Alan the ex, I'd only guided him into my pussy, never really seeing his cock. How many vaginas had this penis fucked? I found myself wondering as I gazed at the small bridge of skin running from the back of his knob to his foreskin. How many girls had taken his purple globe into their mouths and sucked out his sperm? *Take what you can when you can.*

Leaning over, my open mouth only inches from Alan's beautiful knob, I hesitated. What was wrong with me? I wondered. Jackie would have gobbled his knob, eagerly, taken the full length of his penis into her wet mouth and sucked him to orgasm. There again, Jackie had fingered another girl's pussy and God only knew what else in the name of cold lust. Finally plucking up courage as Alan moved forward on the sofa, his penis swelling in my hand, I tentatively kissed his purple globe.

Breathing heavily, he reclined as I leaned over and sucked his plum into my hot mouth. Uncharacteristic thoughts hurling around the wreckage of my mind, I ran my tongue around the bulb of his silky-smooth knob, the salty flavour tantalizing my taste buds as I moved my hand up and down his solid shaft. Alan was going to come in my mouth, I knew as he clutched my head and began to tremble. Was this what I'd wanted? I didn't *know* what I wanted as I instinctively bobbed my head up and down, his swollen glans repeatedly driving to the back of my throat. I felt like the tart in the book. Mouth-fuck. Mouth-sperm. Was I a tart?

Easing his balls out of his jeans, I gazed at the hairy bag as his sperm-spheres rolled and heaved. His solid shaft between my taut lips, his bulbous knob deep within my mouth, I watched his balls move within the thin bag of his scrotum as he gasped in his male pleasure. What did sperm taste like? I wondered as his body became rigid. Mouth-fuck. Mouth-sperm. *Take what you can when you can.*

His sperm finally gushing into my mouth, the salty liquid bathing my tongue, filling my cheeks as his cock rhythmically twitched, I swallowed hard. I'd done it, I thought excitedly. I'd actually brought a man off in my mouth. I wished that Jackie could have seen me as I drank from Alan's orgasming knob. But no. She'd probably laugh and inform me that she'd sucked her first knob when she was twelve years old. Twelve, for God's sake!

The white liquid running down his veined shaft and over my hand, I sucked out his orgasm until he pushed me away and doubled up as if in pain. Sitting upright and licking my lips as he recovered, I suddenly sobered up and realized that I'd behaved like a common slut. Alan would think that I'd taken him back to my flat to seduce him. He'd think me a slag for . . . All I'd done was taken what I could when I could. Was that a crime?

'Jade,' he whispered, tugging his zip up. 'Jade, that was something else.'

'Good,' I murmured, not knowing what to say as I felt my face flush. 'You'd . . . you'd better go now.'

'Yes, right.' Standing up, he adjusted his jeans and smiled at me. 'I'll be in the pub tomorrow night if . . .'

'I'm not sure what I'm doing tomorrow,' I said, knowing full well that I had nothing planned. I could feel sperm running down my chin. 'I might be there,' I murmured, wiping my mouth with the back of my hand.

'I hope you turn up. It'll be good to see you again. I—'

'Go now, Alan,' I broke in before he could say anything stupid about love. What was love?

'Jade, I feel that I . . .'

'Go now,' I repeated, rising to my feet and seeing him to the door before he had a chance to proclaim his undying love for me. 'I'm sorry about the coffee.'

'Don't apologize,' he chuckled. 'You were fantastic.'

Returning to the lounge, the taste of Alan's sperm lingering on my tongue, I couldn't believe what I'd done. Fantastic? He must have thought me a slut, a whore. To suck off a virtual stranger was so out of character for me. And, to make matters worse, I'd instigated the sordid episode. I felt disgusted with myself. There was no way I was going to that pub again, I decided. After the way I'd behaved, I knew that I could never face Alan.

At least I could now write about blow jobs as well as masturbation, I thought, pondering on the dreadful term. Lying full-length on the sofa, I wished that I'd not gone out with Jackie, or invited Alan back or sucked him off or . . . What was done was done.

But I'd never do it again.

I was about to close my eyes and drift off to sleep when the front doorbell rang. 'God,' I breathed, thinking that the musician had come back for more as I almost fell off the sofa. And never again would I drink too much. Perhaps he'd returned to inform me that he'd fallen in love with me. Love? That would be all I needed! Walking through the hall, I brushed my hair back with my fingers and took a deep breath. Perhaps I should pretend to be asleep in bed, I thought, hovering by the door. Best to get it over with, I decided.

'Hi, Jade!' Jackie trilled as I opened the door. 'Thought I'd come round for coffee.'

'At this time of night?' I sighed. 'It's almost twelve.'

'So what? Put the kettle on and we'll have a chat.'

'How was the nomad?' I asked as she followed me into the kitchen.

'The what?'

'That dreadful man you were groping in the pub.'

'His name's Dave. He's great. We went to the park and walked by the pond.'

'And?'

'Well, you know.'

'Yes, I believe I do. How many men have you had?'

'Don't know, I lost count. Anyway, what about you?'

'Me?'

'How did you get on?'

'Alan came back for coffee.'

'Not another Alan?' she grinned. 'Did you do it?'

'Do it? Jackie, sex isn't . . . No, we didn't do it. We talked about writing books and poetry and music, and then he went home.'

Pouring the coffee, I eyed Jackie's dishevelled hair. There were grass stains on her skirt, and I imagined her on her back in the park as the nomad fucked her to orgasm. I couldn't help thinking that her pussy would be full of sperm. I was about to tell her that she'd behaved no better than a slut, but then I realized that I'd been as bad, if not worse. The pot calling the kettle black, as my father always said. I wanted to tell Jackie that I'd been mouth-fucked, but thought better of it. I was the pot, the sperm-pot.

'There,' I smiled, passing her a cup of coffee. 'So, are you seeing him again?'

'I doubt it,' she replied dismissively. 'He's broke, so there's not much point. Mind you, he was good in the park.'

'Those are your criteria, then? Money and good in bed. Was he clean?'

'Clean?' Jackie frowned.

'He looked dirty. I doubt that he's washed in weeks.'

'He was scruffy, but clean,' she returned. 'You're such a snob, Jade. That's why you never have any fun. You're too haughty to mix with normal people and enjoy life. What do you think you've got in your knickers? Some sort of priceless treasure to be kept secret from the world? We've all got cunts, Jade. Whether you like it or not, all women have cunts.'

'I know that. What I meant was . . . Anyway, I'm not a snob. It's just that I don't agree with screwing around. And I don't like the word . . . The C-word.'

'You won't even write about sex, let alone do it.'

'As it happens, I . . . I gave Alan a blow job.'

'You sucked him off?' she shrieked, holding her hand to her mouth.

'Yes, I did. So you can forget about snobbery and my never having any fun.'

'Good God. Jade the prude sucking a bloke's knob on the first night. Did he fuck you?'

'No, he didn't. I don't want to talk about it, Jackie.'

'But you'll write about it?'

'I might.'

Wishing that I'd kept my mouth shut, with both Jackie and Alan, I sat at the table and toyed with my coffee cup. Hanging my head, I felt embarrassed. Jackie was gazing at me – I could feel her stare burning into me. Was I a snob? I wondered. I'd always had a thing about clean clothes, noticed what people were wearing and whether they'd washed or not, but that wasn't snobbish. Perhaps my attitude towards sex *was* prudish, but that didn't make me a snob.

Turning my thoughts to erotic fiction, I gazed at the swell of Jackie's breasts exposed by her partially open blouse. I wanted to see her nipples, compare her breasts with mine. Wondering about her sex crack, I took a deep breath. Why was I thinking like that? I mused as Jackie leaned forward, partially revealing her lacy bra. Reckoning that she knew what I was thinking, I sipped my coffee and talked about the hot weather we'd been having.

'It's the middle of June,' she laughed. 'That's why it's been so hot. Getting back to the blow job, did he come in your mouth?'

'Jackie, I don't want to talk about it,' I snapped.

'Did you swallow?'

'For God's sake. Yes, he came in my mouth and yes, I swallowed. OK?'

'Great! Was he big?'

'Yes . . . Oh, I don't know. I'm beginning to wish that you'd been there. You could have seen for yourself.'

'I wish I had. I watched my sister suck her boyfriend off once.'

'You watched Christine suck her boyfriend?' I gasped in disbelief.

'Our parents were out and we were mucking about in the bedroom. Christine got Mike's cock out and sucked him off.'

'You never cease to amaze me,' I frowned.

'And then *I* sucked him.'

'You sucked him while your sister . . .'

'It was a laugh, Jade. We were having some fun, that was all. I don't know what this thing is that you have about sex.

It seems to me that you look upon sex as some kind of sacred act. That's why I've never talked to you about it.'

'Not sacred, exactly. But it is something to be shared with the one you love.'

'Oh, so you *love* Alan now?'

'No, of course . . . OK, you win,' I conceded.

'I'll tell you what we'll do. You get Alan round here again and I'll join in. It'll be fun.'

'No, Jackie! Certainly not!'

'Come on, Jade. Climb down from your pedestal and live for once. Besides, if you're going to write about sex, then you'll need all the experience you can get. We'll wank him, take turns to wank him and watch his spunk shoot out.'

'Jackie, I am *not* going to take part in . . . in a threesome.'

'It's not a threesome. We'll just have some fun with his dick, that's all.'

Shaking my head as Jackie left the room to go to the loo, I wondered what Alan would think if she arrived and joined in. He'd think we were a couple of sluts. Take turns to wank him and watch his spunk shoot out? I'd thought I'd known Jackie well, I reflected. Obviously not. Was it *her* attitude towards sex that was abnormal, or mine? Was a penis merely something to enjoy and have fun with? My strait-laced upbringing had suppressed my sexual feelings and desires, I knew. But was my outlook really that odd?

'My panties are soaked with spunk,' Jackie complained unashamedly as she returned and sat at the table.

'I don't think I want to know about the state of your panties,' I said, shaking my head.

'At least you swallowed the stuff,' she grinned. 'Fancy giving a bloke a blow job on the first night. I can't believe it.'

'Jackie, will you please stop going on about it?'

'I'll ask you one more thing, and then I'll shut up. How many cocks have you sucked?'

'That was my first. And don't laugh or call me a prude. I've just been a little slower than you.'

'Slower? Bloody hell, you've been standing still. Anyway, how about the thing with this Alan bloke? Shall we have some fun with his dick?'

I must admit that by now I was in two minds over her proposition. It wasn't so much that I wanted to have some fun with Alan's dick or experience the sordid act to help me with the book. I think that I was intrigued rather than anything else. The thought of Jackie and I wanking Alan, playing with his cock and making him come, grabbed my fascination. But I didn't think Alan was the sort of person to . . . I didn't know what sort of person he was. He'd not thought it a good idea for me to write about sex. There again, he might jump at the chance of having two attractive girls wank him off.

'No,' I finally replied. 'Anyway, I doubt that I'll be seeing him again.'

'That's a shame,' she sighed. 'It would have been great to share a bloke.'

'Share a bloke? For goodness' sake, Jackie. The very notion is . . . It's awful.'

'Where's the harm in having a laugh? Sex should be fun. Not a serious act solely for the purpose of having kids. If you do see him again, get him round here and we'll have some fun. Anyway, I'd better be going.'

'And I'd better get to bed. I'll ring you some time.'

'Ring me when you've lured Alan here, OK?'

'I doubt that I'll see him again.'

'If you do, ring me. Right, I'll see you soon.'

When Jackie had gone, I wandered into my bedroom and slipped beneath the quilt. Pondering on her disgusting proposition, I was sure that the sordid episode would lead to group sex. I couldn't see Jackie playing with Alan's dick without wanting him to slip it into her pussy. And then he'd screw me and then Jackie would touch me and expect me to . . . My imagination was running away with me. All she wanted was to have some fun with his dick, not with my pussy. Didn't she?

Chapter Three

To my surprise, Alan rang at ten the following morning. Ex-Alan, not musician Alan. After a year without any contact, he suddenly announced that he wanted us to get back together. The tart had found someone else and he should never have left me and he wished he could turn the clock back and he'd realized just how much he loved me and . . . I listened to his drivel until boredom set in and I finally interrupted him.

'I've got someone else,' I announced proudly.

'*What?*' he gasped in surprise. 'You've been seeing someone else?'

'Of course. Surely you didn't expect me to stay celibate.'

'Who is he? I mean, where did you meet him? How long has this been going on?'

'He's called Alan. The Pub. And for about two months.' I didn't want to tell him I'd only met the young musician the evening before.

'Alan?'

'Ironic, isn't it?'

'Jade . . . Are you busy today?'

'I'm working on my new book.'

'I've got the day off. I'll call round, if that's OK?'

'Well . . . I'm not seeing Alan until this evening so you can come round for coffee, if you so wish. Not for long, though. I have a lot of work to do.'

'And we have a lot of talking to do.'

'Talking?' I echoed with a giggle. 'What about?'

'Us . . . I mean . . . I'll be about an hour.'

'Whenever,' I said dismissively, and hung up.

That was a turn-up for the books, I mused as I showered and dressed. I'd been alone for over a year, and within twelve hours I'd sucked a man off and Alan the ex wanted us to get back together. *Things always happen in threes*, I mused. What was the third surprise? Another cock to suck? No, I wasn't going to play the field. I had my writing to get on with. The last thing I needed was men disrupting my life. Love brought pain, I recalled sadly. And, inevitably, desolation. Perhaps Jackie's thinking made sense after all. No love, no commitments – just raw sex.

Although I felt guilty, I also felt proud of myself. Sucking Alan to orgasm and drinking his sperm had been like passing my driving test. I'd done it. I'd actually done it. I'd pulled a young man in the pub, taken him home, hauled his cock out and wanked and sucked him until he'd spermed in my mouth. A triumph, a first, a pioneering leap forward . . . Realizing that I was being stupid, I bashed away at the computer keyboard until the doorbell rang.

'Hi,' I said as Alan stepped into the hall. 'How are things?' I hoped that they were really bad. He deserved a taste of loneliness and desolation.

'I'm dossing on a friend's sofa,' he murmured dolefully. Did he want sympathy? 'Angela said that . . . The flat's in her name so I've had to leave.'

'How sad for you,' I grinned sarcastically as he followed me into the kitchen. 'Still, there are plenty of other slags around.' Was *I* a slag?

'It's good to see you again, Jade.'

'Is it?' He was a two-faced, cheating liar.

He leaned against the worktop as I filled the kettle. Looking him up and down from the corner of my eye, I thought that he didn't look too bad. He'd shaved and was wearing a clean shirt and pressed trousers. His hair was neat and I reckoned that he'd at least been looking after himself since the tart had evicted him. It seemed strange, having him in the flat after all that time. He'd been sleeping in her bed, fucking her and coming in her cunt . . . We were like strangers, I mused. Musician Alan and I had been strangers until—

'So, who's this bloke?' Alan asked, interrupting my thoughts. I detected a hint of jealousy as he hung his head.

'I told you, his name's Alan.'

'Serious, is it?'

'Serious enough,' I lied. Was it a lie? 'He's a musician. So, you and the tart are no longer.' I had to rub it in. 'Finished, split up . . .'

'I should never have left you,' he sighed. 'Jade, I—'

'What's done is done,' I broke in. Including sucking the sperm from a stranger's cock. 'We can't turn the clock back, Alan. Not that I'd want to.'

'So, you wouldn't consider us getting back together?'

'I was no good in bed. You said that Angela was into oral sex and just about everything else, unlike me. Besides, my Alan thinks that I'm brilliant in bed. What was it with Angela? Did she find someone who was better than you in bed?'

'No, it wasn't that. Perhaps we could have a drink or a meal some time.'

This really was ironic. He'd devastated me with his cruel words and was now almost begging me to take him back. It wasn't in my nature to be heartless, but I considered playing games with him. Perhaps I wanted revenge? I didn't know

43

what I wanted. But I *did* know that, for the first time in a year, I felt good inside. I had the musician after me, and now Alan the ex. The dirty book that the literary agent had given me constantly on my mind, I decided that I would have some fun with him. I wanted to show him that I'd changed, that I was no longer the prude. Did I want to shock him? More than likely.

'It's strange that you said I was no good in bed,' I persisted, pouring the coffee. 'Angela has dumped you for another man, and I've got a man who reckons that I'm a nymphomaniac. You seem to be the common denominator when it comes to being no good in bed.'

'It wasn't that,' he returned irritably. 'She was looking for something. I don't know what she wants and I don't think she does. But I do know that I don't want *her*. My biggest mistake was leaving you. I said things at the time that I didn't mean.'

Passing him a cup of coffee, I frowned. 'Didn't mean?' I echoed, feigning astonishment. 'If my memory serves me correctly, you said that I was asexual. You also informed me that I had no idea how to please a man and you were delighted because you'd found a proper woman at last.'

'Yes, but I didn't mean—'

'It was a year ago, Alan,' I broke in dismissively. 'Let's not drag up crap from the past. So, you're dossing on a friend's sofa? What plans do you have? Are you still working for the insurance company?'

'Yes, I am. As for plans, well . . . I'd thought that we might give it another go.'

'I've had a dozen or more men since you dumped me, Alan.'

'What? But you were never . . .'

'I've been living. I'm enjoying life now I'm free of the

constrictions of a possessive, jealous and dominant man who has no idea how to treat a woman.'

Standing before him, I rubbed the crotch of his trousers, feeling his penis through the tight material. He stared at me as though in a state of shock while I massaged his swelling organ. I didn't know why I was behaving like that. I supposed it was part of my plan for revenge. Plan? I had no plan. I didn't know what I was thinking as I contemplated pulling his cock out and wanking him. But I was enjoying the game. *Dangerous games*, I mused as his cock became fully erect. *Dangerous games, dangerous pleasure*.

Recalling the tart in the dirty book, I realized how easy it was to seduce men. I could have had Alan eating out of my hand, if I'd wanted to. Both Alans, in fact. I wanted to show ex-Alan that I'd not only changed, but was enjoying life to the full without him. He'd always thought I'd needed him, couldn't survive without him. He'd been wrong. I didn't want him to think me a tart, but . . . Perhaps I did, after all. Perhaps I wanted him to think me a common slag. *Revenge is sweet*, I reflected, slowly pulling his zip down. From angelic innocence to carnal lust – I was changing.

His eyes widening as my hand delved into his trousers and squeezed the warm shaft of his penis, I wondered what Alan the ex was thinking. I knew what *I* was thinking as I pulled his solid cock out. I was thinking that I needed experience to write my own dirty book. Feeling the fleshy shaft of his penis, I recalled the first time it had entered me, driven into the virginal duct of my pussy and spermed me. *Those were the days*, I reflected. *Days of innocence and naivety, trust and stupidity*.

'Jade . . .' he murmured as I wanked his hard penis. I grinned at him as I ran my hand up and down the twitching shaft of his cock, massaging his purple knob. Wanked? I thought about the word. I'd need to expand my vocabulary for my dirty book. Wank, fuck, shag . . . Cunt? I'd always hated the C-word. It was crude, cold, barren as the fields in winter. As was the act I was committing. Wanking Alan to orgasm wasn't really the sort of experience I needed, but it was fun. And it might be fun to utter one or two expletives, I chuckled inwardly, again recalling the book. *Do my arse. Spunk my arsehole and then come in my cunt and my mouth.*

Alan's gasps growing louder, I kneeled before him and took his swollen knob into my wet mouth. Looking up at his expression of astonishment, I ran my tongue over the silky-smooth crown of his glans and sucked harder. Pulling his heavy balls out of his trousers, I wondered when he'd last come. Perhaps he'd been wanking since the tart had thrown him out. Perhaps he'd been wanking and shooting his sperm while he'd been thinking of me, of my wet cunt. Cunt.

His sperm finally jetting from his throbbing knob, filling my gobbling mouth, he clutched my head and let out long low moans of pleasure. Swallowing the salty liquid, I had it in mind to make up for lost time, to catch up with Jackie. No, that was impossible. To catch up with Jackie would require me to screw about and suck six men every day for a year. *Nothing's impossible*, my thoughts urged me. *Screw and suck.*

'God,' Alan sighed as I sucked the last globules of sperm from his solid glans. Quivering, he leaned back on the worktop as I lapped up the spilled sperm from his deflating shaft, licked it off the wrinkled bag containing his sperm-spheres. Staring at his penis as it hung like a pale dead slug over his hairy balls, I recalled again the time he'd taken my virginity. We'd gasped and loved in our loving union. We'd touched and caressed, whispered words of love and fucked and come. And then he'd taken up with that slut and left me to cry rivers of tears while he spurted rivers of sperm over her cervix.

'You're not as big as my boyfriend,' I complained, rising to my feet and licking my sperm-dripping lips. 'And you come too quickly. Still, you always did.'

'Why did you do that?' he asked, puzzlement reflected in his brown eyes.

'Why not?' I grinned. 'I like sucking men off. I'm sorry, didn't you *want* me to suck your cock?'

'Yes, but . . . You *have* changed, haven't you?'

'As I said, I'm living. I'm enjoying life now.'

'This bloke's not living with you, then?'

'No. He stays some nights but he has his own house. It's a lovely place. Too big, really. Rather like his cock,' I giggled.

'Shall I call round again? If you're not busy, I could come round for coffee.'

'Coffee or a blow job?'

'Well . . .'

'I don't know, Alan. I suppose you could call round on the odd occasion. There again, there's not much point.'

'Why? What do you mean?'

'When you left me, you said that I was no good in bed. I've since discovered that it was *you* who was bloody useless in bed.'

'Useless?'

'The orgasms I've had with other men have been . . . You never fingered and licked my bottom.'

'Is that what you're into now?'

'You bet I am. I suppose we weren't compatible. Perhaps we were too young.'

'We're older now, Jade.'

'Older and wiser. Give me a ring some time.'

47

'Yes, I will.'

'Right, I have a lot of work to do. The money's been pouring in,' I lied. 'Things are really looking good.'

'I'm pleased to hear it.' He smiled, finishing his coffee. 'I'll ring you, then.'

'You do that.'

Seeing Alan the ex to the door, I felt a mixture of emotions. I felt sorry for him, I felt like a tart – and I was overwhelmed by a terrific sense of elation. Tasting his sperm on my lips as I closed the door, I thought about my book. At least I was a little more confident now. Not only confident about writing erotic fiction, but confident with myself. *Two Alans?* I reflected, imagining sucking two knobs at once. I couldn't believe that I'd sucked two men to orgasm within a matter of hours. At this rate, I'd be bashing out chapter after chapter of unadulterated filth. I was set to be a pornographess.

At this rate? Which sexual act would I experience next? I wondered. I wasn't out to experience every crude act imaginable. Alan the musician had been a one-off. And as for Alan the ex . . . I felt that the situation was running away with me, soaring out of control. All this because David had suggested that I should write erotic fiction, I mused. It was probably best to forget about both Alans. Was it best to forget about my clitoris and masturbation? Definitely not, I concluded as I poured myself another cup of coffee. Thinking again about anilingus, I tried to imagine what it would be like to have my bottom-hole licked. *Quite pleasurable*, I decided, realizing that my panties were becoming very wet.

The phone rang. 'Jade, David Stevens,' the dark brown voice breathed as I answered it. 'I've put a book in the post for you.'

'Another dirty one?' I asked, rather too eagerly.

'No. Well, not really. It's a dictionary of naughty words.'

'Smutty words?'

'No, no. Proper words such as "huffle".'

'What on earth does that mean?'

'Shagging someone's armpit, to put it bluntly.'

'Fascinating, I must say. And this book's going to help me write erotica?'

'If nothing else, it might give you some ideas. By the way, I was talking to a publisher this morning. I mentioned you and he came up with an idea.'

'Oh?'

'A diary of a Victorian lady. You know, what she got up to sexually and the like. We thought you might include letters in the book and—'

'That's a dreadful idea, David,' I returned, recalling Jackie mentioning a book written in the form of diaries. 'Besides, I've already started the novel,' I blurted out.

'Great! What's it about?'

'Sex, what else?'

'Give me a rough outline.'

'I'm not saying anything. You'll read it when I'm ready.'

'The first two chapters, that's all I need to—'

'When they're ready, you'll have them.'

'OK. Get off the phone and hammer that keyboard.'

'I will. Speak to you soon.'

Hammer the keyboard? Hammer out filth? Feeling that I was losing my bearings in life, I began to wish that I'd never met David. He'd put ideas into my head, ideas that were haunting me, rattling around in the back of my mind and confusing me. I'd always been strong, known what I'd wanted and gone for it. As with the romantic novel, I reflected dolefully. I'd thought I'd known what I'd wanted, only to waste three years chasing a dream. Perhaps I *did* need someone like David to guide me in the right direction.

Mooching into my den, I hammered the keyboard for an hour or so and then read my work from the beginning. There was a story, of sorts, but it was weak. The plot was obviously nothing more than a vehicle to carry the sex. Grabbing the mouse, I made a rash decision and deleted all I'd written. 'Truth is stranger than fiction,' I ruminated, deciding to write about a young woman's sexual exploits, her journey along a path scattered with failed relationships and punctuated with crude and illicit sexual acts.

Crystal, the twenty-two-year-old heroine, was based on me. No, she was to be my fantasy. She reflected the woman I wasn't and yet perhaps secretly desired to be. Crystal was to live out the dreams of Jade Kimberly. How the book would end, I had no idea. Where would my life take me? I wondered as I thought about Crystal's thirst for sexual gratification. To protect my identity, I decided that she'd be a photographic model rather than an author. She had money, owned a nice flat and . . . and what?

Why would Crystal crave any and every sexual act imaginable? Was that my own quest in life? No, of course it wasn't. I'd sucked two men to orgasm, which was completely out of character, and I didn't intend to broaden my sexual experience by indulging in casual fucking. Fuck. A beautiful and yet a vile word. Beautiful in its vileness. Fuck. A word that society never actually permitted to sink completely out of sight into the murky swamp of depravity where many believed it belonged. Fuck.

What was driving Crystal? I mused. What was goading her to commit crude sexual acts with both men and women? Simply stating that she was a nymphomaniac wasn't good enough. She had to have a reason to fuck freely. Feeling despondent, I reclined in my chair and gazed out of the window. Wondering what the difference was between erotica and pornography, I felt that my book should cross every boundary, smash the barriers of convention. Complete and utter filth without being gratuitous. Was I making my job unnecessarily difficult? Or downright impossible? Did David want erotica or pornography? Relationships were inherently pornographic, I concluded.

I worked for several hours and then made a ham salad for my lunch. Picking at my food, I felt that I was getting to know Crystal. Looming from my mind, from the computer screen, she was coming to life. I knew what her likes and dislikes were, how she'd react in given situations. She dressed in revealing clothes and had an air of sensuality about her. She oozed sex, but she wasn't a tart. Crystal was all woman, feminine in the extreme, sought after by men, gracious and refined – but a whore in the bedroom. Unlike me.

Spending the afternoon at my desk, I was surprised to find that I'd completed the first chapter in such a short time. Reading my efforts, I was also surprised by how well it had come together. It was as if I'd typed unconsciously, not knowing what I'd written until I read it back. Crystal's insatiable thirst for sex had been instigated by the ending of her relationship with a man she'd desperately loved. Just like Alan, he'd left her for another woman. She was out for revenge. Hating men, she used and abused them in an effort to seek vengeance. Was *I* out for revenge?

I was feeling pleased with myself. Then the doorbell rang. I hoped it wasn't Alan the ex. I didn't need his whining and whinging about Angela the tart and how he'd been missing me and wanted us to get back together. Crystal would have told him where to go in no uncertain terms. Walking to the front door, I decided to seek my own vengeance by rubbing his cock through his trousers and sending him on his way with an erection. What would Crystal have done?

'Oh,' I breathed, opening the door to find Alan the musician standing on the step. 'Er . . . Come in.'

'Thanks,' he smiled. 'I was just passing and thought I'd say hi.'

'Yes, well . . . Hi.'

'You're not working, are you? I mean, I hope I haven't interrupted you.'

'No, no. I've finished for today,' I replied, leading him into the lounge.

'I would have phoned but I don't have your number.'

'That's OK. Er . . . coffee?' I asked, again wondering what Crystal would have done. Would she have phoned Jackie and invited her to play with his dick? 'She would have asked you to leave,' I murmured.

'Who would?'

'Sorry, I was thinking about my book. I find that I become so engrossed in my work that . . . I suppose I almost become the character I'm writing about. It's a strange feeling.'

'Yes, it must be,' he grinned, making himself at home by plonking himself in the armchair. 'Particularly if it's a man.'

'No, no. She's a young woman. Crystal, a photographic model.'

'And she would have asked me to leave?'

'She wouldn't like anyone turning up unannounced. She leads a busy life and couldn't have people arriving at her flat out of the blue. She wouldn't have been rude, though. She'd have explained that—'

'You really have got into this character, haven't you?'

'I seem to have done,' I laughed. 'It's never been like this

52

before. I've always been removed from the characters but, with Crystal . . . Perhaps I see myself reflected in her.'

'That's interesting. What's she like?'

'Funnily enough, she's not at all like me.' Did I want to be like her? 'She's very attractive, for starters.'

'And so are you, Jade.'

'If only. She's got money, she's successful and . . . I won't bore you. I'll go and put the kettle on.'

Leaving the room, I realized that I couldn't get Crystal out of my mind. The more I thought about her, the better I knew her. She seemed so real, and I wondered on whom I'd based her character. It certainly wasn't me! Perhaps, subconsciously, I'd based her on someone I'd once known. But I couldn't for the life of me think who. Maybe this was a sign that the book was working, I mused as I made the coffee. Did Crystal masturbate? Yes, she did. She had no qualms about her sexuality, or about deriving pleasure from her naked body.

'What would Crystal do in this situation?' Alan asked as I placed the cups on the lounge table.

'How do you mean?' I said, contemplating my knee-length skirt. Crystal wore miniskirts.

'Alone here with me. OK, she'd have sent me packing but, now that I'm here, how would she react?'

'Crystal's dominant. She takes what she wants. If she wanted sex, she'd drag you into bed. Once satisfied, she'd spit you out. She's refined, ladylike, attractive, sensual . . . She's also an animal in the bedroom. A man-eater.'

'Quite a woman,' he chuckled.

'She certainly is.'

'Would she fall in love?'

Fall in love? No, that wasn't her style at all. Monogamy wasn't possible for a girl like Crystal. She chose her partners not only for their sexual prowess but for what they had to offer. She liked to be wined and dined, showered with gifts – and then spend the night entwined in lust. She was a hunter. Men were her prey. Had I based her on Jackie?

'No, I wouldn't fall in love,' I finally replied abstractedly.

'*You?*' he echoed. '*You* wouldn't fall in love?'

'I mean Crystal,' I grinned sheepishly. '*She* wouldn't fall in love.'

'Sounds like you're going through an identity crisis.'

'As I said, I become engrossed in my work.'

'To the point where you actually become the character?'

'No, no. I . . . I'm my own person, Alan. Crystal is a fictitious character in my book, nothing more.'

'Who are we, really? What are we? Perhaps we're all figments of our own imaginations.'

'How do you mean?'

'Perhaps we act out our fantasies to the point where we become fantasy characters. As they say, you are what you think you are.'

'What do *you* think you are?'

'Lost, I suppose. I drift around wasting my time with this and that while life passes me by.'

'Like a rudderless ship. What about your music?'

'I suppose my music has shaped me. I try to come across as a bohemian, but it's not the real me. I have no idea what the real me is. The inner man, and all that. Who are you?'

'I'm . . . I'm just plain and simple old me. Have your coffee before it gets cold.'

Alan's philosophical ramblings made me feel uncomfortable. The real me? I didn't want to know what lurked within the depths of my subconscious. But I did want to be like Crystal. She was fast becoming a role model, someone to look up to and admire. She had a streak of bohemian in her.

She was a mysterious woman of great depth. A complex character, she was looking for something that probably didn't exist. What was *I* looking for?

'Let's talk about you,' Alan said, sipping his coffee. 'What are you like?'

'Terrible,' I laughed. 'I've had too much sex with too many men, I drink too much . . .' Hesitating, I wondered whether it was Crystal or me talking. 'I'll try anything once and, if I like it, I'll try it again and again.'

'Did you like last night?'

'Last night has gone. Like a page of a book, turned over and . . .'

'Gone but not forgotten. Did you like it?'

'I . . . Yes, I did.'

'You can always turn back to that page.'

This was my chance to play the role of Crystal, I mused. And the chance to experience sexual acts I'd never even dreamed of. Alan had the equipment and I was hungry to learn. No one would ever know what I'd got up to in the privacy of my flat, I tried to console myself. No matter what I did, it would be my secret. I wouldn't even tell Jackie. I could fuck, have Alan lick and finger my bottom-hole, sperm over my breasts and . . . and when Crystal had finished with him, she'd spit him out.

'I want you,' I said huskily, standing before him. 'Unveil my body.' As Alan tugged my skirt down, I felt as if I was dreaming. The room spinning, my mind out of control, I allowed him to slip my panties down my thighs and gaze at the most intimate part of my young body. I didn't know what I was doing. I wanted to experience cold sex, crude sex, raw sex, but . . . but what? Were the confines and restrictions of society goading me to conform? Was Crystal trying to rule my head?

Feeling Alan's hot breath on the fleshy pads of my vaginal lips, I shuddered as his tongue delved into my sex crack and tasted me there. My clitoris swelling, my arousal soaring out of control, I breathed deeply as he licked the full length of my valley of lust. Valley of lust? I'd been reading too much of that dirty book. Was it dirty? No, I concluded as Alan teased my clitoris with his wet tongue and sucked it into his hot mouth. It was heavenly.

'God, no,' I breathed as my orgasm stirred deep within the very core of my being. My legs trembling, my heart racing, I spread my feet wide as Alan expertly sucked and licked my swollen clitoris until the explosion of orgasm ripped through my defenceless body. Never had I known such incredible sensations as I clung to his head and shook violently. Never had an orgasm immersed me so deep into the sea of sexual satisfaction. Again and again my clitoris pulsated, transmitting tremors of sheer lust through my young body. Alan's fingers entering the tight duct of my pussy sending me into raptures of pure sexual elation, my juices of lust squelching, a feeling of pure decadence gripped me. I was pornographic. Life was pornographic.

'Fuck me,' I gasped as Alan thrust his fingers in and out of my tightening pussy. 'For God's sake, fuck my cunt.' My orgasm receding as he slipped his fingers out of my drenched pussy, I lay on the floor and slipped my panties over my ankles. The power of lust had overwhelmed me, I knew as he positioned himself between my parted legs and pulled his penis out. His knob pressing against the dripping folds of my inner lips, I let out a rush of breath as his male length thrust deep into my tightening vagina. Rocking his hips, his solid knob battering my cervix, he gasped and grunted in his fucking as I cried out in my ecstasy.

'Fuck me harder!' I screamed, my body jolting with the

forceful pistoning of Alan's rock-hard cock. His balls slapping my firm buttocks, I listened to the beautiful sound of my vaginal juices squishing as my pussy tightened around his shaft, lovingly hugging his solid organ. I was Crystal, I mused, my clitoris swelling against the pistoning shaft of his magnificent cock. I was Crystal in all her sensuality, her depravity, her feminine glory. 'Come inside me,' I murmured, desperate for the feel of sperm gushing into my cunt, bathing my cervix. Cunt. It had been over a year since I'd been fucked and spunked, I reflected. And I was desperate to hear the heavy breathing of a man fucking my cunt and spunking up me.

'Yes,' he breathed, his sperm finally shooting from his knob and filling my cunt. 'God, you're beautiful.'

'Call me Crystal,' I gasped in my sexual delirium. 'Tell Crystal that you're fucking her cunt.'

'I'm fucking your cunt, Crystal,' he murmured, obviously perplexed by my request. 'Coming in your beautiful cunt, Crystal.'

My second climax finally erupting within my ballooning clitoris, my juices of arousal gushing from the bloated opening to my cunt and wetting my inner thighs, I rolled my head from side to side as Alan fucked me senseless. On and on he fucked my quivering body, his sperm filling my cunt, his knob pummelling my ripe cervix until he finally collapsed in a trembling heap on top of me. The smell of sex filling my nostrils, the burning lips of my cunt gripping his deflating cock, I swam in a warm pool of self-satisfaction. I'd done it, I reflected through the sexual haze of my mind. I'd been fucked and spermed. Crystal had been fucked.

'You're something else,' Alan breathed as he raised himself on his arms, his cock sliding out of the spermed sheath of my tight cunt.

'You weren't too bad,' I murmured dismissively. Was I being cruel?

'Was I too quick for you?'

'I'm used to men lasting at least . . . No, you were OK.'

'Why did you want me to call you Crystal?' he asked, zipping his trousers as I clambered to my feet.

'Why not?' I grinned. The time had come to spit him out. 'You'd better go now.'

'Go?'

'I have things to do, Alan.' Why was I being so cold and cruel?

'Oh, OK. Will you be in the pub this evening?'

'I don't know what I'm doing yet. I might be. Then again, I might not.'

'Perhaps I'll call round again tomorrow,' he said, hope mirrored in his dark eyes as he moved towards the door.

'Whatever,' I smiled, grabbing my panties from the floor. 'I might not be in tomorrow. And if I am, I might be busy.'

As Alan left, I flopped onto the sofa and hung my head. I'd behaved like a common slut and then treated him abominably. He was a nice person, and I'd been cold, cruel and heartless. I'd also acted completely out of character. Clutching my panties, I began to wonder whether I was losing my mind. Crystal was a fictional character, I reminded myself. She wasn't a reflection of my inner self, she didn't exist. She was nothing more than words. Nothing more than a figment of my pornographic imagination.

'Yes?' I snapped, grabbing the ringing phone.

'Hi, it's me,' Alan the ex said.

'And?'

'I . . . I thought I might come round.'

'Again?'

'Are you all right, Jade? You sound odd.'

'I'm fine, Alan. What do you want?'

'As I said . . .'

'OK, come round – if you have to.'

Slamming the phone down, I reclined on the sofa and grinned. Another conquest, another plaything, I mused. But why was I doing this? Reading a dirty book hadn't turned me into a wanton tart. And writing my own mild erotica certainly hadn't affected me. I desperately wanted to be like Crystal, I concluded. Having led a sheltered life, experiencing boring straight sex with my one and only boyfriend, I wanted to live like Crystal. But Crystal wasn't real. She was a fantasy, a dream. I recalled leaving a cinema and wanting to be like the heroine of the film. I'd tried to act like her, tried to become her. I wanted to be like Crystal.

Waiting for Alan to arrive, I paced the lounge floor. I felt as if something deep within me had been woken. Prince Charming had kissed Sleeping Beauty, and given her life. Alan the musician had fucked me, and given me life. And now Alan the ex was coming round again to . . . to what? Fuck me? Was Jackie planning to give me life?

Chapter Four

The doorbell ringing at last, I raced through the hall, realizing that I was still clutching my wet panties. Did Crystal wear panties? Wondering whether to send Alan the ex packing, I thought about ringing Jackie and inviting her round to play with his dick. Maybe that wasn't such a good idea, I giggled inwardly, opening the door to Alan the ex. Alan the bastard.

'Oh, it's you,' I breathed dismissively, tossing my panties beneath the hall table.

'You don't seem very pleased to see me,' he murmured dejectedly, following me into the lounge.

'Why should I be pleased to see you, Alan? I saw you this morning, and now you're here again.' I didn't mean to be rude to him. Then again, perhaps I did.

'I don't know. I just thought that, after . . .'

'What is it you want from me?'

'Want? I don't want anything.'

'I thought you might want coffee or another blow job.'

'Well, I suppose . . .'

'I'll fill the kettle,' I sighed, leaving the room.

I don't know what it was about Alan that bugged me. I didn't want revenge. If anything, I was pleased to be rid of him. Had we still been together, he'd have been trying to force his cock into my mouth and I'd be shunning his advances. I didn't know what it was about myself. Something was getting to me, I knew. Something was bugging me. Perhaps it was that I'd wanted to have my romantic novel published and was now being forced to write erotic fiction. Forced? I was becoming desperate for money so, in effect, I *was* being forced. I was prostituting myself.

Taking the coffee to the lounge, a blend of sperm and vaginal juice running down my inner thighs, I gazed at Alan the ex. Had he come round for another blow job? More than likely. He'd come to visit the pornographess in the hope that she'd suck him off and swallow his spunk. Feeling decadent, a wicked plan coming to mind, I sat on the sofa and began talking about sex. Sex with Alan the musician, how he fucked me senseless, how he made me come again and again.

'I don't really want to know, Jade,' he finally sighed, plonking himself in the armchair.

'Sorry, I was forgetting that you don't have a sex life at the moment.'

'It's not that.'

'Now that Angela's thrown you out, you don't have a tight, juicy cunt to fuck and spunk.'

'What?' he gasped, his face grimacing.

'I didn't mean to say that,' I murmured, wondering where the crude words had come from.

'God, you've changed.'

'We're all changing, Alan. Changes bring about changes. So, you were saying?'

'I don't want to know what you and your boyfriend do in bed. You're so different, Jade. You're not the girl I once knew. What's happened to change you so much?'

'You leaving me, that's what changed me. That's when I began to live.' Or had I died?

'I wasn't that bad, was I?'

'You seemed to think that you owned me. You were possessive and became insanely jealous if I chatted to other men. I felt restricted, suppressed, suffocated. If I went anywhere without you, you questioned me, gave me the third degree. Look at that hen night I went to. Who did you meet? Who were you talking to? How long were you there? Was there a male stripper? Did you talk to any men? Did you go straight home afterwards? It nearly drove me mad. I was sad when you left me, but also relieved. I wasn't going to tell you this, but you said that I was no good in bed and complained because I never sucked you off.'

'I didn't mean . . .'

'Yes, you fucking did, Alan.'

'OK, OK. There's no need to get riled about it.'

'Your obsession, your jealousy and continual suspicion and questioning . . . That's what drove me to . . . Shall I tell you what it drove me to?' I didn't know what I was saying. 'I didn't want your cock in my mouth because, towards the end of our farcical relationship, I was sucking someone else off.'

'*What?* You were cheating on me?'

'You were screwing Angela, so don't come the fucking moralist with me.'

'Who was he? Anyone I know?'

'You didn't know him. We were at school together. We used to play about in a haystack down on Turner's Farm. I bumped into him about three months before you left me. And we fucked and sucked and licked each other.'

'Christ. And I thought . . . I don't know what I thought. Or what to think now.'

'I'll tell you what I think . . .' I began as the phone rang. 'Wait there.'

Grabbing the phone in the kitchen, I was pleased to hear

Jackie's voice. I hadn't told her about Alan the ex and decided to update her. She went very quiet when I said that he'd been to see me that morning and had turned up yet again. Thinking that she was worried that I might take him back, which would spoil her plans for a threesome with musician Alan, I asked her what the problem was.

'He hasn't split up with Angela,' she informed me. 'I saw them together this morning, leaving their flat and kissing in the street.'

'Are you sure?' I asked surprisedly.

'Of course I'm sure, Jade,' she returned. 'I've known them long enough to recognize them. The way they were kissing, I can tell you that they haven't split up. It looks as if Alan is trying to sow his oats elsewhere.'

'He told me that they'd split up because she's got someone else and . . .'

'He's a lying bastard, Jade. You of all people should know that.'

'That's an understatement. He's a fucking—'

'Calm down,' she broke in. 'I've never heard you swear before.'

'I don't usually swear. But when a fucking bastard like that . . .'

'Shall I come round?'

'He's here now so . . . Yes, come round. Don't let on that you know anything.'

'No, no, of course not. You haven't . . .'

'Had sex with him?'

'Yes.'

'Er . . . No, I haven't. And I don't intend to. He's a lying fucking cunt, he really is.'

'Hey, hey. Relax, for God's sake. They're all the same, believe me. I'll see you soon.'

Returning to the lounge, I smiled at Alan, wondering how he could have spun such a sob story just to have his wicked way with me. There again, I'd instigated the cocksucking. I also wondered why I'd sworn on the phone. It wasn't like me to swear. In fact, it was so out of character that I wondered what was getting to me. Alan was getting to me. I'd sucked him off, swallowed his sperm – and he'd gone home to the tart and probably fucked her rotten. He might even have fucked her before I'd sucked him off. God, his penis might have been covered with the slag's pussy juice. He was going to pay for this, I decided. I was out for revenge.

'Sorry about that,' I smiled sweetly. 'It was my boy-friend.'

'You're lucky to have someone,' he said softly.

'Yes, I am. You must be feeling very lonely, Alan.'

'I am. Dossing on a sofa isn't much fun. I spend the evenings sitting on my own.'

You lying bastard! 'I wish I could help somehow.'

'It's nice being able to come here and talk to you.' He smiled and let out a chuckle. 'I liked what you did to me this morning, Jade. It's a shame we can't . . .'

'We can be friends,' I said, smiling brightly. I hated him, hated his very being. 'I know I was a bit offhand but . . . Let's be friends, shall we?'

'Yes, I'd like that.'

'It's a shame about you and Angela. I know that I called her a slag but . . . I saw her the other day. I wasn't going to say anything, but she was with a man. Obviously, it was her new man.'

'Oh?' he frowned. 'Where was that?'

'They were going into a pub in town. They were kissing and groping each other . . . Well, you don't want to hear about that.'

'What did he look like?'

'Oh, I don't know. Dark, tall, good-looking. To be honest, I didn't take too much notice.'

As he fired several questions at me, I replied with the appropriate lies. If nothing else, I'd cause trouble between them and appease my thirst for revenge. No, causing trouble wasn't revenge enough. I hadn't nearly finished with him. In fact, I'd barely started. Leaving the room to answer the door, I didn't tell him that it was Jackie who'd just arrived. No doubt he was hoping for another blow job, or more. He'd be really pissed off when he realized that Jackie was staying for a while.

'Hi, Alan,' she smiled, walking into the lounge.

'Oh, er . . . Hi,' he stammered, rising to his feet and shaking her hand.

'How's Angela?'

'She's OK.' He hung his head. 'Actually, we've . . . we've split up,' he sighed. I hate self-pity, especially when it's false.

'Oh, I'm sorry to hear that. Are you two back together again?' she asked, turning to me.

'We've talked about it,' I replied. 'We're sort of meeting up now and then to see how we get on. Jackie, why don't you come and give me a hand with the coffee?'

'OK. You know, I always thought you two were made for each other.'

'Yes,' Alan murmured. 'I . . . I believe we are.'

'I reckon we'll be back together soon,' I smiled as I left the room.

Jackie danced around the kitchen as if she'd won the lottery. Her face beaming, she suggested that we both play with Alan's dick. She then suggested that we drop him in it with Angela. Leaving her to babble on about telling Angela that Alan was screwing around, I made the coffee. Jackie loved the situation, I knew. Excited, bubbling over with enthusiasm about having Angela catch Alan coming in my mouth, she finally calmed down and let me get a word in.

'We're not going to get his dick out,' I said, fighting my inner thoughts as I placed the coffee cups on a tray. Would Crystal have sucked and licked his knob? *Do it. Suck his knob.* 'No, I . . . Stop it, for God's sake.'

'Are you OK?' Jackie asked.

'I'm a little confused, that's all.' *Suck the sperm out of his knob.* 'I don't want to suck his knob.'

'I will, then,' she grinned. 'I'll tell you what. You go upstairs and I'll seduce him, get his cock out and wank him off.'

'Jackie!' I whispered loudly. 'We are not . . .'

'You can walk into the lounge and catch us,' she interrupted me. 'And then we can both tell Angela.'

'I don't know,' I murmured pensively. 'The idea's crazy.' *Do it.* 'I can't do it.'

'Come on, Jade. Have a laugh, for once. Say that you're going up to your den to make a phone call. Say that you'll be a while and, when you've gone, I'll . . .'

'Maybe,' I broke in, walking into the hall. 'Let's see what happens. Play it by ear.'

As we returned to the lounge, I thought about Jackie's idea, but I still had misgivings. I certainly wanted to drop Alan in it, but Angela would never believe that he'd been to my flat and that Jackie had wanked him. It would have been far better to have her see me out with Alan, going into a pub or a restaurant. *Do it. Do it.* My head aching, I wished that my mind would stop playing tricks on me. Passing Alan a cup of coffee, I turned and grimaced at Jackie as she reminded me that I had an important phone call to make.

'Go and ring your agent now,' she persisted. 'I'll entertain Alan while you're gone.'

'In a minute,' I replied, realizing that she wasn't going to give up. Crystal would have done it. *Do it*.

'I'll go if . . .' Alan began.

'No, no,' Jackie broke in. 'Stay and have a chat. I haven't seen you for ages.' Turning to face me, she frowned. 'Go on, then,' she urged me. 'You were saying how important the call was.'

'OK, OK,' I finally conceded. 'I'll be about . . . about ten minutes.'

Leaving the room and hovering in the hall, I wished that I'd never agreed to such a crazy idea. I felt as if someone was in my head, goading me to do things against my will. Was I going crazy? What the hell was Jackie going to do? I wondered, listening to her chatting to Alan. Rip his trousers down and grab his cock? And what was I supposed to do? Walk in just as he was shooting his spunk? There was no point in playing stupid games, I concluded. He wasn't my boyfriend and I really didn't care about dropping him in it with Angela.

Spying through the crack in the door, I shook my head. I was going to make my entrance before Jackie'd started seducing him but she'd already moved in. Kneeling at his feet, she was whispering something and trying to yank his zip down. Almost raping him as she yanked at his trousers, she had no qualms whatsoever. How she could behave like that without becoming embarrassed, I really didn't know. I wished that I was Crystal more than ever.

'Come on,' she said huskily. 'She'll be ages yet.'

'Jackie, we can't do it here,' he complained.

'Stop wasting time and get your cock out. I want to suck your knob.'

'Bloody hell,' he whispered as she finally managed to haul his stiffening penis out of his trousers. 'You're some bloody woman.'

'I've always wanted to do this to you,' she grinned, pulling his foreskin back and sucking his purple knob into her pretty mouth.

This was ridiculous, I mused, watching Jackie gobbling – and Alan squirming and writhing in his illicit ecstasy. What was I supposed to say when I made my untimely entrance? *Oh, God, what's going on? Alan, how could you betray me yet again?* As he gasped and clutched her head, I reckoned that he was close to coming. The bastard had already come in my mouth that morning, and now he was going to sperm Jackie's mouth. Gripping his solid cock by the base, she bobbed her head up and down, moaning through her nose as she mouth-fucked herself. Clenching my fists and grimacing in preparation for my dramatic entry, I took a deep breath. This was it, I knew as he let out a gasp. His spunk was about to flow. Mouth-fuck. Mouth-sperm.

'God,' I breathed, walking into the room. 'Alan, what . . .'

'Oh,' he cried as Jackie slipped his glistening knob out of her mouth. His sperm shooting through the air, he tried desperately to conceal his cock. 'Oh, God. I . . . I was just . . .'

'Sorry,' Jackie said, clambering to her feet, sperm dribbling down her chin. 'He went on and on and in the end . . . Well, I did it.'

'There's no hope for us now, Alan,' I sobbed, wiping my eyes.

'But . . .'

'I shall ring Angela and tell her that dumping you was the best thing she ever did.'

'No, don't ring her,' he gasped.

'I'm not surprised that she went off with another man.'

'Whatever you do, don't ring her.'

'Why not? What's it to you?'

'I think I'd better be going,' Jackie said, moving to the door.

'Yes, I think you had,' I replied with feigned outrage. Judging from her expression and discreet pointing gestures that she was going to wait in the kitchen for me. 'And don't bother coming back.'

'Jade,' Alan said, taking my arm as Jackie scurried out of the room. 'Please don't ring Angela. I don't want her to think that . . . Anyway, this has nothing to do with her. We're not together any more so . . .'

'I'm going to tell her that you not only came in Jackie's mouth but in my mouth too.'

'You . . . you don't know the number,' he stammered, his eyes widening as he realized that I meant it.

'Don't I? Get out, Alan.'

Tugging his zip up, his sperm splattered down his trousers, he finally made his exit. Shrieks of laughter came from the kitchen as the front door slammed shut. Jackie was loving every minute of the game, I knew as she bounded into the lounge. I supposed that it had been fun, but I felt guilty. Should I tell Angela? I wondered as Jackie flopped onto the sofa. Again wondering why Jackie seemed to have no inhibitions, I thought she might contact Alan and arrange to meet him for sex. Knowing her, I wouldn't have put it past her.

'We'd better not tell Angela,' I said.

'Why not?' she frowned. 'The bastard cheated on her, for goodness' sake. If you won't tell her, then I will.'

'I suppose so. It's just that . . .'

'Just that what?'

'I don't know, Jackie. I don't know what's happening. My life was so quiet and . . . Well, normal. Everything seems to be happening at once. What with Alan the musician and then Alan the ex turning up, I don't know what's going on.'

'You're enjoying yourself – at last. That's what's happening.'

'Enjoying myself?'

'You sucked off the musician. I'll bet you enjoyed that.'

'I also sucked off Alan the ex.'

'Really? My God, you're a dark horse. When did this happen?'

'He came round this morning. I don't know why I did it.'

'That's great!' She beamed. 'It won't be long before we're both sucking one dick. You wank and I'll suck, then I'll wank and you—'

'Jackie, that's not what I want,' I sighed, sitting next to her.

'I don't understand you, Jade. We could have some real fun together. We ought to team up and seduce men. Just think of the ideas you'd get for your book. We could call ourselves the cum-sluts.'

'Jackie, you're terrible. *The cum-sluts?*'

'Or the facial females.'

'What do you mean, *facial*?'

'Don't you know anything? Facial as in sperm all over your face. Cum-slut as in a girl who loves spunk all over her face and in her mouth.'

'I'm beginning to realize how little I do know,' I sighed. 'There's no way I'll be able to write a dirty book . . .'

'Let's team up, Jade.'

'No, I don't want that.'

'Call it research. We'll grab a bloke from the pub, bring him back here, and seduce him. What better way of gaining experience?'

'I'd be too embarrassed. It's one thing being alone with a man, but to . . . to suck a cock with you watching me . . .'

'I wouldn't be watching. I'd be sucking, too.'

'This is getting out of hand. I've sucked two men, and now you want us to team up and . . . and seduce men.'

'That's not all I want to do.'

'What do you mean?'

'I want to seduce *you*, Jade.'

Running her hand up my inner thigh, she pressed her fingertips into the swell of my naked vaginal lips. I was stunned, unable to utter words of protest or move for several seconds. Finally managing to press my legs together, I thought of Jenny Hardbrooke. What the hell did Jackie think she was doing? I wondered, grabbing her arm and trying to remove her hand from between my thighs. The girls at school might have enjoyed mutual masturbation. Jenny Hardbrooke might have . . . But I wasn't interested in lesbian sex.

'No panties,' Jackie breathed huskily as I again tried to push her away.

'Jackie, don't,' I protested as she managed to push her fingers into my wet sex crack. 'For God's sake, stop it.'

'Relax,' she murmured, forcing my thighs apart. 'I want to teach you, Jade. Teach you how to enjoy your body.'

'Jackie, this is wrong,' I murmured. What would Crystal have done? 'Jackie, please don't.'

Closing my eyes as her finger slipped between my fleshy vaginal lips and drove deep into my hot pussy, I gasped. I shouldn't be doing this, I knew as she expertly massaged my drenched inner flesh. This wasn't right. But no one would know what I'd done in the privacy of my flat, I reflected. Privacy of my flat? Did that give me *carte blanche* to commit illicit sexual acts with anyone who visited me? *Take what you can when you can.*

The sensations driving me wild, I relaxed, allowing my thighs to part further. I'd lost all control – I knew that as I felt my womb contract and my juices bubble within my hot cunt. 'God, that's nice,' I breathed without thinking as she lifted my skirt up and buried her face between my thighs. The words weren't mine, they were Crystal's. 'Oh, God. Don't stop.'

My sex juices and Alan's sperm squelched as Jackie thrust her finger in and out of my tightening pussy and I tried to tell myself that I wasn't enjoying the lesbian encounter. This wasn't normal. I wasn't a lesbian. My womb quivering, rhythmically contracting, I couldn't deny the immense pleasure another girl was bringing me. Would she want me to masturbate her? I wondered as my body shook uncontrollably. Did I want to finger her pussy? Crystal wanted to tongue-fuck her sex-juiced cunt.

'Lick my cunt,' I whispered, clutching her head as she pushed her face against the swell of my girl-wet pussy lips. Slipping her finger out of my spasming vaginal sheath, she ran her tongue up and down my naked sex valley. I could feel her wet tongue, licking, teasing, tantalizing, tasting. Alan the ex had licked me there, tried to make me come, but his tonguing had done nothing for me, unlike the oral expertise of Alan the musician. Alan the ex had been rough, licking too hard in his desperation to take me to orgasm. I'd hated it, the sound of his wet tongue between my soft sex lips. But Jackie . . . Jackie knew exactly what to do.

'Nice?' she asked, lapping at the sensitive pink flesh surrounding my vaginal entrance. Unable to answer, I breathed deeply as her tongue entered me, licked the creamy-wet walls of my burning cunt. Cunt. A battle still raging in my mind between Crystal and me, I tried to imagine that it was a man licking my cunt. I was Crystal, Jackie was a man. But the aroma of Jackie's perfume filling my nostrils, the feel of her silky-soft hair as I clutched her head, her feminine gasps as she mouthed and licked between my pussy lips . . . There was no denying that it was a female tongue that was darting in and out of my drenched cunt.

'Oh, God,' I murmured as she moved up my sex valley and licked the delicate flesh surrounding my solid clitoris. Teasing me, she worked her tongue around my solid pleasure spot, deliberately avoiding the sensitive tip as she took me closer to my orgasm. Holding me on the threshold, she slipped her fingers into my spasming cunt and massaged my G-spot. I was desperate to come, but she held me there, teetering on the verge of orgasm until I begged for the relief I craved.

'Please,' I cried, pushing my hips forward and grinding the inner flesh of my wet cunt hard against Jackie's pretty face. 'Please, I need to come.' Sucking my clitoris into the heat of her wet mouth and licking the pulsating tip, she took me to an orgasm so powerful that I felt as if my mind had left my body. My very being centring on my orgasming clitoris, I shuddered and writhed, wailing my pleasure as I floated through swirling purple clouds of sex far above my quivering body.

As Jackie sustained my ecstasy, I floated through hues of pastel blues and greens, drifting into another world. The intensity of my pleasure increasing, silver sparks of orgasm exploded around me, flashes of brilliant white light bathed me. Again and again my pleasure peaked, sending bolts of euphoria through my blown mind. Finally drifting back down into my shaking body as my pleasure subsided, I lay sprawling on the sofa like a rag doll. Done in my illicit coming. Fucked. Girl-fucked.

'God,' I whispered shakily as Jackie's slender fingers gently pistoned the burning sheath of my drenched cunt. My head lolling from side to side, my eyes rolling, I breathed heavily as her fingers finally slipped out of my lust duct. In a sexual daze, I gazed through my eyelashes at her grinning face. Her tongue licking her fingers, lapping up my orgasmic juices, I saw her lips moving. I couldn't hear her words. Still drifting, floating, I felt as if I was in a semiconscious state. One word wafted through the haze, and then another.

'Jade,' said Jackie, shaking my shoulder. 'Jade, are you all right?' I managed to smile at her as she stroked my flushed cheek. Kissing my perspiring forehead, she pulled my skirt down and veiled the sex-matted blonde pubes of my fiery vulva. 'Jade,' she whispered again as I began to return to consciousness.

'I'm OK,' I murmured, dragging my limp body upright. 'I'm OK.'

'I thought you'd passed out,' she smiled.

'So did I. I thought I was losing my mind.'

'Was it all right?'

'All right? God, Jackie, I've never . . . never known anything like it.'

'Only a girl knows how to pleasure another girl,' she giggled. 'What do men know?'

'Not a lot, it would seem.'

'So, are we going to join forces?'

'Jackie, I didn't want to . . .' *Crystal wants to.* 'No, she doesn't.'

'Who doesn't what?' Jackie frowned.

'Nothing. I was thinking aloud. It's not right to . . .'

'Before you start harping on about lesbians, let's get one thing straight, Jade. We are *not* lesbians.'

'What the hell are we, then?'

'Two girls having some fun – sexy fun.'

'OK, so what would we have to do to be classed as lesbians?'

'You do complicate things, don't you? Lesbians are . . . All right, put it this way. A bloke wanks his mate. He's heterosexual, but he has a laugh and wanks his mate off. Does that make him gay?'

'Well, yes.'

'Of course it doesn't.'

'If he wanks his mate, as you put it, every day, then surely . . .'

'You're splitting hairs, Jade.'

'Am I?'

'Yes, you are. Anyway, it's my turn.'

'What do you mean?'

'What do you think I mean? After all I did to you, I'm really turned on and need to come.'

'No, Jackie. I . . .' I squeezed my eyes shut as my mind seemed to speak to me. *Crystal would have jumped at the chance.* 'This isn't what I want.' *Crystal wouldn't have hesitated.* 'I've already been feeling that I'm losing control of my mind. I sucked off Alan from the pub and then Alan the ex. Now you've . . . you've done things to me. I feel that I'm being dragged downstream and I've nothing to cling onto.'

'And what's downstream? Where are you being dragged to?'

'I don't know. The unknown, I suppose.'

Was this another chance in a lifetime? I knew there'd be

other opportunities to indulge in lesbian sex with Jackie, but not opportunities like this. The time seemed right, the feel of the situation seemed right. Wondering what another girl's juices of arousal tasted like, I realized that my clitoris was swelling as I thought about examining Jackie's intricate sex folds. After the immense pleasure she'd brought me, I owed it to her to reciprocate. My stomach somersaulting, I knew that I had to go for it. But something was holding me back. And Crystal was urging me on.

'Jackie, I can't,' I murmured as she stroked the smooth skin of my inner thigh.

'Want some help?' she smiled.

'What do you mean?' *Crystal wants Jackie.* 'No . . .'

'You're probably embarrassed, feeling a little shy. Add that to your crazy battle between what's right and wrong, normal and abnormal, and I reckon that you need some help.'

As Jackie raised her buttocks and pulled her panties down to her ankles, I shook my head. I so much wanted to taste her, to bring her as much pleasure as she'd brought me, but knew I couldn't do it. *You can do it*, my mind whispered. Kicking her shoes and panties across the room, she lifted her skirt up over her stomach and perched her naked buttocks over the edge of the cushion. As she spread her young thighs, I gazed at the sparse pubic hair covering the delicate rise of her mons. *Take what you can when you can.* Focusing on her gaping vaginal valley, the pink protrusions of her inner sex lips, I took a deep breath and plucked up as much courage as I could.

Glancing at Jackie's pretty face as she closed her eyes, I knew that she was leaving me to my own devices. She wasn't going to interfere or tell me what to do. She was offering me her body to do with as I wished. It was up to me. What I did and how I did it was entirely up to me. No, it was up to Crystal. *Crystal doesn't exist, for fuck's sake*, I tried to convince myself.

I didn't know what the hell was going on in my head as I began by parting the swollen lips of Jackie's pussy. Crystal was a figment of my imagination, she didn't exist. And yet I could hear her voice in my mind, goading, urging. Jackie breathed deeply, her stomach jerkily rising and falling as I examined her most secret place. I wasn't in control of my actions as I parted the wings of her inner lips and ran my finger up and down her drenched sex groove. It wasn't my doing, I knew as I located the entrance to her vagina and thrust my finger deep inside her young cunt. But it *was* my doing. I couldn't blame a fictitious character for my wanton act of lesbianism.

'God, you're beautiful,' I breathed – Crystal breathed. I didn't know where the thoughts, the uncharacteristic words, were coming from. I was in a dreamlike state, lucid and yet drifting out of control in a mist of confusion. My mind was dissolving in a liquid flow of confusion. I could hear a voice in my head, a girl's voice. Wicked laughter, giggling. Fingering Jackie's tight pussy, I felt that I was possessed. The squelching of her copious vaginal juices resounded around the room, filling my ears, battering my mind.

'No,' I murmured, leaning over her thigh and burying my face between her legs. Breathing in the scent of her young sex, I pushed my tongue out and licked the hot folds of her wet cunt. *Cunt*. It wasn't my word, was it? Where had it come from? Who was talking to me? Crystal didn't fucking exist! And yet she was there. Like a ghost lurking somewhere within the dark depths of my mind, she was there, goading me to commit crude acts of lesbian sex.

Jackie parted her young thighs further, opening the very

centre of her young body to my inquisitive tongue. Her juices of lust flowed in torrents as I pushed my tongue deep into her fiery cunt. *Cunt*. Licking, sucking out her lubricious sex juices, I lost myself in my sexual delirium. I wanted more girl juice, more sex. Sliding off the sofa, I knelt on the floor between her feet and forced her long legs wide apart. She moved forward, her rounded buttocks clear of the cushion as she lay on the sofa in expectation.

'Wider,' I whispered, parting her knees until her vaginal slit yawned, exposing the intricate inner flesh of her young cunt. Her sex-hole exposed, I focused on the juices trickling from her inner sheath, running down between the firm moons of her naked buttocks. Pushing my face hard against her pinken flesh, I locked my mouth to her open love-hole and sucked out her sex cream. She quivered, trembling uncontrollably as I repeatedly swept my tongue up her open valley of desire. Her exposed clitoris swelling as my tongue ran over the solid tip of the small protrusion, she gasped and writhed, begging me to make her come.

'When I'm ready,' I murmured, sucking her clitoris into my wet mouth. I'd barely started, I mused. I'd tease her, take her close to her orgasm and hold her there, teetering on the brink. Her juices of lust would gush from her young cunt, flooding my face as I drank from her vaginal sheath. Again, she begged me for the release of orgasm, grabbing my head and trying to force me to concentrate on her ripe pleasure bud. No, I wasn't going to allow her the pleasure – yet.

Locking my wet mouth to Jackie's open lust-hole again, I sucked hard. Her juices flowed, filling my mouth as she whimpered in her debased pleasure. Slipping a finger between the warm spheres of her buttocks, I teased the brown portal to her young bottom. This was wrong, I tried to convince myself. *This is love*, my mind whispered, Crystal whispered. 'No,' I murmured, moving up Jackie's gaping vaginal crack and sucking on her pulsating clitoris.

'Yes,' she breathed as her body became rigid. She was there, I knew as her orgasmic juices gushed from her bared sex-hole, flooding my face as I snaked my tongue around her swollen pleasure spot. Massaging her anal inlet, I couldn't push my finger into her bottom. I desperately wanted to finger her tight bum-duct, but couldn't bring myself to commit the vulgar act, the beautiful act. Her back arched, her stomach quivering, she gripped my head and gyrated her hips as I sustained her girl pleasure with my hot mouth, my sweeping tongue, my teasing finger.

At last, Jackie's trembling body began to calm as her orgasm subsided. Her eyes rolling, her nostrils flaring, she lay on the sofa with her legs wide apart, her open cunt forced against my girl-wet face. Panting for breath as she recovered, her eyes closed, she pushed my head away. I gazed at her open sexual centre as I sat back on my heels. Her creamy juices of lust oozing from her bared sex-hole, her clitoris receding beneath its protective pink hood, she finally closed her legs and dragged her young body up. Smiling at her as she locked her gaze to mine, I hoped that I'd brought her as much pleasure as she'd brought me. I was pleased with my efforts, my expert clitoris-sucking – but a tidal wave of guilt drowned me.

'You're good,' Jackie murmured as I clambered to my feet. 'Very good.'

'Jackie . . .' I began, not knowing what to say.

'Don't. Whatever you're about to say, don't. I'll go now.'

'No, don't go.'

'You need time to think,' she said, tugging her panties up her long legs and standing up. Moving to the door, she turned and grinned. 'This was your first time, Jade. You'll be mixed up, not sure what it is you want. You need time to think about us.'

The front door closing, I flopped onto the sofa. What had I done? I asked myself, the taste of her orgasmic juices lingering on my tongue, the aphrodisiacal scent of her pussy folds filling my nostrils. Time to think about us? What had Jackie meant? What had Crystal done? Jackie was my best friend and I'd . . . I couldn't face her again. I had to get both Alans and Jackie out of my life and find some normality again. Normality? I had to get Crystal out of my head.

Chapter Five

I'd had no contact with anyone for two days. Working solidly on the book, I'd not answered the phone or the door. I was pleased with my efforts. Crystal was enjoying one crude sexual encounter after another. She was larger than life, and I believed as much in her existence as I did in Jackie's. No longer a fictitious character, Crystal was getting inside my head, goading me to call Jackie and invite her round. There had been times when I'd been hammering the keyboard that I'd thought I was my own sexually predatory heroine. The experience had been almost frightening. Crystal seemed to be trying to take over.

Finally needing contact with the outside world, I called Jackie. She complained about my not answering the phone and, once she'd calmed down, updated me with the local gossip. Alan and Angela were having problems. Giggling, she told me that it might have had something to do with her chatting to Angela and happening to mention that her man was screwing me. For good measure, she had also informed the distraught girl that she, Jackie, had been having a fling with the three-timing bastard.

'You shouldn't have told her,' I said.

'Why not? Anyway, sod her. So, any chance of a coffee if I come round? Or are you too busy writing smut?'

'Yes, come round. There's every chance of coffee.'

'And?'

'And what?'

'Coffee and?'

'Sorry, I'm not with you.'

'You will be soon. I'm on my way.'

'OK, I'll put the kettle on.'

I'd known what she'd meant, but hadn't known what to say. Writing about lesbian sex had somehow removed the guilt, my wanton act of oral sex with Jackie becoming fictitious, like a dream. But now that Jackie was on her way to see me again, the emotion was returning with a vengeance. Every time I'd thought of what I'd done with her, I'd written another lesbian scene. I'd supposed I was trying to push the reality out of my mind by turning it into fiction. The idea had worked well, but now?

Jackie arrived wearing a red microskirt and a loose-fitting white blouse. I made the coffee and we sat on the patio, talking about anything and everything other than lesbian sex. Her long dark hair shining in the morning sun, her eyes sparkling lustfully, she radiated sex. I couldn't take my eyes off her naked thighs as I sipped my coffee. She noticed my gaze, I was sure as she parted her legs, displaying the tight triangle of red pantie silk covering the swell of her fleshy pussy lips. I'd licked her there, sucked out her juices of desire and taken her to orgasm.

'It's a lovely day,' I murmured abstractedly, my stomach somersaulting as I imagined pushing my tongue into the wet heat of her vaginal sheath.

'It is,' she replied. 'So, you've not seen anything of the infamous Alans?'

'Nothing. As I said, I got stuck into the book and ignored the phone and the doorbell.'

'How's the book coming on?'

'OK. I'm on chapter five.'

'Out of?'

'Fifteen, I reckon. Jackie, we're sitting here talking about nothing when . . .'

'When what?'

'I don't know. After the other day, I don't know what to think.'

'Don't think anything. After all, what is there to think about? We had some sexy fun, and that's it.'

'You said something about *us*. My needing time to think about us.'

'Yes, I did.' She fidgeted in her chair and then locked her dark gaze to mine. 'What I meant was . . . Should you want to do it again . . . Have you thought about it? Us having sex again, I mean.'

'I've written about it,' I sighed. 'I've been trying to push the act onto the heroine in my book. I've been trying to . . . I don't know what I've been trying to do,' I confessed. 'I'm talking crap, aren't I?'

'No, you're not. You've been trying to push your guilt onto the character in your book. That's right, isn't it?'

'Yes, I suppose so. The thing is . . . She's real to me, Jackie. I'm not making sense, am I?'

'Yes, you are.'

'It's as if she wants to live her life through me. In the past, I had control and power over my characters. Even to the point where I could kill them off. But this character seems to have control over *me*.'

'Well, let's hope that *she* doesn't want to kill *you* off,' she giggled, crossing her long legs. 'Seriously, Jade, I wouldn't worry about it. I would have thought it a good thing to believe in your characters.'

'Yes, it is. But not to the extent where they take over.'

'You've been working too hard. Take a break and gather your thoughts.'

'I've decided not to work until after lunch. Crystal, that's the heroine—'

'It's a lovely name,' Jackie interrupted me, frowning. 'But I don't think you should use it, Jade.'

'Why not? I don't know where I got it from. It just sort of came to me.'

'Oh, I thought you'd got it from Crystal Marshall.'

'Who?'

'Crystal Marshall, the girl at school.'

'Oh, yes. I remember her. She was in the class above me, so I didn't really know her. Anyway, I didn't get the name from her.'

'You obviously haven't heard.'

'Heard what?'

'They reckon that she might be dead.'

'God,' I breathed. 'She was only a year older than us.'

'Yes, I know. Haven't you read the local paper?'

'No, I've been too busy working.'

'Crystal disappeared a week ago. Apparently, there were signs of a struggle in her bedroom. It seems that she was into prostitution.'

'God,' I breathed again. 'She was so attractive and . . . Why on earth did she become a prostitute?'

'Why does anyone turn to prostitution?'

'I'd better change the name. I don't want people to think that—'

'Call your character Jackie, after me.'

'Yes, I might do that.'

Finishing my coffee as Jackie wandered down the garden, I pondered on the matter of Crystal Marshall. That she would become a prostitute and end up dead was unbelievable. The girl, from what I remembered, had been into athletics and very much full of life. And, as far as I knew, her parents hadn't been short of money. But one never knows what goes on behind closed doors – or closed minds. Obviously, something had driven her to sell her young body for sex. What her parents were going through, I couldn't begin to imagine.

'I thought I saw something in the bushes,' Jackie said, wandering across the lawn towards me.

'It was probably a cat,' I replied, looking down the garden. 'There are several around here.'

'No, it wasn't a cat. I thought I saw . . .'

'What?' I frowned.

'There was a face, peering out of the bushes.'

'A face?' I laughed. 'What, a peeping Tom?'

'No, it was a child's face. Are there kids next door?'

'Not as far as I know. I don't know about the house at the end of the garden. They might have kids.'

'It was a girl. She looked about twelve years old, with long blonde hair.'

'I don't know, Jackie. It doesn't matter if there are kids playing about. Leave them to it.'

'I suppose so,' she mumbled, sitting on the patio chair.

'Are you OK?' I asked. 'You look pale.'

'It was the girl's face,' she replied, not taking her eyes off the bushes. 'She looked tormented.'

'There's no one there now. I wouldn't worry about it.'

Jackie seemed nervous and fidgety as we finished our coffee. The prospect of lesbian sex had blown away on the wind, which was probably a good thing. I'd wanted sex with her, but knew it was wrong. The battle was still raging in my head. Right, wrong, immoral . . . I wished I'd not experienced sex with another girl. It had helped my writing no end, but it had also left me in a quandary. *What you haven't had, you don't miss*, I reflected. But I'd had it.

'I'd better be going,' Jackie said, moving to the back door.

'Already?' I asked. 'I thought you might want to stay and have lunch with me.'

'No, no, I can't. I'll ring you later.'

'OK. How about the pub this evening?'

'Maybe. I'll ring you.'

Seeing her out, I closed the front door and walked back to the garden. The girl's face, or whatever it was, had obviously worried Jackie. I reckoned that, since she'd been wearing her microskirt and flashing her panties, she'd planned to have sex with me. She must have been concerned about something. It was unlike her to turn down a chance of sex. Wandering down the garden, I peered into the bushes. There was nothing there, other than a high fence. Kids couldn't get over the fence, and there was no other way into the garden. Jackie had been imagining things, I concluded, dashing back to the house as the phone rang.

'Jade?' a female voice asked.

'Yes.'

'It's Angela.'

'Oh. Er . . . Hi.'

'Hi. I'm sorry to ring you but . . . I have to know something.'

'What's that?' I asked, knowing what she was about to say.

'You and Alan. Have you been . . .'

'Fucking him?' I giggled. They weren't my words, I knew as she gasped. 'Sorry, I meant . . .'

'I know what you meant,' she broke in.

'Angela, you stole my man, so don't come whingeing to me about—'

'I didn't steal him, Jade. He came to me because you were screwing around behind his back. I felt sorry for him and . . .'

'Is that what he told you?'

'Yes, it is.'

'Are you busy this morning?'

'No, why?'

'Come round. We'll have coffee.'

'OK.'

Alan seemed to be rather economical with the truth at times. Particularly when it came to pushing his cock into girls' pussies. To tell Angela that I'd been screwing around behind his back was despicable. Jackie had been right. Telling Angela of his infidelity had been the right thing to do. He was going to pay for his bastardy, I decided. And pay dearly.

Angela finally arrived and plonked herself at the kitchen table. She looked dejected. Her long chestnut hair was dishevelled and it was obvious that she had been crying. She'd put on weight, I observed. Perhaps I was being catty, but she'd definitely put on weight. Making her a cup of coffee, I thought how funny it would be if Alan turned up, hoping for a blow job. There again, I doubted that he'd show his face again after I'd caught him sperming in Jackie's mouth. He didn't care where he stuck his cock. Any girl's mouth would do. Or any girl's pussy.

'You're better off without him,' I said, placing the coffee cups on the table.

'He's such a liar,' she sighed as I sat opposite her. 'He told me that you'd been screwing around. He said that you were . . .' Her words tailed off as she caught my gaze.

'What?' I asked. 'What did he say about me?'

'He said that you were nothing but a tart.'

'*Me?* Good God, he's a lying sod,' I shot back. 'A tart? I was faithful to the end, Angela. That's more than he can say. Where is he now?'

'At work. He said that you'd seen me with another man.'

'He told me that you two had split up. I didn't believe him, that's why I said I'd seen you with someone else. He wanted sex and . . . I was testing him. Anyway, it doesn't matter who said what to whom. What are you going to do now?'

'It's my flat, so he can get out. Who's that?' she asked, looking through the open back door.

'Where?' I frowned, following her gaze.

'There was a girl in the bushes down the garden. She's gone now.'

'Er . . . Next door's kids,' I lied, wondering who on earth the child was.

We chatted about Alan and men in general as we drank our coffee, and I felt that we were getting on pretty well. We might even rekindle our friendship, I mused when she said that Alan would be out on the street that night. I couldn't blame her for being taken in by his lies and suggested she came round for coffee again. I couldn't wait to see Alan homeless, and decided to play games with him. Perhaps I'd invite him round and pull his dick out, tease him and send him on his way with his balls full.

'She looks upset,' Angela said, gazing down the garden again.

'Who?' I asked.

'The girl. Oh, she's gone again.'

'She's . . . she's always crying,' I smiled. 'She'll be all right.'

'Well, I'd better get home. I have Alan's things to pack.'

'And throw out into the street?' I giggled.

'And throw out into the street,' she laughed. 'It's been nice seeing you again, Jade. We'll definitely get together again.'

'Any time. I work from home, so ring me.'

'I will. And thanks for everything.'

For sucking your man's cock and swallowing his sperm?

'Don't forget to call me.'

'I won't.'

When she'd gone, I raced down the garden in search of the elusive child. There was no way anyone could get into the garden, I again observed, gazing at the high fence behind the bushes. Jackie might have been mistaken, but not Angela as well. Spending an hour or so on the patio, I saw nothing. It was only when I finally went into my den and slipped into fiction mode that I put two and two together. If Crystal Marshall had died . . . My Crystal was becoming frighteningly real to me, a mysterious young girl's face had emerged from the bushes . . . And Crystal Marshall was dead.

'A ghost?' I breathed. 'Don't be so silly.' Shaking my head as I switched the computer on, I decided to bring a ghost into my story. I had no idea how to do it, or whether David would like the idea, but the notion gripped me and I spent several hours hammering the keyboard.

After dinner, I printed the chapter I'd written that afternoon and wandered out onto the patio with a bottle of wine. As the evening sun sank behind the trees, I began to read the chapter. 'This isn't right,' I breathed, flicking through the sheets of A4. *Crystal grimaced as the young man forced his fist into her inflamed anal canal. A girl's teeth sinking into her hairless vulval lips, a solid knob ramming to the back of her throat, she shook violently as the leather whip flailed her naked breasts.*

Reading through the pages, I shook my head in disbelief. I hadn't written one word of this sexual torture. This wasn't my work. Lifting my head, I looked down the garden, thinking about the mysterious young girl. Dusk falling, I could barely make out the bushes. Was there something there? I wondered, straining my eyes. Feeling cold, I grabbed what was left of the wine, went into the kitchen and locked the back door.

There were no such things as ghosts, I tried to convince myself. If Crystal Marshall had been murdered, my Crystal . . . 'The idea's ridiculous,' I breathed, walking into the lounge as the phone rang. A ghost lurking in the bushes? Grabbing the receiver, I decided to put ghosts and ghouls out of my mind. But I couldn't explain chapter six. Pressing the phone to my ear, I sighed as Alan the ex began rambling. He'd been thrown out and he'd not meant to lie to me and he wanted to come round and talk and the thing with Jackie had been a mistake and . . .

'All right,' I conceded finally. 'Come round for a chat. But you're not sleeping here.'

'Thanks,' he said. 'It's just that I need someone to talk to.'

'And that's all you're going to do,' I stated firmly.

'Of course,' he agreed. 'I'll be about ten minutes.'

As I waited for him, I wondered why I was bothering to speak to him, let alone have him round for a chat. He'd lied to everyone and didn't deserve any sympathy. He certainly wasn't going to doss on my sofa, if that was what he had in mind. Again pondering on chapter six, I paced the lounge floor. Someone had written it, but . . . No one could have got into my den. Obviously I had written it. I must have had some kind of mental block and forgotten what I'd written.

When Alan arrived, I took him into the lounge and gave

him a glass of wine. He looked tired and drawn, and I wondered what Angela had said to him. I found myself staring at the bulging crotch of his jeans as he sat in the armchair and rambled on about his great love for me. The last thing I'd intended to do was seduce him, and yet I felt compelled to unzip his jeans and drag his penis out. My thoughts muddled, I poured myself another glass of wine and tried to clear my mind of ghosts and Crystal.

'Why don't you strip off?' I breathed as Alan talked about moving in with me. I couldn't for the life of me think why I'd said that.

'Great,' he smiled, leaping to his feet and unbuckling his belt.

'Hurry up, then,' I whispered, wondering what the hell I was doing. They hadn't been my words and yet . . . 'I want your cock spunking in my mouth.'

Watching him pull his jeans off and slip out of his shirt, I couldn't believe what I'd said. I was either tired or . . . Perhaps I'd been working too hard over the last couple of days, I thought. And I'd probably had too much wine, which was blurring my thinking. It would be best to get rid of Alan and have an early night. Staring at his naked body, his erect penis, I was about to tell him to go when there he was, standing in front of me.

'You taste good,' I murmured, retracting his foreskin and licking the silken globe of his purple knob. Kneading his heavy balls as I sucked his knob into my wet mouth, I dug my fingernails into his scrotum. He twitched as he felt the pain, and I tightened my grip on the sensitive skin of his ball-bag Complaining, he tried to push me away but I clenched my hand, gripping his hairy sac until he cried out. I felt my cunt decanting its juices of arousal into my panties.

'Christ,' he said, grabbing my arm. 'You're hurting me.'

'I'm sorry' I chuckled, releasing his scrotum. 'I didn't mean to hurt you. I'll tell you what I'd like to do.'

'What's that?'

'I'd like to tie you up with rope,' I grinned, licking the shaft of his solid cock.

'What?'

'I said, I'd like to tie you up with rope. Don't you want to have some fun?'

'Yes, of course,' he replied eagerly.

Leaping to my feet, I moved to the door. 'I have a washing line in the kitchen cupboard. I'll go and get it.' On my way through the hall, I stopped briefly to peel off my uncomfortably sopping-wet panties and sling them under a small table.

Returning to the lounge with the line and a pair of scissors, I grinned at Alan and he stared at me. I didn't know why I was acting the way I was, and neither did he. All I knew was that I had to commit vulgar sexual acts with him while I had the chance. It must have been writing filth that had made me like this, I reflected. But I hadn't *really* written chapter six, had I? Instructing Alan to lie on the floor with his limbs spread, my mind brimming with wicked ideas as he complied, I kneeled at his feet and cut the line into four lengths.

'This will be fun,' I grinned, tying one length of line around his right ankle and securing the free end to the radiator. Yanking his feet wide apart, I tied another length of line to his other ankle and fixed the end to one of the sofa legs. Crawling across the carpet, I tied the last two lengths of line to his wrists and pulled his hands behind his head. Tying one free end to the other sofa leg and the other line to the TV stand, I stood up and gazed at his spreadeagled naked body.

'Perfect,' I murmured as he pulled on his bonds and asked what I intended to do. 'You've been a naughty boy, Alan,' I replied huskily. 'I'm going to have to punish you.'

'Sounds like fun,' he chuckled. 'You know, we're really good together.'

'Aren't we just?'

'I was hoping that you'd . . . Well, you know.'

'Want sex with you?'

'Yes.'

'Of course I want sex with you, Alan. I've been hoping you'd call me.'

'I know how much you want me, Jade. And I want you. Angela was . . . I don't know why I ever bothered with her. It was you I loved all along. I suppose she enticed me with her lies and I fell for it.'

'Well, you're here with me now so you needn't worry about her. As you said, we're really good together. And we're going to get better.'

The only good thing was that I was about to have my revenge and vent my anger on the lying bastard. Whether I was being driven by Crystal the heroine or my own craving for revenge, I didn't know or care. And as for Crystal Marshall . . . Prostitution? Had a client abducted her and . . . She'd seek revenge, given half the chance. But that was impossible, seeing as she was . . .?

Picking up the scissors from the floor, I settled between Alan's splayed thighs and began snipping the dark hairs covering his balls. Lifting his head, he protested as I cut away the pubic curls above his erect penis. Ignoring him, I worked around the base of his cock until nothing but rough stubble covered his pubic area. He was beginning to annoy me with his continual complaints, so I darted into the hall, grabbed my wet panties from beneath the table there, raced back into the lounge and stuffed them into his mouth.

'That'll keep you quiet,' I smiled. 'Now I can enjoy myself in peace.' I don't know what had possessed me to cut his pubes off, but I decided to finish the job. I slipped into the bathroom and grabbed my razor and a can of shaving foam. He'd look like a little boy by the time I'd finished with him. And he'd have some explaining to do if he was lucky enough to pull a slut. Sitting between his thighs again, I squirted the foam over the stubble of his pubes and began shaving him. He wriggled and moaned through his nose, but there was nothing he could do to halt the depilation of his genitalia.

Finally wiping the foam away, I studied my handiwork. 'Smooth as a baby's bum,' I murmured, running my fingertips over his rolling balls, the swell of his naked pubic mound. Looking into his wide eyes as I stood towering above him, I grinned. 'The time has come,' I whispered, placing my foot on his stomach. 'The time has come for you to receive your just reward for your lies and deceit. You're about to be punished.'

His terror-stricken eyes following me as I walked across the room, I wondered what he was thinking. He'd be in two minds, I concluded, opening the bureau and taking out a wooden ruler. On the one hand, he'd trust me not to hurt him or do anything stupid, apart from shaving his pubes off. On the other hand . . . He didn't really know me. I'd changed, and he couldn't be sure what to expect of me. I didn't know what to expect of myself.

'Angela came round earlier,' I said, sitting by his side and tapping his flaccid penis with the ruler. 'Apparently, you told her that I was a tart. You went running to her with your stories of my unfaithfulness and your lies about me screwing around behind your back.' He winced as I tapped his slug-like organ a little harder. 'You lied about me. And you lied about her. You said that you were dossing on a friend's sofa. She hadn't thrown you out, Alan. You lied to get your hands inside my wet knickers.'

Tapping his hairless balls with the ruler, I giggled. He was terrified, and so he should have been. He was a lying, cheating bastard and deserved everything he was going to get. But what *was* he going to get? I wondered, flicking his limp penis from side to side with the ruler. Realizing what I was doing, as if waking from a dream, I focused on his shaved pubic mound. Recalling chapter six of my erotic work in progress, I began to wonder what was happening to me. This recent behaviour was so uncharacteristic that I couldn't believe I'd written the chapter, or shaved Alan's pubes off.

'I'll wank you,' I smiled, dropping the ruler to the floor and grabbing the soft shaft of his cock. The fear left his eyes as his penis stiffened in my warm hand. He was finding trust in me, confidence. 'Is that nice?' I asked, running his foreskin back and forth over his swelling knob. He nodded his head, his eyes smiling as he relaxed. Leaning over, I sucked the purple globe of his solid cock deep into my hot mouth and moaned through my nose. His naked body writhed, his heavy balls rolling as he wallowed in his pleasure.

Pleasure before pain. The words reverberating around my mind, I again wondered about the young girl's face emerging from the bushes. Wishing I'd seen her, I wondered whether she was the ghost of Crystal Marshall. I didn't believe in ghosts as such, but thought that some form of projection of the mind was possible. Perhaps Crystal's thoughts had been so powerful just before she'd died that they'd somehow materialized. But why in my garden? Was there a link between my fictional character and Crystal

Marshall? If there was such a link, then I had no idea what it was.

As Alan breathed heavily through his nose, his orgasm nearing, I couldn't stop wondering what the link was. I'd not known Crystal Marshall, so why would she haunt me in death? Simply using her name in a book wouldn't summon her from the grave. What was I thinking? It hadn't been established that the girl was dead. Summon her from the grave? I should be writing horror, not erotica, I reflected as Alan's moans grew louder. He wanted to come. He wanted me to wank him faster and bring out his sperm.

'I fancy a cup of tea,' I said, leaping to my feet and leaving the room. In the kitchen, I happened to notice a carrot in the vegetable rack. Wicked ideas filling my mind, I grabbed the carrot and ran my fingers along the tapered shaft. Would I really do it? I wondered, picturing Alan's face as I forced the carrot deep into his rectal canal. To write about anal sex, I'd need to watch the brown tissue surrounding his bottom-hole expand to accommodate the shaft. A carrot penetrating a man's bottom or a penis entering a girl's bottom, the effect would be the same. Male or female, carrot or penis, the brown tissue would stretch wide open just the same. I had to witness the enforced opening of an anus, I decided in my new-found wickedness as I returned to the lounge.

Alan's penis was still erect, and no doubt in dire need of wanking to orgasm. But he'd have to wait until I'd satisfied my curiosity about his anus. The thick end of the carrot was almost two inches across. I reckoned Alan knew what I intended to do as he watched me examining the vegetable. Would he enjoy the experience? I wondered, kneeling between his thighs and parting his tensed buttocks. Two inches? It might be possible. There was only one way to find out.

Pressing the thin end of the carrot against the delicate tissue of his brown ring, I twisted and pushed until the tip slipped past his anal sphincter muscles and drove on into his tightening rectum. He writhed and moaned through his nose as I eased the orange shaft further into his private duct. Since his penis was still solid, I reckoned that he was enjoying the experience. Perhaps I'd slip a carrot into my own bottom later, I mused. God, what *was* I thinking? And what the hell was I doing to Alan?

I tried to halt the crude act but my hand continued to push the carrot into his inflating anal canal. Watching the brown tissue expand, I felt a quiver run through my con-tracting womb. My arousal heightening, I forced the carrot into Alan's rectum until only the end protruded between his rounded buttocks. His head lolling from side to side, his penis rock-hard, I knew that he was deriving pleasure from my debased action. But I hadn't intended to bring him pleasure.

My mind awash with gross thoughts, I grabbed the wooden ruler and sat by Alan's side. A loud slap resounded around the room as the ruler struck the back of his penis. Another slap, and another until the organ shrank and fell limp over his hairless balls. I continued to slap his penis as he writhed and moaned through his nose. He'd wanted to come so much, and all I was doing was thrashing his cock. *Poor Alan*, I thought, striking his deflated member again and again. *Poor used and abused bastard.*

'Oh, it's turning scarlet.' I grinned. 'And it's all soft and limp. You obviously didn't enjoy the ruler. There again, *I* don't enjoy being called a tart and being cheated and betrayed.' Alan pulled at his bonds as I struck his crimsoned cock again. 'It's no use, Alan,' I whispered threateningly. 'You can't escape me. I'll tell you what I'll do. I'll go out for a drink and leave you here for the evening. When I get back, I'll wank you and make you shoot your spunk all over your stomach. But only if you're good.' The doorbell ringing, I leaped to my feet. 'Don't go away,' I chuckled. 'I'll get rid of whoever it is and then give you a good cock-thrashing before I go out.'

Jackie was standing on the step, grinning. Wearing her microskirt and revealing blouse, she was obviously ready to go out. Not sure what to do as she stepped into the hall, I closed the lounge door and asked her to wait in the kitchen while I got ready.

'Hurry up,' she said, wandering into the kitchen. 'It's late enough as it is.'

'I thought you were going to ring me,' I called from my bedroom as I changed.

'Was I? I thought we were going to the pub and . . . What does it matter? I'm here now.'

'OK, let's go.' I smiled as I walked into the hall. 'I'll tell you all about Angela's visit.'

'She came here?' she gasped.

'Yes, for a chat. I'm looking forward to having a drink. Having been stuck in the flat working for the past couple of days, I'm really looking forward to going out.'

Closing the front door, I followed Jackie down the path. I'd deal with Alan when I got back, I decided. I'd leave him to ponder on his wickedness for a few hours, and then thrash his cock and his balls. Wondering whether his rectum could take two carrots, I could hardly wait to get home.

Chapter Six

Alan had somehow managed to free himself and had gone by the time I'd got home from the pub. Jackie had suggested coming in but I'd told her that I'd wanted to go straight to bed. The last thing I needed was her finding Alan's naked body spreadeagled on the lounge floor. But I needn't have worried. Alan had left me a note informing me of his anger and threatening to deal with me – whatever *that* meant. Screwing the note up, I climbed the stairs and slept like a log.

Waking early the following morning, I slipped out of bed and drew the curtains. The sun was shining and it was going to be another beautiful day. But I had work to do. I couldn't waste time sunbathing when I had a book to write. Pondering on chapter six as sleep left me, I went into my den and switched the computer on. I couldn't believe what I'd written as I flopped into the swivel chair and brought the chapter up onto the screen.

The brown entrance to her anal canal stretched tightly around his wrist, he repeatedly thrust into her shaking body as she begged him for mercy. The other man's fist bloating her vaginal cavern, she coughed and spluttered as the huge penis fucking her mouth shot out its copious flow of white spunk. They weren't my words, I knew. It just wasn't my style. Having said that, what I'd done to Alan was hardly my style.

Looking down at my naked body, I decided to have a shower and dress. I'd planned to spend the day writing, but if I was going to churn out several thousand words and not have a clue as to what I'd written . . . I must have had some sort of memory lapse, I concluded as I wandered into the bathroom. But what I'd done to Alan could hardly be called a memory lapse. Still, since I'd been angry, I supposed I'd acted out of character. I must have been more than angry, I thought as I stepped into the shower. I must have been enraged to the point where I'd lost control of my senses.

I wrote for a couple of hours, repeatedly reading each page to ensure that I knew what I was doing. They were my words this time, and I thought again that tiredness and anger had influenced me during chapter six. I wasn't convinced but I could come up with no other explanation. Deciding to have a ten-minute break, I grabbed a can of cola from the fridge and sat on the patio.

The carrot and lengths of washing line were still in the lounge. Making a mental note to remove all signs of my sexual debauchery before I had any visitors, I chuckled as I recalled Alan's face when the carrot had slipped into his bum. Although my behaviour had been totally out of character, I found the memory of the evening hilarious. Shaving him, slapping his cock with the ruler, forcing a carrot up his bum . . . It served him right. I doubted that he'd be back in a hurry.

Swigging from the can, I almost choked as I looked down the garden and saw a young girl's face emerge from the bushes. Standing and walking towards her, I was determined not to take my eyes off her. If she was going to disappear, then I wanted to know which way she went. As I approached her, I frowned. Her pale face was screwed up with anguish. She appeared to be frightened, her pained expression reflecting torment. As the phone rang, I instinctively turned and looked at the back door. By the time I looked at the bushes again, my visitor had gone.

'Shit,' I breathed, searching the bushes as the phone continued to ring. There was no sign of the girl, and I finally dashed back to the house and leaped into the kitchen just as the phone stopped ringing. 'It's always the bloody way,' I murmured. As I was about to return to the bushes in search of the girl, it rang again. It was Alan the ex, Alan the ex-pubes. And he was far from happy.

'You're a bitch,' he hissed.

'And you're a lying, cheating bastard,' I returned. 'But you have a lovely cock. I was looking forward to sucking you off when I got home, but you'd gone.'

'You weren't going to do anything of the sort. You . . . you were going to torture me, for fuck's sake.'

'Don't be ridiculous. Torture you? I was having some fun, Alan. I thought that's what you wanted?'

'I didn't want to be shaved and then left tied up while you pissed off out.'

'So, I take it that you won't be coming to see me again.'

'I don't know. I mean, I'd like to but I don't want—'

'You can visit me whenever you want to. But the sex will be the way I want it.'

'What, stuffing a carrot up my arse?'

'If that's what takes my fancy, yes. I don't know why you're complaining. I thought you were into the kinky stuff.'

'Yes, but . . . . I have to go, the boss is on the warpath. I'll call you some time.'

'I'll get some fresh carrots in,' I laughed, and banged the phone down.

Alan hadn't complained nearly as much as I'd thought he

would. As I wandered down the garden I reckoned that he was looking forward to coming round again. Next time, I'd allow him the pleasure of shooting his spunk into my mouth, I thought as I searched the bushes and checked the fence. I couldn't understand where the girl had got to. I'd only turned my back for a few seconds. There was no way she could have dashed past me. Pondering on ghosts again as I ambled back to the kitchen, the notion didn't seem so far-fetched. A ghost, or a thought projection? Whatever the answer, I decided that the girl wasn't human.

I cleared up the lounge and spent the rest of the day hammering the keyboard in my den. I couldn't stop thinking about the girl in the bushes, her tormented face continually looming from the depths of my mind. If it had been only I who had seen her, I would have questioned my sanity. But Jackie and Angela had seen her. If she was a ghost – and I thought the idea ludicrous – then she must want something. Unless ghosts hang around in bushes just for the hell of it. Hell?

'Yes?' I snapped, snatching up the ringing phone.

'Guess what?' Jackie asked.

'Jackie, I am not in the mood for guessing games,' I snapped.

'Oooh,' she giggled. 'PMS or just a bad hair day?'

'I'm busy, Jackie. What do you want?'

'It's about your ex-boyfriend. I don't want to say anything on the phone so . . .'

'Don't play games. I'm really busy and haven't got time to—'

'I'll be there in ten minutes. This is something that'll blow your bollocks off.'

'Jackie, for your information, I don't have any bollocks.

Men differ from women in several ways, one of them being—'

'OK, it'll blow your ovaries off. See you soon. And put the bloody kettle on.'

What with ghosts, my shaving Alan's pubes off and spanking his penis, and now Jackie playing mind games, I began to wonder in which direction my life was taking me. I'd been a quiet girl, minding my own business and writing my romantic novel without the hassle of relationships and . . . I'd sucked two men off, fucked one of them, had lesbian sex with my best friend, started writing dirty books – and been subjected to the antics of the dead. Shaking my head despondently, I ambled into the kitchen and filled the kettle. *I might as well open a bloody coffee shop*, I reflected, grabbing two cups. *And a knocking shop.*

Jackie arrived bubbling over with excitement, but I also detected an element of seriousness in her tone as she blabbered on about Alan the ex. She wasn't making any sense so I ordered her to sit at the kitchen table and start from the beginning. She was obviously eager to tell me her news, but she still wanted to play her mind games.

'You'll never guess what,' she repeated for the umpteenth time.

'OK, OK,' I sighed. 'It has something to do with my exboyfriend, right?'

'Right,' she beamed.

'You arranged to meet him in the park and he fucked you senseless?'

'No, of course not.'

'I wouldn't put it past you.'

'I'll tell you.'

'No, you won't. You've been asking me to guess and I'm going to.'

'Actually, it's not funny,' she murmured, her smile fading.

'Go on, then.'

'Crystal Marshall, right?'

'Right.'

'She was a prostitute.'

'Yes.'

'She had clients.'

'Jackie, if she didn't have clients, she couldn't sell her body for sex. If she couldn't do that, then she wasn't a prostitute. It's like calling someone a shopkeeper when they haven't got a shop.'

'One of her clients was Alan.'

'*My* Alan?'

'Yes.'

'How do you know?'

'I was talking to a girl whose boyfriend knows someone who . . .'

'OK, cut out the friend-of-a-friend-of-a-friend crap. Alan visited Crystal Marshall?'

'Yes. He was a client.'

'I can't believe it.'

'It's true. The police are trying to track down Crystal's clients. It's pretty obvious that one of them abducted her. You'd best keep away from Alan.'

'He's not a killer,' I murmured pensively. 'But he is the link.'

'The link?'

'The link between Crystal and . . .' I decided not to mention ghosts. 'It was just something Alan was saying,' I smiled.

'I wonder where he's living now that Angela's thrown him out?'

'I don't know, or care.'

My mind wandering, I imagined that Crystal Marshall was somehow influencing me. She'd wanted to get back at Alan, and had used me as a tool. I'd never have tied him down, shaved him, spanked his penis and shoved a carrot up his bum. That was Crystal's doing. What would she influence me to do the next time he came round? Perhaps she wanted to get back at men for the way they'd used and abused her. Perhaps she'd influence me to kill him. But who was the girl in the bushes?

Had Crystal influenced me when I'd been wondering what to call the girl in my book? I thought that my imagination was running wild. Ghosts influencing me? The way I'd behaved was down to talking to Jackie about sex, reading the book David had given me and writing my own erotic fiction. But why had I enjoyed lesbian sex with Jackie? Pushing my face between her warm thighs and licking her erect clitoris to orgasm had driven me wild. That was most unlike me.

'Heard anything from the Alan you met in the pub?' Jackie asked.

'No, nothing,' I replied, wondering where he'd got to. 'I thought he might be in the pub last night. I expect he's busy with his band.'

'Probably.'

'Jackie, I can't stop thinking about Crystal. I never saw her around town.'

'She lived in one of those old cottages near Turner's Farm.'

'A cottage?' I echoed, my heart sinking.

'You know, the ones along the lane leading to the farm.'

'God,' I breathed.

'What's the matter?'

'Let's go there.'

'Now? What for?'

'I have to check something out. Come on, we'll take my car.'

Jackie didn't stop questioning me as I drove to the farm. I didn't want to say what was on my mind until I'd made sure that I was right. I hoped to God that I *wasn't* right as I pulled up in the lane. The pieces were beginning to fit together. The name, the cottage . . . Climbing out of the car, I stared at the row of cottages. The one with a policeman guarding the door catching my eye, I turned and gazed at Jackie.

'That must be the one,' I said.

'Yes, but what's this all about?'

'Look at the front garden. There's a laburnum tree. And a well.'

'So?'

'Crystal, the girl in my book. She lives in a cottage with a laburnum tree and a well in the front garden.'

'We played here as kids, Jade. You probably remembered this place and—'

'No, I don't think so.'

'I remember this place only too well. The haystack used to be through the trees over there. Shall we take a look?'

'You go ahead. I'll catch you up.'

'OK,' she murmured, heading for the trees. 'Don't be long.'

Gazing at the cottage, I imagined Alan visiting Crystal. He'd have parked his car in the lane and . . . Trying to think back to when I'd started the book, I wondered exactly when I'd come up with the name of the heroine. It was after Alan

the ex had visited me. Had he mentioned the name? I
wondered. He certainly wouldn't have mentioned the cottage. No, he hadn't talked about Crystal, or uttered her
name. It was coincidence. I'd dreamed her up, and the
cottage. As I was about to follow Jackie and take a look at
the site of the infamous haystack, the policeman guarding
the cottage wandered over to me.

'Are you all right, Miss?' he asked.

'Yes. I was just looking at the cottage. I went to the same
school as Crystal.'

'It's a sad affair,' he sighed. 'So young and attractive. It
makes you wonder what's gone wrong with society.'

'It does,' I agreed. 'I didn't exactly know her, but I do
remember her from school. I thought her parents were well
off. Why she had to turn to—'

'They moved to Australia when she was twelve. She lived
here with her aunt. In poverty, by all accounts. When the
old lady passed on, Crystal turned her hand to writing.'

'Writing?' I echoed disbelievingly.

'She wrote several novels but they were never published.
She finally ran out of money and . . .'

'Her novels . . . Are they in the cottage?'

'Yes, but I can't let you see them. The girl might still be
alive. If you have a vested interest, then . . .'

'No, no,' I murmured. 'It's all right.'

'Well, I'd better get back.'

Jackie came bounding towards me as the policeman
returned to the cottage. Complaining that a house had
been built where the haystack had once stood, she rambled
on about her schooldays and how she'd had many a good
time in the woods with Jenny Hardbrooke. Climbing into
my car, I took little notice of her as I drove down the lane. I
couldn't believe that Crystal had written novels. None of

the recent events had been coincidental, that was certain.
Crystal Marshall wanted something from me. But what?

Parking outside my flat, I asked Jackie in but she said
that she had things to do. I was relieved in a way as I wanted
to sit alone and think. The girl in the bushes intrigued me.
She was about twelve years old, the very age Crystal had
been when her parents had left her and gone to Australia.
Why hadn't they taken her with them? Why dump her on an
old aunt?

Standing in the back garden, I decided to help Crystal
with whatever it was she was trying to do. I didn't think that
she wanted to hurt Alan. She wanted revenge, perhaps, but
not to the point where she'd cause him harm. Did she want
to live out her lesbian fantasies through me? Was that why
I'd derived immense pleasure from licking Jackie to orgasm? Dashing into the kitchen, I rang Alan on his mobile
and invited him round for the evening.

'Are you going to tie me down?' he asked.

'Of course,' I giggled. 'But this time I'll make you come.
Not just once, though.'

'OK, I'll be there at seven,' he said enthusiastically. 'At
least you won't be able to shave my pubes off.'

'Not for a few weeks, I won't. Don't be late, will you?'

'Of course I won't.'

Phase one of the plan completed, I rang Jackie and
invited her round. I didn't tell her what I had in mind,
but I made her promise to arrive at seven-thirty. I reckoned
that she knew something was going on because she asked
me what she should wear. I rather liked her red microskirt,
and we settled for that. She said she'd bring a bottle of wine
and a little surprise for me. She'd always loved secrets.

I was in two minds as to whether or not I should invite
Angela to my little gathering. Perhaps not, I concluded as I

wandered into my den. She might not be the type to enjoy debauched sex. I had time to kill, and decided to work on my book. Or was it Crystal's book? I'd write for a few hours and then prepare the lounge for Alan's arrival. Ropes, carrots, the ruler . . . Or a garden cane? I deliberated. I was in the mood to write about sex, and hammered the keyboard for several hours.

His face beaming, Alan arrived at seven on the dot. Wasting no time, I had him stripped and his naked body spreadeagled on the lounge floor within minutes. I'd secured the lengths of washing line properly this time. There was no way he could escape. He was a pathetic sight, and I couldn't help laughing at his hairless balls. He looked like a schoolboy with his milk-white pubic mound and naked scrotum. Pulling my girl-wet panties off, I stuffed them into his mouth and grinned at him. He seemed happy enough to be bound and gagged, I observed as his eyes smiled. Happy enough – for the time being.

Closing the lounge door, I hovered in the kitchen, waiting for Jackie to arrive. Of course, I'd have to explain why a naked man was tied to the lounge floor. God only knew what she'd think of me, but I didn't care. I was doing this for Crystal Marshall, wasn't I? Was she lurking in the bushes? I wondered, gazing out of the kitchen window. I couldn't see the young girl, and again wondered what she had to do with Crystal. If the girl was a ghost, which I still very much doubted, what was she doing lurking in the bushes? And how had she got there?

My thoughts turning to Jackie, I knew that she'd have no real interest in the reasons why Alan was bound and gagged. She'd simply be only too delighted by the prospect of crude sex and would dive straight in. It occurred to me that I might feel embarrassed. If we both played with Alan's dick, wanked him and watched his sperm shoot out of his knob, I was sure I'd turn scarlet. And what would Alan think of me for inviting Jackie to join in? On reflection, though, I didn't give a toss what he thought.

Jackie arrived on time, for a change, and I took her into the kitchen to explain what the evening was all about. The way she frowned at me when I announced that Alan the ex was ready and waiting for us, it was obvious that she didn't believe me. Leaning against the worktop, her panties almost showing below her microskirt, I could hardly wait to get my hands on her beautiful body. How would I react with Alan watching me? I wondered. Licking and fingering Jackie's beautiful pussy while he watched . . . I was thinking like a nymphomaniac. Was Crystal influencing me? I thought not as I eyed Jackie's shapely thighs. This was my thinking, I was sure.

'God,' Jackie gasped as I led her into the lounge. 'I thought you were joking.'

'I never joke about sex,' I smiled, gazing at Alan as he frowned and pulled hopelessly on his bonds.

'He's . . . he's shaved,' she breathed, holding her hand to her mouth. 'How did you . . . I mean, this just isn't like you, Jade.'

'Isn't it?'

'No, it's not. God, how you've changed.'

'Don't worry about me. He's ready and waiting for you so dive in. You did want us to share a dick, didn't you?'

'Yes, but . . . God, I never thought . . .'

'Don't think, Jackie. What is it you're always telling me to do? Ah, yes. Have some fun.'

I started the ball rolling by grabbing a huge carrot from the table and settling between Alan's splayed thighs. The expression on his face was priceless as I parted his firm buttocks and exposed the brown ring of his bottom-hole to Jackie's wide eyes. Easing the thin end of the vegetable into his tight brown orifice, I felt wicked in the extreme. Alan grimaced and moaned through his nose as I forced the carrot deeper into his anal duct. But this was nothing, I mused. The fun had barely begun.

Jackie sat on the sofa gasping as she focused on the carrot, staring in disbelief as I forced the orange shaft deeper into Alan's rectum. His penis didn't stiffen, which was disappointing. I supposed he was too embarrassed to have an erection. And I'd thought that I'd be swamped with embarrassment, I reflected, twisting the carrot. He'd soon overcome his humiliation and his cock would rise to the occasion.

It wasn't long before Jackie settled on the floor beside Alan and started fiddling with his limp dick. Pulling his foreskin right back, she leaned over and sucked his purple knob into her mouth. Pistoning his rectum with the carrot, I watched his naked balls jerk as she sucked and wanked his stiffening cock. Bobbing her head up and down, she was obviously desperate for his sperm. I'd allow him some pleasure, but I didn't want him to come. He was going to have to wait a long time for the release of orgasm, for the spurting of his sperm.

Parting his buttocks as wide as I could, I gazed at the delicate brown tissue of his bottom-hole stretched tautly around the massive carrot. Imagining that this was a girl's bottom and the carrot a penis, I took mental notes. The previously wrinkled tissue of his anus was now smooth and paler in colour. As I withdrew the carrot, his anal ring clung to the vegetable, as if being sucked out of his anal canal. Pushing the natural dildo back into his rectum, the brown tissue looked as if it was being drawn into his body. This was what I'd needed to experience, I reflected. But it was only the beginning.

'Not yet,' I said as Jackie fervently wanked and sucked his rock-hard penis. 'We don't want him to come yet.' Releasing Alan's cock, she smiled as she gazed at my knickerless pussy. Sitting cross-legged, I'd not deliberately exhibited all I had. I'd genuinely forgotten that I'd taken my panties off. Her wide-eyed gaze locked to my gaping vaginal crack, she reached out and stroked my swollen outer lips. I spied the tight material of her panties as she lifted her thigh. I wanted her tongue inside my cunt, tasting, licking, teasing. I wanted to tongue-fuck her wet cunt.

As she reclined on the floor and lifted her buttocks, I watched her pull her panties down her long legs and toss them across the room. The crack of her vagina was drenched, running with her creamy girl-juice. My mouth watering as I imagined sucking out her juices of lust, I frowned as she straddled Alan's naked body. Her gaping vaginal valley hovering above his erect penis, I lay on the floor between his thighs to watch his cock enter her young cunt. *More experience*, I mused as she grabbed his cock and pressed his swollen knob between the dripping inner petals of her pussy. Only inches away from the penetration, I focused on his veined shaft as she lowered her trembling body and completely impaled herself on his solid penis.

Jackie's swollen outer lips pressing against Alan's hairless balls, I gazed in awe at the brown ring of her succulent bottom-hole. Would she like to have one of my carrots pushed into her bum? I wondered. Feeling decadent, I stood up and pulled my skirt off. Wicked ideas swirled around my confused mind as I looked at Alan. His gaze catching mine as I stood with my feet either side of his head, he must have again wondered what on earth had changed me from a prude into a rampant nymphomaniac.

Squatting, my vaginal crack stretching wide open only inches above Alan's face, I smiled at Jackie. She leaned forward and locked her full red lips to mine in a passionate kiss. *Another first*, I thought as her tongue entered my mouth, seeking my tongue as she breathed heavily through her nose. I was learning fast. I'd loved to have pulled the gag out of Alan's mouth and forced my hot cuntal flesh hard against his face, but I wanted him to remain silent for the time being.

As Jackie moved back and bounced up and down on Alan's erect penis, I felt an overwhelming desire to commit an act so vile that I shuddered. It was one thing to have Jackie join in with Alan and me, but there were limits. Standing up, I left the room and went to the kitchen to try and clear my head. I could hear Jackie gasping as she fucked my ex-boyfriend, and I began to realize that I was turning my flat into a den of iniquity. Again, I felt an urge to commit a vile act. The terrible notion crashing around the wreckage of my confused mind, I knew that Crystal was near by.

'I won't do it,' I murmured, leaning on the table to steady my trembling body. My head spinning, I closed my eyes and breathed deeply. Through the mist of my mind, I saw a naked girl, her arms outstretched, her face contorted with anguish. It was like a dream, a nightmare. I tried to open my eyes but couldn't. Hearing Jackie's orgasmic cries some-where in the distance, I finally managed to break out of my strange mental state and look about me.

Unbuttoning my blouse, I slipped it over my shoulders and let it fall to the floor. Releasing my bra, my firm breasts tumbling out of the silk cups, I watched my nipples grow and stand proud from the chestnut discs of my areolae. I was ready, I knew as I made my way to the lounge. I had to commit the vulgar act. Jackie was sitting on the floor, gasping after her orgasm. Alan's cock was limp, a blend of sperm and girl-juice glistening on his shaft, running over his naked balls.

'Where did you get to?' Jackie asked as I squatted over Alan's face. Leaning over his tethered body, I licked the blend of sperm and Jackie's orgasmic juices from the shaft of his flaccid penis. Lapping up the creamy cocktail of sex from his naked balls, I projected my rounded buttocks, exposing my anal entrance to my victim. He'd be gazing at my anus, I knew as his penis rolled towards his stomach and began to swell. When I was ready, I'd commit the vile act.

'Jade,' Jackie murmured. 'Are you all right?' Remaining silent, I sucked the swollen knob of Alan's wet cock into my mouth and ran my tongue around his salty globe. His balls rolled, his cock stiffening fully as I lowered my head and took his ballooning glans to the back of my throat. Reaching behind my thighs, I sank my fingers into my drenched vaginal crack and yanked the swollen lips of my pussy wide apart. Alan would be gazing longingly at my inner folds, the bared entrance to my hot vagina. I was ready.

'Jade!' Jackie cried as she settled behind me. 'What the hell are you doing?' I could hear the splashing as Alan's body writhed beneath me. His face, his hair . . . He'd be drenched, I knew as I relaxed my muscles and showered him with the hot liquid. 'I can't believe you're doing this!' Jackie wailed. The panties stuffed into Alan's mouth would soak up the downpour. He'd taste it as the liquid permeated the gag and trickled into his mouth. He'd taste my golden rain.

Alan obviously had no complaints, I thought as his penis swelled and twitched within my hot mouth. Moaning through his nose, his body becoming rigid as my golden flow began to stem, he pumped his sperm into my mouth. Fervently sucking and licking his bulbous knob, I swallowed his orgasmic cream as he writhed in ecstasy beneath me. I could hear Jackie's little gasps as my golden liquid dribbled from my gaping cunt, splattering Alan's face as he continued to pump his sperm into my gobbling mouth.

Suddenly realizing what I'd done, as if waking from a dream as I sucked out the last of Alan's spunk, I sat upright and clambered to my feet. Jackie gazed at me, disbelief mirrored in her sparkling eyes as I sat on the sofa. I didn't know why I'd behaved like that, I reflected as I looked at Alan. His face and hair drenched, the soaked panties sticking out of his mouth, I couldn't think why I'd done it. Jackie said nothing as I reclined on the sofa and closed my eyes. She was obviously too stunned by my crudity to speak.

Hearing movements, I watched Jackie through my eyelashes as she slipped the carrot out of Alan's rectum. Pulling the wet panties out of his mouth, she turned and looked at me. Pretending to doze, I listened as she asked Alan whether he was all right. He asked her to untie him, and she again looked at me. I couldn't allow that, I mused. I hadn't finished with him. I hadn't fucked him or pushed my open vaginal crack hard against his mouth and ordered him to tongue-fuck my cunt.

'I don't know what's come over her,' Alan whispered.

'Neither do I,' Jackie rejoined. 'She was always such a prude. Did you . . . did you enjoy what she did?'

'Yes,' he chuckled softly. 'I must admit that no one's ever done that to me before, but I quite liked it. I also liked it when you slipped my cock into your cunt, Jackie. We must meet up somewhere. Don't tell her, though.'

'I'd better release you before she wakes up.'

'I'll do that,' I grinned, leaping to my feet. 'Alan will be staying the night, so I'll release him when you've gone.'

'Gone?' Jackie echoed. 'But it's early. We haven't had a drink yet. And I haven't shown you the surprise I brought.'

'Another time,' I said, grabbing her panties and passing them to her. 'Alan and I have to talk, don't we, Alan?'

'Er . . . Yes,' he replied hesitantly. 'But I'd rather you untied me before Jackie leaves.'

'No, we'll wait until she's gone.'

Seeing Jackie to the door, I told her that I'd ring her in the morning. She looked puzzled as she turned and asked whether I was feeling all right. Reassuring her, I opened the door and told her not to worry. After all, she had nothing to worry about.

But Alan did. Returning to the lounge, I stood over his naked body and looked down at him. He had that same puzzled look as he gazed up at me. The same look he'd had the last time he'd been tied up in my lounge.

'What's the matter?' I asked.

'I was just wondering what all this is about,' he replied. 'Are you going to release me now?'

'No, not yet. Did you enjoy fucking Jackie?'

'Well, I . . . Yes, I did.'

'And did you enjoy fucking Angela?'

'No, she . . .'

'What about Crystal Marshall?'

'Who?'

'Crystal Marshall. Did you enjoy fucking her?'

'Crystal was—'

'I know what she was, Alan. Did you enjoy fucking her?'

'Jade, what's all this about?'

'Did you know that she's dead?' I asked, grabbing a cushion from the sofa and pushing it beneath his head.

'I know that she's gone missing, but . . . Wait a minute. Surely you don't think that I—'

'We'll talk about it in the morning, Alan,' I smiled, walking to the door. 'I need an early night. Sleep well.'

Chapter Seven

I woke the following morning with an aching back. I hadn't slept at all well. Dreams had haunted me. Dreams of Crystal's naked body dumped in the woods, her wide eyes glazed, staring sightlessly at the trees high above her. Was it a dream? Climbing out of bed, I suddenly remembered that Alan was in the lounge. As I raced through the hall I couldn't for the life of me think why I'd left him there. I must have been out of my mind. Either that or . . . Possessed?

'For Christ's sake, let me go,' he hissed as I walked into the lounge. 'Jade, what the hell do you think you're playing at? Leaving me here all bloody night and—'

'Shut up, Alan,' I hissed. 'Just shut up. Now, listen to me. You were screwing around when we were together. You cheated on Angela and were quite happy to have Jackie suck you off after telling me that you wanted us to get back together. And to top it all, you'd been visiting a prostitute.'

'I have *never* been to a prostitute,' he returned indignantly.

'Crystal Marshall was a bloody prostitute.'

'Crystal? Of course she wasn't.'

'Jackie said that she was into prostitution.'

'I don't care what Jackie said. The police said that it was a *possibility*, seeing as the neighbours reckoned that she had a lot of male visitors.'

'Have you been to the police?'

'No, why should I? I hardly ever saw her.'

'When were you last there? And how come you knew her?'

'I haven't been to see her for several weeks. I met her at a party and, before you ask, we were only friends.'

'I don't believe you,' I snapped. 'You can't have females as friends. You have to fuck them.'

'I don't give a toss what you believe. Just release me and let me get out of here.'

'No, I won't,' I stormed, leaving the room.

I thought that I must be going mad as I wandered into the kitchen. Crystal probably had nothing to do with prostitution, and no one had said that she was definitely dead. She might have gone anywhere, gone away for a couple of weeks to think about her life. I'd lost my senses thinking that she was a whore and that one of her clients had abducted and murdered her. But, gazing through the kitchen window at the bushes down the garden, I was sure that she was dead. It all added up. The cottage with the laburnum tree and the well, the girl's face in the bushes, my book and . . . If Crystal Marshall was alive and kicking, then who – or what – was getting to me?

'Will you shut up!' I screamed, bursting into the lounge as Alan repeatedly called me.

'For Christ's sake, Jade. Let me go!'

'That should keep you quiet,' I grinned, stuffing the soaked panties into his mouth. 'I don't like shouting at the best of times, and certainly not early in the morning.'

I didn't know what the hell was going on as I flopped onto the sofa. What had I been thinking? What had I done? Alan tied up on the floor with my urine-soaked panties stuffed in his mouth, his pubic hairs shaved off . . . What had happened to my life? Ghosts, faces in the bushes, Jackie fucking Alan, me pissing over him . . . I had to take control, I knew as Alan writhed and struggled to break free. I had to backtrack and return to normality. That wouldn't be so difficult, I mused. Let Alan go, forget the dirty book and lesbian sex with Jackie . . . Realizing that I was naked, I looked down at my firm breasts. What Alan thought of me, I had no idea. I doubted that I'd ever see him again. Which probably wasn't a bad thing.

This is your chance. Jumping as my mind whispered to me, I really did think that I was going crazy. I'd been working too hard, I concluded. Staring at the computer screen day in and day out had made me tired and muddled my thinking. Eyeing Alan's flaccid penis, I wondered about my uncharacteristic thoughts. My last chance? Yes, it was. Once I'd released Alan, he'd run like hell and never come back. I couldn't let him go – not yet, not before I'd . . .

'I want you to come in my mouth,' I said huskily, leaving the sofa and sitting by his side. 'No, I have a better idea.' Toying with his flaccid penis, I retracted his foreskin and stroked his glistening knob. This was my last chance. I'd not seen musician Alan for a while and once Alan the ex had gone I'd be manless. There was Jackie, of course. But returning to normality didn't mean having a sexual relationship with my best girlfriend.

Pulling my panties out of Alan's mouth, I squatted over his face and ordered him to lick my bottom-hole. I felt embarrassed as I yanked my firm buttocks apart and exposed my small brown ring. But I had to feel a tongue there, licking, tantalizing, teasing my delicate anal tissue. My anal sphincter muscles tightening as his tongue licked my private hole, I closed my eyes. The sensation was heavenly. His wet tongue lapping, tasting me there, I breathed deeply and began to tremble as my sex juices oozed between the splayed lips of my young pussy. My fingers within my anal crease, I pulled my bottom-hole wide open and ordered Alan to push his tongue deep into my bum. Shuddering as he complied, the wet warmth of his tongue delving into my sensitive rectal duct, I let out little gasps of debased pleasure.

Another first, I reflected as Alan tongue-fucked my bottom. From nervous prude to lascivious female experienced in crude sex, I was changing fast. But there was another act that I needed to experience before I gave Alan his freedom. Anal intercourse. Would my anus stretch enough to allow his bulbous knob entry to my inner duct? Would my rectum be able to accommodate his huge shaft? My private hole well lubricated with saliva by now, I moved down his naked body and positioned myself over the swollen glans of his erect cock.

'Jade,' he murmured as I pushed the swollen knob of his penis against my bum's inlet. Closing my eyes and trying to relax my muscles, I managed to force his purple globe past my tight ring and into the heat of my anal canal. *So far, so good*, I mused, slowly lowering my naked body. His solid shaft driving into my tight rectum, the stretching and bloating sensations were heavenly. My juices of desire coursing from my open pussy hole, my clitoris painfully swelling, I completely impaled myself on his rock-hard cock.

I wanted to feel Alan's spunk gushing into my bowels, filling me to the brim as he fucked my arse. I was desperate for the sensation of sperm swirling within my tight anal duct, lubricating his pistoning shaft. I felt decadent, crude in the extreme as I gently bounced up and down, fucking my tight arsehole with his beautiful cock. My firm buttocks repeatedly meeting his naked balls with loud slaps, his knob massaging the velveteen walls of my tightening rectum, I felt my clitoris swell and pulsate as my arousal went through the roof. Never had I known such beautiful sensations as the pistoning of his cock in my anal cylinder, the rhythmically expanding and contracting walls of my burning sheath.

As Alan's gasps grew louder, I knew that he was about to come. I bounced up and down faster, the sensitive tissue of my anus sending electrifying sensations of crude sex deep into my quivering pelvis, and slipped my fingers between the swell of my vaginal lips to massage my erect clitoris. Our orgasms exploding together, I felt his sperm gushing into my rectum, lubricating the illicit union as my climax sent heavenly tremors of debased sex coursing through my naked body.

'Yes,' I breathed, massaging my clitoris faster and sustaining my mind-blowing orgasm as my anal duct filled with sperm. The lubricating liquid oozing from my inflamed bottom-hole, squelching as I bobbed up and down on Alan's huge cock, I reached such incredible heights of sexual ecstasy that I felt that I'd lost my mind. Swirling colours engulfed me as sparks of orgasm showered my very being. I was floating, drifting through purple clouds of sex in another world. My very soul in the grip of sexual euphoria, I became oblivious to my surroundings.

I bounced up and down again and again, fucking my arse, spunking my hot bowels. The delicious sound of squelching sperm filling my head, gasps, low moans of pleasure, buttocks slapping balls, heavy breathing . . . My orgasm peaking, I threw my head back, my nostrils flaring, my eyes rolling as I rode the crest of sexual ecstasy. My neglected vaginal sheath yearning for my massaging fingers, I imagined that there was another huge penis fucking my cunt.

Two fleshy shafts thrusting in and out of my inflamed sex-holes, the sensations blowing my mind away on the wind of pure debauched lust.

Finally drifting down from my sexual heaven, I hung my head, gasping and panting for breath as my anal sheath gripped Alan's deflating cock. Two penises? I pondered. That was something that I had to experience, I knew as my trembling body rolled to one side and Alan's cock left my inflamed arsehole with a loud sucking sound. Quivering on the floor, sperm oozing from the burning eye of my gaping anus, I lay in a warm pool of debased sex.

'Christ,' Alan murmured as I searched through the mist of sex and found my mind. 'You really are something else.' Releasing his ankles, I untied his wrists and clambered to my feet. Moving to the door as he dragged his naked body off the floor, I left him to dress. I didn't want to speak to him, there was nothing to say. There were no words. I'd used him to further my sexual experience, which was all I'd wanted from him.

After a shower, I emerged from the bathroom to find him gone. That was that, I reflected. Another encounter, another experience, another chapter for my erotic book. Dressing in a miniskirt and loose-fitting blouse, I flopped in my swivel chair and switched the computer on. Sperm oozed from my bottom-hole, my arsehole, and seeped into my tight panties. A stark reminder of my debauched act. I didn't want to think about Alan or Jackie or Crystal. I needed to work with a clear mind, concentrate on my writing. Would my sperm-oozing bottom allow me to concentrate? Arse-fuck. Arse-sperming.

The phone had rung a dozen times during the day. I'd stopped for nothing, ignoring the phone and the doorbell and even going without lunch. By four o'clock, I'd written chapter seven and printed out the text. The first seven chapters should be more than enough for David, I mused, parcelling up the manuscript. I should have read the story so far, but I knew that if I did I'd only spend several days rewriting it. Grabbing my bag, the wrapped-up manuscript under my arm, I walked down the road to the post office.

That was that. It was posted. There was no turning back now. Whatever subsequent thoughts and ideas I had for the book, it was too late. Walking home, I wished that I'd done this and that to the manuscript. Should I have changed Crystal's name? Perhaps she should have lived in a flat rather than a cottage. But no. I'd wasted three years writing my romantic novel and I certainly didn't intend to waste another three years on my dirty book.

Sitting in the garden, I decided to wait for David's reaction before writing another word. If he turned it down, then . . . then what? Then I'd remain broke and have to find a regular job. Pushing the book out of my mind, I closed my eyes and relaxed in the afternoon sun. Pondering on ani-lingus and anal intercourse, I grinned. I'd experienced more crude sex in the last week or so than I had in my entire life. My grin fading as I recalled pissing over Alan's face, I again wondered what he must have thought of me. And as for Jackie . . . I could never face her again, I was sure. She'd witnessed my vile act and must have thought me a filthy little slut. A cum-slut. A piss-slut.

I was surprised when she turned up that evening. Inviting her in, I could feel my face blushing as we walked into the kitchen. No doubt she'd come to question me, I thought. Watching me piss over Alan's face must have shocked her to the core. There again, the things she'd done in the haystack with Jenny Hardbrooke had quite taken *me* aback.

'What time did Alan leave last night?' she asked as we walked out onto the patio.

'He left this morning,' I replied. 'And, before you ask, no, he didn't sleep with me. I left him on the lounge floor.'

'What?' she gasped. I spied her pink tongue and imagined her licking my cunt. 'You left him tied up all night?'

'Yes, by way of punishment for his cheating and lying. By the way, Crystal Marshall wasn't a prostitute.'

'People are saying that she was.'

'Well, they shouldn't.'

'I heard on the news today that there's still no sign of her. It seems that there was a struggle in her bedroom and . . .'

'How do they know that? I mean, she might have just left the room in a mess.'

'Apparently, ornaments were smashed and the room had been turned upside down. Anyway, I bumped into Brian Marchant this morning.'

'Who's he?'

'He's a friend of Ian's, my ex. He said that Crystal was running some sort of business from the cottage, which backs up the prostitute rumour.'

'A business?'

'No one knows what it was, but she had plenty of male visitors. She was on the game, Jade. There's no doubt about it.'

'It does rather look that way,' I sighed.

'How's the book coming on?'

'I posted the first seven chapters to the literary agent this afternoon, so it's fingers crossed.'

'Are you going to let me read what you've written so far?'

'No, I'm not.'

'Just a quick look?'

'No, you're not going to read a word of it until it's published. Jackie, have you ever had anal sex?'

'Well, almost,' she giggled. 'It was with Ian. He couldn't get it in. We tried, but there was no way he could get it in. Why do you ask?'

'I was just wondering what it's like. I'm bringing a scene into my book and . . . Having never experienced it, it's not easy to write about it.' I didn't dare tell her the awful truth.

'That's easily put right.'

'How?'

'Jade, after what you did to Alan last night . . . I think the time has come for me to teach you a thing or two. I realize that you're trying to experience various sexual acts for . . . well, for research purposes.'

'What are you getting at?'

'Jenny Hardbrooke . . . I'm still in touch with her.'

'Really?'

'Yes. I wasn't going to say anything, but . . . Jenny and I . . . We still, you know.'

'God,' I gasped. 'You have sex with her? But she's married and—'

'She's having an affair with me. And has been since we were at school.'

'I don't know what to say.'

'There's more. I'm only telling you this because you seem to have come out of yourself recently. There's no way I would have said anything had you remained the prude you were. Anyway, Jenny and I have these parties. There's one tonight. That's why I've come to see you.'

'I haven't been to a party in ages.'

'Yes, well . . . It's not a party, exactly. Jenny will be there, and me, of course. So will her husband and two other men.'

'Is it at her place?'

'No, my place this time. Interested?'

'Yes, I am.'

'We all have sex, Jade.'

'What? All at once?'

'Together. A groupie.'

Stunned, I held my hand to my mouth. I'd thought I'd known Jackie . . . I'd thought I'd known myself. Three men, Jackie, Jenny and me . . . No, I couldn't do it. I was sure. The experience would be more than helpful, but there was no way I was going to strip off and have sex with three men and two other girls. Crystal would have joined in.

'Be at my place at eight,' Jackie said, walking into the kitchen. 'If you want to experience real sex, then be there at eight.'

As the front door slammed shut, I stood on the patio, frozen to the spot. Finally managing to look at my watch, I wondered what to do. It was already seven o'clock. I had one hour to make up my mind. *Three men?* I mused, picturing three erect penises stabbing at my pussy. And my bum and my mouth. This was a chance in a lifetime if ever there was one. But I couldn't do it. My mind whispered to me, goading me to go to the orgy. But I knew I couldn't do it.

I'd set out on some daft quest to experience unusual sexual acts, and that quest had already taken me across thresholds I'd never dreamed I'd cross. I'd had notions of ghosts, I'd masturbated, had anal sex with my ex-boyfriend, pissed over his face, had lesbian sex with Jackie, sucked Alan the musician . . . My life had run wild. Everything turned upside down and inside out, I'd lost completely my direction in life.

Ambling down to the end of the garden and gazing at the bushes, I wondered where Crystal Marshall was. Had she been abducted? If she was still alive, she might be enduring crude sexual acts. I imagined her tied up in a basement, her naked body abused by her abductor. If she was dead, then . . . The police had to find her, and soon. All the time I didn't know whether she was dead or alive, I couldn't think straight. The girl's face in the bush, the cottage, chapter six . . . I had to know one way or the other.

As I was about to head back to the kitchen, a crazy idea came to me. My back garden was completely secluded. No one could see me, spy on me. The evening sun warming me, I slipped my blouse off and tossed it to the ground. Tugging my skirt and panties down, I kicked them aside and un-hooked my bra. Standing naked on the grass, I moved forward and walked into the bushes. The sharp leaves and branches scratching me, I forced my way past the bushes into the small clearing by the fence.

I didn't know what I was doing or why as I looked about me. I'd had the crazy notion that the ghost of Crystal might have been attracted to the bushes by my nakedness, but the idea was ridiculous. Had Jackie seen me, she'd have suggested that I visit a psychiatrist. I felt strangely aroused as the leaves caressed my naked body. Like a thousand tiny fingers, they stroked me, tickled my naked flesh. The fence giving way as I leaned against it, I just managed to keep my balance. To my surprise, the fence wasn't a fence. It was a gate opening onto a narrow alley.

'*That*'s where the child came from,' I murmured to myself, peering into the alley. I felt such a fool. The ghost of a dead girl peering out of the bushes? I must have been completely mad to think that I'd seen a ghost. And standing naked in the bushes, I reckoned that I *did* need a psychiatrist. Forcing my way back though the bushes to the lawn, I grabbed my clothes and dashed into the kitchen. 'Bloody kids mucking about,' I breathed irritably, rubbing my scratched arm as I dressed. 'What a bloody fool I've been.'

Pacing the lounge floor, I didn't know what to do about Jackie's so-called party. Half of me wanted to go but the other half told me to keep away. I was torn between trying to return to some sort of normality, and enjoying a life of . . . Enjoying life by finding sexual freedom and satisfaction? Pondering on my dirty book, I realized why David hadn't been interested in my romantic novel. 'Closing the bedroom door on the horny couple,' I chuckled. Was I closing a door? By not going to Jackie's party, was I closing a door that might never open to me again?

'Sod it,' I murmured, grabbing my bag and leaving the flat. I had to go to the orgy. Losing my mind and standing naked in the bushes – that was no way to run my life. I had to get out of the flat and have some fun. It was a lovely evening. The sun still hot, there wasn't a breath of wind and I decided to cut through the park. I rarely went to Jackie's flat. She didn't have a garden and her place was small in comparison to mine so she usually came to me or we met in the pub. It made a change to get out, I thought again. Being stuck in my den wasn't so bad in the winter, but not during the summer months.

'Hi,' someone called from behind.

'Oh, hi,' I smiled, turning to see Alan the musician running towards me.

'I thought it was you. How are things?'

'OK,' I replied. He hooked his hair behind his ears. He was wearing his Jimi Hendrix T-shirt and I wondered whether he'd taken if off since I'd last seen him. 'How are you?'

'I'm fine. I called at your flat a couple of times but you weren't in.'

'Ah, yes,' I grinned sheepishly. 'Actually, I *was* in but I didn't answer the door. Don't take it personally, Alan. I was working on my book and ignored the doorbell and the phone.'

'Oh, right. I'm on my way to the pub. Isn't your friend coming along?'

'The pub?' I frowned.

'I'm playing there tonight. I thought you were going to . . .'

'Er . . . Saturday,' I mumbled. 'Yes, yes. I have to call round to a friend's place first.'

'We start at nine. It'll be great to see you there, Jade. I've written some lyrics just for you.'

'Oh, er . . . I don't know what to say.'

'Don't say anything until you've heard the song. I wrote the music a long time ago. Meeting you gave me the idea for the lyrics.'

'I might not get there until after nine,' I said, forcing a smile.

'That's OK. We'll wait until you arrive before we play your song.'

'My song. Right. Well, I'd better be going.'

'OK, see you later. I'll save you a table. And get you a vodka and lime. I have some cash now.'

As he walked away, I felt terrible. I'd completely forgotten about Alan and his bloody band. To be honest, I'd thought today was Friday. That was the trouble with working from home. I never knew which day it was. I couldn't let him down, particularly as he'd written a song for me. But I really didn't want to sit in the pub on my own. Apart from that, I'd made the decision to go to Jackie's sex party. There were always complications, I reflected, making my way across the park. Nothing was ever straightforward.

Sitting on a bench, I had to decide between the pub and
Jackie's party. I was going to let one of them down, but
which one? Perhaps I could leave Jackie's flat at ten and
then go on to the pub. Or perhaps I should go to the pub
and then . . . 'It's my life,' I sighed, again wondering why
things were always so bloody complicated. Recalling standing naked in the bushes, I shook my head. Again pondering
on my life and where it was taking me, I wished I could go
back to the way things were. All right my book had been no
good and I hadn't had a sex life. Boring though my
existence had been, at least I'd known what to expect each
day. There were no surprises.

Wondering what to do, I checked my watch. Eight
o'clock. Perhaps it was best to go home and forget about
Jackie and Alan. Watching a young lad walking across the
grass, I wished that I could go back a few years to my mid-
teens. His hands in his pockets, he was whistling as if he
didn't have a care in the world. Nearing the bench, he
smiled at me, and I wondered whether he'd be as happy in a
few years' time when he had a relationship and bills to pay.

'Hi,' he said, standing before me. 'Cool day, isn't it?'

'I thought it was warm,' I replied, immediately realizing
my mistake. 'Oh, *cool*. Yes, I see what you mean.'

'Mind if I join you?' he asked, sitting next to me before I
could answer. 'I was supposed to be meeting my girlfriend
but she didn't turn up.'

'You don't seem too worried.'

'I'm not bothered, really. Well, I suppose I am but what
the hell. You been stood up, too?'

'No, no,' I laughed. 'I'm on my way to . . . I'm just out
for a walk.'

'I could have gone out with the lads tonight but it's too
late now. I don't know. Saturday night and nowhere to go.'

'Where were you going with your girlfriend?'

'Only down the pub.'

'To watch a band?'

'No, no. Live bands are great but she reckons they're too loud. We were going to the White Horse.'

'I was thinking of going to a pub this evening. A friend of mine plays in a band and he's there tonight.'

'Yeah? What's the band called?'

'The Gremlins or something.'

'The Gremlins from Hell?'

'That's it.'

'They're great. I've seen them at the Frog Pond. I'll come with you, if that's OK?'

'Yes, why not?'

That was that settled, I thought happily as we walked to the park gates. I could watch Alan play without having to sit alone. Jackie's party . . . There'd be others, I knew. Besides, it probably wasn't a good idea. As we neared the pub, it occurred to me that I didn't know the lad's name. I also wondered whether he was old enough to drink. His dark hair flopping over his forehead, his fresh face unblemished, I found myself wondering whether he was a virgin. But he had a girlfriend, and I reckoned that he'd had at least some sexual experience.

'What you having?' he asked, pulling a ten-pound note from his pocket as we walked to the bar.

'Vodka and lime with ice, please,' I replied, scanning the pub for Alan. The band were setting up on a small stage but Alan wasn't around. The pub was beginning to fill up and there was nowhere to sit other than at a table in a secluded corner. I doubted that we'd have a good view but I needed to sit down. 'I'll be over there,' I said as my companion ordered the drinks.

Taking a seat, I wondered how Jackie was getting on at the orgy. Perhaps I should have gone, I ruminated, wondering what I was doing in a pub with an under-age boy as he brought the drinks over. Orgy? No, it was best that I kept away from such things. I was becoming bad enough as it was without taking part in orgies.

'You're OK,' the lad smiled as he sat beside me.

'Oh, thanks,' I replied with a chuckle. 'I'm Jade, by the way.'

'My friends call me Mog. Don't ask why.'

'I won't. But I will ask how old you are.'

'Almost old enough to drink this,' he grinned, taking a gulp from his pint. 'And you?'

'You're not supposed to ask a girl her age,' I giggled.

'Why not? I reckon you're . . . I'll go for nineteen.'

'That'll do. How old is your girlfriend?'

'Libby? She's fifteen.'

'Is that all?'

'Yeah. Too young, really, but there we are. I'd be better off with a girl like you. Where do you work?'

'I . . . Oh, there's my friend.' I waved at Alan who held his guitar up and grinned. No doubt he was wondering what I was doing with a young lad. It might be an idea to say that he was my brother. 'So, your girlfriend's only fifteen?' I said, turning and facing Mog.

'That's right. She's still at school, of course.'

Better off with a girl like me? I wondered as he talked about his girlfriend. I wasn't a cradle-snatcher, but he *was* rather good-looking. No, I dared not get involved with a young lad. I was having trouble enough with men in their twenties, and with women. Wondering why he was called Mog, I found myself gazing at the crotch of his tight jeans as he drank his beer. So young and fresh and—No, I mustn't.

My hand seemingly moving of its own accord and settling on his thigh, I wondered what the hell I was playing at. He reacted immediately by placing his hand on my inner thigh and running his fingers up under my short skirt to my tight panties. *Talk about a fast mover*, I thought anxiously. But I'd instigated the physical contact. As he pressed his fingers into the warm swell of my panties, I looked around to see whether anyone was watching. Since the illicit act was taking place beneath the table, we were safe enough. But I couldn't allow him to go any further.

'Mog,' I whispered urgently, again wondering at his strange name as he massaged my vulval cushions through my moistening panties. 'Mog, don't.' Ignoring me, he pulled the crotch of my panties aside and slipped his fingers into the wet valley of my yearning pussy. Trying to push him away without attracting attention, I gasped as he drove a finger between the wet petals of my inner lips and thrust deep into my tightening vagina. 'Mog, *no*,' I breathed, involuntarily parting my thighs to give him better access to my spasming sex sheath.

My hands trembling as he massaged the velveteen walls of my drenched cunt, I felt my clitoris swell and pulsate. What the hell was I doing sitting in a pub with a stranger's finger up my cunt? Not only a stranger, but a young lad. Despite his youth, he knew exactly what he was doing. Slipping his wet finger out of my hot sex sheath, he moved up the engorged valley of my vagina and gently massaged my ripe clitoris. I couldn't allow myself to come, I thought, breathing deeply as I quivered and writhed in my rising ecstasy.

'No, Mog,' I breathed, grabbing his arm in an effort to stop him. Saying nothing, he glanced around the pub as he continued to masturbate me. I looked at the stage to see

Alan setting up his equipment. People were too busy drinking and chatting to notice our intimate game in the shadowy corner. I again made a perfunctory move to stop Mog, but I had succumbed to my arousal. My clitoris pulsating, I knew that I was going to come and prayed that I'd not cry out.

'You've got a nice cunt,' Mog breathed in my ear as I shook uncontrollably. His crude words driving me wild, my body becoming rigid, I lowered my head and bit my lip as my clitoris exploded in orgasm. Gasping, stifling my moans of illicit pleasure as he expertly sustained my mind-blowing climax, I clutched his thigh. On and on my orgasm rolled, my juices of lust gushing from my neglected cunt and soaking my panties. Praying for my pleasure to subside, my whimpers growing louder, I parted my thighs and tossed my head back.

His fingertip deftly encircling my pulsating sex bud, my skirt up almost over my stomach, I grimaced as my orgasm peaked. My womb rhythmically contracting, my clitoris pulsating wildly, I prayed that no one was watching as I slipped into a state of semi-consciousness. Again, I drifted in swirling clouds of pastel colours, the voices and laughter in the pub fading into the distance as my mind flew away. On and on I rode the crest of my orgasm, the beautiful sensations rocking my very being, shaking my soul.

'Are you OK?' a distant voice finally asked. Slowly opening my eyes, the sounds of the pub growing louder, I looked about me as Mog pulled my skirt down to conceal my drenched panties. 'Hey, you all right?'

'Yes, yes,' I gasped, shuddering my last shudder as my clitoris pulsated in its deflating. 'You shouldn't have done that,' I admonished him, my face burning as I grabbed my drink.

'Didn't you like it?' he smiled.

'Of course I bloody well liked it,' I whispered. 'But not in a pub surrounded by people.'

'The danger of getting caught makes it more exciting,' he said as I gulped down my drink.

'You might think so, but I don't,' I replied.

My body finally calm, I brushed my long blonde hair away from my flushed face as I reclined in the chair. My panties had slipped into my sex crack, my juices flowing from my burning pussy and soaking into the material. My arousal high, my womb fluttering, I needed another drink, I knew as Mog finished his beer. But I wasn't going to get wrecked on vodka and invite him back for coffee. Would Alan expect to come back to my flat for a blow job? I'd have to leave the pub before he'd finished playing, I decided as Mog placed his hand on my naked thigh.

Groping for his zip as he massaged my drenched outer lips, I managed to pull his erect penis out. His shaft felt warm, granite-hard, and I again wondered how old he was. Old enough, I decided, moving his foreskin up and down over the globe of his youthful cock. He gasped and closed his eyes as I wanked him faster. *Payback time*, I thought wickedly as the band started playing. All eyes were focused on Alan as his guitar wailed. I looked down at Mog's erect penis. He was a big lad, I observed, wondering if I should slip beneath the table and suck his glans into my sperm-thirsty mouth.

Groaning as if in pain, Mog trembled uncontrollably as he pumped out his sperm. I could feel the tepid liquid running over my fingers and down my hand as I continued to wank his beautiful cock. His orgasm seemingly never-ending, his sperm gushing in torrents from his young knob, I had it in mind to take him home with me and initiate him in the fine art of clit-sucking. No doubt he'd already experienced oral sex, I mused, his body shuddering wildly as the last of his spunk jetted from his purple glans and ran over my hand.

'Bloody hell,' he breathed as I released his deflating cock. 'You're OK.'

'Why, thank you,' I smiled, lapping up the white liquid from my hand as he watched in disbelief. He must have thought me a whore. I *was* a whore.

'I'd better go and sort myself out.' Zipping his jeans and standing up, he grinned at me. 'Don't go away,' he said. 'I like you. You're a cool bird.'

'A cool bird?' I frowned. 'Will you be in the park tomorrow?'

'I can be. Will you be there?'

'Yes. About eight?'

'OK. Hang on, I'll be back in a minute.'

As he walked through the crowd, I made my way to the door. Guilt consuming me, I left the pub and hurried down the road. I shouldn't have allowed him to slip his hand up my skirt. And I should never have wanked him. Cutting through the park, I pondered on Jackie and her orgy. What were things coming to? I wondered. Jackie at an orgy, me picking up a young lad in the park and . . . I was definitely going to return to normality, I decided. I'd go home to bed and start afresh in the morning.

Chapter Eight

The phone was ringing when I woke at nine the following morning. Pulling the quilt over my head, I guessed that it would be Jackie wanting to know why I'd not gone to the orgy. I couldn't talk to her, not until I'd fully woken. I couldn't face listening to the sordid details of her sex session with three men and another girl. Had the men all entered her orifices at once? I wondered. One in her pussy, another up her bum and the third fucking her mouth?

Memories of Mog filtering into my mind, I slipped my hand between the welcoming heat of my thighs. My outer lips sticky and swollen, my sex crack drenched with my juices of desire, I wished I'd brought him home and . . . What the hell was I thinking? I wondered. I had to forget about crude sex. Crystal Marshall haunting me, Jackie inviting me to a sordid orgy, wanking a young lad in the pub . . .

'A fresh start,' I breathed, slipping out of bed and heading for the shower. I'd made my decision and was determined to stick to it. Jackie might be happy with her life of debauched sex, but that wasn't the way I wanted to go. I'd originally thought that I'd meet a decent man one day and settle down. Not launch myself into one crude sexual encounter after another in the name of cold lust.

After my shower, I had poached eggs on toast for breakfast and took a cup of coffee into my den. I didn't want to get the dirty book up on screen and decided to go through my romantic novel. I was backtracking, I knew, but wasn't going to throw away three years' hard work. Reading through the book, I laughed when I reached the end of chapter two. Elizabeth, the heroine, slipped into the bedroom with her husband-to-be and closed the door. In comparison with Crystal's sordid exploits, Elizabeth led a totally sheltered life and was virtually asexual. Was that the real me? I wondered.

'Jade, it's David,' the familiar voice announced as I answered the phone at midday. 'I've been reading the manuscript. It arrived this morning.'

'That was quick,' I said. 'I only posted it—'

'You've done it, Jade,' he said enthusiastically. 'You've hit the nail right on the bloody head.'

'You like it?' I asked surprisedly.

'Like it? It's fucking brilliant. The sex is . . . is just incredible. Where the hell did you get your ideas from?'

'Er . . . My imagination, I suppose.'

'Chapter six is . . . It's amazing stuff. When can you finish the book?'

'Well, I don't know.'

'I'm showing it to a publisher this afternoon. They'll take it, I have no doubt about that.'

'That's good.'

'You don't sound very excited.'

'I am. I'm a little surprised, that's all.'

'OK, you get writing and I'll be in touch. We'll talk about money and get the contract drawn up. Speak to you soon.'

So much for making a fresh start, I mused, bringing the dirty book up on the screen. Was writing smut my forte? At least I'd earn some money, I reflected, wondering why I'd not asked David how much he thought I'd get. The way my finances were going, every penny I earned would help. I had to work hard now, I knew. The romantic novel would have to be shelved for a while. Trying to forget about Mog and the dreadful act I'd committed in the pub, I got stuck into the book and managed to get in a good day's work.

Jackie rang and complained that I'd neither turned up at her so-called party nor bothered to answer the phone and informed me that I'd missed a really good night. She was keen to call in and see me and, as I'd got on pretty well with the book, I agreed. I was determined not to fall prey to her lesbian charms and end up having sex with her. As much as I wanted to slip my tongue into her hot vagina, I had to stop thinking about lesbian sex. It was wrong, I knew only too well. What I'd done in the pub had also been wrong, but I'd at least been with a male. Was I trying to justify the fact that I'd behaved like a wanton tart?

When I answered the door to find Mog standing on the step, I almost had a heart attack. This was all I needed, I thought anxiously, wondering how on earth he'd found out where I lived. Had he got chatting to Alan before leaving the pub? No, Alan wouldn't have given him my address. So how the hell had he traced me? More to the point, what did he want? And this was supposed to be a fresh start?

'What are you doing here?' I breathed, looking up and down the street, although I didn't know what I was looking for.

'I've come to see you,' he said matter-of-factly.

'How did you know where—'

'I saw you leaving the pub last night and decided to follow you. I was about to go into the loo and happened to see you leaving. I thought you might not want to see me again.'

'Mog, I . . . You'd better come in for a minute.'

143

Taking him into the lounge, I prayed that Jackie wouldn't turn up and get the wrong idea. Or the right idea, more like. I was pretty annoyed to think that he'd followed me to my flat, but then, I had walked out on him, which had been extremely rude of me. He was dressed in tight blue jeans and a white T-shirt, and looked even younger than before. My insatiable clitoris swelling, my mind torn, I didn't know what to do. Again telling myself that I was starting afresh, I tried desperately to push all thoughts of sex from my mind.

'I told you I'd meet you in the park,' I said firmly.

'Yes, but when I saw you leaving the pub . . . You could have at least said goodbye. After what we did, the least you could have done was tell me that you were leaving.'

'I know. I'm sorry, it's just that . . .' Looking him up and down, I frowned. 'How old are you, Mog?'

'What does it matter?'

'It matters to me. I'm twenty-one, and I can't . . .'

'OK, I'm eighteen.'

'You're lying.'

'What's the point in asking my age if you're not going to believe me?'

'You're nowhere near eighteen. Your girlfriend's only fifteen and I reckon you're about the same.'

'What if I am?'

'It's illegal, for a start.'

'Are we going to stand here and discuss my age for hours on end?'

'Look, I have a friend coming round soon. I said that I'd meet you in the park. I don't want you coming here uninvited.'

'I only called in to see whether you were going to meet me this evening. After you walked out, I thought you might have changed your mind.'

144

'Mog, I like you very much,' I began, feeling a little sorry for him.

'So, you'll be there at eight? As the time's getting on, we might as well go there together.'

'No, I . . .'

'You're only three years older than me, Jade.'

'And the rest,' I sighed. 'OK, I'll be there.'

'Really?'

'I promise you, Mog. I'll be there at eight.'

'Great. I'll see myself out.'

'OK.'

As he left, I held my hand to my head and wondered what the hell I'd let myself in for – yet again. The fact was that the attraction to Mog was that he was attracted to me. I couldn't believe that such a good-looking young lad was interested in me. Admittedly, I was only a few years older than him. A few? But there was more to it than flattery. I have to confess that, to my horror, I really did fancy him. Had I been sixteen, then . . . but I was twenty-one, and there was no changing that.

Thanking God that Jackie hadn't turned up while he'd been there, I began to wonder where she'd got to. Perhaps she'd run into Mog, I reflected, imagining her seducing him in the street. She'd love to wank him, bring out his sperm and . . . Not thinking straight, I paced the lounge floor. I had to meet Mog at eight, giving me little time to talk to Jackie. I couldn't let the lad down. I'd meet him and explain that I couldn't see him again. Although he was good-looking and brilliant company, he was too young for me.

'It's me,' Jackie announced as I answered the phone.

'Where are you?' I asked irritably. 'I thought you were coming straight round.'

'I got held up. How about meeting in the pub later?'

'It'll have to be much later. Say, nine?'

'OK, see you there.'

'Or even later than nine.'

'Whenever. I'll be there until closing.'

Replacing the receiver, I checked my watch. Seven-thirty. Only half an hour to go before . . . before what? Before having sex in the park with an under-age boy? I was supposed to be working flat out on my dirty book and getting my life together, not committing sexual offences in the bloody park. I'd talk to Mog and explain that . . . But I couldn't help myself, I knew as I went to my bedroom and changed into a miniskirt and loose-fitting blouse. I needed sex, the feel of a fresh young penis swelling within the hugging sheath of my wet vagina. I was going to the park to seduce the boy, and I couldn't deny it.

Leaving my flat, I walked down the road with a spring in my step. I didn't know whether it was because the youngster fancied me or because I was desperate to touch and feel his fresh penis that I felt so elated. Perhaps it was the element of danger that excited me. The illicit affair between a woman and a young . . . I dreaded to think how old he was. Reaching the park, I realized that I was behaving stupidly. Crystal wouldn't have done this, would she? She went for mature men, men of experience. But I wasn't Crystal, was I?

Sitting on the bench, I checked my watch and realized that I was about fifteen minutes early. Jackie would think me terrible if she knew what I was up to, I mused, wondering whether I'd make it to the pub later. I might be jeopardizing my career as a writer of erotic fiction. If it came to light that I seduced young lads in the park . . . I was being ridiculous. No one would know of my clandestine meeting.

While I waited, I pondered on the young girl in the

bushes. She must have lived nearby. Sneaking through the back gate and spying on me, she was probably only playing about. But she'd appeared to be so anxious and tormented. I'd have to discover where she lived, I thought. Deciding to nail the gate closed, my thoughts turned to Crystal Marshall. She was somewhere. Dead or alive, she was somewhere. The sooner the police discovered where she was, the better. I had to get her out of my mind and concentrate on my book. And as for the cottage with the laburnum tree and the well . . .

'Jade,' Mog called as he ambled towards me. 'I didn't think you'd turn up.'

'I made a promise,' I sighed, gazing longingly at the bulge in his tight blue jeans. 'I don't break promises. Well, not very often.'

'Fancy a walk in the woods?' he asked, his wide eyes focused on my naked thighs.

'Sit down, Mog. We have to talk before . . . We must talk.'

'What about?' he asked, sitting beside me.

'First of all, how old are you?'

'You have a thing about my age, don't you?' he chuckled.

'Just answer the question, Mog.'

'I told my girlfriend to sod off,' he announced proudly. 'She was playing around with another . . .'

'Mog?'

'Oh, right. Er . . . I'm eighteen. I told you that last night. My age isn't important, Jade. I like you and you like me, so what's the problem?'

'The problem is . . . There's no problem,' I conceded as he placed his hand on my thigh. My clitoris stirring, my juices of desire seeping into my tight panties, I had to have him. 'Come on, then,' I smiled, trying not to appear too eager. I'd never been so bloody eager for sex. 'We'll take a walk in the woods.'

Following a path through the trees, I wondered just how experienced Mog was. Illegal though it was, he'd probably screwed his girlfriend, I mused. Had he licked and sucked her young pussy? Had he pushed his knob into her mouth and spermed over her tongue? Many girls of fifteen could easily pass for twenty, I reflected. And I was sure that many of them were more experienced than I was. I had to relax, I knew as I again pondered on the prospect of committing an offence. No one would know that I'd screwed . . . But I'd bloody well know.

Emerging from the trees into a clearing by a high fence, I turned and looked at Mog. Wondering what his real name was, I decided to ask him about his sexual experience as I sat on the short grass and rested my chin on my knees. He could see my bulging panties, I knew as I followed his gaze. I was a tart, wasn't I? Joining me, he stared longingly at my naked thighs, the swell of my tight panties, and I imagined his young penis fully erect, in dire need of my hot wet mouth. Mouth-fuck. Mouth-sperm.

'Your girlfriend,' I began. 'Did you . . .'

'No,' he smiled. 'She wouldn't let me.'

'Just as well, seeing that she's only fifteen. Have you had many girlfriends?'

'Not really. I mean, I know what to do but . . .'

'You certainly do,' I giggled.

'I know what you're building up to,' he sighed.

'Do you?'

'I've never done it,' he confessed. 'That's what you wanted to know, isn't it?'

'No, no. Why did you want me to come into the woods, Mog?'

'You know why. I'm a virgin, OK?'

'Would you like me to teach you?'

'You don't have to teach me,' he replied. 'I do know what to do.'

'All right,' I grinned, standing up. 'You can begin by undressing me.'

His dark eyes looking up at me, he tugged my skirt down to my ankles with an eagerness that stated in no uncertain terms that he was desperate to lose his virginity. But I was in no rush to have him penetrate me and shoot his fresh sperm over my cervix. As he pulled my panties down and gazed longingly at the blonde fleece covering my vulval flesh, I stepped out of my clothes and stood before him with my legs wide apart.

I felt as though I had power. For the first time in my life, I was with a male who was less experienced than I. Engulfed by an overwhelming desire to teach him all I knew, I unbuttoned my blouse and tossed it to the ground. Mog watched with bated breath as I unhooked my bra and let it fall clear of my firm breasts. My nipples stiffening in the relatively cool air of the shady clearing, I massaged my sensitive milk buds as I ordered him to strip naked.

Eagerly complying, he almost ripped his clothes off and stood naked before me with his young penis fully erect. Kneeling, I fully retracted his foreskin and kissed his glistening purple knob. He shuddered, his penis twitching expectantly as I tentatively licked his ripe plum. His girl-friend wouldn't have done this, I knew as I engulfed the bulbous head of his cock in my wet mouth and gently sucked. Not wanting him to shoot his spunk too soon, I slipped his knob out of my mouth and licked up and down his solid shaft. He gasped, his naked body trembling as my tongue worked its way over his heaving balls. Being so

149

young, he'd probably have enough stamina and spunk to be able to fuck my mouth and my cunt, I mused in my rising wickedness.

'That's nice,' Mog breathed as I drew his swollen glans into my hot mouth again. Moving my head forward, I took his knob to the back of my throat and gently sank my teeth into his young shaft. Kneading his youthful balls, I slipped my hand between his thighs and ran my fingertip up and down his buttock crease. Barely able to stand on his trembling legs, he clung to my head as I teased the sensitive brown ring of his anus. Unable to control myself as he gasped and writhed, I pushed my finger deep into the heat of his rectum and massaged the inner flesh of his tight bottom.

His knees bending as I sucked his glans between my wet lips and snaked my tongue over its silky-smooth surface, he let out a long low moan of pleasure as his spunk gushed from his throbbing knob. Sucking and mouthing as he pumped out his sperm, I pistoned his hot bottom-hole with my finger, sustaining his orgasm as his naked body sagged with pleasure. Swallowing his spunk, fervently gobbling his orgasming knob, I wanked his rock-hard shaft with my free hand until I'd completely drained his heavy balls.

Mog was unable to speak as I withdrew my finger from his anal canal and sucked the last droplets of sperm from his purple plum. Finally collapsing to the ground, he lay in a heap of quivering limbs. Feeling not only proud of myself but in complete control as he rolled onto his back, I squatted over his face and yanked the swollen lips of my pussy wide apart. My knees either side of his head, I lowered the open centre of my naked body, forcing my inner cunt flesh hard against his gasping mouth.

'Tongue-fuck my cunt.' I breathed in my devilry, manoeuvring my hips and aligning my open sex-hole with his hot mouth. I felt his tongue delve deep into my drenched cunt, tasting me, licking the creamy walls of my sex sheath as I writhed and gasped above him. I had an hour or so before meeting Jackie in the pub, but I wasn't going to waste any time. Young Mog was going to be subjected to more crude sex in an hour than he'd probably thought he'd experience in a lifetime. My juices of desire bubbling from my tongued sex-hole and filling his mouth, I felt my clitoris swell and throb. My orgasm was nearing, I knew as he reached up and squeezed the firm spheres of my young breasts. He'd come in my mouth, and now I was going to fill his mouth with my orgasmic juices.

'Suck my clitoris,' I gasped, swivelling my hips and pushing the hard nodule of my pleasure bud into his pussy-wet mouth. The heavenly sensations driving me wild as his tongue swept over the sensitive tip of my sex button, I tossed my head back and looked up at the trees towering above me. My womb rhythmically contracting, my vaginal fluid gushing from my open sex-hole, I cried out as the explosion of lust ripped through my naked body.

Leaning back, my cunt lips gaping, I rested my hands on the ground either side of his hips as my cunt milk flooded his already drenched face. Lifting his head, he licked the full length of my bared sex valley, his wet tongue sweeping over my pulsating clitoris as my screams of ecstasy resounded through the trees. Again, my orgasm peaked, my pussy cream gushing over his face as I rode the crest of my illicit climax. His tongue entering the burning sheath of my cunt as my orgasm finally began to retreat, I closed my eyes as he drank the juices of desire from my open body. Fervently sucking and licking, he cleansed me, swallowing every last drop of my girl-come before resting his head on the ground.

'Not bad for a first-timer,' I grinned, hauling my trembling body up and sitting on his firm chest. 'Now you may attend my bottom-hole.' Turning, I lowered my naked body until my rounded buttocks rested against Mog's wet cheeks. 'Tongue-fuck my bottom,' I breathed, eyeing his solid penis, his rolling balls. As his tongue licked my anal crease, seeking the small hole of my rectum, he finally located the brown eye of my anus. Teasing the delicate tissue there, he yanked my firm buttocks wide apart and pushed his tongue inside me.

'Yes,' I breathed as his tongue delved further into my rectum. My girl-juice flowing between my inner lips, I again tossed my head back and looked up at the trees as he tongue-fucked my arsehole. Tongue-fuck. Arse-fuck. Losing all sense of time, I revelled in the lewd sensations, my naked body trembling as wondrous ripples of crude sex drifted over my naked flesh. But this wasn't enough, I knew as my mind flooded with lewd thoughts. Crystal would have used and abused him, she'd have delighted in—

Whisperings drifting through my mind, I slipped off Mog's face and grabbed a branch from the ground. As if possessed, I ordered him to roll over onto his stomach. His eyes frowning, he did as I'd asked and lay with his firm buttocks perfectly positioned for the birch. He'd no doubt complain and protest, I knew as I raised the branch above his tensed bottom orbs. But I had to live out a fantasy.

Bringing the branch down with a loud swishing noise, I grinned as it struck the unblemished moons of his young buttocks. Crying out, Mog tried to roll over as the branch flailed his tensed anal orbs again. His pale skin reddening as I continued the merciless thrashing, I finally discarded the branch and yanked his crimsoned buttocks wide apart. Focusing on his brown ring, I pushed the tip of my finger past his anal sphincter muscles and drove it deep into the heat of his rectal duct. Reaching beneath his balls with my free hand, I grabbed his solid cock and pulled it up between his parted thighs.

'No,' he gasped as I pressed the solid shaft of his penis against his balls, his swollen glans forced up between the backs of his thighs. 'Jade, what are you doing?' Ignoring him, I thrust my finger in and out of his bottom-hole and rolled his foreskin back and forth over the globe of his swollen glans. Would he shoot his spunk over his own buttocks? I wondered, wanking his young cock faster. Struggling, he seemed to be in pain as I tried to force his knob between his firm buttocks. My finger slipping out of his hot anal sheath as he finally managed to roll away from me, I grinned.

'Don't be a naughty boy, Mog,' I said huskily.

'You were hurting me,' he complained.

'You can get your own back now,' I said, passing him the branch and positioning my naked body on all fours. Projecting my rounded buttocks, I turned my head and looked at him. 'Give me a gentle thrashing,' I ordered him. 'And then you may fuck my wet cunt.'

Kneeling behind me, he brought the branch down with such force that I fell forward, my head meeting the grass as the burning sensation permeated my naked bottom. Again, the branch lashed me, the loud smacking sound sending the birds fluttering from the trees. I couldn't believe the incredible pleasure I was deriving from the crude thrashing as the branch repeatedly lashed my burning buttocks. My cunt juices coursing down my inner thighs, my sensitive nipples scraping the ground, I sank my fingernails into the grass as I endured the lewd beating. I wanted Mog's tongue in my bottom again, licking me there, massaging my inner rectal flesh. This was my chance to enact any number of crude acts and I was determined not to let the opportunity pass me by.

'Fuck my cunt,' I murmured as the branch thrashed the fiery globes of my naked bottom. He immediately dropped the branch and pressed his swollen knob between the engorged cushions of my pussy lips. He was about to lose his virginity, I mused as his glans entered the hot wet shaft of my tightening cunt. He was going to fuck me and spunk me – and discover manhood. 'Grab my hips and fuck me hard,' I instructed him in my lechery. 'I want to feel your beautiful cock fucking my wet cunt.'

Ramming into me, his gasps floating on the warm air, his swinging balls battering my puffy sex lips, Mog fucked me with a vengeance. My clitoris swelling, I reached beneath my naked body and massaged the sensitive protrusion. I wanted our orgasms to explode together, his sperm filling my tight cunt as my clitoris erupted in ecstasy. He slapped my stinging buttocks as he pistoned my vaginal sheath with his rock-hard cock. The sensations ripping through my contracting womb, I breathed in the scent of the grass as my ecstasy heightened. I was going to come in a flood of vaginal juice, I knew as my erect nipples scraped over the rough ground. My buttocks on fire as he spanked me, I thought of Crystal, wondering what she would have done with the virginal lad.

'Push your cock up my arse,' I breathed, wondering at my crude words. 'I want you to fuck my tight arse.' I couldn't believe the depths my debauchery had plunged me to as I felt his penis slip out of my spasming cunt. His bulbous glans pressing hard against my sensitive anal ring, I again dug my fingernails into the ground as his solid knob slipped past my tight portal and pressed into my anal tract. From the prude to the whore, I was turning.

'You asked for it,' he chuckled, grabbing my hips and ramming his entire length into my tight anal channel. I felt as though I was going to split open as my spasming duct inflated, my delicate brown tissue tautly stretched around the root of his rock-hard penis. My pelvic cavity bloated, my naked body convulsed fiercely as he began spanking my burning buttocks. Loud slaps resounding around the trees, he withdrew his huge organ and rammed into me again.

Repeatedly withdrawing his hard cock and driving back into my tight arse, his swinging balls battering my swollen vaginal cushions, his lower stomach slapping my tensed buttocks, Mog fucked my naked body as if I were a rag doll. Rocking back and forth, my face pressed against the grass, I massaged my clitoris to a massive orgasm. Quivering, crying out as my pleasure heightened, I heard him groan as his sperm gushed from his bulbous knob and flooded my hot bowels. Imagining another penis fucking my wet cunt as another pumped spunk into my thirsty mouth, I began to wish that I'd gone to Jackie's orgy and allowed the three men to use and abuse my naked body. But there'd be another opportunity, wouldn't there?

As Mog slowed his crude arse-fucking, my orgasm began to wane and he finally stilled his trembling body. Gasping for breath, my sperm-oozing anal tissue gripping the base of his deflating cock, I again wondered at the murky depths of my crudity. How far would I plummet into the vile swamp of decadence? I wondered as his cock left the spunk-flooded sheath of my arse. Sperm running from my inflamed bottom-hole and trickling into my yawning vaginal valley, I thought I'd reached the bottom of the pit of sexual depravity.

'You're quite a girl,' Mog chuckled, slapping my stinging

buttocks as I rolled over and lay on my back. 'I wish Libby had been like you.'

'She's fifteen, Mog,' I murmured, sitting upright. 'Far too young for—'

'Here we go,' he sighed. 'You're on about age again.'

'It's just that . . . It doesn't matter. Look, I have to go. I'm meeting a friend later for a drink.'

'Male or female?'

'Female.'

'Safe enough, then.'

'Yes, yes, safe enough,' I grinned.

'See you here tomorrow?'

'God, I don't know.'

'Why don't you know? I'm a man now.'

'I don't know because . . . I just don't know.'

'You either want to meet me or you don't.'

'All right, I'll be here. Eight o'clock, OK?'

'OK.'

As Mog dressed, I managed to stagger to my feet and tug my panties up my sagging legs. This was going to become a regular thing, I knew as I pulled my skirt on. But was that so bad? If we only met in the park for crude sex . . . I didn't know what to think. I didn't know what I wanted, where my life was taking me or . . . I was about to become a published writer, I mused as Mog finished dressing. A writer who fucked young lads in the park? It was different, that was for sure.

'I'll walk through the park with you,' he said as I buttoned my blouse and stepped into my shoes.

'No, I'll stay here for a while,' I smiled. 'I need some time alone, time to think.'

'OK. Well, it's been . . . I don't know what to say, Jade.'

'Say nothing, Mog. Go now. I'll see you tomorrow evening.'

'Great. Bye, then.'

'Bye.'

Watching him follow the path through the trees, I took a deep breath and sat on the grass. Jackie would be waiting for me in the pub. Desperate to talk about her orgy, she'd be bubbling over with excitement. But I had a sex life of my own, now, I mused. No longer stuck in my flat hammering out romantic fiction on the keyboard, I now had an enviable sex life. Enviable? I was sure that my mother wouldn't have been envious. And my father would have been positively disgusted with his baby girl had he known the things I'd done. 'Baby girl,' I breathed, aware of my tight panties filling with a blend of sperm and girl-juice as my sex-holes drained.

Once so innocent in my tender years, my young body barely grown, my breasts only buds, the crack of my vagina devoid of hair . . . The baby had grown into a girl and then a woman and then a slut. My sex-crack, once so private and tightly closed, was now on offer to virtually anyone, yanked wide open to display my intricate inner folds – the wet entrance to my cunt. Tongue-fuck. Arse-fuck. Mouth-fuck. Cunt.

Was it me or society that I was worried about? I mused. My thoughts were private. My sexual exploits shared with only a select few. If I were to fuck Mog in the park every evening, then only he and I would know. Our secret. Until I opened my mouth to Jackie. Opened my mouth to her? I'd loved locking my lips to her pussy lips and drinking the slippery girl-milk from her hot cunt. I knew that, if I went to the pub that evening, I'd ask her back to my place for coffee and we'd have sex. Was that so wrong? I couldn't get my mind around the idea of a lesbian relationship. Shit. I couldn't get my mind around *any* bloody relationship.

Walking through the trees, I crossed the park and wandered home. It had been a good day, a bad day. The news from David about the book was good and bad. The sexually depraved acts I'd committed with Mog had been good and bad. Opening the front door as the phone rang, I knew that it would be Jackie. Where was I? What was I doing? Why wasn't I going to the pub? Perhaps it was Alan the ex. I didn't care who it was, I wasn't going to answer it.

Sitting on the sofa, I tugged my wet panties down to my knees and examined the crotch. Spermed, cunny-juiced, sexed . . . Pulling the garment over my ankles, I lay on the sofa and breathed in the sex-scent of my wet panties. My clitoris swelled, my juices of arousal oozed. I needed to come, yet again. I'd sleep for a while and then masturbate, I decided, dropping my panties to the floor and closing my eyes. Sleep and then masturbate and finger my cunt and my bottom-hole and pump out my juices of desire and come again and again until . . .

Chapter Nine

I slept on the sofa until the sun rose the following morning. Hauling my aching body up and holding my hand to my head as the phone rang, I sighed. 'Not until I've had coffee,' I murmured, making my way to the kitchen. Filling the kettle, I gazed out of the window and saw the girl's face peering through the bushes. Rubbing my eyes, I looked again. She was there, watching, spying. This was my chance to grab her, I thought, opening the back door. As I meandered down the garden looking at the flower beds, I was sure that she didn't realize that I'd seen her.

'Hallo,' I smiled as I approached the bushes and looked her in the eye. 'What's your name?' She disappeared like a flash of lightning. Leaping into the bushes, I couldn't understand how she'd slipped through the gate into the alley at such speed. 'That's it,' I murmured, deciding to nail the gate shut as I wandered back to the kitchen. I didn't know who the girl was or what she wanted, but I wasn't going to have her sneaking into my garden and spying on me. The phone ringing again, I grabbed the receiver and sighed as Jackie began complaining.

'I couldn't make it to the pub,' I replied.

'I waited until closing time, Jade. Where the hell did you get to?'

'I was with a friend. I thought I'd be able to meet you but . . .'

'That Alan was there asking about you.'

'Oh?'

'He said that you'd been there with a young lad.'

'Yes, that's right. He's a friend of a friend.'

'Alan reckons that you were pretty close to each other.'

'No, of course we weren't. We bumped into each other and had a chat, that was all.'

'That's not what I heard.'

'Jackie, I've had a bad night. I'm not interested in rumours.'

'What are you doing today?'

'I've only just got up. I suppose I should work.'

'All work and no play . . . I thought you might want to come round. It must be my turn to make the coffees.'

'Er . . . OK, then. We'll have a chat and then I'll come back and work on the book. I've got to get ready so I'll be a while.'

'All right, I'll see you soon.'

I had the feeling that Jackie was up to something, although I didn't know what. She loved sitting in the sun in my garden. It was most unusual for her to invite me to her place for coffee. No doubt I'd find out what was going on, I mused as I showered and dressed. Feeling guilty as I finally left my flat, I knew that I should be working on my novel. David would soon be nagging me for the rest of the book, and I'd have no excuse. But it was early days, I consoled myself. There was plenty of time, wasn't there?

'Come in,' Jackie said as she opened the door.

'What are you up to?' I asked, following her into the kitchen.

'The young lad you were with in the pub.'

'What about him?'

'You were seen.'

'So you said.'

'What you were doing to him. Your friend Alan saw it all.'

'He couldn't have done. All I did was—'

'Wank him off beneath the table. You're getting as bad as me, Jade.'

'God, I didn't realize that . . .'

'How old is he?'

'Eighteen.'

'Eighteen, my foot.'

'I'm not interested in him or your foot. I have some news.'

'Oh?'

'My agent rang yesterday. He wants my dirty . . . my *erotic* novel.'

'Jade, that's brilliant,' she beamed excitedly. 'How much will you get?'

'I don't know yet.'

'What did you write about?'

'Sex, what else?'

'Tell me about it. Was it cocks and pussies or—'

'You'll read it when it's published.'

'Is there a sixteen-year-old boy in the book?'

'No, Jackie, there isn't.'

'What was his cock like? Fresh, stiff, big and—'

'Jackie . . . I thought we were having coffee?'

'Did he spunk over your hand?'

'Jackie!'

'Sorry. Come into the lounge. I have a surprise for you.'

Following her through the hall, I thought about Mog. I don't know why I felt so guilty. OK, so he was young. So what? He was *too* young – but did that really matter? He had a beautiful penis, hard, fresh, unblemished in youth. He was desperate for sexual experience, desperate to explore the female form, to learn. Why should he be denied pleasures of the flesh because of his age? But my conscience still nagged me. He should be playing around with girls of his own age, not being seduced by an older woman. Older? I was only twenty-one.

'What do you think?' Jackie asked as we entered the lounge.

'What's that for?' I breathed, gazing at a massage table set in the middle of the room. 'I didn't realize that you were into—'

'Jade, you are silly,' she giggled. 'I'm not a masseuse.'

'Then why . . .' I began in my naivety.

'I have handcuffs, whips, vibrators . . . Want to give it a try?'

'No, I don't. Jackie, you amaze me.'

'*Me?* What about you? Tying Alan down and pissing over his face and—'

'Well, yes.'

'Get on the table and I'll give you a massage.'

'No, I don't think . . .'

'It'll relax you. Strip off and lie on the table and I'll go and get some oil.'

'Well . . .'

'Come on, Jade.' She smiled. 'You look tense, all wound up. You've been working too hard. A massage will do you good.'

As she left the room, I slipped my blouse over my shoulders and tugged my skirt down. I *was* tense. My shoulders and neck felt tight and my back ached. But the sort of massage Jackie had in mind wouldn't help. There again, it might be relaxing. Slipping my panties off, I unhooked my bra and climbed onto the padded table. So much for coffee, I reflected, gazing at the ceiling. My arousal rising as Jackie returned, I wondered again about my so-called fresh start. She was going to masturbate me, I knew as she stood beside me and eyed my naked body.

'Just relax,' she whispered, kneading the firm mounds of my breasts. Her fingertips encircling my erect nipples, she told me to close my eyes. Watching her sprinkle oil over the mounds of my breasts, my heart rate slowing, I began to relax. As her oily hands ran down over the smooth plateau of my stomach, I breathed deeply and closed my eyes. Sex with Mog was frenzied, our fucking crude and ferocious. But Jackie was sensual, her fingertips gently teasing the delicate rise of my mons, tracing circles over the sensitive flesh just above my moist sex-crack.

My mind drifting, I almost fell asleep as she ran her fingers up my inner thighs, massaging oil into my soft flesh. I'd never felt so relaxed, so calm as I breathed in the scent of the oil. This was what I'd needed, I knew as I parted my legs. Slouching over the keyboard for hours on end and worrying about sex and Mog's age and Alan . . . I'd become physically and mentally tense. Oblivious to my surroundings as Jackie massaged oil into the swell of my engorged outer lips, I drifted, floated, swam through swirling clouds of pleasure.

I didn't know how long I'd been in a sleeplike state but, when I woke, I couldn't move my arms or legs. In her devilry, Jackie had spread my legs wide and tied my feet. My arms pulled down on either side of the couch, my wrists tied to the frame, I couldn't move. I was about to protest but her fingertips ran up and down the gaping crack of my pussy, sending ripples of pleasure through my pelvis. I was hers for the taking. My naked body was hers to do with as she wished.

'Nice?' she asked, her finger slipping between the sensitive petals of my inner lips. Letting out a rush of breath, I closed my eyes as her finger entered me, penetrated the tight, hot sheath of my young cunt. Massaging oil into the softness of my girl lips with her free hand, she slipped a second finger deep into my tightening cunt. My head lolling from side to side as the sensations rippled through my tethered body, I recalled her words. *Only a girl knows how to pleasure another girl.* She was right, I knew as she drove another finger into the bloated sheath of my spasming vagina. My body tingling with sex, I gasped as she pushed her tongue into my navel. Licking the small indentation, she kissed and nibbled the soft flesh of my stomach. Arching my back, my breathing now fast and shallow, I desperately needed to feel her wet tongue between the swell of my pussy lips.

'My clitoris,' I murmured as Jackie fingered my pussy, my juices of lesbian desire squelching with the beautiful pistoning. Ignoring my request, she continued to finger-fuck me, massaging my girl lips with her free hand and sucking my navel into her hot mouth. She was teasing me, I knew. Deliberately neglecting the solid protrusion of my clitoris, she was tormenting me. My naked body trembling, my breasts heaving, I gripped the metal frame of the couch as she managed to thrust another finger into the wet duct of my burning cunt.

'Please,' I gasped, my juices of love decanting, running over the small bridge of skin dividing my love-holes to the brown eye of my anus. Parting my fleshy girl lips, she stretched the ravine of my vagina wide open and exposed my inner folds. My erect pleasure bud emerging from its pinken hide, ripe for massaging to orgasm, I prayed for her to masturbate me. I couldn't take much more, I knew as my clitoris painfully swelled and pulsated. My vaginal muscles gripping her thrusting fingers, my naked body jolted as she pressed the buzzing tip of a vibrator against the solid nodule of my clitoris.

'God,' I cried, the sensations transmitting deep into my contracting womb as my clitoris ballooned and pulsated. The explosion of orgasm rocking my tethered body, I screamed as shock waves of pure sexual bliss shook my very soul. Again and again my orgasm peaked, gripping my shaking body, tossing my mind on the wind of ecstasy. In the distance, I could hear Jackie's breathing, the squelching of her fingers thrusting in and out of my fiery cunt.

'Keep coming,' she breathed, pressing the buzzing vibrator harder against my pulsating clitoris, the intense pleasure of my lesbian coming almost agonizing as my juices of lust gushed from my bloated cuntal sheath. My inner thighs drenched with my vaginal milk, my outer pussy lips engorged, the vibrator sustaining my mind-blowing orgasm, I thought my ballooning clitoris was going to burst. Powerful tremors of sex surging through my tethered body, reaching every nerve ending, I sang out in my coming, wailing my appreciation as Jackie sank her teeth into my stomach.

Never had I known such wondrous sensations. My nostrils flaring, my head tossed back, I arched my back as my cunt tightened around Jackie's thrusting fingers. Again, the vibrator heightened my orgasm, taking me to hitherto unknown heights of sexual elation as my girl-juice gushed from my dilated cunt and sprayed my inner thighs. My eyes rolling, my body shaking fiercely, I begged Jackie to stop. I really couldn't take the agonizing pleasure any more. The vibrator seemed to buzz louder as she ran the tip around the nodule of my solid clitoris. My head spinning, my cunt squelching with the girl-fingering, I again cried out, begging her to release me from my climax.

The vibrator finally silent, I lay quivering uncontrollably as Jackie slipped her fingers out of my cunt with a loud sucking sound. Convulsing wildly, my muscles involuntarily spasming, I panted for breath as I gently drifted back into my sated body. I could feel Jackie attending the pouting lips of my burning cunt, wiping my cream away with a cloth. Shuddering, I finally managed to lift my head and focus on her smiling face.

'Well?' she breathed. 'What do you think?'

'That was incredible,' I gasped.

'I mean, what do you think about your pussy?'

Lifting my head further, I gazed at the hairless rise of my mons. 'God,' I cried, focusing on the smooth hairless lips of my vagina. 'Jackie, what the hell have you done?'

'It was hair-removing cream,' she enlightened me, stroking the soft hillocks of my outer labia.

'I thought it was oil. Jackie, I hate you.'

'No, you don't. You look beautiful, Jade. A schoolgirl, once again.'

'Why the hell . . . Let me go, for God's sake.'

'Not yet,' she grinned. 'I have another surprise for you.'

'I don't want any more bloody surprises,' I snapped, my wide eyes transfixed on my hairless vulval flesh.

'Lie back and relax. You'll enjoy *this* surprise.'

As she left the room, I laid my head on the padded table and sighed. It would take weeks before my pubic hair once more veiled my pussy lips. How she could have done such a thing, I had no idea. What would Mog think? I wondered. There again, it was probably best not to see the boy again. Jackie was a right bitch, I mused, looking again at my schoolgirl lookalike vulva. Hair-removing cream? 'I'll give her bloody hair-removing cream,' I sighed.

'Your surprise,' she grinned leading a naked man into the room.

'Jackie!' I screamed, gazing at the man's erect penis, the purple globe of his knob.

'It's time you learned a thing or two about sex,' she giggled as another man walked into the room.

'Jackie!' I cried again as the men stood either side of the table, their erect penises pointing to the ceiling.

'This is Tom, Jenny's husband,' she said, gazing at the dark-haired man. 'And this is Lenny, a friend of the family.'

'You planned this,' I returned. 'You tricked me and—'

'And this,' she interrupted me as the door opened. 'This is Don.'

Gazing at the third man as he entered the room and stood by the table, I couldn't believe what was happening. Slipping out of her clothes, Jackie asked the men what they thought of my hairless pussy. Humiliated beyond belief, I lifted my head as the men examined my pouting vaginal lips, commenting of the beauty of my cunt. Jackie was going to pay for this, I decided as fingers stroked the soft hillocks of my love mouth.

'Right,' she beamed, standing beside me. 'Now we're all naked, we'll have some fun. Jade is writing a dirty book and she needs to experience a few things.'

'I'll give her some experience,' Tom chortled, pressing the bulbous glans of his huge penis against my mouth.

'I believe she'd benefit from having three penises spunking her holes. Her mouth, her bum and, of course, her hairless pussy. Before that, do whatever takes your fancy.'

Remaining silent since protesting would have been futile, I closed my eyes as my ankles were untied and my legs placed in a new position to either side of the couch. The ropes securing my ankles again, the bared crack of my cunt gaping between my splayed thighs, I opened my mouth and sucked on the penis pressing against my lips. The man gasped as I rolled my tongue over the silky-smooth glans of his erect cock. Three penises sperming me? I pondered as someone adjusted the table. A penis-head stabbing at my vaginal entrance, I realized that the bottom half of the table had either been removed or lowered.

'Yes,' a man breathed as I felt a huge penis glide into the tight sheath of my sex-wet cunt. I could feel his balls pressing against my tensed buttocks as his ballooning knob met my cervix. The cock in my mouth swelling as I snaked my tongue over its velveteen surface, I wondered whether I'd be forced to take a cock up my bum. But they couldn't get to me, I knew as my tethered body rocked with the vaginal fucking. There was no way a man could enter my anal canal while I was on the massage couch.

As Jackie sucked my elongated nipple into her hot mouth and sank her teeth into the sensitive bud, I resigned myself to the fact that I was going to have to offer my body for crude sex. I'd eventually be allowed to stagger home, I mused, sucking and mouthing the twitching knob. I'd shower and then sit at the keyboard and write like I'd never written before. After all, that had been the experience I'd often thought of. Three men and a girl using and abusing my naked body. That's what I'd wanted, wasn't it?

Sperm suddenly gushing from the swollen knob within my mouth, flooding my tongue and filling my cheeks, I swallowed repeatedly. The other penis pumping sperm deep into my vaginal throat, I shuddered as my orgasm erupted within my solid clitoris. Squelching and grunting sounds resounding around the room, I drank from the cock fucking my mouth as my cunt overflowed and spunk splattered my inner thighs. My tethered body shaking violently as the men crudely fucked my mouth and my cunt, I moaned through my nose as Jackie repeatedly bit the sensitive bud of my erect nipple.

I couldn't believe the crude sex I was experiencing as my naked body shuddered and my cunt tightened around the pistoning cock. For a year I'd not set eyes on a penis or had one orgasm, but now? Would I become a regular visitor to Jackie's sex parties? The man fucking my spermed mouth forcing his swollen glans to the back of my throat, my lips stretched tautly around the root of his huge cock, I knew I'd visit Jackie's den of iniquity again. From strait-laced prude to wanton slut, I was turning.

Sperm oozing from my mouth and running down my face, I licked my full lips as the man finally withdrew his spent cock. My orgasm subsiding as the other man shot the last of his sperm into my drenched cunt, I lay shaking on the couch in the aftermath of my incredible coming. Releasing my sore nipple, Jackie stood beside me and grinned. What had she planned for me next? I wondered as she adjusted the table. As she lowered the top section, my head falling back over the edge of the table, I gazed at the third man's erect penis as he stood behind me.

Pulling his scrotum up, he stood with his legs either side of my head and rested his heavy balls on my mouth. Pushing my tongue out, I licked the wrinkled sac, breathing in the scent of his genitalia as fingers entered the spermed duct of my fiery cunt. Opening my mouth as wide as I could, I sucked his balls inside. *Another first*, I reflected as the man gasped in his debased pleasure. His balls jerking, I knew that someone was wanking his knob. Guessing that it was Jackie, I gazed at the man's brown anal eye as I tongued and sucked his balls.

'You're going to come over her face,' Jackie giggled. 'She doesn't know what a facial is, so you're going to show her.'

His balls slipping out of my mouth, my head upside down, I watched as Jackie wanked his solid shaft. His purple glans only an inch from my mouth, I pushed my tongue out as his spunk jetted from his glistening glans. The white liquid splattering my face, running into my nose, I lapped up as much as I could while Jackie wanked him faster. Finally thrusting his knob into my mouth, his balls pressed against my nose, he pumped his spunk down my throat.

Coughing and spluttering as another penis drove deep into the wet heat of my young cunt, I wondered when the debauchery would end. Never had I been used and abused like this, and I began to wonder about my lechery as I drank from the orgasming knob filling my mouth. To what depths would the crude sex plunge me? What would I become? I could never enjoy a loving relationship with a man, I knew. Mouth-fucked, arse-fucked, cunt-tonguing, arse-licking . . . Never would I be able to make love again. Sex ruled me now. Crude sex for the sake of lust.

The swollen knob leaving my spermed mouth, I gazed in disbelief as Jackie stood with her thighs either side of my head and bent over. Aligning her bottom-hole with my mouth, she ordered me to tongue-fuck her arse. My cunt filling with sperm, I pushed my tongue into her private hole and tasted her there. Yanking her bottom orbs wide apart, her small hole opening, she instructed me to push my tongue deep into her anal canal. My tongue entering the dank heat of her rectum, my nose between the swell of her wet vaginal lips, I sealed my mouth to her brown tissue and sucked hard. She gasped as I licked the velvety walls of her anal canal. Writhing, whimpering, she was obviously de-lighting in the crude act.

'Push your tongue right up my arse,' she ordered me. My body jolting with the enforced vaginal fucking, I pushed my tongue deeper into the tight tube of her rectum. Savouring the bitter-sweet taste, I breathed in the heady scent of her cunt as her girl-juices gushed from her sex sheath and drenched my face. The cock finally sliding out of my inflamed vagina, I tongued Jackie's tight bottom-hole until she turned round and instructed me to lick her cunt out.

Complying as she stood with her feet wide apart, I lapped up the vaginal cream oozing from her bared sex hole, swallowing her offering as she trembled and whimpered in her lesbian lust. As one of the men stood in front of her with his knob between her pouting cunt lips, I watched in amazement as she swivelled her hips and sucked his bulbous glans deep into her young quim. His balls battering my forehead, I watched his girl-wet shaft pistoning Jackie's tight sex duct. The lewd sight only inches away from my wide eyes, I focused on the taut lips of her vagina rolling along his veined shaft as he fucked her.

A tongue entering the wet shaft of my cunt, my face splattered with girl-juice and spunk, the taste of Jackie's anal canal lingering on my lips, I knew I could sink no further into the mire of depravity. I had enough experience to write erotica now, I knew as I watched the crude fucking. The man's swinging balls slapping my forehead, Jackie's come-juice spraying from her bloated cunt-hole and splattering my face, I knew that I could write about sex in all its crudity, its beautiful decadence. Cocks fucking cunts, spunking arseholes, sperming mouths . . . Cum-sluts, facials, cunt-licking, arse-fingering, face-pissing . . . There wasn't much I'd not had the pleasure of experiencing in the last couple of weeks. But there was so much more I was to experience, so much more I was to learn.

Sperm pouring from Jackie's fucked cunt as the man gasped, I opened my mouth and lapped up the aphrodisiacal blend of the decadent union as Jackie cried out in her coming. Her thighs pressed against my ears, his balls rolling over my forehead, I licked the wet shaft of his huge cock as he thrust his purple knob in and out of her drenched vaginal sheath. The tongue slipping out of my cunt and snaking up my valley of desire to my swollen clitoris, I again gripped the metal frame of the couch as my orgasm exploded.

The man's knob leaving Jackie's vaginal duct and nestling between the crimsoned folds of her inner lips, I opened my mouth wide as a long strand of spunk hung from the purple head. Reaching my tongue, the thread of spunk left the knob-slit and dropped into my mouth. Swallowing the salty liquid, I watched as more sperm oozed from the bared entrance to Jackie's flooded cunt. The penis moving back, Jackie lowered the open centre of her young body and pressed the wet lips of her vagina against my mouth. I instinctively sucked the blend of girl-come and male cream from the hot cavern of her cunt, repeatedly swallowing as I drained her young body.

It had been quite a morning, I reflected as Jackie moved away from my sex-wet face. I'd felt guilty for neglecting my book, but this was research, wasn't it? Wondering whether I'd be released and allowed to go home, I lifted my head and gazed in horror at Jackie as she lashed my hairless cunt lips with a leather strap. Crying out as the excruciating pain permeated my vulval flesh, I knew that I couldn't take the vaginal torture as the strap repeatedly lashed the swollen hillocks of my sex lips.

'No!' I cried as the strap landed across my reddening love lips with a loud crack. 'Jackie, for God's sake!' Chuckling wickedly, she continued with the vulval beating until the lips of my cunt swelled and turned ruby-red. As the men kneaded my breasts, rubbing their sperm-covered knobs over my naked body, I tried desperately to break free of my bonds. 'No!' I screamed again as the strap caught the wings of my inner lips.

'Now you can write about cunny-thrashing,' Jackie grinned, bringing the strap down with such force that my body convulsed wildly. Finally discarding the strap, she released my ankles and ordered the men to lift my legs and push my knees against my breasts. Obeying, they held me in the degrading position while Jackie ran a length of rope over the backs of my knees and secured the ends beneath the couch. My pussy hole gaping, the entrance to my bowels fully exposed, I guessed what I was to endure as Jackie massaged oil into the delicate tissue surrounding my bottom-hole.

Lifting the top section of the table, bringing my head in line with my body, she grinned at me. Frowning, I didn't know what to say as she began explaining that the men were going to take turns to pump their spunk into my bowels. I'd been arse-fucked before, but not by three men in succession. Wondering what was going on as one man clambered onto the table with his knees either side of my hips, I watched Jackie move to the end of the table. Guiding his solid cock deep into my spermed cunt, she moved aside and grinned at me again.

'One in, one to go,' she whispered huskily. Feeling a bulbous knob pressing against my well-oiled anal entrance, I knew that I was to experience the ultimate sexual depravation. Two huge cocks forced into my tight sex-holes, fucking me and spunking me? But that had been my fantasy, hadn't it? No, my fantasy had been *three* cocks fucking my orifices. My bottom, my cunt and my mouth. I was developing an insatiable thirst for sperm. The beautiful mother-of-pearl liquid, lubricious, salty . . . I was also acquiring a taste for girl-come. And the heady blend of the two substances was pure nectar to me.

My bowels were going to be filled with sperm, I knew as the swollen knob slipped past my defeated anal sphincter muscles. The solid penile shaft gliding slowly into my tight anal channel, dilating my secret passage, I felt that I was going to split open. My pelvic cavity bloating as the penises drove fully home, I couldn't believe the wondrous sensations rippling deep into my contracting womb. The mouth of my rectum stretched tautly around the base of one erect penis, the inflamed lips of my vagina encompassing the root of a second cock . . . This was sheer heaven, I thought as Jackie turned my head to face the third man's bulbous glans.

'He's going to fuck your mouth while the others fuck your tight holes,' she said excitedly. Taking the ripe plum into my mouth as the double fucking began, I again pondered on the frightening depths of depravity to which I'd plummeted. My young body rocking, my love-holes repeatedly inflating and deflating, I snaked my wet tongue over the purple knob. Teasing the sperm-slit, licking the hard rim of the swollen crown, I was desperate for the gushing of sperm. Depths of depravity or heights of ecstasy?

Listening to the squelching and grunting sounds of crude sex as I gobbled and sucked on the ripe plum of the man's penis, I thought of Mog. I'd use and abuse him, use him for cold sex, raw sex. At my beck and call, he'd become my plaything. I'd order him to attend my naked body, pleasure me, spunk over me and in me, take me to orgasm. Perhaps I could get my hands on his girlfriend, I mused as the penis fucking my wet mouth swelled. There again . . .

'Coming,' the man breathed as his sperm jetted from the purple sphere of his beautiful cock. Bathing my snaking tongue, filling my cheeks, he pumped out his orgasmic cream. Savouring the heady taste, a river of sperm coursing down my flushed face, I finally swallowed his male offering. The other men breathing heavily, I felt sperm gushing into the core of my bowels, jetting over my cervix. I'd done it, I reflected, the hot orifices of my naked body crudely fucked and spunked. Three men using me to satisfy their base desires, filling me with their spunk . . . The ultimate in sexual depravity. Or was it?

I'd not yet had two knobs in my mouth, the purple globes of two penises fucking and sperming my thirsty mouth. Could I manage to suck *three* men at once? I wondered as I snaked my tongue around the rim of the orgasmic glans. My inflamed bottom-hole oozing with spunk, squelching as the penile shaft massaged my delicate brown tissue, I wondered whether Mog had any young friends who might be interested in having a girl use and abuse their youthful bodies. From prude to cum-slut I was turning. I *had* turned.

My erect clitoris exploding in orgasm again as the shaft of the penis fucking my tight cunt massaged its sensitive tip, I swallowed the sperm pumping into my mouth, gobbling and sucking in my ever-deepening quest for lust. Rocking with the three-way fucking, my naked body tingling with illicit sex, I moaned through my nose as my climax took me through swirling mists of pastel hues. Sailing, floating high above my trembling body, I again saw visions from another world. Was it my mind, my subconscious? Or was I really visiting a lustful world of perpetual orgasm? Unseen beings touched me, caressed my mind. Was Crystal Marshall there?

The spent penis finally leaving the spunked orifices of my exhausted body, I writhed in a semi-conscious state as I was released from my bonds of lust. I could hear voices mur-

muring in the distance, floating through the mist of my delirium as I lay shaking uncontrollably on the padded table. Had they finished with me? I wondered. Were they going to force two penises into the burning sheath of my sperm-brimming cunt? Perhaps they planned to double-fuck my arsehole.

There was so much I had to experience, I reflected as my abusers left the room. A double cunt-fucking, double arse-fucking . . . A triple mouth-sperming? Falling into a deep sleep, I dreamed my dreams of lust and debauchery, crude sex, orgasming knobs, spunk jetting over the mounds and crevices of my young body, girl-come filling my thirsty mouth, men fucking my beautiful cunt, wanking up my arse . . .

Chapter Ten

Jackie had gone out by the time I returned from my dreams and dressed. Staggering home, the holes between my thighs oozing with sperm, I let myself into my flat and flopped onto the sofa. It had been quite a morning, I reflected. Expecting a cup of coffee and a chat, I'd ended up living out a fantasy. Now I had to work on the book. David would soon ring and ask how I was getting on. I was getting on very well with sex, enjoying every minute of it. But I wasn't writing about it.

Taking a shower, I gazed at the hairless flesh of my vulva and wondered at Jackie's audacity. What would I say to Mog the next time he stripped me? How would I explain? The next time? I was supposed to be meeting him in the park that evening. Hadn't I had enough sex for one day? No, I hadn't. He was young, fresh, his penis unblemished, pure in its unknowing. He probably wanked, I mused as I washed the sperm and girl-come from my naked body. He'd probably been wanking for several years, shooting his sperm over his stomach, over the floor.

Taking a summer dress from the wardrobe, I sat on my bed and raised the hem. The dress was turquoise, low-cut and extremely flimsy. 'My new look,' I murmured, donning the item and gazing at my reflection in the full-length mirror. I'd taken the hem up rather too much, but it didn't matter. I had good thighs, worth showing off. Mog would appreciate it, I mused. Particularly as I hadn't bothered with panties or a bra. I felt free with the hairless crack of my vagina completely unveiled, my nipples unrestricted by tight material. Making a sandwich, I sat at my desk and switched the computer on. It was a lovely day, the sun beating down, the air warm and still. But I had to work. I'd already wasted the morning and . . . Wasted? Hardly!

I hammered the keyboard until five o'clock. Three men using and abusing a young girl's naked body, another girl forcing her to suck the juices of lust from her open cunt, she'd spent several hours being fucked and spunked. *Auto-biographical?* I mused, acutely aware of my hairless pussy. It was a dream brought out into the light of day. *Dreams sometimes come true*, I reflected. *Be careful what you want for you just might get it.* I'd got it, all right.

There'd been no phone calls, no interruptions, which was unusual. I'd at least expected Jackie to ring to discover my thoughts and feelings on the . . . the rape? Was that what it had been? Technically, I'd been raped. The notion arousing me, my juices of sex oozing between the inflamed petals of my inner lips, I recalled Jackie's vibrator. The sensations had been wondrous, the vibrations transmitting deep into my womb as my clitoris pulsated wildly beneath the buzzing tip of the phallus. I'd have to get myself a vibrator, I mused, deciding to ring Jackie.

'I wondered when you'd call,' she said.

'I thought *you*'d ring me after . . . after you'd watched me being raped by three men.'

'Raped?' she giggled. 'You were a consenting adult, Jade.'

'Consenting? Tied down and . . . Why the hell did you use hair-removing cream on me?'

'I thought you'd like it.'

'Like it? You are a cow, Jackie.'

'Oh, thanks. So, what do you think of your girlie pussy?'

'I think it looks terrible. Anyway, where did you get to?'

'I went out for lunch with the men. You were sleeping, so . . .'

'Unconscious, more like.'

'I thought we'd go to the pub this evening.'

'I . . . I don't know, Jackie. I've so much to do.'

'Writing?'

'Er . . . Yes. I really have to get on with the book. Maybe tomorrow evening.'

'You're going out somewhere, aren't you?' she asked suspiciously.

'No, no. I have to work. I'll give you a ring tomorrow.'

'OK. Presumably you'll be coming to my next party?'

'I'll ring you, Jackie.'

Next party? I didn't know what I was going to do, apart from nail the gate shut before my visit to the park to meet Mog. Grabbing a hammer and a jar of nails from beneath the kitchen sink, I wandered down the garden and slipped into the bushes. If Mog was going to be a regular visitor, which I reckoned he was, then I didn't want kids creeping into the garden and spying on us. Managing to nail the gate shut, without hitting my thumb with the hammer, I grappled my way out of the bushes.

That was that little problem dealt with, I mused, deciding to go to the park early and enjoy the early-evening sun. I should have cooked a meal but wasn't feeling very hungry. Besides, I couldn't be bothered to cook. Standing before the hall mirror, I brushed my hair and grinned. I was attractive, even though I thought so myself. I had a good body, a body I'd at last discovered. And I was determined to . . . But Mog was so young, I thought again, anxiously.

Walking down the street, a warm breeze wafting up my dress and playing around the hairless lips of my moistening vagina, I felt alive with sex. I was going to meet Mog, my secret lover, my young plaything, my toyboy. He was Romeo and I was Juliet – and we'd fuck rotten. Right or wrong, I didn't care. In my view, he was a male with a beautiful penis and he was able to fuck me to orgasm. Besides, he'd bought alcohol in the pub and had as good as said that he was eighteen. Almost eighteen. *What the fuck?* I giggled inwardly as I walked across the park to the bench, our bench.

It occurred to me as I relaxed beneath the evening sun that I knew nothing about Mog. I didn't know where he lived, or what his real name was. But it didn't matter. My ignorance added mystery to the relationship. He was an unknown quantity, enigmatic, inexperienced in his youth . . . And I wanted his perfect body. The time would inevitably come when he found a girl of his own age, I pondered sadly. As the years passed, he'd develop an eye for the younger girls. I was twenty-one. By the time I was twenty-five, he'd be . . . My thinking was silly. I wasn't in love so it didn't matter. *Enjoy the moment*, my ageing aunt used to say. There would always be a supply of fresh teenage boys for the taking. There'd always be an abundance of muscular young lads only too willing to attend my naked body and pleasure me.

Checking my watch, I looked around the park. With over half an hour to go, I decided to take a walk across the grass to the trees. As I wandered past a row of bushes, I happened to notice a figure in the distance. Wondering whether it was Mog, I watched as the figure grew larger. It was a woman. She appeared to be walking slowly, cautiously, as she made her way towards the trees. Slipping behind the bushes, I watched her. Why I was hiding, I didn't know. Perhaps it was guilt. I might have known the woman and she'd think it odd that I was hanging around by the trees in a dress so short that . . .

As she approached, she looked about her. I didn't recognize her, but I had the notion that she was looking for me. Intuition? I didn't know what it was as she followed the row of bushes and finally slipped into the trees. She was wearing a short skirt and blouse, not unusual for the time of year. But she was carrying a large bag. There was something about her, something that made me feel uneasy. Mog would arrive shortly, I mused. Perhaps the mysterious female was searching for him. Whatever it was that she wanted, I could hardly have sex in the woods with Mog, knowing that she might be lurking nearby. Creeping through the undergrowth, I was sure that there was no way through the woods; the path didn't lead anywhere. I could hear twigs cracking underfoot, but saw no sign of her until I was close to the clearing.

Looking about her as she dumped the bag on the ground, she checked her watch. Sign enough that she'd arranged to meet Mog, I decided. But why would he ask another woman to join us? I wondered. Taking a closer look at her face, I realized that she was in her teens. Perhaps it was Mog's girlfriend, I pondered fearfully. A fifteen-year-old? It was time to leave, I decided, squatting behind a bush. But not until Mog had arrived and I'd discovered exactly what was going on. I didn't have to wait long. He emerged from the trees and stood in the clearing, smiling at the girl.

'She'll be here soon,' he said.

'I don't think this is a good idea,' the girl sighed.

'It's a brilliant idea,' he replied. 'You'd better get ready.'

'There's plenty of time. Besides, we'll hear her coming.'

'Get ready now, just in case. Have you got everything?'

'Yes,' she murmured, picking the bag up.

'I'll see you later, back at the pub.'

'OK,' she said, and wandered into the bushes.

I watched Mog for several minutes, wondering what on earth was going on. The girl was hiding in the bushes, he was waiting for me . . . Suddenly realizing what they might be planning to do, I bit my lip. I couldn't leave without the bushes rustling and twigs cracking. But I didn't dare show myself. Wondering what to do as Mog sat on the ground, I knew that I had to face him.

'Hi,' I smiled, walking into the clearing.

'You look great,' he beamed, eyeing my naked thighs.

'Thanks. I'm afraid I can't stay.'

'Why not? I thought we were going to . . .'

'Yes, I know. It's just that something's happened.'

'Oh,' he sighed, glancing at the bushes. 'I was looking forward to . . . Well, you know.'

'So was I, Mog. The thing is, someone saw us together. Not in the pub. I mean here, in the woods. Because of your age—'

'Who saw us?'

'A girl. I don't know her name but a friend of mine knows her and . . . It's a long story.'

'A girl? But—'

'She's going to blackmail you, Mog. And me. I wouldn't be surprised if she'd followed us here and was hiding somewhere.'

'Who's this friend of yours?' he asked, again glancing at the bushes.

'Just a friend. If you'd like to, you can come round to my place. We'd be safe enough there. I'd better go home now. I don't want to be seen hanging around here.'

'Yes, right. I'll . . . I'll call round later. Say, half an hour?'

'That would be nice. I'll be ready and waiting for you.'

Leaving the clearing, I felt quite proud of myself. The girl had been going to take photographs of us having sex. She would then have demanded money from me in return for keeping quiet about the illicit affair. It was a pretty good plan. No matter what Mog's age, they knew that I'd be worried and would pay up. Not that I had any money. I might even carry the scam a little further, I mused as I crossed the park. I could make out that the girl had been in touch with me and had threatened to expose us. Whatever happened, I was looking forward to an evening of rampant sex with the lad.

Deciding to tidy up before Mog arrived, I grabbed the pile of freebie newspapers from behind the front door. I was about to put them in the bin when I noticed a small package among them. It was the book from David. Grinning as I flicked through the pages, I wondered when it had arrived. 'Autopederasty?' I murmured. 'The insertion of another's penis into their own anus.' Now that was an interesting idea, I thought, recalling pulling Mog's penis through his legs and pressing his glans against his buttocks.

Tossing the book onto the hall table, I thought about Mog and his wicked plan to blackmail me. He'd ruined all we could have had together, I reflected. It was only sex, but . . . I didn't know what to think as I dumped the newspapers in the bin. We certainly couldn't meet in the park again. He'd put an end to our fun and games in the woods. But why had he brought the girl in to blackmail me? He might have thought that I had money, but to blackmail me . . . The doorbell ringing, I checked myself in the hall mirror.

I seemed to be changing, I observed. I had a look of . . . I

183

didn't know what it was as I brushed my long blonde hair away from my face. A look of wickedness about me? My lips seemed to curl into a salacious smile, my eyes reflected an inner desire. A young lad calling round for sex? I pondered, opening the front door. What would Crystal have done with him?

'Hi,' he smiled, stepping into the hall. 'This friend of yours—'

'I don't know what's going on any more than you do, Mog,' I interrupted him. 'All I know is that we were seen in the woods by some girl or other and she thought it was a good idea to blackmail us. As far as I know, she was going to drop me in it for screwing an under-age boy. Anyway, it's been dealt with.'

'Dealt with?'

'She won't be interfering any more. Come through to the lounge.'

That had put the frighteners on him, I knew as he sat in the armchair. I supposed it was because I'd kept harping on about his age that he thought I was really worried. Which I was. The last thing I'd needed was . . . I had no need to worry, I was sure as he gazed longingly at my naked thighs. I'd put an end to his silly games, and we were now free to enjoy crude sex. Wondering what he'd think of my hairless pussy, I sat on the sofa and parted my thighs a little.

'I'm not under age,' he murmured solemnly.

'I know you're not, Mog,' I smiled, parting my thighs a little further. 'Do you know what I'd like to do to you?'

'No,' he smiled, catching sight of my hairless vaginal crack. His eyes lighting up, he leaned forward. 'Tell me what you'd like to do to me.'

'I'd like to . . . Come over here and I'll show you.'

Leaping to his feet, he stood before me with his face

COLLAR'S

28 Church Street
Enfield, Middlesex
EN2 6BB
Tel: 020 8363 6060
Fax: 020 8363 6464

1st Mar 2006 15:46

CASHIER 2 DANI

0079745/WE/23 FIRST HAND   6.99

TOTAL   ITEMS   1   6.99

Cash   20.00
CHANGE Cash   13.01

Head Office: St John's House,
72 St John's Road, London, SW11 1PT

Vat No: 561997200
Company Reg No: 2133199

beaming as I unbuckled his belt. He'd been stupid to think that he could blackmail me. There again, that was only my theory. But why else would a girl be hiding in the bushes? She must have had a camera and been ready to take incriminating photographs of me screwing Mog. I'd have to teach him a lesson, I reflected, pulling his jeans down. Naughty little boys had to be punished by Crystal.

'Turn round,' I ordered Mog as he kicked his jeans and shoes off his feet. 'And take your T-shirt off.' Turning, his pert buttocks facing me, I stroked the smooth skin of his anal globes. His T-shirt dropping to the floor, I ordered him to stand with his feet wide apart and bend over. His balls hung alluringly between his thighs, the brown eye of his anus exposed within the ravine between his rounded buttocks. Kneading his balls, I reached between his legs and grabbed his solid penis. His body was perfect, I observed. Not a blemish on his beautiful buttocks, his penis rock-hard, his balls rolling, I leaned forward and kissed his firm bottom cheeks.

Squeezing his solid penis, I puckered my lips and pushed them into his anal valley, teasing the sensitive tissue of his anus with the tip of my tongue. The bitter-sweet taste driving me wild, I released his cock and yanked his buttocks wide apart. My tongue slipping into his rectum, I lost myself in my debauchery as he gasped with pleasure. I couldn't help myself as I licked and sucked. This is what Crystal would have done, I mused, moving back and gazing longingly at his open hole.

'This is what I want to do,' I whispered huskily, pushing a finger deep into the heat of his anal canal. He writhed and quivered as I massaged the greasy inner flesh of his tight tube. In my wickedness, I'd have loved to guide a stiff penis into Mog's tight bum. I doubted that he'd enjoy the

185

experience, but I'd have loved to watch him getting arse-fucked. He hadn't been subjected to my carrots, I reflected, wondering at his reaction to such a debased act. Would that be punishment enough for his crime of attempted black-mail?

'Let the punishment begin,' I murmured involuntarily.

'The what?' he breathed as I slipped my finger out of his tight anal channel.

'Crystal . . .' I began. 'I want to tie you up, Mog.'

'Tie me up?' he echoed, turning to face me.

'You've heard of bondage, haven't you?'

'Yes, but . . . It's the woman who gets tied up, isn't it?'

'Not necessarily.'

'I don't want to be tied up,' he murmured.

'Oh, come on,' I smiled, stroking his heaving balls. 'I want you all trussed up, Mog. I want to suck the sperm from your beautiful knob. I'll lick your balls and your bum. I'll wank you, rub my cunt all over you and then fuck you. Wait there. I won't be a minute.'

Grabbing the lengths of washing line from the kitchen cupboard, I suddenly wondered what I was doing. This was madness, I reflected, running the line through my fingers and thinking about thrashing Mog's naked buttocks. After the session of depraved sex with Jackie and her friends, I was now going to use and abuse a young lad. Gazing out of the kitchen window, I saw the girl's face peering out of the bushes. 'Jesus,' I breathed, wondering how the hell she'd got into the garden. There was something weird going on, I knew as I watched the girl retreat into the bushes.

'Hurry up,' Mog called from the lounge. Opening the back door, I wandered down the garden and gazed into the bushes. The girl wasn't human, I knew as I looked at the gate. I'd not made a professional job of nailing it shut, but there was no way she could have opened it. Reckoning that Crystal Marshall was dead, I returned to the house. This was eerie, I thought, closing the back door. And probably dangerous.

'You'd better go,' I said, returning to the lounge.

'Go?' Mog frowned, gazing at the lengths of washing line dangling from my hands.

'I can't explain, Mog.'

'I don't want to go, Jade. I've come here for sex, and that's what I'm going to get.'

'All right,' I grinned. 'Lie on the floor, on your back, and I'll give you sex.'

His face beaming, he lay on the floor with his erect penis pointing to the ceiling. He wanted sex, and he was going to get it, I mused, going about my job of bondage. There was a scene in my book that I'd been thinking about for some time. A young man trussed up and abused by his girlfriend. But things had gone too far and the girl . . . I didn't know where my ideas were coming from as I gazed at Mog's erect penis. Taking an elastic band from the bureau, I settled by his side and pulled his scrotum away from his body.

'What are you doing?' he asked, raising his head. Ignoring him, I slipped the rubber band over his balls. 'Jade, what—'

'That's not too tight, is it?' I asked, the band now around the neck of his scrotum.

'No, but . . .'

'Your balls look nice like that, Mog. Your scrotum's tight, outlining your sperm eggs beautifully.' Where were my words coming from? I pondered. Sperm eggs? 'And now I'll show you what I enjoy doing to men's bottoms.'

Racing into the kitchen, I grabbed the biggest carrot I could find. My juices of arousal seeping between the hairless

187

lips of my vagina, I desperately needed Mog's cock fucking my tight cunt, spunking my cervix. But I had to prepare him before allowing myself the pleasure. Returning to the lounge, I sat between his thighs and parted the firm moons of his arse cheeks.

'You'll like this,' I grinned, forcing the thin end of the carrot past his anal sphincter muscles as he tensed his buttocks.

'Jade, I don't want . . .'

'Be quiet, Mog. Unless you want me to gag you.'

'Gag me? I thought we were going to have sex, not—'

'One more word, and I'll gag you.'

Easing the carrot deep into Mog's anal canal, I watched his brown ring gradually stretching wider. His balls hugged by his tight scrotum, his anal inlet dilated, I pushed the carrot fully home and pulled his foreskin back. His purple globe inviting my wet mouth, my tongue, I wondered how many times he'd be able to come. Two, three? He remained silent as I slowly wanked his solid cock, rolling the loose flesh of his foreskin back and forth over his glistening knob. I could see his anal sphincter muscles spasming as his cock twitched. Gripping the carrot, his bottom-hole would be sending amazing sensations through his young body

As the phone rang, I released Mog's rock-hard cock and leaped to my feet. I thought I'd better answer it in case it was Jackie wanting to come round. She'd have loved Mog's young body, but I had no intention of sharing him. Or it might have been Alan the ex wanting a blow job.

'Hi,' Jackie said. 'Guess what?'

'I haven't got time to guess, Jackie,' I returned.

'Crystal Marshall is alive.'

'Really?'

'It seems that she'd had a row with her mother on the

phone and then wrecked her room before running off. Anyway, I thought I'd let you know that she's OK.'

'Yes, I'm glad you did,' I murmured pensively.

'I'll come round, OK?'

'Yes, OK,' I replied without thinking.

Replacing the receiver, I thought about the girl in the bushes and the heroine in my book. If Crystal Marshall was alive, then . . . then what? Had my imagination been running away with me? Perhaps it was coincidence that I'd called my character Crystal. And the girl in the bushes was probably . . . I didn't know what or who she was. Now that I knew that it wasn't the ghost of Crystal Marshall haunting me, I felt relieved but more confused.

'Jade, what's happening?' Mog asked.

'Nothing. Right, where was I? How does your bum feel?'

'It's . . . I don't know, really. It's nice.'

'Good. So you'd like me to wank your cock and bring your spunk out?'

'Yes, I really need to come. I think it's the carrot. It's making me feel like coming.'

Settling by his side, I grabbed his penis and wanked him as fast as I could. My idea was to bring out his spunk and then restiffen his cock. Once he'd shot his first load, he'd be able to maintain an erection for quite some time. He'd come again, of course, but it would take him that much longer, giving me more time to enjoy his young cock. Watching the eye of his knob appear and disappear as I moved his foreskin up and down, I couldn't wait to watch his spunk jet out and run down my hand. His tight balls jerking, he gasped as I moved my hand up and down his solid cock and thrust the carrot in and out of his tight rectum. His naked body becoming rigid, the white liquid shot out of his knob, jetting at least a foot above his body before raining down over his stomach.

'Keep coming,' I ordered Mog, wanking him even faster. His spunk flying through the air, his foreskin squelching with spunk, I didn't stop until the flow of sperm had ceased and he seemed to be in pain. 'You needed that, didn't you?' I asked, lapping up the sperm running over the taut bag of his balls. Licking his shaft clean, I moved up to his stomach and sucked up the little pools of spunk. Finally cleansing his purple knob, I licked my hand and grinned at him.

'You're going to come again now,' I said. His flaccid penis snaking over his balls, I took my wooden ruler from the bureau and settled between his thighs. 'I said, you're going to come again now,' I snapped, slapping his wet cock with the ruler. 'Be quiet!' I hissed as he protested. 'I want you to come again, so stiffen your cock immediately.' He looked at me with fear mirrored in his wide eyes as I grabbed the end of the carrot and pistoned his rectal cylinder.

'Let me go, Jade,' he said shakily. 'Please, let me—'

'What was that girl doing hiding in the bushes?' I asked, slapping his limp penis again.

'What girl?'

'The one . . . You know what I'm talking about. What was the plan?'

'There was no—'

'Right, you'll be severely punished for lying.'

Try as he might, he could not escape his bonds as I repeatedly slapped his penis with the wooden ruler. To my surprise, his cock began to stiffen as I continued the spanking. Finally becoming fully erect, I realized that the so-called punishment was bringing Mog immense pleasure. Slapping the crimsoned flesh of his solid penis harder, I was amazed as he began to gasp with arousal. Would he come? I wondered, flailing his cock even harder as his purple knob ballooned and his balls heaved within their taut bag.

'That's amazing,' he breathed, his cock twitching as the ruler repeatedly struck its solid shaft. Praying for him to come, I knew that this would make an ideal scene for my book. *Talk about truth being stranger than fiction*, I mused, beating his cock harder. I'd never have dreamed that I could make a man come by thrashing his cock. *Perhaps I should spank my clitoris*, I thought as Mog let out long moans of male pleasure.

'Come,' I urged him, desperate to see his spunk shoot out of his swollen knob. Again and again I struck his rock-hard cock with the ruler, the slaps resounding around the room as my juices of desire gushed out of my burning cunt and drenched my inner thighs. 'Come,' I said. 'I want your spunk.' I didn't think he'd be able to make it as I continued to spank his solid penis. As I was about to halt the thrashing and wank the spunk out of his cock, he cried out in his ecstasy as a long thread of sperm left his knob-slit.

'Yes!' I cried excitedly, thrashing his cock harder and faster as he pumped out his sperm. Lost in my sexual delirium, I continued the merciless beating until the front doorbell rang. Mog's stomach was covered in sperm, the white liquid running in rivers down his sides and pooling on the carpet, and I wondered what the hell Jackie would think of me as I leaped to my feet. Mog was in no fit state to realize that we had a visitor. His head lolling from side to side, his eyes rolling, he was oblivious to his surroundings.

'Come in,' I smiled, opening the door to Jackie. 'Come and see what I've got in the lounge.'

'You haven't got Alan tied up again, have you?' she giggled.

'No,' I replied, leading her into the room. 'But I do have a fine young specimen for you to play with.'

'Jade!' she gasped, her wide eyes gazing at Mog's scarlet penis. 'What the hell have you done to him?'

'Thrashed the spunk out of his cock,' I grinned. 'Take your clothes off and—'

'No, I'm not staying,' she said, much to my surprise. 'I don't want to be a part of this.'

'Of what?' I asked, somewhat perplexed by her attitude. 'I thought you were into cock-sharing.'

'Come with me,' she said, pulling on my arm and leading me out of the room as Mog, bleary and confused after his orgasms, asked what was going on.

In the kitchen, Jackie shook her head despondently as she paced the floor. I really couldn't think what her problem was. OK, so Mog might not have been very old, but he was certainly old enough to have sex. Sixteen? I pondered. He was at least sixteen, I thought. Perhaps she'd not liked the idea of thrashing his cock with the ruler. There again, with the things that went on at her sex parties, I couldn't imagine why she wouldn't want to share Mog with me. Was it the carrot I'd stuffed up his bottom or the elastic band I'd placed around his balls? Unless it was just *me* that worried her, the changes in me.

'You know who he is, don't you?' she whispered, closing the kitchen door.

'No, I don't,' I replied. 'His nickname's Mog, but—'

'He is Jeremy Brentwhistle.'

'Who?'

'Have you not heard of Jonathan Brentwhistle?'

'The name rings a bell, but . . .'

'The MP?'

'Oh, right. But—'

'Jade, that's his son you have tied up on your lounge floor.'

'Oh, shit,' I gasped.

'Exactly. If your publisher or agent or whoever finds out that you've been—'

'That explains the girl,' I murmured.

'Girl?'

'Never mind. I'd better get rid of him. You wait here.'

'If this got into the papers, you'd be finished.'

'Yes, I realize that.'

'I'm going. You get rid of him and I'll see you in the pub this evening.'

'Yes, all right. I'll be there.'

'Right. I'll see you later.'

As she left, I realized what the lad's game was. The girl in the bushes had probably had a camera and would threaten to expose us. Mog would reveal his true identity and tell me to pay the girl otherwise his father would find out and I'd be in the papers, accused of God knows what. They'd probably only have asked for a thousand or two. I'd have found the money somehow, borrowed it or whatever, to keep the girl quiet. Mog would pretend to be as worried as I was, of course. He'd say that his father would have me locked up for seducing his 'under-age' son and my only choice would be to pay the girl off. *What a little bastard*, I mused, returning to the lounge.

'There's been a development,' I said, sitting on the floor beside him. 'It seems that someone has taken photographs of us together in the woods.'

'No, she . . .' he began. 'No one knew we were there.'

'*Someone* did, Mog. I've just been shown a photograph. I really don't think your father will be very impressed to hear that you've been boozing in pubs and screwing girls in the park. So, you'd better get out of here before—'

'It wasn't meant to be like this,' he said, pulling at his bonds.

'Wasn't it? You'd better tell me exactly what's going on.'

'All right, all right,' he finally breathed. 'I'll tell you everything.'

It transpired that Mog's accomplice in the bushes was Libby, his girlfriend. Their plan had been just as I'd expected. But what I hadn't realized was that they'd actually targeted me. Mog hadn't simply been strolling in the park. He'd seen me several times and thought I looked gullible, which I was. He'd followed me to the park and chatted me up. Like a fool, I'd fallen for it.

'I'm sorry,' he said when he'd finished his confession.

'So am I, Mog. We could have had a good thing going, but now. . .'

'We still can,' he said enthusiastically. 'I really like you, Jade.'

'So much that you were going to blackmail me?'

'No . . . well, I suppose so.'

'You have a girlfriend, Mog. Go back to her and, when you've grown up, come and see me.'

'I want to see you now,' he sighed. 'I *have* grown up, believe me.'

'What, in the space of a few seconds?'

'Yes.'

Taking his flaccid penis in my hand, I slowly wanked him. Would he come again? I wondered, gazing at the crimsoned shaft of his young cock as it swelled and hardened. Grown up? I wondered. He should have been with a girl of his own age, not a nymphomaniac in her early twenties who was bent on crude sex. His cock fully erect, Mog began breathing heavily as I moved my hand up and down his shaft faster. Youthful as he was, he could come again and again, I reflected. It would be a shame to send such a fine young man packing. But I had to, didn't I? I didn't dare see him again.

'Coming,' he gasped, his white spunk jetting from his purple knob and landing on my hand. Spurt after spurt flying through the air, splattering his stomach as I wanked him, I leaned over and sucked his orgasming knob into my thirsty mouth. Drinking from his fountainhead, swallowing his copious flow of sperm, I continued to wank his twitching shaft as he gasped and writhed in his male pleasure. No, I couldn't send him packing, never to see him again.

Lapping up the sperm from the firm plateau of Mog's stomach, licking his young balls clean, I finally released his naked body and ordered him to dress. I'd used and abused him, thrashed his penis to orgasm, taught him things that he was too young to know about. Perhaps *I* was too young to know? I mused as he finished dressing and looked at me with anticipation reflected in his wide eyes. Moving to the door, he turned and opened his mouth as if about to speak.

'Mog,' I smiled. 'Tomorrow night about eight. I'll be here waiting for you.' Beaming, he walked through the hall. Hearing the front door close, I shook my head despairingly. *Another huge mistake*, I reflected. Would I never learn? Gathering up the evidence of sexual debauchery, I climbed the stairs to the bathroom. I was hooked on Mog, I knew. But it was only cold lust, wasn't it? Raw sex.

Chapter Eleven

I went to the pub that evening and waited an hour for Jackie to arrive. I didn't mind sitting alone as it gave me time to think. Alan the ex, musician Alan, Mog, lesbian sex with Jackie, taking part in her orgy . . . I realized what a mess my life was in. I didn't know what I'd been trying to do, apart from gain sexual experience to help me write the book. And to top it all, I'd come close to being blackmailed.

A new start was what I needed. Hadn't I thought that before? How was I going to start afresh? I'd have to move to another town well away from Mog and the two Alans. Jenny Hardbooke's husband had screwed me, I'd been screwing a young lad in the park . . . I didn't want to be in the same town as the Hardbrookes, the Alans or anyone else. I'd tell Jackie that I was thinking of moving.

'You took your time,' I said as she arrived and sat down opposite me.

'I was held up,' she breathed. 'Have you been here long?'

'About an hour,' I sighed. 'Jackie, I've got to change my way of life.'

'Why?' she asked, hooking her long black hair behind her ears. 'Apart from getting mixed up with that boy, you've been having a bloody good time recently.'

'A good time? I don't think it can be described as a good time. I've become . . . I don't know what I've become. This isn't me, this isn't the way I am.'

'This *is* the way you are, Jade. You've changed and now you're different.'

'The old me is still there, somewhere inside my head. Yes, I have changed. But I've changed into something I'm not. Do you understand what I mean?'

'You enjoyed the sex, didn't you?'

'Yes, I can't deny that. But the point is . . . It's just not me, Jackie. To me, sex should be something between two people who are in love.'

'I don't know how you can say that after pissing on Alan's face,' she giggled. 'I can see that you're going to harp on about this for hours, so I'm going to get a drink. Want one?'

'Yes, thanks.'

I was sure that she knew what I was talking about. Most people pretend to be something they're not at times, and some do it all the time. Admittedly, it had become quite easy for me to strip off and enjoy debauched sex, almost second nature. But it wasn't the real me. *You are what you think you are*, Alan the musician had said. What did I think I was? I thought I was a whore. I didn't want to bore Jackie by going on about it and decided to change the subject.

'I'll tell you what I think,' she said as she placed my drink on the table and sat down. 'I think that you should stand back and evaluate the situation. Take a look at yourself from the outside. I know it's not easy, but try to look at yourself from a different angle. I think you'll find that the real you, as you put it, is someone who enjoys sex.'

'Of course I enjoy sex, but not with lots of different people.'

'Why not? I know that you'll say that I'm being shallow or whatever, but what's wrong in having two or more relationships on the go?'

'To be honest, Jackie, I don't think there's anything *wrong* with it. It's just not the way *I* want to be.'

'Ah,' she grinned triumphantly. 'You're now saying that it's not the way you *want* to be. But it's the way you *are* and you can't deny that. Look what you were doing to that lad. For God's sake, you've been having tremendous sex with several different people.'

'Yes, but—'

'There are no buts, Jade. I'm going to the loo. If you're chatted up by anyone while I'm gone, ask if they have a friend and also ask whether or not they fuck rotten.'

'Jackie!'

'See you in a minute.'

Shaking my head as she left the table, I had to laugh. She was so . . . I didn't know what. So normal and down to earth, I suppose. But I was more confused than ever. I'd thought that the old me was the real me, and now I wondered whether the new me was the real me. It was best to allow life to carry me in whichever direction it did and see where I ended up. If I felt like sex, then I'd have sex. If I felt like licking Jackie's pussy, then I would. *But it's not right*, I mused. 'For God's sake, forget about right and wrong,' I breathed, watching a young man wander up to the bar.

It was Mog. 'Shit, that's all I need,' I whispered as he looked around the pub. He didn't notice me, thankfully, and I hoped he wouldn't. I reckoned that he was right. One can grow up in the space of a few seconds. Grow up? No, just become wiser. He'd probably become wiser. After his ridiculous blackmail attempt, he'd learned his lesson. I must admit that thrashing his penis to orgasm had really turned me on. I wanted to see him again, but . . . It would only lead to illicit sex and I'd behave uncharacteristically and . . .

Uncharacteristically? *You are what you think you are.* I wanted crude sex with Mog, so what did that make me?

'Bloody hell,' Jackie murmured as she returned. 'I just had a call on my mobile. Guess who's going to join us this evening?'

'I don't know,' I sighed. 'And I don't think I *want* to know. In fact, I don't want to stay here.'

'Why not?'

'Because I've just come to a decision.'

'Oh?'

'I've decided that, from now on, I'm going to do what the bloody hell I want to do. I'm fed up with people telling me that I should do this or that. One thing that really bugs me is when someone says, *you know what you want to do?* In other words, I'm telling you what you want to do.'

'Jade, what the fuck are you talking about?'

'I'm talking about me, as a person, an individual with thoughts of my own.'

'Oh, right. Anyway, your ex-Alan is on his way here. He got my mobile number from my mum and . . . he's on his way.'

'Good,' I grinned. 'I could do with some fun. By the way, I didn't mean you.'

'What?'

'When I said that I'm fed up with people telling me that I should do this or that. I didn't mean you. Actually, I *did* mean you. Fuck it. I *did* mean you, Jackie.'

'Oh, thanks.'

'For fuck's sake, what's the fucking matter with the world?'

'How many have you had?'

'Nowhere near enough. Mog's over there. Go and tell him to join us.'

'Jade, Alan's on his way and I really don't think he—'

'Tell Mog to bring me a drink.'

'No, Jade. I'm not getting involved with him.'

I really didn't know what I was doing, what I was thinking. What the hell did Alan want? And why had Jackie told him where we were? I should have been hammering the keyboard in my den, not sitting in the bloody pub wasting my time and money. Money? That was a joke. I was just about penniless. I desperately needed the advance for the book. I'd have to ring David, I thought, gazing at Mog and wondering again what I was doing.

'What with Mog over there and Alan on his way, I'm leaving,' I said as Jackie sipped her drink.

'Leaving?' she frowned. 'I thought you wanted to have some fun with Alan?'

'I did, but . . . Oh, I don't know. What's the point?'

'We'll see what he wants and take it from there.'

'He wants me to take him back, Jackie. He's been on about us getting back together, trying again and—'

'And allowing me to suck him off. He's OK for a fuck, but nothing more.'

'You have a wonderful way with words.'

'If I were you, I'd tell him to bog off.'

'Bog off? You are funny,' I smiled. 'OK, I'll tell him to bog off.'

Alan finally arrived and sat next to me. He made several odd facial expressions at Jackie, indicating that he wanted to be alone with me. Jackie, in her wisdom, stayed put. Mog remained oblivious to me as he leaned on the bar, knocking back several beers, and Jackie began chatting about the party she'd had and how much I'd enjoyed myself.

'Alan doesn't want to hear about the party,' I interrupted her when she began talking about sex.

'Jade,' Alan smiled, sipping his beer. 'I've been thinking.'

'So have I,' Jackie grinned. 'Thinking that we should go on to a nightclub.'

'That's a good idea,' I said, just to annoy Alan.

'Jade, I need to talk to you,' Alan sighed, obviously pissed off with Jackie.

'What about?' I asked.

'In private.'

'Whatever you have to say, you can say it here.'

'All right. Crystal wants to talk to you.'

'Crystal?'

'Crystal Marshall.'

'To *me*? But why? She doesn't know me.'

'She rang me earlier. She didn't say what it was about, but she wants to talk to you.'

'OK,' I said, catching Jackie's frowning gaze. 'When and where?'

'She wants you to go to her place. I have the number here – give her a ring.'

'Thanks, I will,' I murmured, taking the piece of paper.

'Here,' Jackie smiled, offering me her mobile phone.

Leaving the pub, I sat on a wall and dialled the number. The rough bricks biting into my naked buttocks as I waited for Crystal to answer, I wondered what on earth she wanted. Alan might have said something about me, but why would she want to see *me*? Perhaps she wanted to talk about writing. She'd obviously heard something about me.

'Hallo,' a soft voice finally answered.

'Crystal, this is Jade. Alan asked me to—'

'Oh, yes. How are you?'

'Intrigued, to say the least. I remember you from school but we didn't know each other.'

'Jade, I need to see you,' she said with an urgency that I found worrying. 'Can you come to my place?'

'What, now?'

'Yes.'

'No, not really. I'm in the pub. I've had a few drinks so I can't drive.'

'OK, I'll come to your place. It's extremely important, Jade.'

'All right. Say, half an hour?'

'I'll be there. Alan told me the address.'

'Did he now?'

'I hope you don't mind.'

'No, of course not. I'll see you soon.'

I had the feeling that I was about to discover something that would shock me. The girl in the bushes, the character in my book, and now Crystal Marshall ringing me? The jigsaw puzzle was about to be completed, I was sure as I entered the pub. Giving Jackie back her phone, I made my excuses and moved to the door. Alan looked somewhat perplexed, as did Jackie, but I didn't have the time to explain.

Walking home, I had a feeling of déjà vu. I was on my way to meet someone, a young woman. She was going to tell me something that would frighten me. I was being silly, I tried to convince myself as I reached my flat. A thousand questions thronging my mind, I paced the lounge floor. Suddenly realizing that I was wearing a very short dress and no panties, I was about to go and change when the bell rang.

'Crystal?' I asked, opening the door to a tall slim girl.

'Yes,' she smiled. 'I'm pleased to meet you, Jade.'

'So, what's all this about?' I frowned, showing her into the lounge.

'Where to begin?' she sighed, seating herself in the arm-chair. 'Where to begin?'

Tossing her long golden locks over her shoulder, she smiled at me. She was extremely attractive. Far removed from the lanky little girl I remembered from school. Her make-up was impeccable, as was her long blonde hair. She didn't look as if she'd been on the run, I mused, eyeing her naked thighs.

'Alan told me that you're a writer,' she said as I sat on the sofa and tried to push thoughts of lesbian sex out of my mind.

'Well, I've only just started,' I replied, eyeing her small breasts clearly defined by her tight blue dress. 'I was a journalist for many years and I'm now trying to get into fiction. Why are you here, Crystal?'

'Because . . . Initially, I didn't take a great deal of notice when Alan said that you write.'

'Why was he talking about me in the first place?'

'We were discussing relationships. Anyway, when he said that you write erotic fiction, I became interested. I've been writing erotica for some time now and—'

'You write filth? I mean, erotica?'

'Yes, I do. This is so complicated that I don't know where to start. Alan said that you'd changed.'

'What did he say, exactly?' I asked accusingly. 'I hope he hasn't been—'

'Don't get me wrong, Jade. All he said was that you were doing things he'd never thought you'd do. Don't worry, he didn't go into any details.'

'But I still don't know why you're here.'

'I've come to see you because I've changed too. While I was away . . . I'll explain why I ran off later. While I was away, I had several sexual relationships and . . . To be honest, I did things that were downright disgusting.'

'Something's been happening to me, too,' I said, wondering what the hell was going on. 'I'm halfway through my book and the strange thing is, I've set my story in a cottage with a laburnum tree and a well in the front garden. *Your* cottage, *your* garden.'

'God,' she breathed.

'This is really uncanny. I've named my character *Crystal.*'

'I . . .' She turned pale, her hands visibly trembling. 'Tell me about your book.'

Relating the story of Crystal and her exploits, I wondered whether to go back to the pub and forget all this business. It was bad enough to think that I'd changed so dramatically. Add to that the fact that Crystal Marshall had not only made contact but was sitting in my lounge, I'd just about had enough. I rambled on for another ten minutes or so, wondering why I was wasting my time, and then decided that she'd heard sufficient.

'I believe I know what's happening,' she said mysteriously. 'This is going to sound crazy, I know. But I firmly believe that your writing is influencing me.'

'That's ridiculous,' I returned. 'OK, so I've used the name Crystal for my heroine. But that's purely coincidence.'

'The cottage, the tree, the well . . .'

'Yes, but—'

'Jade, listening to your story was like listening to someone telling me about the things I've been doing lately. All that you've written has happened to me.'

'*What?* Even the part about the girl enduring an anal fisting?'

'Even that.'

'So you're saying that whatever I write happens to you?'

'Yes.'

'I don't like this,' I murmured, the hairs on the back of my neck standing up. 'I don't like this at all.'

205

I wanted to mention the girl in the bushes, but didn't dare in case Crystal had seen a similar girl. But the idea was crazy. I was becoming annoyed, not only with Crystal and with Alan for getting me involved with her, but annoyed with myself. The situation was ludicrous. The way my life was going was ludicrous. As Crystal spoke of the things that had happened to her of late, I began to wonder whether she was lying. Alan was the only link between us, I reflected. He must have been up to something, trying to cause trouble or, knowing him, trying to get inside Crystal's knickers.

'Is there anything between you and Alan?' I interrupted her as she rambled on about the crude sex she'd endured.

'No, nothing. Initially, he wanted more than friendship but . . .'

'He would,' I laughed. 'He chases anything in a skirt.'

'He doesn't chase me, Jade,' she smiled. 'He's not had thoughts like that about me since I told him that I'm a lesbian.'

'You're a . . .' I gasped.

'Are you OK with that?'

'Yes, of course. But the girl in my book—'

'That's what worries me. I told you that I've changed. There's been a major change in me recently. I've always been a lesbian, Jade. That's why my parents dumped me on my aunt when I was twelve years old. They knew then what I was and they couldn't handle it. Recently, and for the first time in my life, I've been going with men. I have no idea why because . . .'

'Apparently, you have a lot of male visitors. I heard that . . .'

'Yes, I've heard the rumours, too. I'm not a prostitute. I write erotic fiction to order. I have several clients who call at the cottage to collect their stories. The money helps.'

'Yes, I suppose it does,' I murmured.

Feeling more confused than ever, I didn't know what to think. I felt as if I was going mad as I gazed at Crystal's long legs, her naked thighs. A lesbian? The way she'd changed, the way I'd changed . . . Was my book really influencing her? What if I killed my character Crystal off, had her jump over a cliff or something? I dreaded to think of the consequences. Deciding to prove this one way or the other, I asked the real Crystal whether she'd been with a young girl who had tied her down to a bed and shaved her. It hadn't happened in the book, so . . .

'No, I haven't,' she frowned. 'Is that what happens in your book?'

'Yes,' I smiled.

Suddenly wondering whether she was lying, I thought that she might be in this with Alan. He'd probably told her about me, the terrible things I did to him. Between them, they might have decided to play games with me. Crystal pretending to have changed, making out that what I'd written had happened to her . . . But how would they have known what I'd written? Alan might have seen my book, I reflected. If he still had a key to my flat . . . It would have been easy enough to bring my book up on the computer. All he had to do was take a few notes and . . . But why would be bother?

'The other day, I wrote about Crystal visiting a girl who'd shaved her pubic hair off,' I said, watching for her reaction.

'I haven't visited anyone recently,' she murmured pensively.

'I didn't tell you about Crystal's long-term relationship, did I? She's been seeing a man for some time,' I lied. 'It starts in the first chapter. They have sex, but only in shop doorways. It's a thing Crystal has. A sort of fetish.'

'No, that hasn't happened to me either,' she murmured.

'I don't believe that my book is influencing you,' I giggled. 'There are one or two coincidences, but that's all.'

'All the other things you told me have happened to me, Jade,' she persisted. 'Did your Crystal go to a wine bar and meet a man?' she asked.

'Er . . . no,' I lied, my heart racing as her words assaulted my mind.

'I went to a wine bar and met a man and . . . Terrible though it sounds, we had sex up against the bar.'

That's exactly what *my* Crystal had done. Trying to conceal my shock, I offered her a cup of coffee and left the room. She'd either seen my book or . . . or she was being influenced by what I'd written. I recalled watching some film or other with a similar storyline. But things like that only happened in the movies. There was one way to discover the truth. Write a sex scene and see whether the same thing happened to Crystal Marshall. My thinking was crazy, I knew as I poured the coffee. She must have known about my book. Alan must have seen it and told her. He'd been into my den and read the manuscript. But why? What was their plan? Why pretend that my writing was influencing her?

'There we are,' I smiled, placing the coffee on the table. 'As I was saying, the whole thing is nothing more than coincidence.'

'No, it's not,' she murmured, locking her sky-blue gaze to mine.

'If it isn't, and you really are being influenced by my character, then you have quite a shock coming,' I laughed.

'What do you mean?'

'I finished another chapter this afternoon. Crystal is kidnapped.'

'No,' she gasped, feigning shock quite well. 'Jade, you must change it.'

'Don't be silly,' I grinned. 'My Crystal doesn't look like you, she hasn't had sex in a wine bar, and she doesn't have pubic hair. She shaves regularly and—'

'So do I,' she said, holding her hand to her mouth.

'I don't believe you,' I returned. 'You're making this up as you go along.'

'I am *not*,' she snapped, rising to her feet and pulling her dress up. Standing before me, she tugged her blue panties down. 'Look.'

Gazing in disbelief at her hairless vaginal crack, I really didn't know what to think. My Crystal *did* shave regularly. It had been an idea I'd had when I'd started the book. Staring at the swell of Crystal's smooth outer lips, the pinken wings of her inner lips protruding invitingly from her valley of desire, I licked my lips. She *was* being influenced – but how? Perhaps there *was* a ghost or whatever at work. No, of course not, I reflected. This was Alan's doing. He'd told me to call Crystal, given me her phone number . . . He was up to something, and I was determined to discover what it was.

'All I can say is that's coincidence,' I said, smiling at her as she tugged her panties up and adjusted her dress. 'As it happens, I shave regularly. A lot of women do.'

'I'm not convinced,' she sighed.

'You know what happens next in the book, don't you?' I asked as she paced the floor.

'What?' she breathed, her face turning pale.

'If you're right and my writing is affecting you . . . After Crystal is kidnapped by two men, she's taken abroad where she's sold as a sex slave.'

'No,' she cried, moving to the door.

'Sit down,' I ordered her. 'I was only joking.'

'For God's sake, Jade. Don't do that to me.'

As she flopped into the armchair, I began to wonder whether she was telling the truth. She seemed genuinely frightened but . . . She was lying, she had to be. This was some daft plan of Alan's to . . . to whatever. Perhaps he was behind her running away, I reflected. Why wreck her room and then run off like that? She must have known that the police were looking for her. And Alan hadn't seemed too bothered when she'd gone missing. Whatever was going on, Alan the ex was behind it.

'Why did you run off?' I asked.

'Because I'd been feeling down. Money was tight, I found out that my long-term girlfriend was two-timing me, I'd rowed with my mother on the phone . . . I wrecked my room and then went off. It was stupid, I know. But I needed time and space to think. I didn't realize that the police were concerned. Anyway, that's all OK now. I'd better be going.'

'Crystal,' I murmured. 'I'm also a lesbian.'

'Are you?' She frowned.

'Yes.'

'But Alan said that you were with him for . . .'

'Alan left me because . . . He discovered that I had lesbian tendencies and he left me. Would you like to stay for a while longer?'

'Yes, yes, I would,' she beamed. 'This isn't in your book, is it? Crystal and an authoress . . .'

'No, it's not.'

I noted that she'd suddenly lost her fearful look. In fact, she seemed to be positively glowing with enthusiasm, which I found odd since she'd been terrified only minutes previously. Whatever was going on, I'd find out eventually, I knew as she crossed the room and sat beside me on the sofa.

I wasn't bothered about Alan and whatever he had planned. And I didn't really care about Crystal. All I wanted was sex with the girl. After that, she could go and rot in hell.

That wasn't the real me thinking, I reflected fearfully. Go and rot in hell? I'd never thought such a thing about anyone. Eyeing the girl's naked thigh as her dress rode up, I felt that I was succumbing to a goading inner voice. I thought that I was going mad as I placed my hand on her thigh. I'd wanted to be like the Crystal in my book, and now I was about to have sex with Crystal Marshall. Leaping up, I walked to the window and took a deep breath.

'Are you all right?' she asked, her blue eyes frowning.

'Yes, yes,' I replied, forcing a smile. 'It's just that I have one or two things on my mind.'

'Come back here and I'll relax you,' she whispered huskily.

'Crystal, I . . .'

Crossing the room, she kneeled at my feet and lifted my dress. I could feel her warm breath on my hairless vulval flesh, the tip of her wet tongue tracing the contours of my swollen outer lips. My legs sagging, I parted my feet, my valley of desire opening to her intimate caress. Lapping at the pink folds of my inner flesh, Crystal breathed heavily as I let out little gasps of pleasure. I was weaker than ever in my lesbian arousal, I knew as my clitoris swelled and pulsated in expectation. My pussy devoid of hair, my vulval flesh was acutely sensitive, the sensations driving me wild as I clung to her head to steady myself.

'Lick my clitoris,' I murmured as my sex budlette emerged from beneath its protective hood as if seeking the caress of her wet tongue. My legs trembling, my knees bent, I hung my head and closed my eyes as she pushed a finger between the dripping inner wings of my vagina and drove it deep into my tightening cunt. 'God,' I breathed as she massaged the creamy-wet walls of my sex sheath. Oblivious to my surroundings, I leaned on her head as she expertly fingered my pussy and sucked and licked my pulsating clitoris. I was going to come in her mouth, I knew as I felt my juices of lesbian lust coursing down my inner thighs. My womb rhythmically contracting, I was almost there.

'Sit on the sofa,' Crystal said, taking my hand and leading me across the room. Reclining, I parted my thighs wide as she settled between my legs and eased open the drenched valley of my vagina. My clitoris fully exposed, swollen in anticipation, I gasped as she sucked the small protuberance into her hot mouth and snaked her wet tongue over its sensitive tip. Two or three fingers driving deep into my spasming cunt, I gyrated my hips, grinding my fiery vulval flesh hard against her wet face as she took me ever closer to the threshold of pure lesbian bliss. Opening my thighs further, giving her better access to my sexual centre, I sang out as the birth of my orgasm erupted within my contracting womb.

'Yes,' I cried, my clitoris exploding in orgasm. The squelching sound of my pistoned vagina filling my mind, I drifted through purple clouds of sexual euphoria as my amazing pleasure rocked my very soul. Shock waves of pure lesbian bliss coursing through my trembling body, I tossed my head from side to side as she expertly sustained my incredible climax with her thrusting finger and sweeping tongue. Mog couldn't have done this, I reflected. Jackie was good, but no one came close to Crystal.

'God,' I gasped involuntarily as she slipped a finger between the globes of my tensed buttocks and massaged the delicate brown tissue surrounding my anal inlet. Her finger driving into my tight duct, waking the nerve endings there, she massaged my inner flesh, bringing me immense pleasure as she continued to finger my cunt and suck my clitoris. I thought I'd never come down from my lesbian heaven as my orgasm peaked. Tremors of crude sex rocking my perspiring body, my stomach rising and falling, I thought Crystal was going to drown as my juices of lesbian lust gushed from my bloated cunt and sprayed her pretty face. Never had I come so much. The cream of my orgasm flowing in torrents from my bloated vagina, I knew that I was flooding the sofa as the squelching grew louder.

Driving a second finger deep into the sheath of my bottom, she double-pistoned my sex-holes and sucked and mouthed on my clitoris until I begged her to stop. My orgasm so intense that I grimaced, I released a flood of girl-come, the lubricious liquid flowing between my naked buttocks, lubricating the anal pistoning. Again, I pleaded with her to stop, but she fingered my holes faster and harder and sucked my pulsating clitoris into her wet mouth until I fell into a state of semi-consciousness.

I could hear her voice calling in the distance, her incoherent words floating about me on the breeze like autumn leaves. Floating, drifting, fluttering unheard. 'Jade,' she said, brushing my golden locks away from my burning face. Opening my eyes, I managed to smile at her as she stroked my cheek. Her face was flushed, wet with my juices of orgasm. She was so pretty, feminine, sensual . . . My sex-sheath spewing out my cream of orgasm as my vaginal muscles spasmed, my clitoris receding beneath its protective hood, I lay quivering on the sofa as Crystal sat beside me.

Stroking my protruding inner lips, she whispered words of lesbian lust in my ear as I slowly returned to my body. She loved me, wanted me, needed me . . . I couldn't think straight as she slipped a finger into the hot sheath of my fiery cunt. My mind still floating, drifting, I said nothing as she nibbled the lobe of my ear. She loved me, wanted me, needed me . . . Did she want me or my body? I wondered as she slipped her wet finger out of my tight cunt and sucked it clean.

'Are you all right?' she asked, driving her finger into my tight cunt again. I nodded as she massaged the creamy-wet walls of my vaginal sheath, inducing my girl-milk to flow. Her finger sliding out of my sex duct and dragging my lubricious juices up my hot valley of desire, she encircled the nubble of my clitoris. I couldn't come again, not yet, I knew as amazing sensations of sex rippled though my quivering womb. I had to rest before enduring another mind-blowing climax.

My clitoris swelling, fluttering beneath Crystal's caressing fingertip, I closed my eyes and parted my thighs. As my pleasure built, I thought about Mog, imagined him watching my lesbian act. His young penis would stiffen as he watched Crystal finger my cunt and massage my clitoris. Would he wank? I wanted him to wank his fresh cock and spurt his spunk over my face. A facial. I wanted to be a cumslut. Perhaps he'd bring his young friends to my flat. They'd stand around me, wanking their hard cocks. Their sperm would gush, jet through the air and splatter my face.

'Come for me,' Crystal murmured, locking her wet mouth to mine. Her tongue seeking mine, she massaged my clitoris faster. My orgasm erupting, my entire body shaking uncontrollably, she kissed me passionately as she took me to my sexual heaven again. On and on the waves of pure sexual bliss transmitted through my quivering pelvis, pulsing within my contracting womb. My orgasmic juices gushing from my open cunt, wetting my inner thighs, running over the inflamed tissue of my bottom-hole, I shuddered and writhed in my coming.

Finally drifting back into my sated body, I lay trembling in Crystal's arms, her finger circling the sensitive tip of my clitoris as I gasped for breath. Kissing me, she rose to her feet and left the room. Had she gone? I wondered. Was she coming back to bring out another orgasm? I wanted her. No, I wanted Mog. Where was Jackie? I was confused in the aftermath of my coming. The front door closed.

Chapter Twelve

For two days I did nothing except write. Ignoring the phone and the doorbell, I felt guilty for neglecting Jackie and Mog, but I had to work on the book. Mog would have wondered where I'd got to and no doubt Crystal had been trying to get hold of me. Jackie had probably realized that I was working and . . . Working? I'd written about Crystal seducing a girl, making love to her, fingering the tight sheath of her young pussy and massaging her clitoris to orgasm. 'Truth stranger than fiction,' I murmured as the phone rang. I glanced up at the clock. Half-past four. I'd finished for the day. I could now communicate with the outside world.

'Jade, it's David.'

'Oh, hi.'

'We're on – the publisher wants the book. I've put some stuff in the post for you. How's it going?'

'Very well,' I replied, wondering when I'd get some money.

'They want another two books.'

'Really?'

'Is that OK? I mean, you *can* write another two, can't you?'

'Of course.'

'Good. They thought the sex was amazing, as did I. Where the hell do you get the ideas from?'

'You've asked me that before,' I giggled.

'When you came to my office, you said that you couldn't write about spanking and anal sex and three men with one girl. You've done a bloody good job of it, I must say. What an imagination you have.'

'Yes, it *is* rather good,' I murmured. *Imagination, my foot.*

'The papers I've sent you. Read through them and get them back to me as soon as you can, OK?'

'OK. David . . .'

'Yes?'

'It doesn't matter.'

'You'll see that I've negotiated a deal. As soon as you've signed and returned the papers, I'll get a cheque to you.'

'Oh, right.'

'Synopses, Jade. I'll need them this week, if that's all right.'

'Yes, no problem.'

'You get back to work, young lady. I'll be in touch.'

'OK. And, thanks.'

Money, I mused happily as I replaced the receiver. *And not before time.* Another two books? I was going to have to get some ideas together. Leaving my den, I wandered out into the back garden and sat on a patio chair. Gazing at the bushes, I thought about my book. I'd written a scene where Crystal struck up a lesbian relationship with an attractive girl. The sex was good, but Crystal wanted more. The scene ended with Crystal naked, her body sexually tortured by her lesbian lover. Now that I'd written the scene, would it happen to Crystal Marshall? I wondered. I doubted it very much. Again wondering why Alan and Crystal were playing games with me, I gave some thought to my next book. 'Ghosts,' I murmured, focusing on the bushes at the end of the garden and wondering where the young girl had got to. But ghosts and sex didn't go together, did they?

The sun warming me, I wondered what to do that evening. The pub might be an idea, I mused. Ring Jackie and suggest having a drink. There again, Alan the ex might turn up, or Mog or . . . Crystal Marshall would be wondering about me. I had to make a decision where she was concerned. Should I embark on a long-term lesbian relationship? I'd had so many sexual relationships recently that I didn't know what I wanted. I'd play it by ear, I decided as the phone rang.

'Where have you been?' Mog asked as I grabbed the kitchen phone.

'Sorry, I had to work,' I replied, my stomach somersaulting as I pictured his young penis, his swollen knob. 'What are you doing this evening?'

'Nothing. Would you like to—'

'Do you have any friends?' I asked, wishing I hadn't.

'Of course I have. Why?'

'I . . . Would you like to bring a couple of friends to my place this evening?' I was going mad, I was sure.

'What for? I mean, I *could* bring some mates round, but . . .'

'For sex,' I breathed, wondering what the hell I was playing at.

'Sex?' he echoed disbelievingly. 'You want sex with me and some of my mates?'

'I'm writing a scene . . .' I began shakily. 'A girl is with these lads and—'

'And you want to try it out?'

'Yes. I mean . . .'

'How many?'

'What?'

'How many mates do you want me to bring?'

'Oh, er . . . Two, three . . . I don't know.'

'I could bring half a dozen if you want.'

'Yes,' I said enthusiastically. 'No . . .'

'I'll see what I can do.'

'Yes, right.'

'Give me an hour, OK?'

'OK.'

Replacing the receiver, my stomach somersaulting, my hands trembling, I wondered what on earth I was doing. Six young lads? 'God,' I breathed, my juices of desire seeping between the hairless lips of my pussy and soaking into my tight panties as I imagined six swollen knobs spunking over my face. Pacing the lounge floor while I waited in anticipation, I wondered what to do, how to begin the evening of debauched sex. Ask the lads to strip? Yes, have them standing naked before me. I'd examine their penises, move along the line and taste each purple knob. My panties dripping with pussy juice, I nervously fiddled with my long blonde hair. I shouldn't have asked Mog to bring his friends, I reflected. The idea was ludicrous. What would they think of me? They'd think me a tart, a cum-slut. That was what I was, though, wasn't I?

'Yes?' I breathed, answering the phone.

'Oh, you're back in the land of the living,' Jackie sighed. 'I do wish you'd let me know when you're going on a writing bender.'

'Sorry,' I interrupted her. 'I should have phoned you.'

'How's it going?'

'Very well.'

'What did Crystal Marshall want? Did you see her?'

'Yes, yes. She . . . she just wanted to chat about writing.'

'It's funny, her running off and the police thinking she'd been murdered. Anyway, what are you up to this evening?'

'Er . . . Working,' I lied. 'I really must catch up with my work. Tomorrow, I'll see you tomorrow.'

'OK, I'll ring you in the morning. Are you all right, Jade? You sound nervous.'

'I'm fine. Give me a call in the morning.'

'Right. Don't work too hard. All work and no play . . .'

'No, I won't.'

The doorbell rang and my heart leaped into my mouth. I couldn't go ahead with this, I was sure as I walked through the hall. How many lads had Mog rounded up? What were they expecting? They'd all know where I lived and word would get round that I was an easy lay, a slut. But this was research, wasn't it? Who was I trying to fool? I wondered. Research? It was crude gratuitous sex, raw sex. Taking a deep breath, I finally opened the door.

'Hi,' Mog smiled.

'Hi,' I breathed, counting the lads standing behind him. Six, including Mog. 'Er . . . You'd better come in.' As they filed into the hall, I told them to go into the lounge. 'If you'd all strip off,' I said, following them into the room.

'Jade . . .' Mog began.

'I'll be with you in a minute,' I smiled, moving to the door. 'I want you completely naked. All of you, completely naked. All right?'

'OK,' Mog smiled. 'If you're sure this is what you want.'

'Oh, I'm sure,' I chuckled, leaving the room.

Standing in the kitchen, I leaned on the worktop to steady my trembling body. *Was* I sure? Far from it, I reflected, my stomach somersaulting again. I could hear the low murmurs of their voices and movements as they undressed. They'd be talking about me, asking Mog where he'd found the slag, where he'd picked the slut up. Never in a million years would I have dreamed that I'd be in this situation. Six young lads standing naked in my lounge, all expecting to have crude sex with me? What the hell had I done to my life? I wondered anxiously. David had started all this with his talk of erotic fiction. Or had it been Jackie revealing her sordid lesbian past? If she knew what I was doing . . . Perhaps I should have invited her, I reflected. She'd have loved to play with six young cocks. No, they were my boys, all mine.

Should I strip off? I wondered. No, get the boys to strip me. They'd like that, removing my clothes and gazing at my breasts, my hairless cunt. What would they think? It didn't matter what they thought. They were here for sex, nothing more, nothing less. What they thought of me was irrelevant. I was ready, I was sure as I stood in the hall and flattened my dress with my palms. The stage was set, and I was ready to make my entrance. Ready to seduce six young men. Were they stiff? I wondered. Were they virgins?

'Right,' I smiled, entering the room. They were standing in a row by the fireplace, their penises stiffening, their balls heavy and full. So young and fresh, I thought, sitting on the sofa and looking at their firm stomachs. Eyeing each cock in turn, I licked my lips. Had they pushed their hard cocks into girls' pussies? I wondered. Had they ever been sucked to orgasm? My panties soaking up my flowing cunt-milk, I focused on the openings in their foreskins. I'd tongue them, I decided. I'd pull their foreskins right back and expose their purple knobs. I'd lick around the rims of their knobs, tongue their sperm-slits to stiffen their young shafts.

'One by one, I want you to stand in front of me,' I said authoritatively, my clitoris swelling as I again imagined sucking their ripe knobs. 'We'll start with you.' I pointed at the young lad hovering at the end of the line. 'Come on, I won't bite you.' Mog laughed as the lad moved forward.

Bite? I might just do that, I mused as the young man stood before me. His penis slowly rising, I fondled his heavy balls, kneaded his sperm eggs. Did he wank? I wondered. Yes, he'd wank regularly. He'd picture naked girls in his mind's eye and shoot his spunk. Had he ever seen a naked girl for real?

Pulling his foreskin back, exposing the full globe of his purple knob, I eyed his sperm-slit. 'Nice,' I breathed, cupping his balls and wanking his solid shaft. 'Have you ever been sucked?' I asked as I watched his glistening plum appear and disappear. He shook his head as I leaned forward. 'You'll enjoy this,' I murmured, retracting his foreskin fully and licking the moist surface of his swollen glans. He tasted salty, sexy. Perhaps he'd wanked that morning, I thought, engulfing his knob in my wet mouth. Quivering as I sucked hard, he pushed his hips forward, pushing his knob deeper into my hot mouth.

'Oh,' he gasped as I continued to knead his full balls, running my wet tongue over his solid knob as he trembled in his rising arousal. Wanking his veined shaft, I breathed in the heady scent of his pubes as his penis twitched and swelled. He tasted of sex, smelled of sex, and I almost lost control of myself as I took his ballooning knob to the back of my throat and sank my teeth into his fleshy shaft. He was going to come, I knew as I moved my head back, my wet lips sucking the rim of his glans. Tonguing his sperm-slit, licking the velveteen surface of his glans, I gave him one last hard suck. Slipping his ballooning knob out of my mouth, I licked my salty lips. I didn't want him coming yet.

'And the next one,' I said, my clitoris pulsating as another young lad stood before me. His penis rock-hard, standing proudly to attention above his heaving balls, he thrust his hips forward. The opening of his foreskin close to my lips, I took his hard cock into my mouth. Grabbing his warm shaft, my vaginal muscles spasming as my arousal heightened, I slowly pulled the loose skin covering his shaft back down towards his balls. His foreskin retracting, his swollen knob emerging, the taste of sex filled my mouth as I ran my tongue over his sperm-slit. Fully retracting his foreskin, I held his glans between my lips and worked my tongue round and round his beautiful knob.

I was in my sexual heaven, I knew as I cupped his heavy balls and sucked hard on his purple plum. He breathed heavily, his legs twitching as I snaked my tongue around the rim of his helmet, licking the small bridge of skin running to his foreskin. He wasn't far off coming, I knew as he let out a moan of pleasure. All my boys would come, eventually. They'd all have the chance to shoot their white spunk and drain their young balls.

'Next,' I grinned, his knob leaving my mouth as I moved my head back. 'I'll have two at once this time,' I said as he returned to the queue. I was desperate to experience crude sex, desperate to have my body fucked and spunked. As two lads stood before me, I again licked my lips. They were big, their shafts long, broad and hard. They'd be fucking me before the evening was over, I knew as I pulled their foreskins back. Their knobs would be pummelling my ripe cervix, filling my hot cunt with their spunk. Little did they know, but they'd also be pumping their sperm into the fiery heat of my bowels.

Ordering them to stand closer together as I pictured their hard cocks fucking the tight duct of my arse, I moved my head forward and licked each purple knob in turn. Their gasps resounding around the room, I pressed their ripe plums together, licking the two spheres. Their rounded knobs inflating as I pressed them harder against each other,

I focused on their opening slits. How many times had sperm jetted from their knobs? I wondered, focusing on the small pink lips of their sperm-slits. Had they wanked each other off? Jackie seemed to think that was what young lads did.

'Mmm,' I breathed through my nose, sucking their globes into my hot mouth and licking the silky-smooth surfaces of their beautiful knobs. Wanking their hard shafts, sucking and mouthing their bulbous purple plums, I wanted their sperm to gush and fill my thirsty mouth. I'd intended to make them wait, to suck each lad until they were desperate to shoot their spunk and make them wait. But *I* couldn't wait. I was a cum-slut and I needed sperm.

They had to come together, I thought, as I gobbled their solid knobs and wanked their rock-hard cocks faster in my desperation for sperm. They had to shoot their spunk together, both come at the same time and fill my mouth with their male cream. My lips stretched tautly around the rims of their bulbous globes, my tongue snaking over their throbbing sex-plums, my stomach somersaulted as they gasped and trembled. They were close to coming. Their shafts swelled in my hands, their knobs ballooned in my mouth. Their balls bouncing, I wanked them faster and sucked and licked for all I was worth. This was it, I knew as they clutched my head and let out low moans of pleasure. They were going to come together.

Their spunk suddenly jetting from their orgasming knobs, bathing my darting tongue, filling my cheeks, I repeatedly swallowed. I could feel the white liquid running in rivers down my chin as I wanked and sucked their beautiful cocks. Spluttering as my mouth overflowed, their sperm running down over my hands, I mouthed and suckled like a babe at the breast as they drained their young balls. Moving my head back, their deep purple knobs leaving my

mouth, I wanked their shafts, splattering my flushed face
with their jetting spunk as they clung to my head in their
agonized pleasure. Cum-slut. Facial. Mouth-fuck. I was in
control. They were my sex slaves, and I their mentor. I felt
like a goddess as they spunked my face. Was I the goddess
of sex?

Their balls bouncing as I rolled their foreskins back and
forth over their purple globes, bringing out the last of their
spunk, I watched their scrotums jerking up and down. My
hand drenched, long threads of sperm hanging from their
balls, I wanked them until the flow of spunk ceased.
Gasping as I lapped up the white liquid dribbling from
their knob-slits, their bodies trembling uncontrollably as
they panted for breath, they swayed on their sagging legs.
Running my tongue up their deflating shafts, over the
wrinkled skin of their ball-sacs, I carefully cleansed them.
Giving their beautiful knobs one last suck, I finally ordered
them to get back in line.

Standing up, I moved to the centre of the room and
grinned at the young men. 'You may remove my clothes,'
I said huskily. 'Gather round me and strip me naked.'
Wasting no time, their eager hands running all over my
curvaceous body, they stripped me down to my knickers
and bra. Hesitating, they gazed at the deep ravine of my
cleavage, the swell of my wet panties. 'Don't stop there,' I
murmured. As one of them unhooked my bra, my firm
breasts tumbling from the silk cups as the garment fell
away, I grinned as my panties were tugged down my legs.
They whispered about my shaved cunt, chuckling quietly
and talking about schoolgirls.

Stepping out of my soaked panties, I stood with my feet
wide apart and told the lads to examine my naked body.
'Do as you wish,' I said, my juices of lust flowing from my

spasming vaginal cavern and running down my inner thighs. 'Examine every inch of my naked body.' Hands and fingers eagerly feeling my breasts, cupping the globes of my buttocks and parting the fleshy swell of my pussy lips, I closed my eyes and revelled in the intimate attention. A finger entered the wet sheath of my hot cunt, another sought the tight inlet to my rectal duct. My elongated nipples squeezed and pinched, my erect clitoris massaged, I had at last found my domain.

'Take me,' I murmured, my head spinning, my trembling body alive with sex. 'I want you all to fuck and spunk me.' Laying me on the floor, my slaves surrounded me. Kneading the mounds of my breasts, parting the soft cushions of my pussy lips, they whispered their wicked plans for my naked body. My arms held behind my head, my feet parted, I knew that the crack of my vagina was gaping, the wet entrance to my young cunt crudely bared.

The swollen knob of a penis slipping between the open wings of my inner lips, I let out a rush of breath and closed my eyes as the huge shaft entered me. The sheath of my cunt expanding as the bulbous glans pressed against the soft firmness of my cervix, I grinned as someone turned my head to one side and another knob pressed against my mouth. Parting my lips, I sucked the rounded glans inside as my naked body rocked with the crude fucking. I really was in my element, I knew as my nipples were sucked into hot mouths. Used and abused by six eager lads, I'd have no excuse not to write erotic fiction now.

'Fuck her shaved cunt really hard,' someone murmured excitedly. Perhaps he'd never seen a girl in all her naked glory. I doubted very much that he'd watched a girl having her shaved cunt fucked. The vaginal pistoning increasing in rhythm, jolting my trembling body, I sucked and mouthed on the swelling knob as teeth sank into the dark discs of my areolae. Through my eyelashes, I saw a knob hovering above me, the young lad wanking himself off, no doubt keen to shoot his beautiful spunk over my face. Fingers seeking my clitoris, massaging the swollen protuberance, the teats of my breasts sucked and bitten, I moaned through my nose as my mouth suddenly filled with salty sperm.

The lad wanking above me gasping, his sperm jetting from his knob-slit and splattering my face as I drank from the orgasming knob bloating my mouth, I shuddered as my clitoris exploded in orgasm. Spunk pumping deep into the inflamed throat of my vagina, my face running with the white liquid of male orgasm, I repeatedly swallowed as my mouth overflowed. My naked body attended by hands, mouths, tongues, cocks, fingers . . . I floated in my delirium, drifting through the now familiar purple clouds of orgasm as my body convulsed wildly.

'Let me do her,' someone breathed eagerly as the spent penis slipped out of my sperm-brimming cunt. They were young, I reflected as my orgasm peaked, sending electrifying shock waves of crude sex through my naked body. Young and keen to learn, eager to fuck me, to spunk up my tight cunt. They'd never forget me, I mused as my orgasm began to recede. For the rest of their lives they'd recall the young slut they'd fucked. The slag, the whore, the cum-slut. Shagged, fucked, used and abused, spunked . . . 'She's got a really tight cunt.' As the rock-hard penis entered me, I swallowed the remnants of the sperm oozing from the swollen cock fucking my wet mouth.

What next? I asked myself, my face drenched with sperm as the lad above me slowed his wanking. The deflating cock leaving my mouth, I licked my lips, lapping up as much spunk as I could as the lad on top of me gasped in his fucking. My vaginal juices and the previous lad's spunk squelching as my cunt was pistoned by the solid cock, I waited in anticipation of the inevitable spunking. My slave gasping, he increased his pistoning rhythm, his swollen glans battering my cervix as he eagerly fucked me.

'Yes,' he breathed, his spunk jetting from his beautiful knob. My cunt awash with sperm and girl-come, my naked body rocking back and forth as I was fucked rotten, I knew that I'd be able to write book after book. Bondage, spanking, mouth-spunking, arse-fucking, cunt-fucking . . . There was nothing I hadn't experienced, I was sure as the vaginal fucking slowed, the balls battering my tensed buttocks finally drained.

The limp cock gliding out of my sex sheath, my naked body roughly rolled over, I lay on my stomach, grinning as my legs were yanked apart. The boys were examining my buttocks, pulling the warm globes apart, opening my anal valley and exposing the brown inlet to my bowels. Fingers teased me there, stroking, massaging the brown tissue. More fingers delved between my hairless vaginal lips, seeking the inner folds of my dripping sex valley, thrusting into the spermed channel of my tightening vagina.

'Hold her arse wide open,' a lad breathed as the fingers slipped out of my hot cunt. I could feel him moving between my thighs, the globe of his knob running up and down my creamy sex valley. My eyes wide as he pressed his solid glans against my partially open bottom-hole, I gasped as he unceremoniously thrust his huge knob deep into my rectal duct. 'God, she's tight and hot,' he murmured as the others painfully parted my tensed buttocks, rudely opening my anal crease to the extreme.

Chuckles resounding around the room as the granite-hard cock forcefully fucked my tight arse while the audience watched, I knew that I'd fallen to such depths of debased sex that I'd never turn back. It was too late to be thinking of a fresh start. There was no new beginning now. My naked body was to be used purely for debased sex, for others to use and abuse, to satisfy their base desires and vulgar cravings. What did I get out of it? Pleasure, immense pleasure and power. The lads were using me, but I was in control. I could order them to do this or that and they'd immediately obey me.

'Coming,' my slave cried, fucking the burning duct of my arse with a vengeance as the others looked on. I could feel his spunk jetting into my anal tube, lubricating his pistoning knob as his swinging balls battered the fleshy swell of my hairless vaginal lips. Again and again he thrust his cockhead deep into my bowels, his lower belly slapping my rounded buttocks as he filled me with his lubricious sperm. The delicate tissue of my anus stretched tautly around his pistoning cock, the crude sensations rippling though my quivering pelvis, I wondered whether the other boys wanted to screw my tight arse. Would they take turns to fuck my bottom and spunk my bowels?

'God, that was good,' the male behind me gasped, his spent penis slipping out of my spermed bottom-hole with a loud sucking sound. I heard them whispering again, discussing my naked body, what they should do to me next. My eyes closed, I played dead as I was rolled onto my side. Like a rag doll, my arms flopping, my golden hair veiling my face, I concealed a smile as my leg was lifted high in the air. The well-spunked crack of my vagina gaping, my sex-holes blatantly exposed to my audience, I wondered what crude act they'd decided upon.

A lad settling on the floor in front of me, his swollen knob running up and down my yawning sex-crack, he drove the length of his rock-hard penis into the hot depths of my wet cunt. The filling sensation was heavenly, as was the feel of his balls resting on my inner thigh as my other leg was lifted higher. Someone moved about behind me, and I thought he was going to push his cock deep into my rectum. *A double fucking*, I thought as his solid plum stabbed between my thighs. I needed a double fucking.

I could hardly believe what he was trying to do as he pushed the hard sphere of his knob against the solid shaft of the penis already embedded within my bloated cunt. The tight entrance to my vagina opening, yielding as he forced his ballooning globe hard against my stretched inner lips, I squeezed my eyes shut. I couldn't take two cocks, I was sure as his glans suddenly slipped into my pussy alongside the other penis. My pelvic cavity bloating, the walls of my vagina stretched to capacity, I gasped as the illicit double fucking began.

Finding their rhythm as my leg was lifted even higher, they repeatedly rammed into me and withdrew, sandwiching me between their naked bodies in their crude fucking. One belly slapping the smooth plateau of my stomach, another meeting my lower back, I gently rocked to the rhythm of the double fucking and the accompaniment of male gasps of pleasure. The audience whispering their crudities, I felt decadent in the extreme as wicked thoughts of debauched sex loomed in my mind. This was what Crystal would have loved, I ruminated. She'd have been in her element with two rock-hard cocks fucking the hot shaft of her tight cunt. Crystal, my heroine, my mentor.

'I'm going to come already,' the one behind me gasped. I could feel their cocks swelling within my hugging vaginal sheath. Their knobs pressed together, gliding along the creamy walls of my vagina and meeting my ripe cervix, I felt their sperm jet into me. Again and again they thrust into my spasming cunt, their spunk spraying my cervix, filling my abused sex duct as they gasped in their decadence. The inflamed inner lips of my cunt stretched around the two huge shafts, I thought the delicate tissue was going to tear as they double-fucked and spunked my tight cunt. My own orgasm erupting within the solid nubble of my exposed clitoris, I knew that the evening of debauchery had barely begun.

Whimpering as electrifying tremors of sex coursed through my contracting womb, my cunt overflowing with the double sperming, I wondered whether another two lads would force their young cocks deep into my abused cunt. They'd all have their turn, I knew as I trembled in the grip of an incredible orgasm. Balls slapping between my thighs, my leg lifted high above me, my naked body was like a sex doll. Fucked, spunked, used and abused, licked, sucked, fingered . . . I was nothing more than a slag of a whore-slut.

The penises finally stilling within the bloated sperm-bath of my inflamed cunt, I rested in the wake of my incredible climax, wondering what the next crude act I was to endure would be. Two knobs had fucked and spunked my mouth, two cocks had screwed my tight cunt and pumped their sperm over my ripe cervix . . . I was sure that they'd try to force three penises into my sex sheath if they could. The wet cocks gliding out of my inflamed sex-holes, I lay quivering on the floor as another two young men sandwiched me between their naked bodies.

Someone yanked my buttocks apart as the man in front of me moved forward and pressed his huge knob against the sensitive brown ring of my anal inlet. Suddenly driving his penile shaft deep into my tight arse, he groped between my legs and massaged the wet flesh of my vaginal crack. The man behind me pushing his swollen knob against my taut brown tissue, I cried out in protest. I couldn't take two rock-hard cocks up my arse, I knew as my buttocks were painfully forced further apart. The first penis withdrawing, the second pressed harder against my inflamed arse-ring. Finally slipping past my defeated anal sphincter muscles, the penile head drove into my rectum. Whimpering as both cocks glided along my rectal duct, stretching me to capacity, I was sure that the delicate tissue of my anus would tear.

'No,' I gasped as both cocks completely impaled me, the brown tissue of my bottom painfully taut around the roots of the huge organs. Ignoring my protests, my anal abusers began their illicit fucking, withdrawing and thrusting into me again and again. I knew I'd tear as my inflamed anal tissue ran along the pistoning shafts. The audience chuckling, making lewd comments about my naked body, this was the height of humiliation, of sexual degradation. Nothing could be more humiliating, I knew as a finger groped between my vaginal lips and thrust deep into my neglected cunt.

'No,' I cried again, my constricted vagina forced to accommodate at least three fingers. A swollen knob ramming into my gasping mouth, my cheeks bloating, my head was lifted off the floor and moved back and forth. The knob repeatedly driving to the back of my throat as my head rocked, two knobs forcefully fucking the tight sheath of my arse, I knew that I'd found the bottom of the pit of depravity. Another penis hovering close to my face, the bulbous knob trying to gain entry to my bloated mouth, I had never dreamed that I'd be treated worse than an animal.

'Fuck her mouth,' someone chuckled as the second knob forced my lips open and slipped into my wet mouth.

'Double-spunk her little mouth.' Coughing and spluttering as my head was yanked back and forth, the two ballooning knobs fucking my bloated mouth, I shuddered as the penises within my anal sheath swelled. Sperm gushing from the two slits, lubricating the double pistoning, I squeezed my eyes shut as my mouth filled with sperm.

More fingers entering my burning vaginal duct, I choked and spluttered on the gushing sperm as my mouth over-flowed. I couldn't take any more. My naked body awash with sperm, I prayed for my abusers to leave. I'd thought that I was in control, but they'd taken over. I had no power over them now: there was nothing I could do to halt the dreadful abuse of my naked body.

'Open her bum further,' the male behind me breathed. Hands grabbing my naked buttocks, painfully yanking my anal orbs apart, I struggled to free myself as the double anal fucking continued. Sperm spraying from my rudely dilated bottom-hole, gushing from my fucked mouth, I closed my eyes as another purple knob brushed against my ear and pumped out its sperm. The male liquid filling my ear, running down my neck, fear gripped me as someone pain-fully pinched and squeezed my sensitive nipples.

My entire body subjected to sexual abuse, I again coughed and spluttered on the sperm jetting to the back of my throat. I wanted Mog to order his friends to leave me alone but I knew he wouldn't. I'd instigated this, I reflected as spunk oozed from my ear and ran down my neck. This was what I'd wanted, and it was what I'd got. The phone ringing, I wondered whether it was Alan the ex. What would he have thought of me had he witnessed my wanton debauchery? Cum-slut. Whore.

The penises finally slipping out of my inflamed anal canal, the two spent knobs leaving my spunk-flooded mouth, I rolled onto my back and panted for breath. Completely drained of all energy, totally exhausted, I knew that I couldn't take another spunking. They had to allow me to rest before fucking my inflamed orifices again. My head lolling from side to side, sperm running in rivers over my flushed face, I looked up to see the shafts of several solid cocks hovering above me. The six boys kneeling around my head, they began wanking their young cocks, gasping as their purple plums appeared and disappeared. They were going to spunk my face. No doubt this was to be the last act of degradation before they left.

Their sperm came quickly. Jetting through the air, raining over my grimacing face, splattering my blonde hair, the streams of white liquid seemed never-ending. Gazing through my eyelashes, I watched them wanking, bringing out their spunk as they gasped in their debased pleasure. My naked body trembling, my inflamed arsehole oozing with sperm, my cunt spewing out the blend of spunk and girl-come, I spluttered as the orgasmic liquid filled my gasping mouth.

At last it was over. The youths rose to their feet and grabbed their clothes, laughing and joking as I lay writhing in a pool of spunk on the floor. They were talking about coming back, asking Mog whether they could fuck me again the following evening. He readily agreed, as if he owned me. I was too weak to protest as they told Mog that several other boys would like to come along. Weak in my exhaustion. Weak in my arousal. As they filed out of the room, I hoped that Mog would stay behind. The murmurs fading, the front door closing, they'd gone.

'Mog,' I called, wiping sperm from my face as I clambered to my feet. He'd left with his friends, left me to drown in the sperm. Staggering to my bedroom, I crawled beneath the quilt and closed my eyes. I should have had a shower, I knew as sperm oozed from my sex-holes, the salty liquid stinging my eyes as it dripped from my blonde hair. But all I could do was sleep.

Chapter Thirteen

The morning came all too quickly. Dragging my sperm-starched body out of bed, I wandered bleary-eyed into the shower. Guilt rose from the turbid depths of my mind. Guilt, anger, remorse . . . I was angry with myself. I should have taken control rather than drifting along with my life. As the hot water cleansed my naked body, washing the dried sperm from my matted hair, I recalled every horrendous detail of the events of the previous evening.

How I could have done it, why I'd done it . . . I couldn't begin to imagine. It was as if I'd been driven to commit the vulgar sexual acts by some unseen force. My flat had become a den of iniquity, my mind a filthy swamp, my body an object designed purely to satisfy the base desires of both men and women. I was far removed from the days when I'd been with Alan. Writing my romantic novel, enjoying shopping trips with Jackie, a drink or a meal with Alan . . . From repressed prude . . . I had turned.

Musing on the day ahead, I tried to push all thoughts of sex and guilt from my mind. What was done was done, and that was the end of the matter. I'd gained the sexual experience and knowledge I'd sought. There was no need to continue my quest for crude sex. I wouldn't answer the door to Mog and his friends. Alan the ex and Crystal could make their plans, but I wouldn't get involved. Musician Alan . . . he didn't really figure in my life. Jackie was Jackie.

RAY GORDON

She'd never change and I didn't want to change her. We'd remain good friends, and nothing more.

I dressed and had breakfast and then sat at my desk and brought the text of my book up onto the screen. Wondering whether Alan had crept into my flat and read through my work, I couldn't get the things Crystal had said out of my mind. She reckoned that she'd met a man in a wine bar and had sex with him. That had happened in my book. Alan *must* have been into my den. There was no other explanation. Lifting the phone, I called his mobile. I couldn't concentrate on the book knowing that he might have been poking around in my flat.

'Alan, I'm going away for a few days,' I lied.

'Why tell me?' he asked irritably.

'Because I'd like you to keep an eye on my flat.'

'I suppose so,' he sighed. 'I hear that Crystal came to see you.'

'Yes, she did.'

'What was it all about?'

'About my writing.'

'I don't understand. Why the mystery? She wouldn't tell me what it was about.'

'There's no mystery, Alan. She writes and so do I. We had a chat about writing. So you'll keep an eye on my flat for me?'

'Yes, yes. When are you going and how long for?'

'I'm leaving now. I'll be a couple of days, that's all. Just call round and check the place a couple of times. Oh, and could you water the yucca plant in the lounge? It dries out so quickly in this heat.'

'OK. Where are you going?'

'To stay with a girlfriend. I'll be in touch when I get back.'

'OK. Have a good time.'

Replacing the receiver, I grinned. Water the yucca plant? To do that he'd have to get into the flat. He still had a key, I was sure. If he hadn't, then he'd have asked me how he was supposed to get into the flat. No doubt he'd realize that the yucca could go without water for a couple of days, but it wouldn't occur to him that I was setting him up. He'd probably call round after work. It would be an ideal opportunity for him to take a lengthy look at my text and poke around the flat. What was I going to do? I wondered. Leap out of the shadows and pounce on him?

After a good day's work, I mooched about in the kitchen, wondering whether Alan would make an appearance. Six-thirty. If he was going to arrive, it would be within ten minutes or so. I'd slip out to the patio once I heard a key in the lock. He'd no doubt go straight to my den and switch the computer on. I'd catch him red-handed and . . . There'd be nothing I could do, but I'd at least know that Crystal had been acting in collusion with Alan. As to the reason why, that was another matter.

When the doorbell rang, I wasn't sure what to do. Creeping into the lounge, I spied through the net curtain. It was Crystal. What the hell did she want? I asked myself. Hadn't Alan told her that I'd gone away? Obviously not. Unless he'd given her the key and she'd come to nose around. She rang the bell again, looking up and down the street as she waited. As she turned and walked back down the path, I dashed to the front door. She might have been checking to make sure I'd gone away, I mused as I opened the door. I should have stayed in hiding, but I felt that I had to speak to her.

'Crystal,' I called.

'Oh, I thought you were out.' She smiled, turning and walking towards me.

239

'Sorry, I was in the back garden. Come in.'

'Thanks. I was just passing and thought I'd see how you are.'

'I'm fine,' I replied as she followed me into the kitchen. 'How's Alan?'

'I haven't seen him for a couple of days. Jade, I want to ask you about your book.'

'Oh, yes?'

'The strange things I've been doing lately . . . I know you think it has nothing to do with your book, but I'm sure it has.' Sitting at the table as I filled the kettle, she looked worried. 'What have you written in the last day or so?' she asked, twisting her long blonde hair around her fingers.

'Crystal is sexually tortured by a lesbian lover,' I smiled. 'When I say tortured, she's really all for it, of course. She falls deeper into the pit of depravity and finds that she can only derive sexual satisfaction from pain, torture. Why do you ask?'

'This morning, I went for a walk in the woods. I was a few hundred yards into the trees when I felt an overwhelming urge to slip my panties off and . . . This is going to sound silly. I whipped myself between my legs with a small branch.'

'And you're saying that this happened because of the things I wrote?'

'There's no other explanation, Jade.'

'There's an explanation that's very simple,' I replied, pouring the coffee.

'Oh? What's that?'

'With luck, you'll find out very soon. Can you stay for a while?'

'I suppose so. What's going on?'

'I'm expecting a visitor. Either within the next few

minutes or later this evening. All will no doubt be revealed then. In the meantime, let's go and sit on the patio.'

Again trying to figure out what Alan and Crystal were up to as we went out to the patio, I imagined the girl whipping her vulval flesh with a branch. She was either lying or she enjoyed abusing her young body. Was that why she'd come to see me? I wondered. To try to convince me that everything I wrote happened to her? I'd take a look at her thrashed pussy, I decided. And I might even thrash her myself for her lies and trickery.

'Show me,' I said. 'Show me where you whipped yourself with a branch.'

Rising to her feet, she lifted her skirt. 'There,' she breathed, pulling the front of her panties down.

'God,' I gasped, gazing at the weals fanning out across the swollen lips of her hairless vulva. 'You did that?'

'Yes.' She pulled her panties up and lowered her skirt. 'As I said, I had an overwhelming urge to slip my panties off and abuse myself. I've never done anything like it before, Jade. I just don't know what possessed me.'

'The girl in my book didn't do that to herself. I think you're trying to find a link that doesn't exist.'

'This is more than coincidence,' she persisted.

'Why did you come to me in the first place?' I asked. 'I know that your initial interest was my writing erotica. You said that Alan had mentioned the changes in me and you thought it odd that you too had been through inexplicable changes. But why come and see me?'

'That's why I came to see you,' she frowned. 'Because I was going through changes and so were you. We both write erotica, and we've been going through—'

'It just seems odd that Alan should contact me a year after he'd left, and then you come on the scene.'

'I don't know why Alan contacted you. In fact, I knew nothing about you until he mentioned that he'd been in touch with you.'

Gazing down the garden, I wondered again about the young girl's face that I'd seen in the bushes. Crystal seemed genuine enough and, unless I could discover why she and Alan would be conning me, I had no reason not to believe her. She'd thrashed her own vulval flesh, she'd said that she'd been into a wine bar and met a man . . . That's what my Crystal had done, I again reflected. Both Crystals had had sex with a man up against the bar. If Alan hadn't been into my flat and looked at my work, then how the hell did Crystal know what I'd written?

'You mentioned sexual torture,' she said, locking her blue gaze to mine.

'Yes, Crystal is tortured by a lesbian lover.'

'I want to try something,' she murmured mysteriously, rising from the chair. 'You are a lesbian lover of mine, as you put it.'

'I'm not a *lover*, exactly.'

'After what happened, I think we can safely say that we were or are lesbian lovers. Do you have any rope or . . .'

'*Rope?*' I broke in, frowning at her. 'What on earth do you want rope for?'

'I want you to tie me down, Jade.'

'Is this some kind of joke?'

'Far from it. I need you to tie me down.'

'What, out here?'

'Why not? No one can see into your garden and it's a beautiful evening.'

'There are no trees to tie you to.'

'The lawn,' she smiled. 'Do you have anything we could use as stakes?'

'Stakes? Look, Crystal, I think you'd better go now. I'm not going to stake you to the—'

'I'm serious, Jade. I've not been sleeping because of all this. I've been doing things that are so out of character that . . . Stake me to the lawn.'

'OK, if that's what you really want.'

'I have to discover whether something is trying to influence me. We'll need something to use as stakes.'

'Influencing you? Crystal, there's nothing influencing you.'

'Just do this for me. We'll need some stakes.'

'There's an old croquet set in the cupboard. It used to belong to my grandfather.'

'The hoops will do. Go and get four hoops and a hammer, if you have one.'

Walking into the kitchen, I reckoned that Crystal must have thought me stupid. As if I was going to believe that there were ghosts at work, for goodness' sake. She was determined to carry on with this business of a link between my writing and her actions, I knew as I dragged the box out of the cupboard. Taking four croquet hoops from the box and grabbing the hammer, I wondered what her idea was. Stake her naked body to the lawn and whip her so that she could say *I told you so*? I might as well have some fun with her, I decided, finding her standing on the patio completely naked.

She had a beautiful young body. Curvaceous, firm, alluring . . . The sun on the mounds of her firm breasts casting shadows across her naked flesh, her naked mons rising gently above the tightly closed crack of her pussy, I knew that I had to have her. Gazing at her vaginal lips, crimsoned and inflamed from the thrashing, I reckoned that she'd dreamed up the business of my writing affecting her so she could have sex with me. To ask me to stake her to the lawn had nothing to do with ghosts or whatever. It was simply to have me attend her naked body.

'Just here will do,' she said, lying on her back with her limbs spread across the grass. 'This will prove . . .'

'This will prove nothing,' I interrupted her, placing the metal stakes over her ankles and hammering them into the ground. There again, it proved that she was a nymphomaniac.

'You don't understand, Jade,' she sighed as I secured her wrists to the ground. 'If there's something influencing me, then it will come to me now. Staked to the ground like this, whatever it is will come, I'm sure.'

'You reckon a ghost is going to appear?' I giggled. 'That's crazy. So what am I supposed to do? Shall I whip you with a branch?'

'Don't do anything just yet.'

'Aren't you worried?' I asked. 'Staked to the lawn like that . . . I could do anything to you.'

'It's not you I'm worried about, Jade. It's the girl in your book.'

'She's locked away in the computer somewhere,' I laughed. 'She's not real, Crystal. She won't be bothering us.'

Shaking my head, I walked to the end of the garden and gazed into the bushes. Crystal must be mad, I reflected, turning and glancing at her naked body. Staked to the lawn to entice a ghost to appear . . . But she wasn't mad. It was just her way of getting me to have sex with her. Wondering where Alan had got to, I snapped a branch off the bush and swished it through the air. Should I thrash her pussy? I asked myself. That was obviously what she wanted. Walking towards her, I decided to play along with her.

Settling between her spread thighs, I stroked the soft

swell of her hairless vaginal lips. Crystal breathed deeply as I ran my fingers along the moist groove of her pussy. Her inner petals beginning to protrude from her alluring valley of desire as her arousal heightened, I knew that I was in for another evening of debauched sex. There was no getting away from it, I knew as I slipped my finger into the wet divide between her pouting vaginal lips. I desperately needed crude sex with both men and women, and I couldn't deny it. Why should I deny myself sexual pleasure? I asked myself, driving my finger fully home as the girl writhed and gasped on the lawn.

'That's nice,' she breathed, her head rolling from side to side as I drove a second finger into the burning sheath of her tight vagina. Imagining a ghost materializing, I slipped my wet fingers out of the hot sheath of her cunt and licked them clean. Her milk tasted wonderful, lubricious, warm, creamy . . . It seemed a shame to have to thrash her vulval lips, but that's what she was expecting. There again, it wasn't a shame. It was a delightful idea.

The branch swishing through the air and landing across the swell of her girl-lips with a loud slap, I grinned as Crystal let out a yelp. Again, I brought the branch down, her tethered body convulsing as the rough leaves lashed her vulval flesh. Her yelps becoming screams, I knew that I was going to have to shut her up before continuing with the merciless beating. The last thing I wanted was the neighbours coming round to see what the commotion was about. Slipping my wet panties off, I knelt by her head and smiled.

'This is what you wanted, isn't it?' I asked, brushing her golden locks away from her perspiring forehead.

'No, it isn't,' she whimpered. 'I didn't think you were going to . . . Do you feel as if you've lost control? I mean, are you being influenced in any way?'

'Oh, yes. I'm being influenced, all right. By your beautiful naked body, Crystal. And by my rising lust for your beautiful cunt.'

'Let me go now,' she murmured shakily. 'I don't think this was such a good idea.'

'But it's a *brilliant* idea. You want me to attend your naked body, finger your cunt, lick you, whip you, rub my open cunt over your pretty face and come in your mouth . . . It's a perfect idea, Crystal.'

'No, no, I . . . Let me go now, Jade.'

Stuffing my pussy-wet panties into her mouth, I grinned as her wide eyes stared up at me. Turning my grin into a scowl, I hoped she'd believe that I really had been possessed by a ghost. Settling between her splayed thighs again, I yanked her vaginal lips wide apart and peered into the wet entrance to her beautiful cunt. Eyeing the small pink funnel of flesh surrounding her open lust-hole, I decided to give her vagina a good pistoning before resuming the vulval thrashing. Leaping to my feet, I looked about the garden.

'Yes,' I grinned, walking across the lawn to a trowel embedded in the mud. The wooden handle was thick and smooth with a rounded end. *A perfect dildo*, I mused, grabbing the trowel and returning to my victim. 'This is rather big,' I murmured, easing the wooden shaft past her naked inner lips and driving it deep into the tight duct of her young cunt. She struggled but there was nothing she could do to halt the abuse as I pistoned the phallus, driving it in and out of her vaginal duct. Her juices of lust squelching, I watched her pinken inner lips dragging along the pussy-wet surface of the wooden handle. Wiggling her hips and pulling against the restraints, she moaned through her nose as I slapped her inner thigh.

'This is what you wanted,' I grinned as Crystal lifted her

head and stared at me. Parting the firm orbs of her young buttocks, I slipped the wet dildo out of her drenched cunt and pressed the rounded end hard against her brown anal tissue. Her eyes widening, she shook her head and tried to protest through the gag as I yanked her young buttocks further apart. Pushing the phallus harder against her anal sphincter muscles, I was determined to force the trowel handle deep into her tight rectum.

Twisting and pushing the trowel, I grinned as the end of the broad shaft opened her anal inlet. Her brown ring stretched tautly around the wooden handle, I eased the huge phallus deep into her rectal canal. I was surprised how easily it had slipped into her young duct. Perhaps it wasn't big enough, I thought, looking about the garden again. I needed something longer and wider, I decided, leaving the trowel sticking out from between her tensed buttocks and rising to my feet.

Entering the kitchen, I opened the cupboard beneath the sink. Plastic bottles caught my eye and a wicked idea came to mind. Taking a bottle, I emptied it and washed it out. Filling it with warm water, I felt my juices of arousal seeping between the inner petals of my vaginal crack. I desperately needed sex, the release of orgasm. But not until I'd had my fun with Crystal's naked body. She'd asked to be staked to the lawn – it had been what she'd wanted. And she was going to get it.

'I'm going to wash you,' I grinned, settling between her thighs and easing the trowel handle out of her anal canal. Her golden locks veiling her face, she lifted her head and stared at the bottle as I eased the globes of her firm buttocks apart. Eyeing her tight brown hole, I pushed the open end of the bottle against her inlet. She squirmed and writhed as I managed to ease the bottle past her anal sphincter muscles. I eased the plastic bottle further into her yielding rectal sheath, grinning wickedly as I watched her juices of lust seeping from her bared cunt-hole.

'Here it comes,' I said, gently squeezing the bottle. The warm water rushing into her bowels, Crystal arched her back and tossed her head from side to side. She was obviously enjoying the sensation, and I decided to allow myself the luxury of an enema. But there was so much more I had to do with young Crystal before pleasuring my own naked body. Squeezing the bottle harder, filling her bowels, I finally slipped the bottle out of her anal inlet. The water spouted from her dilated hole, splattering her inner thighs and pooling on the grass. 'And now for the other end of the bottle,' I murmured, parting the tensed orbs of her buttocks again. The bottle was at least two and a half inches in diameter, and I wondered whether I'd be able to force it past her tight anal entrance, let alone drive it deep into her hot rectum.

Wishing that Crystal was on her stomach, allowing me better access to her bumhole, I pushed and twisted the bottle. Squirming and moaning through her nose, her eyes wide, she jumped as the bottle suddenly slipped past her tight inlet and drove into her rectal sheath. I'd done it, I mused, gazing in awe at the brown tissue of her bottom-hole stretched tautly around the huge bottle. Easing the plastic phallus still further into her tightening anal tube, I grabbed the trowel and pushed the rounded end of the handle between her dripping inner lips.

'You'll love this,' I laughed, forcing the handle into the restricted sheath of Crystal's hot cunt. Her stomach rising and falling as I pushed the trowel handle fully home, I gazed at the lewd sight. Her sex-holes stretched wide open, the bridge of skin separating her vaginal entrance and her bottom-hole no longer visible, I was pleased with my handiwork. Pleased, but nowhere near finished with the girl. Taking the branch, I sat by her side and ran the rough leaves over the mounds of her firm breasts, the brown teats of her elongated nipples.

'This is exactly what happens in my book,' I giggled, tapping her breasts with the branch. My Crystal had been sexually tortured, I reflected, scraping the sensitive buds of her nipples with the branch. The circumstances weren't quite the same, but my character had endured the anal and vaginal abuse. She'd also had her vulval flesh thrashed, and her young breasts. But this wasn't coincidence or ghostly in any way. I'd told Crystal of the torture, and she'd wanted to be staked to the lawn. There were no ghosts lurking.

Raising the branch above my head, I brought it down across the swell of her young breasts with a loud swishing sound. She convulsed, her terror-stricken eyes staring at me as I raised the branch again. This had been what she'd wanted, hadn't it? Her naked body jerking with every lash of the branch, I grinned as red weals fanned out across her pale flesh. Her nipples rising, her areolae darkening, I continued the cruel thrashing, bringing the branch down again and again.

The trowel handle shooting out of her cunt as her body convulsed wildly, I lashed the sex-wet lips of her glistening vulva. Was I possessed? I wondered as I kept up the sadistic beating. This was what Crystal had done to herself in the woods, it was what she'd wanted. And it was what I wanted. Abusing a beautiful young girl's naked body, sexually torturing her . . . If I was possessed, then it was only by myself, my own wicked thoughts.

Finally dropping the branch to the ground, I leaned over

the girl's trembling body and ran my tongue up and down the inflamed crack of her vagina. Her breathing slowing as she recovered, her naked body twitching, she was obviously enjoying my intimate attention. Lapping up her flowing juices of lust, I yanked her pussy lips wide apart and gazed at the intricate folds of her inner sex-flesh. Her clitoris erect, fully emerged from beneath its protective bonnet, her cunt-hole oozing with cream, I decided that it was time for Crystal to come.

Licking her clitoris, repeatedly sweeping my tongue over its sensitive tip, I thrust three fingers deep into the tight sheath of her drenched cunt and massaged her vaginal walls. She was going to come if it was the last thing she did, I mused, pistoning her sex sheath and sucking her solid clitoris into my wet mouth. Her juices of lust squelching, her naked body convulsing, I decided to see how many orgasms she could have.

She came in a flood of cunt milk that gushed from her vaginal entrance, covering my hand and spraying her inner thighs. Her clitoris pulsating in my mouth, her vaginal muscles tightening, gripping my pistoning fingers, I forced out her orgasm as she squirmed and writhed in ecstasy. On and on her pleasure pulsed, her body shaking violently, her stomach jerkily rising and falling, her firm breasts heaving. This was the first of many, I mused, slipping my fingers out of her burning sex sheath and grabbing the end of the bottle. Thrusting the phallus in and out of her anal duct, I continued to mouth and suck her pulsating clitoris, sustaining her incredible climax.

Wishing that young Mog and his friends were there with me, I imagined them taking turns to fuck Crystal's tight cunt, filling her vaginal cavern with their fresh sperm. I'd order them to screw her arsehole, force their solid cocks past her brown ring and fuck her tight rectum and pump her hot bowels full of sperm. Would the girl enjoy a gang-bang? I wondered as her orgasm began to subside. Would she enjoy two cocks fucking and spunking her anal canal? It could always be arranged.

Giving her clitoris one last lick, I sat up and smiled at her. Her face flushed, her hair matted with perspiration, I knew she'd enjoyed her lesbian-induced coming. Grabbing the branch again, I decided to redden the flesh of her young breasts a little more. Her erect nipples standing proud from the dark discs of her areolae, inviting the rough leaves of the branch, I knew she'd enjoy another breast-thrashing.

The first lash rocking her tethered body, I raised the branch and brought it down again as hard as I could. Her breasts heaving, her inflamed nipples rising, I continued the thrashing until Crystal managed to spit my panties out of her mouth and scream. Ordering her to shut up, I lashed her sex-wet vulval flesh, bringing the branch down several times to teach her a lesson.

'Please, stop!' she cried, tossing her head from side to side. 'For God's sake, stop!'

'I'll allow you to rest for a while,' I smiled.

'Let me go, Jade,' she whimpered. 'Please, let me go.'

'But this is what you wanted,' I said, frowning as I stared into her tearful eyes.

'No, this *isn't* what I wanted. I thought you might make love to me, masturbate me, but not thrash me like that.'

'But that's what you did in the woods,' I grinned. I wanted to thrash her naked bottom. 'We're waiting for the ghost, aren't we?'

'There is no ghost,' she whimpered.

'Well, that's strange. How come you've suddenly changed your mind?'

'I haven't . . . I mean, I don't think it's a ghost. I believe it's some force or other that has been—'

'And *I* believe it's Alan,' I interrupted her.

'Alan?' She frowned.

'He's seen my book and told you about it. This is all a game, isn't it?'

'No, of course it's not,' she retorted. 'For God's sake, as if I'd do all this for fun.'

'Not for fun, Crystal. I don't know what it is that you two have planned, but I intend to find out.'

'We have nothing planned. I've not seen Alan for—'

'Be quiet,' I whispered, turning and looking at the open back door. 'I thought I heard something.'

Creeping into the kitchen, I listened for movements but heard nothing. If Alan had sneaked into the flat, he might have seen me in the garden. He could have gone into my den and had a quick look at the computer. Had I caught him, he'd have said that he was checking the flat for me, that he still had a key, and he'd act the innocent. Stealing into my den, I gazed at the computer. It was on. Had I left it on? I wondered. I was sure I'd switched it off.

Walking into the lounge, I looked around the room. Nothing had been moved, as far as I could tell. There again, Alan wouldn't have hung around, knowing that I was in the garden. This wasn't proving anything, I knew as I left the room. Standing in the kitchen, I gazed at Crystal's naked body staked to the lawn, the bottle emerging between her rounded buttocks. Had I really done that to her? I asked myself, eyeing the weals adorning her vulval flesh, the mounds of her firm breasts.

'Let me go, Jade,' she said as I approached her.

'Not until you tell me the truth,' I replied, kneeling beside her.

'The truth? The truth about what?'

'About all these coincidences. You saying that you've changed and that my writing is influencing you. I want the truth, Crystal.'

'There is no truth. I have no explanation for the things that have been happening. If I knew what was going on, then I wouldn't have come here and—'

'You came here for sex.'

'I didn't. I came here to talk to you. Yes, I suggested that you stake me to the lawn. But that was because I wanted to—'

'Because you wanted to have sex with me. It's no good, Crystal. I know that you and Alan have been working together to . . . to what, I have no idea. Perhaps you wanted to steal my book. Perhaps you wanted to frighten me, make me believe that whatever I wrote affected you. So tell me the truth.'

'The truth is that I *have* been affected by your writing.'

'You don't know what I've written. Apart from the few things I've told you, you haven't seen the book.'

'Do you mind releasing me? I'm uncomfortable and I can't talk to you like this.'

'No, you'll stay there until you tell me what's going on.'

Her naked body glowing in the evening sun, the hairless lips of her vagina rising alluringly at either side of her wet sex-crack, I decided to enjoy her body for a while longer. I'd eventually free her, but there was no rush. Lifting my skirt, I moved over her body and placed my knees to either side of her head. Pressing the crack of my hairless pussy against her mouth, I ordered her to tongue-fuck my wet cunt. Obeying, she licked the pink entrance to my sex sheath, bringing out my girl-milk as her tongue explored my vaginal sheath. Gasping, I swivelled my hips, aligning my solid clitoris with her hot mouth. I could feel her tongue sweeping over my swollen pleasure-bud, the electrifying sensations transmitting deep into my fluttering womb.

Gently rocking my hips, massaging the inner flesh of my sex valley against the wet lips of Crystal's mouth, I tossed my head back and closed my eyes. Heavenly sensations coursing through my trembling body, I pondered on my new way of life. Crude sex with men and women, masturbation, bondage and spanking, crudely fucked and abused by half a dozen young lads . . . I'd changed beyond recognition. Was this what I'd wanted? I wondered as Crystal's tongue snaked around the solid nubble of my pulsating clitoris. My quest had been to gain sexual experience, not to become a bisexual whore-slag.

'God,' I breathed as the birth of my orgasm fluttered deep within my young womb. Rocking my hips faster, massaging my dripping sex flesh hard against Crystal's open mouth, I shuddered as my orgasm exploded within my solid clitoris. My juices of lust gushing from my open cunt-hole, flooding her face as she sucked out my pleasure, I whimpered in my incredible coming. Wondrous sensations of lesbian sex coursing through my perspiring body, I sang out as my orgasm peaked. Tremors of lust rippling through my pelvis, playing within my contracting womb, I rode the crest of my pleasure to my sexual heaven. The hot juices of my vagina flooding Crystal's face, lubricating the illicit union, my orgasm finally began to wane. Stilling my trembling body, I breathed heavily as the girl licked and sucked the last ripples of sex from my solid clitoris.

'That was amazing,' I breathed, sliding the wet valley of my burning cunt off her juice-drenched mouth. I'd have to release Crystal, I knew as I recovered from my coming. As much as I'd have liked to, I couldn't keep her staked to the

lawn all night. She'd return for sex, I knew. She'd probably
continue with her ridiculous stories of ghosts and uncharacteristic behaviour, but that didn't bother me. Whatever
she was up to with Alan didn't worry me. All I wanted was
her beautiful body, the hairless flesh of her young vulva, the
hot wet sheath of her tight cunt, her pretty mouth and
darting tongue.

'Let me go now,' Crystal murmured. Releasing her, I
watched her slip the bottle out of her tight anal canal and
toss it to the ground. She'd enjoyed herself, I was sure as she
pulled her panties up her long legs, veiling the crimsoned
flesh of her naked pussy. Thrashed and sexually abused,
she'd enjoyed her visit. As she wandered into the kitchen, I
happened to glance at the bushes at the end of the garden.
Was there movement? I wasn't sure as I heard the front
door close. Was the girl hiding in the bushes, spying on me?

Perhaps Crystal had been right, I mused, wandering
down the garden. Perhaps staking her to the lawn *had*
roused some unseen force. No, the idea was crazy. My
thinking was going way off course. As I began walking back
to the patio, I heard a rustling in the bushes. Turning, I
thought I glimpsed a naked girl. It was my imagination, I
was sure as I watched the bushes in anticipation. I was
probably tired, exhausted after my lesbian sex session. I'd
have a shower and then spend the evening working on the
book, I decided. A naked girl lurking in the bushes? My
mind was playing tricks on me, wasn't it?

Chapter Fourteen

I rang Alan's mobile the following morning and told him that I'd been delayed and was leaving within an hour or so. He said he'd be round that evening to check the flat, but he didn't mention a key. I was convinced that he was conspiring with Crystal. But why had they picked on me? Had it been Alan's intention from the outset to introduce me to Crystal? Had they planned this well in advance? I didn't know what to think. The whole business was beginning to interfere with my work. The girl in the bushes, Crystal and her crazy stories . . . I couldn't concentrate.

Leaving the flat, I walked into town. I needed to clear my head and thought that a walk around town might help. It was a lovely day, and I'd not bothered wearing panties beneath my short skirt. The hairless lips of my pussy cooled by a slight breeze, I was all too aware of my intimate regions as I walked along. My naked pussy gave me a sense of freedom and sent my arousal soaring. Passing a couple of teenage boys, I recalled Mog and his friends. The boys smiled at me, and I wondered whether they'd enjoy my naked body. Would Mog come back for more sex? I wondered, stopping and turning to face the boys.

'Excuse me,' I said. 'I'm lost.'

'Where are you going?' one asked.

'The railway station,' I replied. I felt wicked as they gazed at my naked thighs. I wanted to lift my skirt and show them my hairless pussy. 'Can you direct me?'

'Turn left at the roundabout up there and then keep going.'

'Thanks.' I smiled, walking away.

I could so easily have seduced them, I reflected. I could have lured them into an alley and pulled their hard cocks out and sucked the sperm from their purple knobs. As I walked along the street, I found myself gazing at the crotches of men's trousers. I could have had any one of them, I knew as I strolled down a side street. Men were weak, I ruminated. Any man would succumb to my feminine charms, I was sure. The pouting lips of my naked pussy moistening with my juices of desire, I decided to put my theory to the test.

There was a row of metal posts separating the road from the pavement outside a small gift shop. The ornate posts were topped with knobs about an inch in diameter and a wicked idea surfaced from the swamp of my mind. Tentatively sitting on a post, the metal knob slipping between the swollen lips of my pussy, I wriggled my hips. The knob entering the wet sheath of my tightening vagina, I let out a little gasp. The side street wasn't busy. With only a few window-shoppers milling around, I was safe enough pleasuring myself on the post.

Raising myself slightly, the wet knob slipping out of my pussy, I manoeuvred my hips and positioned the knob between the firm globes of my naked buttocks. My body trembling. I slowly lowered myself, the knob pressing against the brown tissue surrounding my tight bottom-hole. Letting out a rush of breath as the knob entered my anal canal, I rested my weight on the post and relaxed. I couldn't believe what I was doing as I gently wriggled my hips, the cold hard knob massaging the dank walls of my rectum. This was depravity in the extreme, I knew as a young couple walked by.

I enjoyed the pleasure of the post for ten minutes or so before deciding to further my decadence. The gift shop looked attractive, as did the young lad behind the counter. Easing the metal knob out of my inflamed rectum, I stood up and went into the shop. The lad watched me as I browsed. Moving behind some shelving, I picked up a small china lighthouse. It was about three inches long and an inch in diameter, perfect for the tight sheath of my yearning pussy. Slipping my hand up my skirt, I drove the lighthouse into my vaginal canal, gasping a little as the rounded end pressed against my cervix.

'Can I help you?' the lad asked as he peered through the shelving.

'I'm just looking,' I smiled. 'Actually, there is something I'm after.'

'What's that?' he asked, walking around the shelving and standing next to me.

'Candles, ornamental candles.'

'Ah, this way.' He smiled.

Following him to the back of the shop, the china light-house massaging the tight sheath of my vagina, I wondered whether he'd like me to suck him off. I could kneel in front of him and take the purple plum of his penis into my wet mouth. He'd gasp as I wanked his solid shaft and licked the silky-smooth surface of his knob. He'd pump his spunk into my mouth, the white liquid bathing my tongue, jetting to the back of my throat.

'Here we are,' he said, waving his hand at a shelf lined with candles.

'They're beautiful,' I smiled, my cunt tightening around

the lighthouse. 'And very expensive,' I added, looking at the price tags.

'They're handmade, madam.'

'I see. I'm sure I'll find one that's the right size.'

'The right size?' he echoed, his dark eyes frowning.

'My boyfriend is away on business at the moment. I'm sure you understand why I need a candle.'

'Oh, er . . . Yes, of course,' he stammered. 'I'll leave you to choose.'

Returning to the counter, the young salesman was obviously stunned by my revelation. Slipping the lighthouse out of my drenched vagina, I placed it on the shelf and grabbed a huge candle. My feet apart, my knees bent, I pushed the candle between my swollen outer lips and forced it deep into my spasming cunt. The sensations creeping into my contracting womb as I walked towards the door, my clitoris swelling, I prayed that the waxen phallus wouldn't pop out of my cunt and land on the floor. I thought I was safe enough as I left the shop and started walking down the street. *That's one way to shoplift*, I chuckled inwardly. Turning as the lad called out, asking me to step back into the shop, I frowned.

'What's the problem?' I asked, following him through the door.

'There's a candle missing,' he said accusingly. 'I know my stock well, and there's a candle missing.'

'Are you suggesting that I stole it?' I gasped.

'May I check your bag?'

'No, you may not,' I returned, feigning shock.

'Then I have no choice but to call the police.'

'All right,' I conceded. 'I don't have time to hang around waiting for the police.' Opening my bag, I emptied the contents on the counter. 'There. Are you happy now?'

'But . . .' he stammered, staring open-mouthed at my bag. 'I don't understand. The candle was on the shelf when you were looking at them.' He frowned. 'I think I know what you've done with it,' he murmured. 'I'll call the police and let them deal with this.'

'There's no need to do that,' I smiled. 'If you believe I have the candle hidden, then search me.'

Looking me up and down, he reached out but hesitated. I lifted my skirt, revealing the hairless lips of my pussy, my wet sex slit. His eyes wide, his mouth hanging open, he stared in disbelief at my naked pussy. Urging him to search me, I stood with my feet wide apart. He kneeled on the floor, gazing longingly at the wet crack of my vagina. Would he dare to slip his finger into my hot cunt? I wondered.

'I haven't got all day,' I breathed. 'Are you going to body-search me or not?'

'I know you have the candle,' he muttered.

'Then look for it.' This was excellent material for my dirty book, I mused as he gazed at the dripping crack of my pussy. 'Are you going to search me or not?'

Reaching out, he tentatively slipped his finger between the rise of my fleshy pussy lips. His fingertip slowly entering my vagina, I gasped and bent my knees. Finally driving his finger into my cunt, he looked up at me. He could feel the candle, I knew as he prodded the end of the wax shaft, but was he able to pull it out? Finally standing upright. I lowered my skirt.

'May I go now?' I asked.

'Er . . . Well, I . . .'

'You want your candle, don't you? Let me look for it,' I grinned.

Kneeling before him, the candle pressing against my

cervix, I tugged his zip down and pulled his semi-erect penis out before he realized what I was up to. Retracting his foreskin, I moved forward and sucked his purple knob into my hot mouth. Gasping, he mumbled something as I took his swelling glans to the back of my throat. I was in my element, I mused as I moved my head back, my lips fastened around the rim of his knob. The salty taste driving me wild, my vaginal muscles tightening around the candle, I was desperate for his sperm.

Wanking his solid shaft as the salesman trembled on his sagging legs, I wondered at my crude behaviour. The metal post, the lighthouse, the candle, and now sucking a stranger's knob . . . There was research, and there was blatant decadence, I mused, sucking hard on the globe of his rock-hard penis. I wasn't going to change now, I knew. There was no returning to the days of romantic novels and shopping trips with Jackie. I'd go shopping alone now. Seeking male shopkeepers, I would haul their cocks out and suck them to orgasm. Why pay for goods when I could get them for nothing?

'God,' the lad murmured, clinging to my head to steady himself. His sperm jetting into my gobbling mouth, he let out gasps and moans of pleasure as I drank from his throbbing glans. My mouth overflowing as he pumped out his orgasmic cream, I swallowed repeatedly. On and on his sperm gushed, and I wondered when he'd last drained his balls. Perhaps I'd become a regular customer, I mused, wanking his solid shaft faster, sustaining his orgasm.

'No more,' he finally gasped, his knees bending, his spent penis slipping out of my wet mouth.

'Did you enjoy that?' I asked, rising to my feet and licking my lips.

'God, yes,' he breathed, tugging his zip up.

'So, we still haven't found the candle.'

'No, no. It doesn't matter about the candle.'

'I thought you might say that. Well, I'd better be going.'

'Will you . . . I mean . . .'

'Call again? Yes, I think I will. I've enjoyed shopping here. I'm sure you'll see me again.'

Leaving the shop, I couldn't help giggling as I walked down the street. The candle massaging my vaginal flesh, the taste of sperm lingering on my tongue, I thought about the chances of finding another shop with a young lad serving alone. No, it wasn't right, I mused. I wasn't a prostitute, for goodness' sake. There again, it *would* be fun. Daring myself to do it again, I stopped outside a small shoe shop. There was a middle-aged man leaning on the counter. It might be worth browsing, I decided, entering the shop.

'May I help you?' he asked, walking towards me.

'I'm looking for some boots,' I replied. 'I noticed a red pair in the window. I'm not sure what size I am.'

'Ah, yes,' he grinned. 'They've only just come in. Take a seat and we'll see what size you are.'

Sitting on the low bench, I stretched my leg out as he kneeled on the floor. He was too busy measuring my foot to notice that I'd parted my thighs. My hairless vaginal flesh was blatantly displayed, I knew as I parted my thighs further. He finally looked up and froze. His eyes almost popping out, his mouth wide open, he gawped at my young pussy. Finally looking up at my face, he cleared his throat and announced that he was going to fetch a pair of boots. He was gone for some time, and I wondered whether he was wanking. I also wondered what the hell I was doing by showing my hairless pussy to strangers. I hadn't just changed, I'd become another person, I thought as he returned with a pair of red boots.

263

'These should fit you like a glove,' he said and smiled, brushing his dark hair away from his face. I reckoned that he was in his forties, probably married, and probably in need of a slut. 'If you'll lift your foot,' he said, kneeling before me. Raising my leg, I watched his expression as I swung my other leg to the side and exhibited the yawning ravine of my dripping cunt. He must have thought that he was dreaming as he fiddled with the boots. His eyes transfixed on my pussy slit, his hands trembling, he mumbled something and stood up.

'Another size,' he mumbled as he grinned. 'I won't be a minute.' I followed him as he went through a door at the rear of the shop. My cunt-milk streaming down my inner thighs, I watched as he reached up to a shelf. He was still shaking, his hands trembling as he grabbed a box. Turning, he noticed me and dropped the box on the floor. He knew what I wanted as I walked towards him, I was sure. Kneeling, I tugged his zip down and pulled his limp penis out of his trousers. He said nothing, standing still as I took his soft shaft in my warm hand and slowly wanked him.

'Come on,' I murmured, pulling his heavy balls out and fondling his shaft. 'Wake up for me.' Retracting his foreskin as his penis began to stiffen, I sucked his purple globe into my wet mouth and ran the tip of my tongue around the rim. Leaning against the shelving as I wanked his now solid shaft, my tongue exploring the velveteen surface of his swollen knob, he gasped with pleasure. The boots were mine, I knew as he let out long low moans of pleasure. Eyeing the label on the box, I could see that they were my size.

His balls rolling, his shaft twitching expectantly, I moved my head back and forth, fucking my wet mouth with his beautiful cock as he breathed heavily. My body rocking with the mouth-fucking, I kneaded his huge balls and wanked his veined shaft. He was about to come, I knew as he rested his hand on my shoulder. His body becoming rigid, his cock swelling, he groaned as his sperm pumped into my mouth.

'Ah,' he breathed as my mouth filled with his gushing spunk. 'Ah, *yes*.' Again and again his bulbous knob drove to the back of my throat, sperm dribbling down my chin as he mouth-fucked me. Did his wife do this for him? I wondered, gripping the globe of his cock between my spermed lips and tonguing his knob-slit. Did she suck him off and swallow his spunk? I doubted it very much as he doubled over as if in pain. His glistening cock leaving my mouth, I grabbed the box and stood up.

'These are the right size,' I grinned, moving to the door. 'I don't owe you anything, do I?'

'No, no,' he gasped, tugging his zip up.

'Good. I'll probably be shopping here again.'

'Yes, of course.'

'I like the service, and you've been most helpful.'

Once in the street, I couldn't stop grinning as I walked along the pavement. I could have anything I wanted, for nothing. Well, almost nothing. Licking the sperm from my lips, I was about to call into a coffee shop when I noticed Jackie across the road. She'd already seen me and came trotting towards me, waving and calling.

'New shoes?' she asked, eyeing the box.

'New boots,' I replied. 'What are you up to?'

'Just window-shopping. I don't have a great deal of money at the moment. You're obviously doing all right. Have you been paid for the book?'

'Er . . . No, not yet.' The candle slipping partially out of my wet vagina, I squeezed my thighs together. 'I was just going to have a coffee,' I said. 'Want to join me?'

'Yes, good idea.'

Walking into the coffee shop, I headed for the loo while Jackie found a table. Slipping the hot candle out of my wet pussy, I placed it in the box with the boots. It would come in very useful, I mused, brushing my hair before leaving the loo. If I ever found myself without a rock-hard cock to play with – which, admittedly, I doubted – then I'd have my candle. Joining Jackie, I placed the box on an empty chair, hoping she wouldn't want to look at the boots as she asked me whether I'd heard any more from Crystal Marshall.

'No,' I lied as the waitress brought two coffees over. 'She was interested in my writing and we had a chat, that was all. We haven't made plans to keep in touch.'

'It's funny that she should contact you like that,' Jackie murmured pensively. 'We'd talked about her, you using the name in your book, and then she makes contact via Alan. And you'd heard nothing from him for a year or so,'

'Yes, it *is* odd.' I smiled.

'It's funny that Alan knew Crystal in the first place.'

'He met her at some party or other. Talking of which, when's your next . . . what should I call it? Orgy?'

'We're planning one for the weekend. I take it that you'll be coming? Excuse the pun.'

'I don't know yet. I'm hoping to see Crystal again, so . . .'

'I thought you hadn't made plans to keep in touch.'

'No, I meant . . . I meant Angela. She said that she'd keep in touch.'

Sipping our coffees, we chatted about this and that, catching up on the gossip and rumours. I couldn't stop thinking about Crystal as I listened to Jackie's account of one of her sex parties. Was she thinking about me? I wondered. After the things I'd done to her naked body, I doubted that she'd forget me in a hurry. Wondering whether she'd make contact, I decided to call at her cottage. It would be interesting to take a look at her writing. And I wanted to discover a little more about her running off and causing all that trouble with the police. Reckoning that Alan knew more than he'd let on, I decided to visit Crystal that evening.

'Right, I have to go,' I said, rising to my feet.

'Already?' Jackie asked.

'Yes, I have one or two shops to call in to and then I must get on with some work.'

'OK. Are you busy this evening?'

'Er . . . I'm not sure what's happening. I'll ring you.'

'I suppose the coffees are on me?'

'Oh, thanks, Jackie.' I smiled. 'I'll give you a ring.'

Leaving the coffee shop with the shoebox under my arm, I decided to try my trick in one last shop. I was pushing my luck, I knew. But I was becoming hooked on the game. Game? I mused. Was I a prostitute? Since I was now taking goods in exchange for sexual services, I reckoned I was. But I was supposed to be an author, not a whore. Still, I was beyond caring. Besides, I liked sucking rock-hard cocks to orgasm and swallowing sperm. And if I got a new pair of boots thrown in, then why not?

Noticing an electrical shop, I eyed the lava lamp in the window. It would look nice in my den, I mused, entering the shop. To my disappointment, the man behind the counter was in his sixties. There again, he had a cock and I was sure that he'd love to be sucked off. The trouble was that he looked rather stern and grumpy. Perhaps a good orgasm would cheer him up. Asking him about the lamp, I waited by the counter while he took it out of the window. Apparently, it was the last one and he couldn't come down on the price.

'I wasn't going to haggle,' I said.

'I've got to make a profit,' he moaned.

'Of course you have.' I smiled, placing the shoebox on the counter. 'We're all out for what we can get, aren't we?'

'I'm not out for what I can get, exactly. I just need to make a sensible profit to survive.'

'I'm always out for what I can get. In fact, I didn't pay a penny for these boots.'

'Didn't you?' he asked, somewhat puzzled as I patted the shoebox. 'Are you saying that you stole them?'

'No, of course not. I offered the man this in return.'

Lifting my skirt up over my stomach, I watched the man's face as he stared in awe at my vaginal valley. 'My God,' he breathed, as if he'd never seen a pussy before. Perhaps he hadn't seen a hairless pussy. But was he going to give me the lamp in return for . . . for what? I wondered. I doubted that he wanted to fuck me, not in his shop. Perhaps he'd like to touch my pussy, run his finger up and down my sex-crack or push it deep into my hot cunt. Moving behind the counter, my skirt still up over my stomach, I grinned at him.

'Well?' I breathed. 'What do you think?' Dropping to his knees, he wasted no time. Licking the full length of my dripping crack, his tongue delving into my sex-hole as he yanked my hairless outer lips wide apart, he was obviously sex-starved. I allowed him to pleasure me for a while, until I was sure that his cock would be stiff and ready for my mouth, and then asked him to stand up. He appeared to be in a daze as he stood and I kneeled. Unzipping his trousers, I yanked his huge cock out.

'God, you're big,' I breathed, focusing on his huge purple plum.

'Suck it,' he gasped as I kicked the salty globe of his penis. 'Suck it hard.'

'How much is the lamp?' I asked, running the tip of my tongue over his sperm-slit.

'It's yours. Just suck me off and it's yours.'

'I thought you might say that,' I grinned. 'OK, you have a deal.'

Taking his bulbous glans deep into my wet mouth, I sank my teeth into his solid shaft and sucked hard. Leaning on the counter, he gasped in his male pleasure as I slipped his heavy balls out of his trousers and cupped them in my hand. He was big and very hard, which surprised me, considering his age. I don't know what I'd expected an ageing man's cock to be like, but his glans was huge, filling my gobbling mouth. How much sperm would he pump out? I wondered as he held my head, gasping as his penis twitched.

'Lick it,' he breathed, pulling back until my lips enveloped the bulb of his cock. Running my tongue around the rim, teasing the slit, I licked and sucked as he quivered on his trembling legs. He'd shoot any time, I knew as I kneaded his heaving balls. 'I want to watch,' he gasped, looking down at his swollen glans being sucked by my wet lips. I'd allow his spunk to splatter my face, I decided. He'd enjoy watching his sperm shooting from his knob and landing on my face. Cum-slut. Facial.

'Oh, God,' he murmured, clutching my head with both hands. As his sperm jetted over my snaking tongue, I moved back, wanking his rock-hard shaft as the white liquid splattered my nose, my cheeks. Taking his throbbing glans into my hot mouth again, I sucked and licked, swallowing the copious flow of spunk. Not only was he big, but he pumped out more sperm that I'd thought possible. Perhaps he'd been saving it up for weeks, I mused, my mouth filling and overflowing. Perhaps his wife only allowed him a monthly fuck, if that.

I'd become a regular customer at the electrical shop, as well as the shoe and gift shops, I decided as his flow of sperm began to diminish. The lamp this week, a portable radio next week . . . There wasn't much I wanted in the gift shop, apart from the lad's beautiful cock, his salty spunk. I'd probably visit the shoe shop regularly. Wondering what other shops I could infiltrate, I slipped the man's spent penis out of my mouth and lapped up the spilled sperm from his glistening shaft. Licking his drained balls, cleansing him, I watched his penis fully deflate before I stood up.

'How was that?' I asked, licking my wet lips.

'God,' he breathed, leaning on the counter as he panted for breath. 'You're quite a girl.'

'I certainly am. No doubt I'll be calling again to see you.'

'I hope so.'

'Thanks for the lamp.'

'Yes, yes. Er . . . When do you think you'll be in again?'

'A couple of days, I would imagine.'

Grabbing the shoebox and the lamp, I left the shop and walked home. The taste of sperm lingering on my tongue, I felt no guilt or remorse as I recalled the three lucky shop-keepers. I didn't suppose it was very often that attractive young female customers called in to suck their knobs to orgasm. Why should I feel guilty? I reflected. They'd got what they wanted and I'd got what I'd wanted. All's fair in lust and sex.

The lamp looked nice in my den, and the red leather boots fitted perfectly. Placing the candle on my desk, I flopped into my swivel chair and switched the computer on. I had quite a lot of writing to catch up on, what with the time I'd spent sucking off shopkeepers. Young Crystal had been busy, and I had to record her exploits while they were fresh in my mind – the sperm fresh on my lips.

If Crystal Marshall contacted me and said that she'd been sucking shopkeepers' knobs to orgasm . . . I didn't know what I'd think. If that did happen, then she'd followed me and witnessed my antics, which I doubted very much. Or she'd somehow discovered what I'd written, and that could only mean one thing – Alan. Initiating a password for each chapter of the book, I smiled. No one else would now gain access to anything I'd written. Wondering why I'd not thought of it before, I settled down to work for the afternoon.

I'd been working for a couple of hours when the phone rang. It was Crystal. She was desperate to see me, but she wanted me to go to her place rather than coming to mine herself. I didn't think anything of it initially, but when she said that she didn't want to come to my flat because of a young girl, I frowned. She knew nothing of the girl in the bushes. Apart from me, only Jackie and Angela had seen her.

'What girl?' I asked.

'I'll tell you about it when you get here.'

'All right. Give me half an hour,' I said, wondering what she was up to.

'You will come, won't you?' she asked.

'Of course I will. Half an hour.'

'OK.'

Slipping into a pair of panties, I grabbed my bag and left the flat. Again, I thought that I was about to learn something, discover something. Driving to the cottage, a thousand thoughts running through my mind, I wondered whether Crystal planned to get her own back. Perhaps she was going to stake me to the lawn and sexually abuse me. The notion sending my juices of arousal gushing into my panties, I realized that I had to get to the bottom of

whatever was going on. I wasn't at all happy with the idea
that Alan had just happened to get to know Crystal and
mention that I wrote. The girl didn't even know me, so why
would they talk about me? Unless he was pouring his heart
out, playing on her sympathy with a view to getting inside
her knickers.

I parked a little way down the lane from Crystal's cottage
and locked the car. Not wanting her to see me arrive, I crept
down an alley between two cottages. I was a good fifteen
minutes early, and I wondered whether I'd learn anything if
I ventured into the woods. Recalling that she'd walked in
the woods, I reckoned that there must be a gate at the end of
her garden. I was right. Slipping through the gate, I hid
behind a bush, gazing at an open window. Perhaps Alan
was there and they were making their plans. Stealing across
the lawn, I felt like a thief in the night. What the hell would
she say if she saw me?

Standing by the window, I listened for movements but
heard nothing. She was probably in the front room, looking
out for me. Trying the back door, I slipped into the kitchen.
I was taking a risk, I knew as I stole into the hallway. But I
could always say that I'd got lost and had found the back
door open. Crystal was in the lounge, talking on the phone.
My heart racing, my hands trembling, I listened intently as
she asked whoever it was to meet her that evening at eight
o'clock.

'She's going to find out sooner or later,' Crystal said.
'Yes, I heard from them this morning. It's all going ahead.
I'm to sign the contract next week. No, of course not. I told
them that Jade Kimberly is my pseudonym. The cheque will
be made out to me. Yes, they're using my real name for the
book. Make sure you clean up properly. OK, I'll see you
later.'

Creeping back into the kitchen, I slipped through the back door and dashed into the woods. Sitting on the ground, I leaned against a tree as Crystal's words tumbled through my mind. They were trying to steal my book! But they'd never succeed. David had the first seven chapters and had found a publisher – they could hardly get the same book published elsewhere. Then the thought struck me like a bolt of lightning. It wasn't my dirty book they were after. It was my romantic novel.

'Shit,' I murmured. I'd sent a copy of the manuscript to a publisher and had heard nothing. Thinking that I'd made the wrong move, I'd gone to an agent. If the publisher had wanted it, they'd have contacted me. Crystal must have been onto them and given them her address, making out that *she* was Jade Kimberly and that she'd moved. It all fitted together. Alan must have been into my flat well before he'd made contact with me. Poking around in my den, he'd obviously discovered who the publisher was and had taken a look at the manuscript.

It was such a fantastic plan that I began to wonder whether I must be mad. They'd never get away with it, would they? The publisher would know of the change of address and . . . But I had the book on the computer. Surely, with my name and address, that was proof enough that I'd written it. 'Clean up properly,' I murmured. I suddenly realized the shocking truth. Alan was on his way to my flat to wipe the book off the computer. But why the games? Why should Crystal pretend to be influenced by my writing? Although I didn't understand, it was obviously part of the plan.

I had to get back to the flat, I knew as I dashed through the woods to the alley. The dirty book was protected by a password, but the romantic novel wasn't. Leaping into my car, I drove like a maniac. It was a crazy plan, I knew. I'd been galavanting around the shops, sucking men to orgasm, enjoying sex with anyone and everyone, while Alan had been poking around my den. Was Jackie involved? I wondered. No, of course not. Angela might have been in on the plan. But to steal my book was a bloody crazy idea. Crazy as it was, they just might get away with it.

Chapter Fifteen

Alan had done the dirty deed and gone by the time I'd got back to my flat. My erotic novel was safe, but the romantic novel had been deleted from the computer. He'd been meticulous in his devilry. The back-up floppy disc had gone, as had all my notes and scribblings. There wasn't a trace left of the book, not one scrap of evidence.

I'd have to contact the publisher the following morning. In the meantime, I was out for revenge. Alan was a lying thief, Crystal was a conniving bitch . . . I was sure that they'd never pull off such a trick, but they could certainly cause problems for me. It might end up in court, with me having to prove that I wrote the book. It could cost a lot of time and money, and I was far from happy. Deciding to ring Crystal, I told her that my car had broken down on the way to her cottage. I suggested that she come round for a drink that evening.

'No, I . . .' she stammered.

'What's the matter?' I asked.

'The young girl . . .'

'*What* young girl, Crystal? Come round for a drink and you can tell me all about it.'

'Well . . . all right,' she finally replied. 'It's a shame about your car. Will it be all right?'

'It's happened before. It won't cost much to put it right. I was halfway to your place when it started playing up. Anyway, come over whenever you're ready.'

'I will. See you soon.'

Thinking about the girl in the bushes, I began to wonder whether Alan had somehow set it up. Perhaps he was trying to frighten me, get me to leave the flat and move away. But I could see no reason why he'd want to do that. *He might be planning to have me certified insane*, I chuckled inwardly. No doubt I'd discover exactly what he and Crystal were up to before long. Grabbing the phone as an idea struck me, I called Jackie

'This evening,' I said, the minute she answered. 'Go to Crystal's cottage and see what you can find.'

'What?'

'Break into Crystal's cottage and—'

'Jade, what the hell are you going on about? Calm down and explain properly.'

I told her everything. Initially, she thought I was wrong. She didn't reckon that Alan and Crystal had taken my book. We discussed it and she finally began to fit the puzzle together. Even so, she wouldn't agree to breaking and entering, as she put it. But she did suggest that she could try to get some information from Alan. Her idea was to 'get his cock out and disorientate him to glean information.' A mad idea if ever there was one, but she was extremely keen to 'wank the truth out of him'. I gave her his mobile number and that was that. I wouldn't know the outcome until the end of the evening.

I was hoping that Crystal would suggest that I stake her to the lawn again, but I didn't reckon she would after her last experience, her sexual torture. I'd just have to wait and see what happened, play it by ear and pray for a chance to torture the truth out of her. When she arrived, I poured her a glass of wine and we sat on the patio enjoying the evening sun. She was wearing a red dress short enough to reveal the alluring swell of her tight panties and low enough to expose the deep ravine of her cleavage. She wouldn't be wearing the dress for long, not if I had my way.

'How's the writing going?' she asked.

'I've had a spot of bother with my computer,' I replied. 'I seem to have deleted the romantic novel I wrote, and I can't find the back-up floppy disc.'

'Oh, no. What will you do?'

'I'm not too worried about it,' I smiled, mysteriously looking about me. 'It wasn't *my* book that I lost.'

'What?' she gasped, almost spilling her drink. 'What do you mean, it wasn't *your* book?'

'I scanned a book into the computer. It was one I'd bought from a second-hand bookshop. I wanted it up on screen so I could play about with it, perhaps borrow a few scenes.'

'But . . .' she breathed, her eyes wide with shock. 'I thought . . .'

'*What* did you think?'

'I thought *you*'d written it.'

'You didn't know about the romantic novel, Crystal.'

'No, I mean . . .'

'Thankfully, my dirty book is quite safe. And the floppy disc is with my agent. As for the romantic novel . . . I pinched most of it,' I laughed.

'That's plagiarism,' she frowned. 'You'd never have got away with it.'

'I only borrowed a few scenes. I changed them here and there, and changed the names of the characters. Actually, I borrowed more than a few scenes, a lot more. Anyway, it really doesn't matter.'

'So you've not sent it to a publisher?'

'I sent it ages ago.'

'And what happened?'

'I never heard anything. It's just as well, seeing as most of it isn't my work. You said something about a young girl.'

'Yes, that's right. The reason I didn't want to come here was . . . Jade, there's a ghost in your flat.'

'A ghost?' I laughed.

'The ghost of a young girl.'

'Perhaps *she* deleted the book,' I giggled.

'I'm serious, Jade.'

'What makes you think there's a ghost here?'

'I wasn't going to say anything . . . When I was on the lawn, I saw her in the bushes at the end of the garden.'

'In the . . . She's not a ghost, Crystal. She lives a few doors away. She's always in my garden, playing on the lawn or in the bushes.'

'But Alan . . .'

'What about Alan?'

'Nothing,' she sighed, obviously wondering what was going on.

Alan had set me up, somehow managed to make the face of a girl appear in the bushes. Now that I'd told Crystal that she was a neighbour, I'd really mucked up their crazy plan. Whatever it was. There were several questions I wanted answers to. Why had Crystal run off and caused the police no end of trouble? Why the ghost scam? And why steal my book? As the phone rang, I moved to the back door and told Crystal that I'd bring the bottle of wine out. Getting her drunk would be a good start, I mused, grabbing the kitchen phone. A good start to getting her knickers down.

'It's . . . it's Mog,' the lad said hesitantly.

'Oh, hi. How are you?'

'I was wondering whether we could come round this evening.'

'We? Oh, you mean you and your mates.'

'Yes.'

'Er . . . All right, Mog. Say, half an hour?'

'Great! I didn't think, after what happened—'

'After what happened, I can't wait to see you all again.'

'Brilliant. OK, see you in half an hour.'

I didn't have any time to waste, I knew as I took the wine out to the patio. Crystal had to be staked naked to the lawn before the boys turned up. Staked and gagged with my piss-wet panties. She was going to pay for her wickedness, and pay dearly. She'd spill the beans once she was surrounded by half a dozen naked lads with their erect cocks hovering threateningly above her. Even if she *did* tell me everything, she was still going to have every hole in her naked body fucked rotten.

'Shall I get the hoops?' I smiled, pouring her another glass of wine.

'No, I . . .'

'Come on, Crystal. Don't be shy.'

'It's not that,' she sighed. 'It's just that—'

'I won't thrash you this time, I promise.'

'Jade, I don't want to . . .'

'Are you afraid of ghosts?' I chuckled.

'Of course not. I just don't want to be staked to the lawn again.'

'Don't you want me to love you?'

'Yes, but . . .'

'Good. I'll get the hoops. You slip your dress off. I won't be a minute.'

Lurking in the kitchen, I watched Crystal through the window. She stood up and lifted her dress. Hesitating, she looked towards the bushes. Was Alan hiding there? I wondered, eyeing the swell of her panties as she finally pulled the dress over her head. Perhaps he planned to have the 'ghost' appear to frighten me. If he was there, there wouldn't be a great deal he could do to save Crystal from her sexual fate. With six young lads fucking the slut, there'd be nothing he could do to save her. As she tugged her panties down and unhooked her bra, I grabbed the hoops and the hammer and skipped out onto the patio.

'Right,' I smiled, eyeing the weal-lined flesh of her naked vulva. 'Lie on the lawn. I promise to be gentle with you.'

'Don't take too long, Jade,' Crystal said softly, lying on her back with her limbs spread. 'Just half an hour or so, OK?'

'OK. Half an hour of immense pleasure, that's what I'll give you.'

Hammering the stakes into the lawn, I felt my clitoris swell, my juices of arousal gushing into my tight panties. Crystal had a beautiful young body. The mounds of her breasts topped with long nipples, her hairless mons rising alluringly above the swell of her vaginal lips, her inner sex petals peeping out from her valley of lust . . . I wanted to lick and suck and finger her tight cunt, drink her juices of orgasm as she writhed and gasped. But first things first.

Squatting over her head, the bulge of my panties only inches from her pretty face, I contemplated the crude act I was about to commit. There were no bounds to my depravity, I knew as I gazed longingly at the moist crack of Crystal's young pussy. Like the girl in my book, there were no depths I wouldn't sink to in my quest for crude lust. The more I thought about my romantic novel, the more incensed I became. Was Angela involved? I pondered. Perhaps they'd *all* ganged up to destroy me.

'What are you doing?' Crystal asked as my bulging

panties hovered above her face. 'I thought you were going to—'

'This is the beginning of an evening of the most corrupt and debased sex imaginable,' I said.

'Half an hour, Jade. You said—'

'Half the night, Crystal. We're being joined by some friends of mine soon.'

'*What?*'

'Six young lads with big cocks in dire need of a young girl's naked body.'

'No. For God's sake, Jade. I'm not having—'

'Oh yes, you are. You're having six young men. Or, I should say, they're having you.'

'Let me go,' she breathed, her naked body wriggling. 'If you think you can . . .'

'Here it comes,' I giggled 'Open wide.'

'Here what comes?'

'The golden rain of lust.'

'The—'

My panties filling with hot liquid, I lowered my head and looked between my legs as I showered Crystal's grimacing face. On and on the gushing liquid splashed over her, soaking her hair and running down her neck as she tossed her head from side to side. My hairless vulval flesh becoming hot as the golden flow streamed between my swollen vaginal lips, I felt my clitoris pulsate. My womb rhythmically contracting, the sheath of my cunt tightening, never had I been so aroused.

'For God's sake,' Crystal spluttered as the flow began to lessen. 'Jade, you filthy bitch.' Giggling, I stood up and lowered my soaked panties as she spat expletives at me. Slipping my panties over my feet, I rolled them up into a ball and pushed them into the girl's mouth. She tossed her

RAY GORDON

head from side to side, desperately trying to eject the hot, wet ball of material as I giggled in my wickedness. She was mine now. Her naked body was mine for the taking.

The doorbell ringing, I dashed through the kitchen to the hall. The lads were going to have the time of their lives, I knew as I opened the door and gazed at their grinning faces. As they filed into the hall, pulling their shirts off and unbuckling their belts in their eagerness, I ordered them to go to the garden once they were naked. Leaving a trail of clothes in their wake, they gathered in the kitchen to finish their disrobing. Sitting on the patio, I grinned at Crystal as she gazed wide-eyed at the back door. She could hear movements and the murmur of male voices as she waited in fear and trepidation.

'Are you ready?' I asked her as she tried to escape from the metal hooks. Shaking her head furiously as the naked lads emerged from the kitchen and gathered around her beautiful young body, she moaned her protests through her nose. 'She's all yours, boys,' I giggled. 'She's ready and waiting for your stiff cocks, your tongues, fingers and, of course, your sperm.' Pouring myself another glass of wine, I relaxed in the evening sun, ready to watch the sex show as the young men settled on the grass around the girl's tethered body. Was Alan hiding at the end of the garden? I wondered as one lad thrust his fingers deep into Crystal's young cunt. Or was he with Jackie? But I didn't really care where he was. My only concern was Crystal, defiling her naked body by way of punishment for her treachery.

Grinning as the wet panties were ripped out of Crystal's mouth and unceremoniously replaced by a bulbous knob, I watched the girl writhe as the crude mouth-fucking began. The fingers slipping out of her tight sex sheath, her naked body bucked as the purple globe of a rock-hard penis

282

slipped between her swollen vaginal lips and sank into the tight sheath of her wet cunt. She was no doubt enjoying herself, I mused as she sucked on the swollen glans bloating her mouth. After a while, I'd thrash her mammary spheres, whip the brown protrusions of her nipples until they rose from her chocolate-brown areolae and stood proud from her firm breasts. Perhaps she could do with another cunt-thrashing, I thought as her tethered body rocked with the enforced double fucking.

'Come on, boys,' I laughed. 'You can do better than that. Look at all the spare cock hanging around. Surely you can find something to do with your knobs.' Grinning, one lad kneeled by Crystal's head and forced his cock into her mouth alongside his friend's solid penis. Coughing and spluttering, the girl squeezed her eyes shut as the two purple globes drove further into her bloated mouth. Her lips stretched tautly around the huge shafts, her cunt pistoned with another rock-hard penis, she moaned through her nose as the crude three-way fucking shook her naked body. I could resist temptation no longer, and leaped up from my chair to sit on the grass by the girl's head.

'Let me help,' I murmured, grabbing the two cocks and positioning the ballooning knobs between Crystal's wet lips. Wanking the warm shafts, the purple plums between her stretched lips, I could hardly wait for the sperm to jet, covering her chin and cheeks and pumping into her thirsty mouth. The lad fucking her cunt gasped and let out a rush of breath as he filled her sex-sheath with his sperm. Spunk jetting from the knobs between her lips, the white liquid running down her cheeks, filling her gobbling mouth, she repeatedly swallowed the products of the male orgasms.

'Keep coming,' I breathed, their balls battering Crystal's spunk-dripping face as I wanked their huge shafts. One knob slipping out of her mouth and spraying spunk up her nose, I continued wanking the hard shafts, sustaining the young men's orgasms until their balls had drained and their shafts began to deflate. Gasping for breath as the organs moved away, Crystal swallowed the remnants of spunk before spluttering expletives at me. Ignoring her, I ordered another lad to kneel on the grass and fuck her spunked mouth.

'Shove your knob down her throat,' I giggled in my lechery. Obeying, he drove his huge glans into her mouth, her sperm-glossed lips rolling along his veined shaft as his balls pressed against her chin. 'Fuck her mouth,' I said, kneading his heavy balls as he repeatedly withdrew his cock and drove his knob to the back of her throat. The spent penis leaving her spunked vagina, I instructed another lad to penetrate her sex-sheath and fuck her. I'd suck the sperm out of her used cunt once she'd been filled by several cocks, fucked hard and spunked to the brim. I wouldn't question her yet, I decided. When she was nearing exhaustion, I'd get her to talk. And if she wouldn't . . . On her head it would be.

Grabbing the young man's cock, I slipped his purple knob out of her mouth and rolled his foreskin back and forth over his swollen crown as her young cunt stretched to accommodate a fresh penis. I wanted to watch his sperm shoot out of his slit and splatter her face. Cum-slut. She'd love it. I'd love it, having spunk shot over my face, pumped into my thirsty mouth. My six young friends would be regular visitors, I knew as my clitoris pulsated expectantly between the rise of my swollen pussy lips. Six fresh young cocks to enjoy, six pairs of heavy balls, enough spunk to satisfy my craving . . . And Crystal's young body to abuse.

The white liquid finally gushing from the young man's

knob, spraying Crystal's grimacing face as he gasped in his ecstasy, I wanked him faster. Her hair matted with urine and sperm, her sex-wet face glistening in the glow of the evening sun, she was in for an evening of sex so debauched that she'd remember it for the rest of her life. Her mouth, her pussy, her rectum, her cleavage . . . She'd drown in sperm before the evening was over. Eyeing the branch as I wanked the rock-hard cock, drenching her pretty face with sperm, I decided that the time had come for a thrashing.

'Get away,' I hissed at the lad as he gasped and shot out the last of his sperm. Frowning, he moved aside as I grabbed the branch and grinned at Crystal. 'So, you stole my book,' I said, stroking the erect teats of her rounded breasts with the rough leaves as the lad between her thighs gasped and pumped his sperm deep into her vaginal cavern. Her eyes widened, her bottom lip quivering as she realized that I knew everything. 'Get away from her,' I growled at the young man spunking her cunt. His fucking completed, he rolled to one side and lay panting on the grass.

'No,' Crystal murmured. 'I didn't steal . . .'

'You're lying,' I spat. 'You stole my book. You contacted the publisher and gave him your address.'

'But . . . How do you know?' she gasped, the realization hitting her that she was about to be severely punished as I tapped her firm breasts with the branch.

'I know everything, Crystal.' My studs gathered on the lawn and murmured to each other as I lashed the girl's young breasts. 'That was just for starters,' I grinned as she cried out. 'Where's Alan?'

'I don't know,' she whimpered.

'What was the idea behind the girl in the bushes?'

'What girl?'

285

I gave her milk-glands another hard lash. 'What was the idea behind the girl in the bush?' I repeated angrily.

'I don't know anything about—'

Another lash of her crimsoning breasts. 'I can sit here and thrash you all night if I have to.'

'Jade, I know nothing about a girl.'

'Liar!'

Thrashing her mammary spheres, reddening the tight flesh of her young breasts, I lost control. Unable to stop myself, I moved down her naked body and thrashed the smooth flesh of her vulva, reddening her pussy lips, the mound of her hairless mons. Again and again I thrashed her, her screams resounding around the garden as her young body convulsed wildly. The branch swishing through the air, landing across the crimsoned flesh of her pussy, I halted the cruel beating when an idea struck me. Stuffing my panties back into her mouth to silence her, I dashed into the kitchen. Returning with a tub of butter, I settled between her naked thighs.

'This will help me to get my fist up your arse,' I grinned, greasing the brown entrance to her rectum with a handful of butter. Her eyes wide as I smeared more butter between the rise of her tensed buttocks, she shook her head from side to side and struggled to break free from her bonds. Driving two fingers into her tight anal channel, I ordered the boys to wank over her tits. Kneeling either side of her, four of them began wanking their beautiful cocks, their purple plums repeatedly appearing and disappearing as they ran their hands up and down their solid shafts.

'You can all piss on her later,' I murmured, forcing half my hand past her tight rectal ring. Her delicate brown tissue stretching tautly around my hand as I drove deeper into her hot duct, I watched my knuckles slip past her anal inlet. I couldn't believe that her tight arsehole had stretched to allow my fist into her rectum. Writhe and struggle as she might, she couldn't halt the crude fisting, her brown tissue gripping my wrist as I flexed my fingers, stretching open her hot tube. Thrusting my free hand into the butter, I drove three fingers into the restricted sheath of her cunt. Lifting her head and gazing at the four cocks, her face grimacing as I managed to force my fist into the hot cavern of her vagina, she tried to spit the urine-soaked panties out of her mouth.

'It's no good,' I laughed, fisting her sex-squelching holes. 'There's no escape.' The boys gasping as they wanked, their spunk jetting from their deep-purple knobs and splattering the mounds of Crystal's weal-lined breasts, I forced my fist deeper into the tight duct of her rectum. Jutting my buttocks out, I ordered one of the boys to push his cock deep into my cunt and fuck me. I was in my element, I knew as my skirt was lifted up over my back and I felt a bulbous knob slip between the swollen lips of my hairless pussy. This was sex in all its crudity, its glorious depravity. The knob gliding along my sex duct, pressing against the soft firmness of my ripe cervix, I gasped as the young man grabbed my hips and began his fucking motions.

'Yes,' I murmured, my body jolting with the vaginal fucking as I watched the spunk flying through the air and raining over Crystal's scarlet breasts. One of the lads pulling my wet panties out of the girl's mouth and thrusting his knob to the back of her throat, I grinned. Arse-fisted, cunt-fisted, mouth-fucked, her tits spermed . . . This was what crude sex was all about. The orbs of my naked buttocks repeatedly slapped by the lad's lower belly, his balls pummelling my gaping vaginal lips, I shook uncontrollably as my clitoris exploded in orgasm.

Tremors of sex rippling through my contracting womb, I

gasped as a finger slipped past my anal inlet and drove deep into my hot rectal tube. Opening my mouth wide as another lad's cock hovered in front of my face, I sucked his knob to my back of my throat. My arse fingered, my cunt fucked, my mouth bloated with a huge cock, I fisted Crystal's tightening sex-holes as her mouth was fucked by a solid penis. Shuddering in my sexual euphoria as my cunt filled with sperm, my mouth suddenly overflowing with the male liquid of orgasm, I became oblivious to my surroundings.

Floating on purple clouds, sparks of orgasm showering my mind, I drifted into a weird state of consciousness. Dizzy in my sexual euphoria, my mind blowing away on the wind of lust, I was only aware of my pulsating clitoris, floods of sperm, the heat surrounding my hands as I fisted Crystal's lust-sheaths. As my orgasm peaked, I felt as if I was swimming through swirling mists, gliding across the sky, soaring, diving. I thought I was dying as bright lights flashed around me, a streak of red, flashes of blue. I never wanted to come down from my sexual paradise, for ever winging through clouds of utopian bliss.

Distant screams echoed through my head, voices, murmurs and grunts. Crystal's cries resounding around the garden, I opened my eyes as I drifted back into my body. Sperm flooding down my chin as the swollen knob left my mouth, I dragged my fists out of Crystal's sex-holes. The penis withdrawing from my bloated cunt with a squelching sound, the finger leaving the inflamed duct of my rectum, I focused on the sperm hanging in long threads from the four knobs hovering above Crystal's glowing breasts.

'Are you all right?' Mog asked as I rolled to one side and lay panting on the lawn.

'Yes,' I gasped, my head lolling from side to side, my eyes rolling in the aftermath of my heavenly coming.

288

'I think we'd better be going.'

'No, not yet,' I breathed, gazing up at the blue sky.

I could hear movements, low murmurs. My boys were leaving me, I knew as I shuddered in the fading throes of orgasmic aftershock. Sperm seeping between my vaginal lips, running down my cheek, I finally managed to sit upright and look about me. The boys were in the flat, dressing after their debauchery. Crystal lay trembling, rivers of sperm coursing down the mounds of her breasts, her face. Tugging on the metal hoops as the front door closed, I released her violated body and helped her to sit up.

'What's happening?' she asked, her eyes glazed as she looked about her.

'You've been fucked.' I smiled. 'Literally fucked senseless.'

'God, I feel drunk with sex,' she breathed.

'I know the feeling. I think we'd better go inside.'

'Yes,' she whispered as she clambered to her feet and staggered towards the back door.

Following her into the lounge, we flopped onto the sofa, breathing heavily as we recovered. My hands sticky from the fisting, my sperm-bubbling vaginal sheath on fire, my anal duct inflamed, I knew that I couldn't take one more cock, one more massive orgasm. Crystal appeared to be sleeping, and I wondered where we were going to go from here. She looked terrible. Her hair matted with sperm and urine, her breasts glowing a fire-red, her vulval flesh burning scarlet . . . Had I overdone it? I wondered, eyeing the sperm glistening on the mounds of her young breasts. No, I hadn't. She'd deserved all she'd got.

She'd stolen my book, tricked me, lied to me . . . I'd ring the publisher and explain. I'd have to finish the dirty book and get it posted to David. The thought hitting me that I was about to become a published author of romantic fiction, I thought about the erotic novel. I'd have to use a pseudonym, I reflected. Keep the love and lust separate. Love? What was love? I knew that I'd never be capable of loving, now that my life was a swamp of crude sex.

Wandering into the kitchen, I filled the kettle. Whatever became of my life, I was determined to enjoy it. It was funny, I mused. The massive change in me, in my life, had come about because I'd started to write erotic fiction. If it hadn't been for David, I'd never have talked to Jackie about sex. She would have carried on with her lesbian relationships, her orgies, and I'd have been none the wiser. I might have told Alan the ex to go to hell had it not been for my dirty book. I'd never have pulled his cock out and wanked him, not before I'd become interested in erotica.

Pouring the coffee, I wandered out to the patio and sat on a chair. The sun sinking behind the trees, I gazed at the bushes at the end of the garden. How Alan had managed to trick me, I had no idea. He must have made a doll's head or something, perhaps stuck it on the end of a pole and leaned over the fence. But the girl's face had looked so real. I doubted that I'd see her again, not after Crystal had spoken to Alan, told him that I'd discovered their treachery.

There was no need to call the police in, I mused. Not unless Alan and Crystal decided not to cooperate. There was no way they'd get away with it, I reflected again. The plan had been ridiculous, futile. It had probably been Alan's idea. He'd always been jealous of me and must have thought that he'd get one over on me. Wondering how Jackie was getting on, I went into the kitchen and rang her. I doubted that she'd be home, unless she'd not managed to get hold of Alan.

'Oh, you *are* there,' I said as she answered.

'It's all done,' she giggled. 'I met Alan for a drink and wanked him off under the table.'

'Yes, but did you learn anything?' I asked, trying to picture the lewd scene.

'In the end, I asked him outright. He said that he knew nothing about your book. I believe him, although I'm not sure why.'

'He must have been involved,' I sighed.

'He said that he had no idea what Crystal was up to.'

'Why do you believe him?'

'Because he told me why Crystal ran away. Apparently, she was in trouble with one of her clients. You know she writes filthy stories for people?'

'Yes.'

'Well, she tried to blackmail a client. She said that she'd tell his wife that they'd been having an affair unless he paid her a grand. He told her where to go so she phoned his wife. She didn't tell the woman that her husband had been cheating on her, but she did plant a seed of doubt. Anyway, the man went ballistic. He went to see Crystal and wrecked her bedroom. She did a runner and only returned when she realized that the police had been called in. She's desperate for money, Jade. She has debts coming out of her ears and is prepared to do anything.'

'Including pinching my novel.'

'Yes.'

'She's still here, sleeping in the lounge.'

'Shall I come round? We'll sort her out once and for all.'

'I've already sorted her out.'

'What happened?'

'I'll tell you tomorrow.'

'I want to know now.'

'You'll have to wait until tomorrow. I want to speak to her.'

'OK, I'll ring you first thing in the morning.'

Replacing the receiver, I thought about Alan and the girl in the bushes. Perhaps I'd been wrong and he hadn't set it up. If that was the case, then who was the mysterious girl? And why had I written stuff that I didn't recall writing? Hearing movements in the lounge, I went to see what Crystal was up to. Lying full-length on the sofa, her bleary eyes looked up at me as I stood over her.

'Well?' I said. 'What have you to say for yourself?'

'Jade, I . . .'

'Don't start lying, Crystal.'

'All right, I'll tell you everything.' She sat up and brushed her matted hair away from her sperm-starched face. 'I know David Stevens.'

'The literary agent?'

'Yes. I was talking to him about a book idea and he mentioned you. It was only in passing. He realized that we lived in the same town and wondered whether I knew you. He mentioned your romantic novel and . . . Well, I thought it might be worth having a look at it. He said that he was going to have to turn it down and I wondered whether I might be able to help you do something with it.'

'So why didn't you?'

'I had some trouble with a client and had to go away for a while. Anyway, when I got back, Alan happened to mention you. He said that you'd cheated on him and had lied and—'

'That sounds like Alan.'

'In view of what he told me, I decided against trying to help you.'

'And decided to steal my work.'

'Yes, no . . . Alan said something about you sending the book to a publisher. I rang a few publishers, saying that I was Jade Kimberly and asking whether my manuscript had been read. They all said that they'd never heard of me, except one. They loved the book and were about to write with an offer.'

'So you said that you'd moved and gave them your address.'

'Yes. I also said that "Jade Kimberly" was my pen name and that I had decided to use my real name.'

'And the girl in the bushes?'

'A friend of yours mentioned her to Alan. I don't know who it was, but it gave me an idea.'

'It must have been Angela or Jackie,' I murmured pensively.

'I decided to frighten you by saying that your flat was haunted. I suppose I thought you'd move and . . .'

'How did you get in here to delete the book from the computer and steal the floppy disc?'

'I didn't.'

'Someone did.'

'It wasn't me, Jade. To be honest, it didn't occur to me that you'd have the book on your computer. I hadn't really thought things out properly. I was hoping that you'd move and not realize that your book had been published. I was going to give it another title and probably use a pseudonym. I realize now that it was a ridiculous idea. I was desperate for cash and . . .'

'What about all this business about my writing influencing you?'

'That's true, Jade. Believe it or not, but it's true. Do you mind if I go and get my clothes?'

'No, of course not.'

Gazing out of the lounge window as she left the room, I thought about the events. It didn't matter whether Alan was involved or not. All that mattered was that the book was published in my name, and that I was recognized as the author. Ghosts, my writing influencing Crystal . . . None of it mattered. I was about to become a published author of romantic fiction. And erotic fiction. Hearing the front door close, I watched Crystal walk down the path. She'd be in touch, I knew as I went to my bedroom to have a lie-down. She'd be back for sex.

Chapter Sixteen

The following day I rang the publisher and said that I'd moved back into my old place. There was no point in going through lengthy explanations about Crystal trying to steal my work. As long as they knew that I was the author of the manuscript, and the cheques came to me, I really didn't care. I arranged to go to London and see them after they mentioned the advance, a sum that would give me financial security for quite some time.

Feeling confident, I decided to pop into town later in the day and do some shopping, *free* shopping. Another pair of boots would be nice, and a portable radio for my den. *First things first*, I mused, ringing David. I didn't mention the romantic novel since I wasn't the type to say 'I told you so.' He was keen on the dirty books, asking whether I'd sent him the synopses and had the contract arrived. Answering yes to the first question and no to the second, I knew that I'd have to come up with some ideas before long. Now the problems had been sorted out, I was free to work. Apart from the problem of the girl in the bushes. And the strange phenomenon of Crystal Marshall being influenced by my writing. Not that it was really a problem because it didn't affect me.

I worked on the dirty book for a few hours and then wandered out into the garden with a cup of coffee. The metal hoops and the branch were lying on the lawn, along with the tub of butter, stark reminders of my sexual debauchery. I was lucky to have a secluded garden, I reflected. It was another hot day, the sun beating down on me from a clear blue sky. Pulling my dress over my head, I ran my hands over the mounds and crevices of my naked body. I felt comfortable without clothes, and extremely sexual. Tracing the contours of my hairless vaginal lips, running my finger up and down my moistening sex crack, I shuddered. I felt my clitoris, hard in its arousal, yearning for the intimate caress of my fingers. I needed to come. Wondering why Jackie hadn't phoned, I stepped into the kitchen. I wanted sex with her, to feel her wet tongue running up and down my yawning valley of desire, her fingers slipping into the drenched sheath of my pussy. Grabbing the receiver as my clitoris pulsated in expectation, I dialled her number. There was no reply, and I wondered whether she was on her way to see me.

Wandering out into the garden again, I gazed at the bushes. I'd ignore the young girl if she appeared. Whether she was a being from another world or a doll's head on the end of a pole, it didn't really matter. Nothing mattered apart from my writing, and my insatiable clitoris. A good sex life and a brilliant career with plenty of money . . . What more could a girl ask for?

Walking across the lawn, I stood in front of the bushes, the rough leaves brushing the sensitive teats of my breasts as I swayed from side to side. I felt alive with sex as I moved forward, the branches scratching the firm mounds of my milk glands, grazing my erect nipples. My naked body was a temple of pleasure, my mounds and crevices designed solely to bring me sexual elation. My orifices were designed to bring others immense pleasure, to satisfy the base desires of men and women. My mouth, my vaginal sheath, the tight duct of my rectum . . . I was a goddess of sex.

Snapping a branch off the bush, I ran it between my thighs, the sharp leaves scraping the swell of my sex pads, raking the delicate wings of my protruding inner lips. Reaching behind my back, I gently whipped the rounded mounds of my naked buttocks, the heavenly sensations permeating my anal spheres as I gasped in my self-loving – my self-abuse. Cupping a breast with my free hand, I lowered my head and sucked my erect nipple into my wet mouth. Sinking my teeth into the sensitive protrusion, I whipped my naked buttocks harder, the firm cheeks of my bottom stinging delightfully as I thrashed myself in my rising decadence.

Halting my punishment, I looked about the garden. I needed something, something to bring me immense pain and pleasure. My mind awash with depraved thoughts, I eyed the holly bush by the fence. Carefully snapping a leaf off the bush, the sharp points pricking my fingers, I leaned over and parted my naked buttocks. Tentatively placing the prickly leaf in the deep ravine between my stinging bottom orbs, I slowly released my buttocks and stood upright. The sharp points digging into the sensitive flesh of my anal valley, pricking the delicate brown tissue surrounding my abused bottom-hole, I grimaced as I walked across the lawn to the patio.

'God,' I sighed, the pain bringing me exquisite pleasure as I grabbed my dress and stepped into the kitchen. I couldn't believe the depths of my depravity as I placed the branch on the worktop. What else I'd do to my once graceful feminine form in the name of cold lust, I dreaded to think. Slipping my dress over my head and veiling my abused body as the doorbell rang, I hid the branch in the cupboard and wandered through the hall. Wondering whether Crystal had decided to call for another session of debauched sex,

I opened the door to find Jackie standing on the step.

'Are you all right?' she asked as I grimaced. 'You look as though you're in pain.'

'No, I'm fine,' I replied, forcing a smile. 'Come through and I'll fill the kettle.'

'It's hot again,' she sighed, closing the door and following me through the hall. 'Too bloody hot for my liking. So, what's the latest? How did you sort Crystal out?'

'I don't think I'd better go into that,' I laughed. 'Suffice it to say that she'll think twice before crossing me again. So, you believed Alan?'

'Yes, I did. As I said on the phone, Crystal had some trouble with a client, and she's heavily in debt. Alan wasn't in on the scam, I'm sure of it. Have you heard from him?'

'No, I haven't. I've heard nothing from musician Alan, either. God knows where he's got to.'

'There are plenty more fish in the sea, Jade. How's that young boy you were sexually abusing?'

'I wasn't sexually abusing him,' I retorted, frowning at her.

'No, right,' she laughed. 'Of course you weren't.'

'I haven't seen him recently,' I lied as I poured the coffee. 'I thought he might have been in touch but . . . Ouch!' I cried as the holly leaf reminded me that it was between my buttocks by pricking my sensitive brown tissue.

'What's the matter? Are you OK?'

'Yes, I . . . I had a pain in my stomach. I think it must have been something I've eaten.'

'A cock?' she giggled. 'Have you been eating cock?'

'No, I've been working on my book.'

'You're going to have a lot of money, what with this romantic novel being published.'

'I certainly am. I'm going up to London to see the publisher. They're sending me the contract and—'

'Are you still going to write dirt?'

'Erotic fiction, yes. I'll use a pseudonym for that.'

'Good idea. How about Jade Edmons?'

'Jade Edmons? That doesn't sound—'

'Jaded mons, get it?'

'Very funny, Jackie. No, I'll use something like Venus Flower.'

'That's crap, Jade. Venus Flower, for goodness' sake. Talk about contrived!'

'I'll think of something. Talking of names, I've set up a new e-mail address.'

'Oh?'

'Girljuice at Hotmail dot com.'

'Girljuice?' she laughed.

'Why not? It rolls off the tongue quite nicely.'

'So does girl-juice,' she smiled, licking her lips provocatively. 'Shall we sit in the garden?'

'OK, I'll bring the coffee out.'

As she stepped onto the patio, I slipped my hand up my dress and pushed the holly leaf deeper into my anal crevice. As the prickles dug into the brown flesh encircling the entrance to my rectal sheath, I gasped. If Jackie knew what I was up to, she'd think me a nymphomaniac. Perhaps I was, I mused recalling the six young lads, their beautiful cocks, their bulbous knobs shooting spunk over the crimsoned flesh of Crystal's thrashed breasts. It was time they attended *my* naked body again, I decided.

'What's that tub of butter doing on the lawn?' Jackie asked as I took the coffee out.

'Oh, I . . . I was going to put it in the dustbin and dropped it. There's your coffee.'

'Thanks. Metal hoops, a hammer, a branch . . . What *have* you been up to out here?'

'Er . . . Clearing out the shed.'

'You haven't got a shed.'

'I mean . . . Jackie, do you feel horny?'

'Horny? I always feel horny, you should know that. Why do you ask?'

'Because the hot weather makes me horny. I just thought you might like to—'

'Have sex?' she grinned, tugging her short skirt up her shapely thighs.

'Yes,' I smiled, eyeing the pussy-lip-bulged material of her tight red panties.

'What sort of sex? Cunny-tonguing? Bum-fingering? Or how about—'

'You *are* crude,' I sighed, sipping my coffee.

'*Me?*' she cried, her sparkling eyes reflecting an inner lesbian desire. 'You can talk.'

'Yes, well . . .'

'God, how you've changed in the last couple of weeks. Never in my wildest sex dreams did I think that you'd be asking me to have sex with you. Mind you, I've always looked at you with sex in mind. You didn't have a clue what my naughty thoughts were. When we used to go shopping and you'd try on dresses, I'd gaze longingly at your straining bra, your swelling panties. And now . . . Well, now here you are asking me to have sex with you.'

'Did you really think that when we were trying clothes on?'

'I thought a lot more than that,' she laughed.

'I'm going to take my dress off,' I murmured, pulling the garment over my head. 'It's too hot to wear clothes.'

'Bloody hell, Jade,' Jackie cried as I revealed my curvaceous young body. 'What have you done to your . . .'

'I thrashed myself,' I replied, turning and displaying my crimsoned buttocks. 'I thrashed my tits, my pussy and my bum. What do you think?'

'God, you *have* changed. You're nothing like the Jade I used to know. You're . . .'

'Take a look at this,' I said huskily. Bending over, I yanked the warm spheres of my buttocks apart. 'What do you think of that?'

'A . . . a holly leaf?' she gasped. 'God, look what it's done to your bum.'

'It's wonderful,' I said, standing up and grimacing with the beautiful pain. 'It pricks my bottom-hole as I walk about. You should try it.'

'Pricks your bottom-hole!' she shrieked. 'I wouldn't mind having my bottom-hole pricked, *and* well spunked. God, look at the state of your body, Jade. It's scratched and sore and . . .'

'Are you going to talk about my body or use it for sex?'

'Come here,' Jackie whispered huskily, beckoning me to her chair.

Standing before her with my feet wide apart, I tossed my head back as she leaned forward and licked the full length of my inflamed girl-slit. Her wet tongue teasing my protruding inner petals, her hot breath tantalizing the soft flesh of my weal-lined mons, I breathed heavily in my heightening arousal. It was amazing to think that, only two weeks previously, there'd been a battle raging in my mind between right and wrong. Right and wrong, moral and immoral . . . All I wanted now was lesbian sex, crude and debased lesbian sex in all its depraved glory.

'Suck my clitoris,' I murmured, closing my eyes as Jackie's fingertips parted the swollen hillocks either side of my milk-drenched girl-slit. Her tongue circling my erect protrusion of love, I shuddered as sensations of pure sexual bliss rolled through my contracting womb. As her slender finger delved into the velvety-wet sheath of my hot cunt and massaged my inner flesh, I whimpered in my incredible lesbian arousal. The needles of the holly leaf stabbing my brown anal flesh, sending delightful ripples of pain and pleasure into my rectal tube, I squeezed my mammary spheres as hard as I could. My nipples inflating as I kneaded the firm flesh of my young tits, my whole body tingled with sexual pleasure as Jackie thrust a second finger deep into the tightening duct of my drenched cunt.

'I need to come,' I murmured as her wet tongue swept repeatedly over the pulsating tip of my ballooning pleasure-bud. 'God, I need to come.' Sucking my swollen clitoris into her pretty mouth, Jackie continued to tongue the sensitive tip, sending wondrous pre-orgasmic tremors through my quivering pelvis. Again and again she snaked her tongue around the nublette of my passion spot, taking me closer to the explosion of orgasm I so craved. A third finger driving into the silken sheath of my contracting cunt, I released my rounded breasts and clung to her head as my body began to sag.

'Yes!' I cried as my clitoris erupted in orgasm, my hot cunt-milk spewing over her thrusting hand, gushing in rivers down my twitching thighs as shock waves of sheer sexual ecstasy rocked my young body. On and on my pleasure rolled, my mind blowing away as I seemed to leave my body and float up to my sexual heaven. Wailing in my lesbian lust, I gripped her head as she sucked hard on my orgasming sex-bud. I could feel the juices of lust gushing from my bloated vagina, my clitoris pulsating, my womb rhythmically contracting. The holly leaf biting into my anal flesh, my exquisite orgasm peaking, I screamed in my euphoria and almost crumpled to the ground.

Again and again Jackie thrust her fingers into my wet cunt as my pleasure rolled through my sated body. I thought I was going to die as my knees finally gave way, the girl's fingers slipping out of my convulsing sex sheath as I flopped to the ground. Rolling about as if in agony, my trembling body writhing like a snake, I gasped for breath as I slowly drifted down from my sexual utopia. Sobbing as the last ripples of orgasm left my clitoris and transmitted deep into my young womb, I lay on my back with my thighs splayed, the inflamed crack of my vagina gaping. I could hear Jackie's voice calling in the distance as my breathing slowed. Through my eyelashes, I saw her licking my pussy juice off her fingers, sucking them clean as she waited for me to recover.

'Christ,' I finally murmured, propping myself up on my arms and bringing my sticky thighs together. 'That was incredible.'

'I had an inkling that you were enjoying it,' she grinned. 'I have a nose for these things. Or, I should say, a tongue.'

'You certainly have.' Climbing to my feet, I turned and bent over. 'Would you take the holly leaf out?' I asked, the pain becoming unbearable.

'My pleasure,' she murmured huskily.

I cried out as Jackie yanked the leaf from my anal crease. Whispering words of lesbian love as she stroked the brown tissue within my inflamed crease, soothing my sore bottom-hole, she kissed my weal-lined buttocks. Her tongue nearing my private hole, I shuddered as she licked me there, moistening the stinging flesh encircling the inlet to my sheath of illicit sex. Gasping, I felt the juices of sex streaming down my inner thighs as the tip of her tongue entered my once-private hole, tasting my inner flesh, waking sleeping nerve endings within my rectal duct.

My naked body jolting as Jackie drove a finger deep into the sheath of my arse, I focused on the branch lying on the lawn. I wanted a thrashing, a naked-buttock-thrashing, a breast-whipping, a vaginal-flesh-spanking. My insatiable clitoris swelling, calling for fingers or a tongue, I was desperate for crude sex. Sensations of crude sex rippling though my rectal canal as Jackie finger-fucked my tight arse, I wanted to commit the most vulgar and depraved sexual act imaginable.

'More fingers,' I gasped in my lechery. My feet wide apart, my naked buttocks projecting, I rested my hands on the ground as Jackie forced another two fingers past my tight anal ring and deep into the inflamed tube of my rectum. 'More,' I whimpered as my vaginal juices gushed between the swollen lips of my pussy and coursed down my inner thighs. I imagined the lewd sight of my anal ring stretched tautly around Jackie's fingers as she crudely pistoned my burning arsehole. Looking up between my thighs, I focused on the gaping entrance to my drenched cunt. I wanted both holes finger-fucked, used and abused by my lesbian lover. I needed a cock, two cocks, three, four . . . 'God!' I cried as Jackie grabbed the holly leaf and slipped it into the gaping ravine of my wet cunt.

Squeezing the hillocks of my vagina together, crushing the prickly leaf within my tightly closed sex-valley, she managed to force half her hand into my inflamed rectum. The leaf spiking my inner sex flesh, digging into the swollen nodule of my clitoris, I cried out as my orgasm exploded and I flew to my sexual heaven. My pulsating clitoris sending exquisite shock waves of sex though my quivering pelvis as the girl crushed the leaf between my ballooning pussy lips, I thought I was going to die. I could take no more, I was sure as her fist drove deep into my rectal sheath, my brown ring hugging her wrist.

'Keep coming,' Jackie breathed, massaging the fleshy swell of my closed pussy lips, the leaf pricking the sensitive folds of my inner lips, stabbing the nubble of my pulsating clitoris. Her hand moving away from the hairless flesh of my vulval lips, she spanked my burning buttocks as hard as she could, her grunts resounding around the garden with every swing of her hand. Again and again she spanked my twitching anal orbs, the wondrous pain mingling with the ecstatic agony within my drenched sex-valley and coursing through my entire body. Finally falling forward in my sexual delirium, Jackie's fist leaving my rectum with a loud squelching sound, I thought my insides had been sucked out as I collapsed to the ground in a convulsing heap.

'Jesus,' I gasped, writhing on the patio like a snake in agony. I could hear Jackie laughing as I drifted in and out of consciousness, my eyes rolling as my body convulsed violently. Thinking that I'd never recover from my massive climax as I panted for breath, I tossed my head from side to side, my muscles twitching uncontrollably as I squirmed in my sexually drunken state. Finally returning to my abused body, I managed to gaze through my eyelashes. Jackie was masturbating. Her panties around her ankles, her fingers deep into the tight sheath of her cunt, she reclined in the chair and massaged her clitoris.

When she reached her climax, gasping and twitching in the chair, I watched the juices of her cunt spewing between her thighs, running over the edge of the chair and pooling on the patio. Never had I seen a girl come so much. Ramming half her hand deep into her young cunt, the beautiful squelching sounds of female sex filling my ears, she screamed in her orgasmic ecstasy as she fervently rubbed her clitoris. I wanted to thrash her naked buttocks with the branch, whip the mounds of her tits, lash the lips of her wet cunt, thrust my fist deep into her anal core and abuse her curvaceous young body.

I'd lost all control, I knew as I crawled across the lawn and snatched the branch. Staggering to my feet, I teetered towards Jackie's convulsing body and raised the branch above my head. The first lash striking the twitching flesh of her inner thigh, I giggled in my lechery as she screamed out. Again, I lashed her inner thigh, the pink weals fanning out across her milk-white flesh as she sustained her shuddering orgasm with her vibrating fingertips and fist-fucked her young cunt. As she rolled to one side and fell to the ground, her fist embedded within the abused duct of her squelching vagina, I whipped the beautiful orbs of her rounded buttocks. The inflamed lips of her vagina hugging her wrist, I grinned as golden liquid sprayed out between her rubbery sex flesh and her hand. Splashing over her legs, the hot water splashing over the patio, I continued lashing her naked buttocks with the branch as she fist-fucked her young cunt.

'No more!' Jackie finally screamed, dragging her fist out of her drenched cunt, her juices of lust mingling with the golden liquid and splattering my feet. Discarding the branch, I flopped into the chair, exhausted from my incredible coming and the thrashing. I watched the girl twitch and convulse as her flow of golden liquid finally ceased. Her panties twisted around her ankles, she rolled off the patio onto the lawn, squirming and whimpering in the aftermath of her abuse.

I'd found my domain, I knew as I lay in the chair, watching the juices of lust and the golden rain of depravity glistening on Jackie's inner thighs. This was my life, my

existence, I mused. Crude lesbian sex, group sex, anal sex
. . . I was now the goddess of debauchery. I was also about
to become a published author of romantic fiction, and of
erotic novels. I'd attained my goal in life. Had that been my
goal? To become a wanton bisexual whore? A cum-slut? I
asked myself. The phone rang. Clambering off the chair as
Jackie lay whimpering in a warm pool of sex, I went into the
kitchen and grabbed the receiver.

'Jade, it's Alan.'

'Ah, Alan the ex,' I replied. 'And what do you want?'

'I was just wondering whether Crystal was there.'

'No. Should she be?'

'I don't know where she's gone. I've been to her cottage
but it's empty.'

'You mean she's moved?'

'It looks that way. Is it OK to come round?'

'What for?'

'Just to—'

'Coffee and a blow job?'

'That sounds good.'

'Yes, why not?' I replied, gazing out of the window at the
metal hoops lying on the lawn. 'In fact, get here as soon as
you can.'

'I'll be at least half an hour, if not longer.'

'OK, as soon as you can, like I said. I'm looking forward
to this, Alan.'

'So am I, Jade. So am I.'

Replacing the receiver as Jackie staggered into the kitch-
en, I clapped my hands together and grinned. She frowned
at me as I burst out laughing. 'Alan's on his way,' I said.
'Alan the ex.' Grabbing the branch from the cupboard, I
lashed the worktop, chuckling insanely as she backed away.

'Jade,' she murmured. 'What are you planning to do?'

'You'll see,' I replied, lashing the worktop again.

'I won't see because I won't be here.'

'Oh yes, you will,' I hissed. 'You'll be here to help me stake him to the lawn and thrash him.'

'I thought that's what those metal hoops were for. You mustn't do it, Jade.'

'Get out of those wet clothes and go and wait on the patio,' I ordered her.

'Jade . . .'

'Do it, Jackie!'

As she slipped her wet skirt off and walked out into the garden, I lashed the worktop again. I knew that Alan had been involved with Crystal, and he was going to pay for his treachery. The phone rang again and I knew it was my lucky day as Mog asked whether he and his friends could visit me. Readily agreeing, I wondered where Crystal had got to. If I had her naked body staked to the lawn . . . No. There were limits even to *my* debauchery, weren't there? Slapping my palm with the branch, I grinned. There were *no* limits to my depravity – I knew that only too well.

Grabbing the rest of the hoops from the box, I wandered into the garden and tossed them onto the lawn. Jackie was naked, her abused body glowing in the sun as she sat on a chair watching me. I knew she was thinking that I was mad, but I also knew that she couldn't resist any opportunity for crude sex. Walking to the fence, I yanked a bamboo cane out of the ground and threw it on top of the metal hoops. The preparations were almost complete, I mused, eyeing the tub of butter. Apart from a few large carrots. Returning to the kitchen, I was about to grab a handful of the orange phalluses when the doorbell rang. If it was Crystal, then I really would be in my element, I reflected, walking through the hall. It was too soon for Alan the ex to arrive, so . . .

'Angela,' I smiled, looking her up and down.

'I hope you don't mind,' she said softly. 'I was just passing and—'

'Mind?' I grinned. 'Of course I don't mind. In fact, your timing is perfect.'

'Perfect?' she echoed as she stepped into the hall.

'I'll explain everything very soon,' I giggled, eyeing the swell of her breasts billowing her loose-fitting blouse. 'Come into the garden . . . On second thoughts, we'll go into the lounge.'

Settling her on the sofa, I gazed at her naked thighs, pondering on her young pussy as she made herself comfortable. Alan the ex had fucked her, I reflected. He'd pushed his cock deep into her cunt and spunked her cervix. She'd not really crossed me by going off with my man. He'd lied to her as he'd lied to me, but she was still in line for a damned good thrashing. And I was sure that Mog and the boys would enjoy her naked body. I had two choices, I mused. I either forcibly stripped her curvaceous body and staked her to the lawn, or she agreed to my vulgar demands.

'Angela,' I smiled, sitting beside her. 'I'm having a little party.'

'Ah, that's what you meant by my timing being perfect,' she said, reclining on the sofa.

'Yes, yes, it is. This is going to be a party with a difference.'

'Fancy dress?' she frowned. 'I have nothing to wear.'

'Nothing to wear. Yes, that's perfect. It's a kind of pyjama party.'

'Oh, right.'

'I have a spare nightie you can borrow. You strip off and I'll go and get it.'

'Undress in here?' she frowned.

309

'Why not? There's no one else here. Slip your clothes off and I'll get the nightie. The others will be arriving shortly.'

Closing the lounge door, I dashed through the kitchen and leaned out of the back door. Jackie was resting in the chair, basking in the sun, the mounds of her pert breasts glowing, her nipples rising alluringly from the chocolate-brown discs of her areolae. Her eyes closed, she didn't see me gazing longingly at her naked body. The scene was set, I mused as the doorbell rang. Jackie, Angela, Alan, Mog and his mates . . .

Looking in on Angela as I walked through the hall, I told her that I was about to grab a nightie. She was in her bra and panties, her face beaming. She was looking forward to the party, I knew as she asked whether the others had arrived. She'd obviously heard the bell and was eager to meet the other party-goers. The other sex-goers, I reflected, telling her to wait in the lounge. Walking to the door, I suddenly realized that I was heading for trouble. Angela would probably cry rape, Alan the ex . . . God only knew how he'd react when he saw Angela standing almost naked in the lounge. Mog and Co wouldn't give a toss what was going on as long as there was plenty of wet cunt on offer. From prude to . . . I had turned.

Opening the door, I frowned at Alan. 'You're early,' I said.

'Only ten minutes or so,' he grinned, stepping into the hall. 'I'd thought I'd be a lot longer. Anyway, it's the early bird that catches the worm. And when you mentioned a blow job . . .'

'I want you completely naked,' I interrupted him, leading him into my bedroom. 'Strip off and join me on the patio when you're ready.'

'The patio?'

'Why not?'

Closing the bedroom door, I cursed as the phone rang. I didn't need any interruptions, unless it was Crystal asking whether she could come round. Now *that* would have made my little gathering complete. Crystal and Angie staked to the lawn, and Jackie . . . Three beautifully wet girl-cracks to lick, I thought in my wickedness as the doorbell rang. Mog and his gang were gathered on the path, their faces beaming as they gazed at my naked thighs. Not knowing what to do, I told them to go out into the garden. Alan in the bedroom, Angela in the lounge, Jackie on the patio . . . What a bloody mess this was, I thought as I dashed into the kitchen and grabbed the phone.

'Jade, there's been a development,' David announced excitedly.

'Go on,' I replied, gazing out of the window and watching the boys surrounding Jackie as she slept in the chair.

'I have two publishers fighting over your book.'

'Fighting?' I echoed.

'There'll be an auction, by the look of it.'

'For a dirty book?' I breathed disbelievingly.

'It's the character, the storyline that's caused all the interest. You've done a brilliant job.'

'So what happens next?'

'You get those synopses to me a.s.a.p. – and more. Whatever it is you're doing, stop it and get to work.'

'I *am* working,' I responded. 'Research work.'

'That's great. Research? How do you research a dirty book?'

'By . . . That's a trade secret.'

'Oh, right. I'll ring you tomorrow, OK?'

'Yes, yes, that's fine.'

'Work, my girl – work!'

311

Replacing the receiver as Angela wandered into the kitchen asking for a nightie, I sighed as Alan appeared in the doorway, completely naked. His penis erect, his purple knob ballooning, I shook my head as Jackie cried out. Mog entering the kitchen with his rock-hard penis waving from side to side, my guests gasping and frowning at each other, I grinned and invited everyone out into the garden.

'What the hell's going on?' Angela asked, following me onto the patio.

'Jade, I thought . . .' Alan began.

'All be quiet,' I said, eyeing the naked group, their beautiful cocks, their girlie slits. 'We're having a party to celebrate the publication of my book. Angela, it's a naked party so get your panties and bra off.'

'But . . .'

'I'll go and grab a few bottles of wine and get out of my dress, and the party will begin.'

Leaving them to chat among themselves, which they did without hesitation, I went back into the kitchen. Watching them through the window, I smiled. They were laughing and joking, obviously getting on well even though they were all naked. Angela had slipped her bra and panties off, which surprised me. There again, Alan was talking to her, probably chatting her up and lying, as was his wont. This was going to be an interesting evening, I mused, slipping my dress over my head and running my hands over the mounds of my firm breasts.

I'd done it. The transition was complete. From strait-laced prude to whorish nymphomaniac, I had turned. Gazing out of the window again, I frowned. The young girl was peering through the bushes. Her expression reflecting torment, she appeared to be anguished. It wasn't a doll's head on the end of a pole, I knew. And I instinctively knew

that she wasn't of this world. *I'll help write the books.*
Turning, I thought someone behind me had spoken. But
there was no one there. The words had been in my head,
drifting through my mind. Looking at the bushes again, the
girl smiled and then disappeared.

'Are you coming?' Mog asked, stepping into the kitchen.
'Excuse the pun.'

'Yes, I'll be right with you,' I replied as he eyed the
mounds of my breasts, my elongated milk teats. 'There's
wine in the fridge and plenty of glasses in that cupboard.'

'Right, I'll take them outside.'

Wandering through the hall to the lounge, I wondered
about the girl. *Help write the books?* What did she mean?
Who was she and where was she from? Sitting on the sofa,
warmth engulfing me, I felt strangely at ease. She had
smiled at me, her torment gone. Perhaps it was because
she'd been able to communicate with me. *Enjoy your
research.* Was my mind playing tricks? No, it was definitely
the girl's voice.

'I will, Crystal,' I murmured, leaving the sofa. 'And I'll
enjoy my new-found wealth, and my life. Let the orgy
commence.'